THE
TOWER
BESIEGED

NATIONAL
LIBRARY
OF AUSTRALIA

THE TOWER BESIEGED

MARK KRAMARZEWSKI

ALSO BY THE AUTHOR

The Tower Between

Book 1 of the Tower Between Trilogy

Follow the Author at:

For Veronica
Missed still,
Loved eternally.

ACKNOWLEDGEMENTS

Another book and another opportunity to thank all those who have been so generous with their support.

My first thanks this time around is, appropriately, for my readers. Thank you for spending time in this strange world I have created, I hope you enjoyed your time in it during the first book, and that you were excited to return to it in this one. Your support, whether it is through words of encouragement, online reviews, seeking me out at book events or simply reading my stories, is greatly appreciated.

And I offer my thanks to those who helped with the publication of this book, in particular, Jess Chaplin for the amazing cover design, Samantha Elley for her detailed editing and Alana Lambert for bringing it all together.

Thanks to what continues to be the greatest of writing communities, I will forever be in debt to the Wabbers. Special thanks to the query support group, Kim, Haley, Sean, Janna, Raechel, Shelby, Lydia and Cayce – more of us have published since I last wrote an acknowledgement, and for the rest, the journey continues. And thanks too, to the beta read group, Perla, Deeanna, Chrissie, Sharon, Allison and Karlynn who provide enthusiasm for drafts in their infancy along with their valuable feedback.

And extra thanks to my generous critique readers. Danni, Becky, Cathie and Devis, I am deeply appreciative of your time and care as you worked your way through various versions of this book helping me slay yet more killable darlings and too many filter words to count.

Special callout to Taryn, who has continued to be patient and generous in answering questions from outside my lived experience, and to Sam who is constantly captured by my late night ramblings about whatever I've been drafting or editing that day.

Thanks to Jamie, Luke, Adam, Siân, Brad, Damien, Matt, Maddie and Deanna, who played in the campaign that inspired this story, and who may recognise some key scenes such as animated daggers and magical shops.

And thanks to my childhood friends. Brad, Michael, Luke, Mark and Nick put up with the kid who always wanted to live in a fantasy world, and were willing to visit him there as long as there were slurpees and doritos at the table next to the dice and the character sheets.

And, as before, the deepest of thanks are reserved for my family.

Thank you to my grandparents, who were all storytellers. Especially Veronica, who I hope would be happy with this story in particular.

Thank you to my parents, Maureen and Andy, who have been constant in their love and support. And to Emma, who read my first book in less than a day, despite how long it took for me to write it. I hope this one doesn't linger on your TBR pile for long.

And most of all, to Lisa, Ava and Nicholas, who continue to fill my days and nights with so much chaos, nonsense and joy that my mind can't help but create fantastical stories just in an effort to make sense of the three of you. I love you.

CHAPTER 1
ACTIVE DUTY

Zack dived behind a wide, moss-covered boulder; his quarterstaff gripped tight in his hand. He calmed his breathing and brushed his dark brown fringe out of his eyes; his short hair was already matted with sweat and grime.

There was a burst of movement to his right and he shifted his other hand back to his staff, ready to swing, when he recognised the tall blonde-haired shape charging through the tropical underbrush. His best friend, Art, slid to a stop next to him, sharing the stony cover. A splash of light green ichor dripped from Art's broadsword and there was a matching splash on his t-shirt.

"Get one?" Zack asked.

"Maybe. Landed a solid hit on it, but it flew off and I lost it in the trees." He wiped the blade clean against a giant palm frond. "Damn!"

"What?" Zack craned his neck around the boulder.

"Just remembered my Business Studies essay is due tomorrow. Barely started it."

"Who knows, maybe we'll die here before you have to worry about it." Zack smiled.

"Nah, I'm not that lucky. Not with my trusty Lifer at my side. C'mon, we have to find the others and get back to the Tower."

"How?" Zack asked. "I got turned around after those things came swarming in and split us up."

Art closed his eyes. "Nope, their minds are too far away for me to pick up."

A flicker of light flashed out through the trees, accompanied by a faint sound of swearing.

"Well, there's Kimmy, at least," Art said, scrambling back to his feet. "Let's go."

Zack followed closely behind and the two of them surged through the jungle. There were no more bursts of light, but the smell of something smouldering guided them.

"She's going to burn this whole place down if she's not careful," Art muttered as they ran.

"I don't think rainforests burn very easily," Zack answered, hoping to head off another argument between Art and Kimmy before it started.

A third boy emerged from the trees and ran along beside them, his black hair pulled back into a ponytail. Bast had no trouble keeping pace with the other two.

"You saw Kimmy's flash too?" Bast asked, giving a quick flourish of his rapier as he bounded along beside them.

Zack nodded, choosing to save his breath. His legs were a good deal shorter than the other boys' and he was pushing himself to keep up.

They reached a clearing where a dark-haired girl stood over the smouldering insectoid corpse of one of their attackers. Kimmy had recently traded her already short black hair for an even shorter pixie cut and had dyed the tips of her fringe bright red. Zack wasn't sure it quite met the uniform requirements of their school but hadn't been surprised when none of the teachers had risked raising it with her.

"There you all are," she said, glaring at Art more out of habit than for any recent offence.

Bast stepped over to look at the dead creature near Kimmy's feet, prodding at its wings with his rapier. "Nice one."

"Ugly one. Know where the others are?"

"We're here," said a brunette, stepping into the clearing. Tabitha had her flail in hand as she scanned the trees.

A tiny, blonde girl walked beside her, gripping a spear. Jackie moved to her brother, Art, who grinned in relief.

"Did you see Kimmy's fireworks as well?" Bast asked.

"Nope, but Max smelled them."

Zack's eyes passed over the wolf-like dog and straight to the girl walking beside her. Charlie's ever-messy honey-coloured curls were trapped in a loose braid to keep them away from the quiver on her back and she padded along beside her furry companion, an arrow nocked in place.

Zack felt himself staring and pulled his eyes away. "Anybody hurt?"

A quick stocktake revealed a few grazes and scratches but little else. Tabitha opened her mouth to speak when the sound of buzzing from across the clearing warned them that the creatures had returned.

"What are they?" Tabitha directed her question at Zack and Art.

"Why would we know?" Art replied.

Kimmy peered towards the treeline as the buzzing increased in volume.

"Because you're into all this fantasy and monster stuff."

"Fantasy and monster stuff?" Art scoffed. "Playing Dungeons and Dragons for a few years doesn't exactly earn us a bachelor's in magical creatures."

Zack stared as the first of the creatures flew into view. They were insectoid with transparent wings, holding aloft spiny black bodies no larger than a cat.

"Actually," he said, "Art, look at their heads. They're a bit like how I imagined those blood-sucking things looked… what were they called?"

"Stirges?" Art answered. A dozen of the creatures were now hovering, observing the group of teens as they gathered their numbers. "But stirges were like insect-bird things. Look at their torsos, they're more humanoid than anything else."

"Stirgans then?" Zack offered.

Art turned back to Tabitha. "Yeah, okay. Tabs, they're stirgans."

"So, what should we look out for?" Tabitha whirled her flail in anticipation.

"No idea."

Kimmy groaned. "You guys are idiots."

The buzzing took on a higher pitched, angrier quality and the hovering creatures fanned out.

"Maybe watch out for their proboscises?" Zack said.

"Their what?" Bast asked, holding his rapier pointed towards the nearest stirgans.

"The pointy beak-nozzle things", Zack replied. "I think they might use them to suck out your blood."

"The giant face needles? Your advice is to avoid being stabbed by the giant face needles?" Bast asked.

"Yeah."

"What are we waiting for then?" Kimmy asked nobody, letting loose a jet of flame before anybody could answer.

The white-hot fire lanced out from her fingertip and into the torso of one of the creatures. It fell to the ground and, as if it was a starter's flag, its companions swarmed forward. Charlie released her arrow. Her target dipped low but wasn't fast enough. The projectile pierced both its wings and it crashed, skidding along the ground.

His friends stepped forward to meet their attackers but Zack stayed back, both hands ready on his quarterstaff. He felt the usual frustration that he couldn't join them in the fray but, as a Life mage, it was his responsibility to be ready to heal them if necessary.

Art and Bast slashed at the creatures with their swords. Art's heavier blade cut deep into the side of one and he brought it screeching down to the jungle floor. Bast's rapier, however, bounced off the stirgan's thick exoskeleton. It countered with a thrust of its sharp proboscis and only Bast's magical speed saved him from being impaled.

Tabitha chanted; her face clenched in concentration. She flung her free hand forward and a gust of wind erupted behind the stirgans. The air swirled around, upsetting their balance and sending them crashing into each other.

Art, Bast and Kimmy charged forward to take advantage of the disarray left in Tabitha's wake. Art and Kimmy lashed out at the creatures, while Bast made deliberate thrusts with his thin blade. The confusion was short lived, however, and the remaining stirgans turned back to the teens, shrieking in a furious rage.

Beside Zack, Jackie summoned half a dozen fist-sized shields to cover the whole group, but the creatures were attacking with claws and proboscises. The stirgans were too many, too small and too fast for Jackie to stop them all. Art and Kimmy grunted in pain as stirgan claws tore at their skin but, as Bast hurriedly parried away two of his attacks, a third flew in beneath his guard and thrust its beak deep into his thigh. He screamed and fell to the ground, dragging the creature with him.

Tabitha was closest and sent the steel head of her chained flail crashing into the stirgans hovering above Bast. They spiralled lifeless to the ground.

Zack followed behind and slammed his staff against the creature with all his strength. The blow cracked its exoskeleton and it fell limp. The force of Zack's strike wrenched its proboscis from the leg and Bast cried out again, blood erupting from the wound.

Zack dropped to his knees and reached for Life. The rainforest was brimming with it and he drew it towards himself with ease. He recited the phrases his mentor, Sara, had taught him and wove his fingers above the bleeding hole in Bast's leg. Sara had forbidden him more complex healing magic but, after weeks of practice, had conceded he was ready for this particular spell. Zack directed a thin stream of Life into the wound, guiding it towards the arteries and veins opened by the stirgan. The blood thickened and slowed and the flow stopped.

Bast was no longer in danger of bleeding out, but the wound would have to remain open until they returned to the Tower. Zack was confident he could have closed the wound, but he didn't dare jeopardise Sara's trust, not when she'd been so close to expelling him a little over a month ago.

"Try to keep your leg still," he said to a pale Bast. "Until I can get it bandaged, it'll be easy for the bleeding to start again."

Bast nodded and gripped his sword. Zack stood up, guarding over his patient. Six of the stirgans remained, flying around the group and seeking an opening for an attack. Art lashed out at one, but his swing was slow and clumsy. Another stirgan darted towards him, but Kimmy pushed it back with the flat of her axe. She and Art were panting; they all were. The run through the jungle and the fight, in the oppressive heat and humidity, had tired them all.

Zack took a deep breath and drew in more Life before opening channels out to the others. Mixing the gathered Life with his own, he pushed it out towards his friends. The flow lasted only a few seconds before the expected ache rippled through his limbs. He held it as long as he could, but as his vision blurred, he let the connection collapse and dropped to the ground beside Bast.

It was enough. The stirgans moved in, on what should have been exhausted prey, and were caught by surprise when Art leapt out to meet them. He knocked one down with the side of his blade before lunging at a second, piercing it through its sternum.

Max was quick on his heels, tearing into the grounded stirgan while Charlie shot at a third. Tabitha swung her flail at one and it flitted to the side, placing it behind another. Kimmy dropped her axe and called forth another ray of fire from her fingertip. The white-hot beam struck the front stirgan before burning through its chest and hitting the other.

The last creature dived towards Zack, its razor-sharp nozzle aiming straight at his neck. He scrambled for his staff when a spear point thrust over his shoulder and impaled the stirgan through the head, killing it in mid-air.

He turned his tired head to find Jackie standing behind him, a determined look on her face. She shook the creature off her spearhead and smiled at him.

"Thanks, Jackie," Zack said.

She nodded with a blush and turned her attention back to the trees.

"I can't sense any more danger at the moment, I think we're good."

Zack didn't second guess her and turned back to examine Bast. The wound was deep, and not particularly clean. He pulled a pocketknife from his jeans.

"Hold still, Bast. I've got to cut away the rest of the leg so I—"

"You're going to cut off my leg?" Bast's eyes were wide.

"What? No. I mean your jeans' leg."

"Oh. Bloody hell, Zack. Yeah, that's fine."

Zack sawed away at the tear in the jeans, trying to block out Bast's hiss of pain.

"Almost done… There." He let the severed length of denim fall around Bast's ankle and pulled out a roll of bandage. "Okay, so this is going to hurt a bit more, but I've got to make it tight or it could start bleeding again."

Bast took a few deep breaths. "Right then, go for it."

Zack wrapped the bandage around Bast's leg, criss-crossing over the wound to concentrate the pressure where it was needed, before tucking the end into the layers. Bast blinked away some tears, looking pale despite his dark skin tone.

Zack helped him up.

"We need to get back to the Tower. Are we done here?"

Tabitha patted the strap of her backpack. "Yep. I grabbed, like, a dozen of those weird purple flowers before those things—"

"Stirgans," Art interrupted.

She met him with a flat stare. "Before those things attacked us."

"Is a dozen enough?" Kimmy asked.

"It should be," Tabitha said. "The bag's nearly full."

Charlie scanned the trees. "Do we know where the gate is?"

Bast pointed to his left. "I can feel it off that way, not too far."

Tabitha nodded. "Okay. Charlie, can you take Max ahead? We'll follow behind."

"No problem. C'mon Max."

Max lingered for a moment; her eyes fixed to one of the bodies.

"No, Max." Charlie stepped towards her. Max inched closer to the corpse. "No. We've discussed this. No eating magical creatures." Max turned to face Charlie, her eyes wide and sad. "Don't give me that. I'll buy you some beef ribs when we get home."

Max gave a quick, excited bark and padded to her side. Charlie scratched her behind the ear before the two of them jogged off ahead. Zack passed his staff to Bast and slipped his shoulders under the taller boy's arm. Together, they followed behind the others, limping through the jungle.

"I'm sorry, Bast. I should be able to just make the wound disappear." Zack looked down at his feet as he spoke.

"It's okay, man," Bast said in between grunts of pain. "You stopped me bleeding out. I can put up with a bit of pain. Still, it'll be deadly when you can."

"I'm working on it. It's mostly just convincing Sara that I'm ready."

"Yeah, she seems super careful. My mentor is a jerk, but he's happy for me to experiment a little. As long as I don't embarrass him. Or try to open any gates on my own."

"I think Life magic is a little more dangerous in unsteady hands." Zack's eyes flickered to Art. The lanky boy was walking ahead of them, looking out in between the trees. Bast followed his line of sight.

"Oh, yeah. Still, don't forget, however screwy the magic went after, it saved his life first."

Zack nodded as he walked.

"I just need to make sure I'm ready before I do anything like that again."

They lapsed into silence as they walked, Zack lost in his thoughts and Bast grimacing through the pain in his leg. After another 10 minutes or so, the two boys caught up with the others to stand before the oval of familiar, shimmering grey light.

Tabitha motioned for Bast and Zack to enter first.

"Let's get out of here."

CHAPTER 2

EASTER

K-pop music streamed from the bluetooth speaker in the suburban backyard. Zack and Art sat against the back fence, each sipping beer from a plastic cup, enjoying a moment of relative quiet away from the party around them.

Zack nodded in appreciation at the taste of the beer. "Nice one, Art."

"I asked for the most expensive keg they had. Dude was so eager to sell it, I'm not even sure I needed any magic to stop him checking my ID." Art drained his cup. "Are you just going to nurse that one all night?"

"Nah, but I do have to go easy. Easter's a big deal with my family, and I can't be hungover in front of all that food."

"Easter." Art looked up at the night sky. "I can't believe it's almost been a year since the alley."

"Almost a year, or only a year?" Zack asked.

Art laughed. "Yeah. Both, I guess. I can't imagine life without this. But it still seems like only yesterday."

Zack took another sip. "And to think, we wouldn't be here if you hadn't tried to trick me into going to the movies with the girls."

"It wasn't quite the outcome I had in mind. But speaking of

girls, I noticed a few hanging out in the kitchen. I'm going to go have a shot."

"I suppose you're going to want a wingman?"

Art dusted strands of loose grass from his legs as he stood up. "Don't worry, I know you're a lost cause."

"Oh, okay."

Art looked him in the eyes with a raised eyebrow.

"Mate, I'd love you to come with me. Do you want to, though?"

"Well, no."

"That's what I thought."

"Good luck."

Art winked. "Don't need it."

The tall blonde boy strode away and into the house, while Zack remained seated, finishing his beer. Closer to the speaker, on the brick paved courtyard beside the house, Bast, Tabitha and Kimmy danced with half a dozen other teens. He envied them and the carefree way they could join in with almost any group of people. But that would never be him.

He took his time savouring his beer and thinking over the last year. Fighting magical creatures, travelling to strange realms and defending the world against invasion. It had all started with a chance encounter walking down an alleyway. The creature that had attacked them that night and stalked them for months through the realms, was now a month dead. Slain by Art's sword and burned to tar by Kimmy just to make sure.

Now they had earned their place among the mages of the Tower and the perks that came with it. Today's foray into the jungle realm of Calypso was the third mission they'd been assigned, in as many weeks and the pay was amazing. He'd made thousands in the last month alone. Zack was beginning to think he needed a better lie for his wealth than tutoring, or his parents would start to think he was dealing drugs. Zack laughed to himself; wouldn't want his parents thinking he was doing something dangerous like that.

Finished with his beer, Zack clambered to his feet and wandered towards the house. Tabitha and Kimmy were lost to the music but Bast, who was dancing with his arms around a guy from a nearby private school, shot Zack a pair of finger guns as he walked by. Smiling, he moved in through the back door. Art had found the group of girls and had his arm around one of them. She was laughing at something he'd just said while she ran her hand down his chest.

Zack paused for a moment. Art had been more successful with girls lately, but even so, that was fast. He decided to give the kitchen a wide berth and slipped into the lounge room, where half a dozen or so teens were watching what appeared to be a bad 90s horror movie. He was about to claim a seat on the edge when he noticed Charlie and her boyfriend Dave amongst the viewers. Charlie's wave was welcoming, but Dave's glare was far from it. Zack returned a hasty wave and hurried down the hallway.

Zack passed the open door of the bathroom and was confronted with a pitiful scene. A guy was on his knees, hunched over the toilet, loudly emptying the contents of his stomach into the porcelain. A girl was standing behind him, making soothing sounds as she rubbed his back.

"I'm sorry," he said, in between retches. "I'm so sorry. I shouldn't drink rum."

"No," she replied, "and you definitely shouldn't try and keep up with Ahmed."

"I know, I'm so sorry."

The girl glanced over to Zack and rolled her eyes.

Zack stepped just inside the bathroom.

"I'll watch him if you want. Maybe he could do with a glass of water."

The girl nodded. "Does that sound good, Jakey? I'll get you some water?"

"Yes, please," he replied, without looking up from the bowl.

She mouthed, 'Thank you,' before slipping past Zack and down the hall towards the kitchen.

"Hey mate," Zack said softly, "not feeling too good?"

"No, man. I can't stop heaving. I feel so sick."

"It's okay. You're going to be fine. Probably start feeling better in no time."

Zack took a quick look out the door and checked nobody was around. He closed his eyes and reached out to the Life floating around. Not too much; he wouldn't need it for what he was going to try. He sent a thin stream of Life into Jakey's head, targeting the regions of the brain responsible for the feeling of nausea, calming them. Only a little. Nausea was a vital response and if he switched it off completely, the guy could poison himself without skipping a beat. But just enough and he might be able to stop heaving, sip some water and start recovering.

Zack's fingertips flared with a gentle turquoise light and startled, he let the flow drop. Using magic had never done that before. His patient levered himself up off the toilet into a hunched stand.

"Actually, yeah. I think that might have been the last of it."

Zack patted him on the back as the girl returned with a glass of water. The two staggered to the lounge room leaving Zack alone in the hall. He stared at his fingers in concern and decided he needed another beer.

The basket of multicoloured boiled eggs was too tempting and Zack nabbed one, rolling it in his hands to crack the shell. The purple dye rubbed off onto his palms and his fingertips as he picked the hard white free of shards.

Ellen, his sister, shook her head in disgust.

"Do you ever stop eating?"

"What?" he said, his mouth filled with egg. "It's Easter."

She rolled her eyes and strode off into the kitchen. Zack reached for another egg, more to spite her than out of any real appetite. His cousin, Luke, snatched an egg for himself and sat down next to Zack.

"I haven't been able to catch you online for a game, lately."

Luke had introduced Zack to PC gaming, as well as having bought him his first set of dice for Dungeons and Dragons.

"Yeah, sorry. I haven't really been playing much."

Luke scrunched his nose in melodramatic nausea.

"I did not blow two months' pay on my new rig to not be able to shoot my little cousin across the map."

Zack rolled his eyes. "Please, I've been destroying you for the last two years."

"Because of the lag. That's why I needed the upgrade. What have you been playing?"

"Nothing, really," Zack answered. "Too busy studying."

One of his uncles tipped his beer towards Zack in loose salute.

"Good work. Last year this year, right?" he asked.

Zack nodded, chewing.

"Until university," Zack's mother added.

"What are you looking at doing there?" his uncle asked.

Zack swallowed. "Medicine, I hope."

"Doctor Marek." His uncle nodded in approval. "Nice to have a doctor in the family."

"I'm thinking of taking a gap year first though; the universities let you defer for a year," Zack blurted out, avoiding his mother's eyeline.

It didn't help. "That's the first I'm hearing of this."

"Medicine, if I do get in, is going to be full on. First there's undergrad, then postgrad and then you're off into internships. I think I'll just need a year to catch my breath."

"Plus, he's going to need to catch up on all the gaming he's missing out on, Aunty Ness," Luke added unhelpfully.

She narrowed her eyes, lips pursed thoughtfully.

"Also, Art's got a line on a promotions job that he and I might be able to get," Zack said. "Decent pay, commission work. Could be fun for a little while."

"Before going to uni the year after," his mother finished.

"Definitely. I really want to do medicine. I just want to be at my best when I do it."

She chewed her lip for a few moments without breaking eye contact. "Okay. You get into the right course and we can talk about a gap year."

With a crisp, concluding nod, she rose from the table, collected some plates and headed off to the kitchen.

The easy lie, second nature now, triggered the familiar stab of guilt. He had sworn an oath to the Tower to maintain the Silence: the secret that magic and monsters were real, but that didn't make it feel any better. He pushed it down and looked out towards the lounge room.

His grandmother was in her usual chair, tracing her index finger around the chubby palm of the family's newest addition. His cousin's daughter, Addison, was only a few months old, and Zack's aunty was helping hold her on his grandmother's lap. Her cancer made her too frail to hold the baby herself, but with Zack's magical help, she had enough energy to stay alert and get to know her great-grandchild. Their gazes met and she peered back with a knowing sparkle in her eyes. He wasn't sure how she knew he was the cause of her unlikely endurance, but she was keeping his secret and he decided that complied with the tenets of the Silence as best he could.

Keeping her awake and alert wasn't good enough for him anymore. Just over a month ago she'd been in the hospital with less than even chances of making it through the night. He needed to keep proving himself to Sara, to further his understanding of Life, until he knew enough to cure her for good.

CHAPTER 3

APPROVAL

Zack and the others crowded around Bast in the centre of the Tower's weapons room. Weapon racks lined the walls, and the training statues stood idle on the far side of the room.

"C'mon Bast, whip it out," Art insisted.

Bast shot him a raised eyebrow and Kimmy snorted.

Art blushed. "Oh, grow up. Let's see it."

"Fine. Fine." Bast pulled loose the cord and the cloth wrapping fell away, revealing a sword: Bast's new rapier. He stepped back and drew it from its scabbard. The long, thin blade whistled as it slid out and its proud owner gave it a couple of flourishes through the air before holding it out with both hands for his friends to have a closer look. The handguard was ornately crafted and gleamed in the light cast by the Tower's flames.

"It's lovely, Bast," said Tabitha.

Zack noticed there was detail engraved into the pommel. "What's that?"

Bast ran his thumb over it, smiling.

"It's an eagle. Dad's mob come from up in the Hunter making us Wonnarua men. And that's our totem. An eagle is a sign that

Kawal is looking over us. It feels right bringing it with me when we're out there."

"How much did it set you back?" Art asked.

"Nearly five grand."

Art winced.

"Should have brought me along, I could have got a discount for you."

"No chance," Bast replied. "I got it through the Tower. I doubt you'd get away with fiddling with their heads. Anyway, it's worth every dollar."

"It is indeed a beautiful blade, Bast," said a voice across the room.

Zack spun around. He hadn't heard Junie enter the room until she spoke. One of the Tower's liaisons - respected members who coordinated the groups of mages doing work on behalf of the Tower - Junie was an officious woman with short blonde hair, a tidy dress and clear dedication to the Tower.

"Thank you," Bast said, sheathing the sword.

"Please gather round. I have the details for your next task."

The teens moved over, forming a quarter circle in front of Junie.

"Today, I'll be dispatching you to rural South Korea. We've detected a small breach." She handed Tabitha a folded map. "Standard procedure. Find the breach, close it, if necessary, destroy anything that has come through and do whatever it takes to maintain the Silence in your wake. I suggest taking only concealable weapons, and Art, head upstairs and find somebody to enchant you with Korean before you go."

"We might not need to, Junie," Art replied. "Kimmy probably knows it."

"Why? Because I'm Asian?" Kimmy glared at him. "That's racist."

"What? No, not because…" Art stammered and looked to the others for help. "You're Korean!"

"That's still racist." Kimmy crossed her arms. "Anyway, unless we're looking to order food and nothing else, my Korean won't be useful."

Art shook his head and headed for the stairs, muttering, "That's all you needed to say."

As usual, Junie's face remained still, free of any indication of her thoughts.

"Zack, before you leave, Sara wanted a quick word."

"Oh, okay." His mind raced. Did she have new concerns about his magic? He snatched a short staff from the racks and strode towards the door. "Um, I'll meet you all in the lobby. Hopefully this won't take too long."

Zack hurried up the stairs, his mind filled with different worrying possibilities. So much so that he almost walked right into Sara as he reached the top of the stairs. The tiny, wrinkled and always alert Honduran woman had been waiting for him.

"Zachary, good. You're here. Follow me please." Without waiting for his response, his elderly mentor turned and paced down the corridor.

Sara walked clear past the door to her study and Zack opened his mouth to ask where they were going before she waved him in through another doorway. Zack swallowed with difficulty. It was the same infirmary room in which Sara had treated Art when Zack's untrained healing magic had gone awry and nearly killed him. The same room where Sara had threatened to exile him from the Tower. Zack worried he was about to relive the same conversation. He was also worried he was about to relive some of his breakfast.

Zack stepped past Sara and into the room. Thoughts raced around his mind and, for a moment, he thought he'd stepped back in time when he saw Art laying in the bed against the opposite wall. He slowed his breathing and his mind, then realised the figure was larger than Art. Much larger.

"Erik!" Zack called out in greeting and relief.

The hulking Norwegian man had always reminded Zack of

a Viking, something he was confident was a deliberate aesthetic choice on the Water mage's part.

"Hey there, young Lifer."

"Are you okay?" Zack asked, approaching the bed.

"You tell me," Sara joined him beside Erik.

Zack was about to reach for his sense of Life before he saw the 10-centimetre gash down the side of Erik's torso.

"Well, clearly not."

"And what would be the best course of action here, Zachary?" Sara asked, her eyes firmly on Zack's face.

It was a test then.

"Well, first, I'd probe the wound with Life magic, determine what tissue has been damaged. Then I'd channel narrow streams of Life to repair the injury. Organs first, then blood vessels, bone, muscle and skin. Then, I might top up his overall Life if he seemed at risk, although, probably not in this case. I'd also look for any sign of infection, just to be safe."

Sara nodded. "Very well, then."

Zack stood for a moment, waiting for Sara to begin. She also stood, watching him. Erik, too, was looking at Zack with a wry half-smile. Realisation rushed forward at him.

"Oh! Okay." Zack stepped closer to Erik, in line with the gash. Closer now, he could see it had probably been bandaged closed until recently, but blood was still seeping and, if it was as deep as it seemed, it wouldn't take much movement on Erik's part for it to open wider.

Zack centred himself and reached out for Life. It came easily to him, especially here in the Tower. He directed his attention to the wound. A single, sharp incision had cut the muscle and fat and damaged multiple ribs. He looked over his shoulder at Sara and she nodded again.

He closed his eyes and sought focus. As expected, his thoughts flooded his mind. The last time he tried to heal a wound, rather than just slow blood loss, he had nearly killed Art, and they had ended up in this room. Would this time be any different? What would happen if he failed? How long before Junie would need to replace him so his friends would have a competent Life mage with them? And where would that leave him? And if he succeeded? Would Sara finally give him permission to use this magic without supervision? Would she teach him more advanced magic? Would he learn to heal his grandmother?

The thoughts raced on, but he had learned not to ignore them, not to push them away, but to embrace them. To gather them together and turn them to a single purpose. To respond to their questions with one response. To do what was needed.

A needle thin stream of life flowed from him and into Erik's side, repairing the damage. No organs had been harmed, so he started with the blood vessels before moving down his mental list. Turquoise light bloomed from his hand and into the wound. Within moments, as the light dimmed, no sign of the gash remained.

"Very well done, Zachary," Sara said, placing her hand on his shoulder.

Erik sat upright on the bed and gave his torso a twist to each side before nodding with approval. "Fighting fit once more."

"That light," Zack said. "It's only just started happening. Am I doing something wrong?"

"Ah, you are seeing the light of your magic?" Sara asked.

Zack nodded.

"You are not doing anything wrong. And the light is not truly there. As we grow in our abilities and our minds become accustomed to magic, we see magic as light. Not enough to see the specific flows, but enough to know someone is working with it. That you can see it now is another sign that you are progressing well."

Zack smiled, wiping the sweat from his brow. "Does this mean…?"

"Yes," Sara answered, "you have my permission to use this healing magic unsupervised."

"Thank you, Sara." Zack was so buoyant he worried he might actually be bouncing.

"And you can start working at the infirmary, if you'd like. I'll ask Tom to do a shift with you to show you how it works." Sara smiled at him. "But you'd best go meet up with your friends. I understand you've got a breach to close."

"Yes, of course." Zack stepped towards the door, before turning back to Sara and Erik. "You didn't cut him just so I could heal him, right?"

Erik erupted into laughter, but Sara looked shocked.

"No, Zack," she said. "With the work the Tower does, there's rarely a shortage of injuries that are not so life threatening they can't wait for an opportunity like this. And far too often, it's Erik with one of those."

Erik beamed. "The work needs doing, the world needs protecting. What can I say?"

Zack hurried from the room and down the stairs to his friends. Art had rejoined them and called out as Zack approached, "All good, mate?"

Zack nodded. "Better than good, actually. Sara just gave me a green light on healing in the field."

They all congratulated him and Bast slapped him on the back.

"Deadly, mate. No more short-term fixes and bandages?"

"Well, I might still bring the bandages along, but no. That is, assuming you're all okay with that. I can understand if you're not comfortable."

"Dude, are you kidding? I trust you completely," Art said, squeezing his shoulder.

"Yeah, Zack," Tabitha said. "We know how strict your mentor is on you. Compared to most of ours, anyway. If she says you're good to go, you're good to go. I'd even let you heal my own mother."

Kimmy shrugged. "I would have let you practise on mine months ago."

Zack ignored the last comment. "Thanks, everybody. Let's get going."

"Yeah, to Korea," Bast grinned. "This should be fun."

"This sucks," Bast moaned, kicking and scattering the pine needles that littered the forest floor. "How much longer do we have to stay out here?"

"As long as it takes," Tabitha replied. "Until we find the breach or whatever came through."

"It's starting to get dark, Tabs," Charlie said. "We may need to rethink our plan."

Charlie had a point. Normally, magical creatures breaching through into the world left some kind of destruction or confusion in their wake that made it possible to track them down. Torn up landscape, panicking witnesses, even just unusual footprints. But here, there was nothing. The nearby town showed no signs of anything unusual, and hours of tromping around in the forested hills had been fruitless.

"I could try to seek Life again," Zack suggested.

"Yeah, maybe," Tabitha agreed, "but don't push yourself too hard. Charlie's right, we might just have to head back and tell Junie we couldn't find anything."

Zack nodded and stepped away from the others, positioning them behind him. He took a steadying breath and looked up into the tree-covered rocky hills. In his mind, as he looked around, he ran through the kinds of Life he knew he'd find. The old pine trees, the wild bamboo, the moss clinging to the rocks. Wildlife too: foxes, mice, birds and insects. He had to ignore all of those and seek something that didn't belong. He was about to close his eyes when, in the distance, he saw a flare of blue light. Faint against the failing sunlight, it disappeared in an instant.

"Hey guys," Zack said.

"Did you find something?" Art asked.

"Yeah, but not with Life. I think I saw something up on that ridge up there."

Charlie peered into the distance. "Are you sure?"

"Nope."

Tabitha looked up into the hills and then back at Zack.

"Can you sense anything up there?"

Zack shook his head. "That's way too far for me to sense. Sorry."

"No, it's all good," Tabitha replied. "I couldn't sense anything using Air in half that distance. Unless there was a storm coming, anyway. Oh well, I guess we'd better start moving up there."

Zack fell in next to Art as the group of teens trudged their way up the hill.

"How sure are you?" Art asked in a whisper.

Zack shrugged. "Pretty sure I saw something, but who knows if it's what we're looking for."

"Well, given we don't know what we're looking for, we might as well look, I guess."

"I'm more worried about being caught out here by the locals. Bunch of teens sightseeing during the day is one thing. Stomping around at night is another."

"Nah, don't worry about that." Art's grin shone in the dimming light. "Nobody will remember seeing us."

"Guaranteed?"

"Yeah. Well, assuming only five or so people found us. But if there were more, I'd figure something out."

The sun had finished setting and Zack judged that they'd made it halfway to where he thought he'd seen the blue light.

"Hold up. Let's take a break and I'll see if I can stretch my sense up there."

"Sounds good," Bast said. "I'll give it a crack too. Maybe you caught a glimmer of a breach or something."

Zack stepped past the others and closed his eyes, willing his mind forward and up towards the ridge. If he'd judged it right, he was now just within range of the blue light. Even so, he could feel the pressure building up behind his eyeballs and against his eardrums. And just as he released it, he felt something, a flicker of Life that didn't belong.

"There's something up there."

"Are you sure this time?" Kimmy asked.

"Yeah, he's sure," Bast answered. "I felt something too, a breach, I think. Feels a lot like a gate."

"Fantastic work, boys," Tabitha said. "Okay, from here on, we move as quiet as possible. No talking. Weapons out."

Zack was already gripping his short staff that passed for a gnarled walking stick but, next to him, Jackie removed the leather stitched 'hand cover' from her own walking stick, revealing the sharp metal spearhead, while the others drew their weapons from their bags. Armed and ready, Tabitha gestured for Charlie to take the lead and she complied, bow in hand, Max by her side.

The group spent the better part of an hour creeping in silence up the hills. The mossy soil gave way to dry, crumbling stone as they climbed higher and Zack stumbled more than once when the rocks beneath his feet shifted and rolled from his weight. He was caked in dust and sweat by the time they reached the ridge. Charlie had scampered ahead with Max and now motioned for the others to join her behind a cluster of boulders. Zack followed Art to the cover in a hustled crawl.

The ridge was wider than it looked from below and an old cabin stood several metres away from the edge. Or at least the remains of one. Time, likely with the help of wind and storms, had robbed it of most of its roof and half of one wall.

"If I was a Korean ghost, that's where I'd live," Bast whispered.

"There's no such thing as ghosts," Tabitha replied.

"You whitefullas are always so sure of what's real. Last year, you'd have said the same thing about wizards," Bast shot back.

Zack closed his eyes and reached out again. He found it, but it was hard to track.

"There's definitely something in there. It's strange though. We should move in, but carefully."

Tabitha nodded and leapt over the boulder, flail in hand. The others followed and, in a wide arc, they approached the ruined building.

Nothing stirred as they closed in on the cabin. Even without the roof, there was enough of a structure to shield the inside from the moonlight and the darkness hid any sign of what may be laying in wait. The teens swapped questioning looks with each other, until Kimmy threw up her hands in frustration and marched in through a gap in the wall. Bast leapt in behind her and the others followed.

Kimmy traced in the air and a fist-sized globe of fire sprang into life, casting back the din and revealing the inside of the cabin. It was as empty and abandoned as it had appeared from the outside and the air was filled with dust glittering in the firelight.

"Looks empty." Kimmy swept her foot across a thick layer of sediment on the old wooden floorboards.

"No." Jackie shook her head, her eyes darting around at the flickering shadows. "There's something here."

Max's growl made Zack jump. The air behind Charlie rippled and a creature emerged. It was the size and shape of a man but had a monstrous face with sharp teeth too long for its mouth and eyes that shone yellow in the dark. It wore, what appeared to be, tattered medieval robes and held a club in its left hand. A club it slammed into Charlie's ribs.

The impact sent Charlie sprawling to the floor and Max leapt at the creature, snapping at its throat. Before Zack could react, there was a flash of blue fire and two more of the creatures appeared.

Jackie's magical shield blocked the swing of one club that had been levelled at her head, but the other bashed Tabitha in her arm and she fell to her knees, dropping her flail.

Art attacked without hesitation, swinging his long blade over Jackie's head and slashing the creature across its chest. It fell back and raised its club in time to parry Art's second swing, blocking the blow that would otherwise have bit deep into its face.

Bast charged across the room at the creature that had attacked Tabitha, but before he could close in on it, it danced to the side and disappeared back into the air.

"Damn," Bast swore, slicing into the empty space around him.

Zack moved to Tabitha's side.

"Help me up," she said with a wince.

He slid his shoulder under her left arm and aided her back to her feet. Zack reached out for her flail, but she waved him off.

"I'm not going to be able to swing that, I can barely lift my arm."

"I could do something about that, maybe."

"Not yet," Tabitha said. "Not until we're safe."

Art grunted as his opponent blocked another of his attacks and the two foes pushed against each other, their weight on their weapons. The creature slipped backwards and Zack thought his friend might have worn it down, but it was a feint. A leathery foot swept up and struck Art in his sternum, forcing him backwards. The creature smiled as it too faded into the dusty air.

The third, borne to the ground by Max's ferocious assault, managed to get its hands underneath the dog's front legs. It gasped in pain as it tore Max away, sending her flying at Kimmy who stood guard over Charlie's prone figure. Max, dark blood staining her bared teeth, skidded along the cabin floor. She scrabbled back towards the creature but, before she could close the distance, it rolled away and faded from sight.

"Close in around Charlie," Tabitha called out and the others moved to obey. "Do we think they're still here?"

"Yeah, they're still here," Jackie said.

"Do you know where they are?" Kimmy asked.

"Sorry," Jackie answered, "it's not them I can feel, it's the danger they mean to us, so it's everywhere."

"I should see to Charlie," Zack said, glancing down at her.

"No," Tabitha said, "you can help her in a moment, but we need to be ready for their next attack."

"But—"

"She's breathing. Sooner we get these uglies, the sooner we can help her. Any idea what they are?" Tabitha asked.

"Not really," Art said. "Kinda look like goblins."

Zack pulled his sense back from Charlie. Her Life was strong enough for now.

"Yeah, but taller."

"Orcs?"

"No, too skinny. Definitely more like goblins. So… goblinoids?"

"S'pose. Doesn't explain the vanishing," Art noted.

"Or the blue fire."

"Yeah, we've got nothing, Tabs."

"Okay. Let's pair up then. Stevensons, you're together. Kimmy with Bast. And you're with me, Zack. Max, I don't know if you can understand me, but you watch Charlie for us, okay?"

Max was staring off into the darkness, but she gave a short, low growl and backed up towards Charlie.

"I'll take that as a yes, I guess," Tabitha said. "Okay, be ready for anything. We might only get one more chance at—"

The injured goblinoid rippled back into view, swinging its club down at Tabitha. Zack swung his staff at its leg as Tabitha heaved herself out of the way. The club thudded down onto the wooden floor, but Zack's attack was rushed and rather than striking the creature in the knee, it bounced off its thigh. The goblinoid wobbled but raised its club for a second attack.

Another creature appeared alongside Kimmy and Bast, swinging its club at Kimmy's chest. One hand on the base of her axe and the other behind its blade, she held it forward in a parry. Braced in her two hands, the axe head stopped the blow, biting into the wood of the club, but the force was still enough to lift her off her feet and knock her into Bast. The two teens tumbled against each other and fell to the floor while the goblinoid wrenched his club free of Kimmy's axe and lifted it for another attack.

The first goblinoid brought its club down at Tabitha, but Zack stepped forward, splitting his grip across his staff and raising it above his head to meet the blow. The club slammed into his staff and the force from it rushed through his arms, pushing him to one knee and nearly tearing the weapon from his hands. Behind him, he heard Tabitha incant and a deafening bang sounded in the space next to the goblinoid's head. Loud enough to make Zack's eyes water, the sonic assault stunned the creature and it dropped its club, clutching its ears in pain.

Zack slid his hands closer together and thrust the end of his staff against what he hoped was similar to a regular kneecap. He felt a sickening crunch and the creature collapsed to the ground. Max leapt from where she had been guarding Charlie and closed her jaws back onto the goblinoid's throat. Within seconds it lay still.

Kimmy and Bast were struggling to disentangle themselves, but neither had a weapon ready to defend against the two-handed swing of their attacker. With a roar, Art leapt across the cabin floor, lunging forward with his sword. The goblinoid spun and, instead of piercing into its side, the tip of Art's blade merely scratched across its arm. The creature shouted back and brought its club down towards him. But its yell turned into a scream as a ray of white-hot fire from Kimmy's fingertips burned into its chest and it fell to the ground. Art reversed his grip on his sword and thrust it through the back of the goblinoid's skull, silencing it.

Zack looked around the cabin for the third creature and saw Jackie standing in the shadows. Art had left her side to make his attack and now she was alone. The air behind her rippled and, as the third goblinoid revealed itself, Zack ran towards her, knowing he could not close the distance before the creature attacked. Jackie took a deep breath and closed her eyes as the club moved towards her skull.

CHAPTER 4

DISCOVERY

In the last instant, Jackie dropped to one knee. The goblinoid lunged after her but overbalanced. In a fluid motion, she planted the base of her spear against the cabin floor, the tip pointed over and behind her shoulder. Off balance, the creature stumbled forward and its weight carried it into the spear, impaling itself. The goblinoid, lifeless, continued to fall forward and Jackie yelped as its body pinned her to the floor.

Art was only a second behind Zack and the two boys hauled the creature off her.

"Are you okay?" Zack asked, looking for any sign of injury.

"Yeah, I'm fine," Jackie replied. She looked at Art as she climbed back to her feet. "I suppose you're going to tell me off or something?"

"Jackie," Art said, taking a deep breath. "That was the coolest thing I've ever seen."

Zack smiled at them before turning and hurrying to Charlie's side.

"Yeah, Jackie," Tabitha said, "that was amazing. I thought you said you couldn't sense exactly where they were."

Jackie blushed. "Not until it was about to hit me. Mr Smith calls it the 'collapse of the danger probability function'."

"Is that like, a real thing?" Bast asked.

"I don't know. I don't understand much of what he says. But…" Jackie gestured to the dead goblinoid.

"Hard to argue with that," Kimmy said.

Zack knelt beside Charlie, and Max gave him a whimper of concern.

"I'm not sure," he replied, guessing at the dog's question. "Give me a moment to find out."

Whether or not that answer satisfied her, Max settled back down, resting her muzzle against Charlie's hand.

Zack probed Charlie's Life with his mind. It was strong and its effort to repair the damage directed Zack to three main injuries. The impact from the club had broken her forearm before continuing through to crack several ribs. The splintered bones had cut through muscle and blood vessels, but no organs seemed to have been damaged. However, it was the third injury that concerned Zack the most. Charlie must have hit her head as she fell to the floor and, while the force of that impact might have been the least of the three, her skull was cracked and Zack could sense a light internal bleed. Zack probed deeper, worried that her brain might have been damaged, and just as worried that he might have to do something about it. Thankfully, beyond the pressure of the broken skull and some light bleeding in between the bone and the skin, the brain seemed fine. At least fine enough to get her home and in front of a more experienced Lifer.

Zack directed a gentle flow of Life into Charlie's skull, willing it to the precise points of fracture and repairing the damage, before moving on to the surrounding tissue and blood vessels. His hand glowed again with the turquoise light of Life, but he stayed focused. Charlie's face relaxed and Max licked her cheek.

"I'm not done yet, Max. Be gentle," Zack said, shifting his focus to Charlie's ribs.

He started with the bones. Memories of Art's overgrown bones pushing out against his skin, caused by Zack's own use of untrained Life magic, threatened to distract him, but Zack accepted the stray thoughts, bending them to his purpose. Charlie's ribs reformed as he worked, the cracks and splinters growing back healthy and strong. Next, he moved the flow of Life towards her muscles and then to her blood vessels and finally to the abrasion he could sense on her skin. He ran his hand over the point of impact to confirm the bones had set in the correct position.

"Gonna buy me dinner first?" Charlie spoke in a weak, dazed voice.

Zack snatched his hand back, hoping the gloom of the cabin hid his blush.

"H— hold still, Charlie. I haven't fixed your arm yet."

"'Kay."

The breaks in the arm were clean, if brutal, and Zack poured Life into the injury with confidence.

"Okay, that should do it. I've kept some of the swelling, it'll help protect your arm if I've missed anything. How do you feel?"

"Good, yeah. A bit spacey, but not sore or anything."

Max yapped in excitement and leapt at Zack, licking his face up and down.

He fell back, before scrambling to his feet. "Yuck, Max."

"She's grateful that you looked after me. We both are." Charlie eased herself up.

Zack gave a stunted nod.

"It's nothing. It's just what I can do. Okay, how's everybody else going?" He turned around and blinked at what he saw.

The room looked different. Kimmy's globe cast a brighter light than before and the shadows had receded further. The walls were marked with strange, arcane symbols and several piles of items cluttered the previously bare floor. There was also the grey light of a breach in the centre of one of the walls.

"What happened?" Zack asked, looking back and forth to the others.

"No idea," Bast replied. "A couple of seconds ago the shadows kind of melted away and all this stuff was here."

Kimmy twitched, her eyes flitting around the cabin.

"Do you think there's another one of those creatures out there?"

Art scratched the side of his head.

"I don't think so. I reckon they were hiding all this, somehow."

"And then when we killed them, their magic faded." Tabitha nodded as she finished the thought.

"Makes sense, I guess," Kimmy said. "But why?"

Bast pointed at the liquid, grey light.

"I reckon that's got something to do with it. Look, it's perfectly elliptical. I was right. That's not a breach. That's a gate. Somebody on this end opened it. I can feel it. And some of these markings on the wall, I don't know what they are, but they feel like Movement magic, maybe anchoring the gate or something."

"Why would somebody do that?" Charlie asked, crouching next to Max.

Art waved his hand through the space above some of the other symbols.

"Also, some of these are Mind symbols, I'm sure of it."

Kimmy burst into a fit of laughter.

"What?" Art asked. "It's definitely Mind magic."

Kimmy waved him off.

"Oh, I believe you. But you get what they were doing, right?"

"Who?" Jackie asked.

"Whoever set all this up." Kimmy pointed at the gate, the symbols and the clutter on the floor. "Look at this stuff. There's jewellery, purses, wallets, a bit of cash. Somebody has used magic to set up a little criminal enterprise."

"Two somebodies," Zack said.

"Huh?" Kimmy turned to face him.

"Two somebodies. One for the Movement magic and the other for the Mind magic."

"So, what should we do?" Charlie asked.

"We close the gate, scratch up the markings and then get the heck out of here, yeah?" Kimmy suggested.

Tabitha pulled her phone from her pocket.

"I want to take some photos of the markings first. Junie will want to see them."

"And we should get rid of the bodies too," Zack added, "to maintain the Silence."

"Where?" Art asked.

Zack pointed to the gate. "Send them home?"

"Fair enough, but Bast, can you be ready in case something on the other side disagrees with us chucking corpses at them?"

Bast laughed.

"Sure thing, mate. Gates are easy enough to slam shut. I'll be ready."

Art and Zack dragged the three goblinoid bodies close to the gate. Zack was panting by the time they were finished; healing Charlie had taken more out of him than he'd realised. He wiped the sweat from his brow and looked at Art and Bast.

"Ready?" he asked.

The other boys nodded.

Doing his best to pretend he was hurling a large sack of potatoes, rather than a corpse, ignoring how the leathery skin was rapidly cooling in the night air, Zack gripped the creature by the shoulders while Art held the legs. Together they heaved it through the grey light. Not waiting for a reaction, they repeated the task until all three bodies were gone and they stepped back to allow Bast to close the gate. Zack noticed a faint orange glow around Bast's fingers as he incanted. Now that Sara had explained it was a sign of his improved sense of magic, he could better appreciate the way the light bloomed from his friend's hand.

By the time they were done, Tabitha had taken pictures of the painted symbols and Kimmy had defaced them with her axe.

"What do we do with all that?" Bast pointed at piles of valuables.

"Bonus?" Art asked with a hopeful smile on his face.

"Art!" Jackie looked horrified. "That all belongs to somebody."

"Well, if we leave it here, it's going to belong to whoever summoned magical goblin ninjas into our world. Do you want that?" Art asked.

Tabitha rubbed her chin.

"Art is right, we don't have any way to get it back to who it belongs to. What if we took the cash and left the rest? Anything else might be hard to explain if we get caught with it."

Art opened his mouth as if to argue but shut it again with a resigned shrug. They all started poking through the piles, pocketing any notes they found. Tabitha winced as she reached toward the meagre hoard.

Zack rushed to her side. "Sorry, I forgot to check if anybody needed any healing."

"Well, you didn't forget everybody," Kimmy smiled, with a suggestively raised eyebrow.

Tabitha ignored her. "Thanks, Zack. I could use some help with my shoulder, my whole arm is throbbing beneath it."

Zack probed the arm with his mind. It was a mess of bruising and pulled muscles and ligaments.

"Hold still," he said, directing Life towards the injuries. Turquoise light bloomed and Tabitha stretched out her arm.

"Wow, thanks Zack. This feels great."

"No problem," he smiled. "Anybody else?"

The others shook their heads or waved him off as they continued hunting through the stolen loot.

"I think that's everything," Charlie said, stepping back from the piles.

"Yeah, I guess so," Art said, with a note of disappointment. "If everybody's happy, I'll take it all, get it exchanged when we get home and share it out."

"Why you?" Kimmy asked.

"Because if they ask any strange questions about why I have so much cash I can deal with it."

Kimmy shrugged and dropped the issue.

"Okay, let's get out of here," Tabitha said. "It's a long way back to the Tower entrance."

The group collected their belongings, left the cabin and then made their way down the rocky slope. The stones gave way to trees and, once they were deep into the forest, Charlie led them around the outskirts of the village.

They had only just made their turn towards the highway when they were met with multiple beams from torches. At least a dozen men, some in uniforms, stepped out from behind trees. One of the men spoke in what Zack assumed was Korean, his voice loud and firm.

Art didn't hesitate. He ran forward at them, screaming in the same language, his arms waving. He gestured towards the trees to the side and screamed. The torchlights turned to where Art had pointed and there was a brief flicker of purple from his fingertips.

As one, the men started screaming, dropped their flashlights and fled deeper into the woods. Art screamed twice more for good measure before turning back to his friends.

"Quick. We need to be out of here before that wears off."

"But what—" Tabitha started to ask.

Art cut her off. "I'll explain later, let's go."

Zack fell in beside Art as they hurried towards the highway.

"That was you 'figuring something out'?" he asked.

"Hey, I said I'd handle it. I didn't say it would be pretty."

Zack claimed a seat on the bus next to Art, enjoying the weight of the cash-filled envelope Junie had given him. Tabitha leaned forward and spoke in hushed tones.

"Junie was rattled by those pictures of the markings."

"How can you tell?" Bast asked. "She always seems cool to me."

"I just can. I spend the most time with her and I'm telling you, she's worried. We can all make it back here Tuesday after school, yeah?"

The others all nodded, except for Charlie, who was distracted by her phone. The device had buzzed five or six different ways within seconds of her turning it back on when they left the Tower.

"Charlie?" Tabitha prompted.

She looked up, her eyes distant for a moment before they focused back on the others. "Yeah?"

"Are you going to be free to come with us to the Tower on Tuesday?"

"Yep, I can do that."

"You sure?" Kimmy asked. "You don't need to check if you have other plans?"

Charlie glanced back at her phone before jamming it into her backpack.

"Yeah, I'm definitely free." She turned away and looked out the window.

Art nudged Zack. "You did good today, man."

"You think?"

"Yeah, mate. Healing magic all over the place, no rib cages bursting out of chests, great work."

Zack grimaced at the mention of his past failure. He still had dreams about the day on the beach when he had tried to save Art's life but failed to control the magic.

"Art, I'm sorry I—"

"No mate, I'm saying it's great. Seeing you patch Charlie and Tabs up; do you know how much safer I feel being out there? How much safer I feel having Jackie out there?"

"I'm just glad I'm finally being useful."

Art scowled. "Finally?"

"Yeah, you know what I mean."

"I know what you think you mean. I swear, I need to find some bit of Mind magic that pulls a guy's head from his arse and lets him see that he's awesome. Fix you right up."

Zack snorted. "Yeah, okay."

"You know what you need?"

"What?"

"A tattoo."

Zack blinked, staring at Art. "I need a tattoo?"

"Definitely. We can easily afford one with what we've been making."

"I can afford a lot of things. Why would I want a tattoo?"

"Because they're cool. And because it'll remind you of how much of a badass you are. I'm kinda getting sick of that being my job, so I'm going to outsource it to some ink."

"We're not old enough."

Art rolled his eyes in response.

"Yeah," Zack agreed. "It's not a problem while I'm with you. But then I go home. Where my mum lives and has eyes."

"But you're a badass," Art said, straight faced. "And badasses don't worry about being caught with tattoos."

Bast's head appeared from over the seat behind them.

"Who's getting a tattoo?"

"We are," Art answered before Zack could shut him down.

"I'm in. The Tower bros, getting matching tattoos."

Zack opened his mouth to object, but Tabitha spoke up, "Tower bros? So, us gentle little ladies can't get tattoos?"

"The hell we can't?" Kimmy's voice was acidic. "I'm going to get a neck tatt of a flame."

"You're not getting a tattoo on your neck, Kimmy." Charlie knelt, leaning over the back of her seat. "Get it somewhere tasteful. I'm going to get mine on my lower back."

"A tasteful tramp-stamp?" Kimmy laughed.

Bast clapped. "Yes, we're all getting ink."

"Well, not all of us." Art tilted his head towards Jackie.

Jackie stared at him in silence, her steady blue eyes looking more the colour of steel.

"Oh, you can't be serious," Art said, shaking his head.

"I'll get it somewhere subtle."

"Where is subtle on a 14-year-old?"

As the argument continued, Zack leant forward, his face in his hands. By the time this was over, they'd all be getting tattoos.

CHAPTER 5

OTHER DUTIES

"What are you so worried about?"

Art's question snapped Zack out of his staring contest with the inside of the staffroom door. He stood up from leaning against a filing cabinet.

"Oh, I don't know, getting caught downloading maths tests?"

"Well, that's just offensive," Art said, swivelling around in his chair to face Zack. "As if my genius can be foiled by a mere teacher."

"What if they run off and tell somebody before you can mindwipe them?"

"Run off to tell who? Zack, they're teachers. They are who you run off and tell things to. They'll stand there and tear into us, in the full comfort and confidence that they hold the power here." Art held his hands out, encompassing the room. "This is literally their space. They'll yell, or ask pointed questions, or gasp at the audacity of us. And then, 'woosh,' not a problem anymore."

"Yeah, okay." Zack's eyes moved back to the door.

"So, I'll ask again. What are you actually worried about?"

Zack took a deep breath.

"My grades. Getting into medical science is going to be tough, even with this." He gestured at the computer. "My exam results are great, but my assignment scores are weighing me down."

Art stroked his chin.

"I could go into the database, up your scores a little. Risky though, a teacher could remember the mark they gave you."

"I don't suppose you could change what they remember?" Zack asked.

"Nah, sorry. Taking out memories is easy enough. And putting emotions in is alright, too. But putting a specific thought in, or a memory?" Art sucked a sharp breath between his teeth. "I'm not there yet."

Zack picked up a Rubik's cube from one of the desks and fiddled with it.

"That's okay, I figured as much."

"Can I ask something?" Art asked, as the transfer progress bar filled up behind him. "Why do you care? I'm not even sure I want to go to uni anymore, let alone something as difficult as medicine."

"You don't want to go to uni?"

Art leaned back, placing his feet up on a desk.

"Why would I? We're making great money with the Tower. Between that and what I can make using a little magic here and there, I'll never need a proper job. Neither will you."

"I don't know. It's important to my parents. But it's more than that. Can you imagine what good a doctor with my magic could do?"

Art stretched back in his chair.

"I like the sentiment, dude. But I think it's a lot of work when there's easier ways."

"Yeah, 'spose. But I like the idea of being a doctor and since I've got to be something..."

"I'm not sure you do. But if you want to be one, then that's enough for me. You're missing out on a lot of gaming time, though. Speaking of which, did you get that copy of Star Defend 3 I sent through?"

"Yeah." Zack frowned. "Thanks. I installed it but haven't played it yet."

"Why not?" Art asked in surprise. "We've been hanging out for it since we stopped playing SD2."

"Exactly," Zack replied. "'We'. You, me and Matt. The idea of playing this one just reminds me of how much we screwed that up."

Art turned back around to face Zack.

"Yeah, that's fair. Have you spoken to him at all lately?

Zack shook his head. "Not really. He doesn't even look at me in English. You?"

"Nah. I don't have any classes with him. I've thought of reaching out to him. I've even thought of 'fixing it'." Art wiggled his fingers in air quotes. "But I'm not sure what the point would be."

"He was our best friend," Zack replied.

"Yeah. And I miss him. That's not what I mean," Art said. "Our friendship didn't end because we had a disagreement or a fight, it ended because we spent no time for him and couldn't tell him why. None of that has changed. Maybe next year, when all we've got on is Tower work, we can reach out again and apologise."

"Yeah, maybe." Zack wasn't hopeful. He pointed to the screen over Art's shoulder. "Download complete."

Art pulled out the thumb drive. "And we're done."

The door swung open. "Just what are you boys doing in here?"

Zack dropped the Rubik's cube as the angry headteacher, red-faced and nostrils flaring, stormed towards them.

"Mr Nelson!" Art smiled, pocketing the drive before standing up. Faint wisps of purple gathered at his fingertips. "It's not what it looks like."

Zack tightened the straps of his wrist guards and clenched his fists, feeling the knuckles press securely into the protective grooves of the hardened plate. His eternal nemesis, the bronze samurai statue, stood waiting, clutching a wooden sword in its hands. Zack squared up to it and took a deep breath. This was going to hurt.

"You got this, man!" Art shouted from the wall.

Zack slid his right foot back and entered his fighting stance.

"I'm going to trust you to react as if my punches hurt you, okay?"

The samurai's only response was to raise its weapon.

"Okay then," Zack said. "Begin."

The statue leapt forward, bringing the sword down in an overhead arc. Zack darted forward and to the left, avoiding the attack and bringing him past the weapon's 'blade'. He took the opportunity to land a solid left jab into the statue's ribs, but his opponent was fast, and lashed out at him with its elbow. The strike cracked against Zack's jaw and, his vision spinning for a moment, he stumbled.

The samurai spun, bringing its sword around in a violent horizontal swing. Zack's vision cleared in just enough time to drop to the ground and, while the weapon completed its rotation, he kicked out hard with his heels and struck the statue's shin. His opponent obliged and dropped to his knee as if Zack's blow had been strong enough to topple the mass of metal. Zack smiled. That is, until the samurai, using that shift in momentum, reversed the path of its sword and brought it crashing into Zack's ribs. Air exploded from Zack's lungs and he hastily tapped the ground next to him, surrendering the match. The statue retreated three steps back and stood at the ready.

Art walked over to Zack's side and helped him up.

"So, turned out you don't got this, man."

Zack nodded and then winced, clutching at his side.

"He break something?" Art asked.

Zack probed his ribs with a thread of Life.

"Small crack. Enough to hurt like hell though." He wove a thicker stream of Life in, directing it into the bone, where it knitted the fracture closed.

"That was wild," Tabitha said from the doorway. Zack looked over and saw that she, Kimmy, Bast and Charlie had arrived and, presumably, seen his walloping. He fought in vain not to blush.

"Why in the world are you training without a weapon?" Kimmy asked. "You should always have one with you. It's not like you can depend on your magic in a fight."

"That's kind of the point," Zack said, trying not to take Kimmy's dismissal of his magic personally. "If I lose my staff, I don't have a backup weapon like you do."

Bast clapped him on the shoulder. "Hand to hand with a statue is crazy. I love it."

Art rolled his eyes. "Not so crazy." He pointed to the other side of the training room where Jackie was moving to stand in between four statues. "That's crazy."

Jackie also hadn't brought a weapon with her into the training pattern, but neither had any of the statues. Instead, each stood next to a crate, resting atop a tall, thin table.

"What's she up to?" Charlie asked.

Art shook his head. "Something stupid. But she won't listen to me." He looked at Zack. "You've got enough juice left if this goes badly?"

Zack nodded, but before he could speak, Jackie bowed, and the four statues leapt into action. Rather than move towards her, they each drew a palm-sized object from their crate and began to circle around the young girl. Without notice, the one behind her hurled its item at her, but Jackie spun and conjured up a shield to deflect it. The projectile bounced off the steely light and skimmed across the training room floor. The solid clacking sound made it clear what it was.

"They're throwing rocks at her?" Tabitha asked.

Art's lips tightened as he nodded again, his eyes not leaving his sister. A second statue hurled its stone at her. This time, Jackie murmured a phrase and her right arm snapped up, batting the stone from the air. Kimmy whooped in support.

The statues kept up their assault, and Jackie maintained her defence, until two stones came at once. She blocked one and ducked the other, but she misplaced her foot and staggered off balance. When the next projectile flew towards her, she wasn't ready and it thudded into her shoulder. The blow knocked her to her knees, but she pushed herself up and batted away the next rock. However, she was slowing and soon another rock slipped past her magical defences. This time, it landed against her jaw and the blow took her off her feet.

"Enough!" Art roared, running towards her.

The statues stopped and moved back to their starting positions. Zack followed Art to Jackie's side, where she was already pushing herself back onto her feet.

"That's enough for today, Jacks," Art said.

She narrowed her eyes at him.

"I decide when it's enough, not you." She rubbed her jaw and winced. "But I've decided that it's enough."

"More than enough," came the rich Spanish tenor of the Commander's voice. The eight foot boulderish form of the Tower's master-at-arms stepped past the statues and into the ring. "Again, I must make the point that you are in an incomplete state and should wait until you have been finished before testing yourself."

Jackie pushed herself away from Art and faced up to the towering mass of stone.

"If I'm so unfinished, how did I block so many attacks?"

The Commander dismissed her comment with a wave of its hand.

"A lump of steel might do a passable job as a club, but it must finish with the forge before it can be tested as a sword. And I will not be blamed for damaging the Tower's newest lump of steel, whether it shows promise or not."

A smile broke on Jackie's face.

"So, I'm showing promise then, am I?"

The Commander turned away without response and stalked

back to the rows of idle statues. Jackie was still smiling, with a thin stream of Life easing her swelling, when Junie entered the room. Their liaison was even more businesslike than normal as she surveyed the room.

"I have a training exercise I need you to undertake. Follow me."

She led them in silence up a series of winding stairwells and to the Gate Room. The first few times Zack had visited this room, he'd pictured it as the highest room of the Tower, but now he wasn't so sure. He wasn't even confident that three dimensional concepts applied to the Tower. Whatever was the case, there were a lot of stairs.

Junie nodded to the woman on duty, who stepped forward and incanted. Orange light bloomed from her fingertips and the grey light of a gate rippled into existence.

"Close it when we're all through and open it again in twenty minutes," Junie instructed.

The woman nodded again and Junie led them through the gate. Zack stepped from the stone floor of the Tower onto sand and shivered at the sudden cold wind of a desert night. The moonless sky was nevertheless bright with the glow of thousands of stars. Junie stood amidst the dunes, showing no sign of chill or discomfort as the grey light of the gate winked out behind them.

"Um, what kind of training are we going to do out here?" Bast asked, peering around.

"None," Junie answered. "I apologise for the deception, but I wanted to speak to the seven of you alone."

The teens stopped shuffling their feet.

"The cabin in Korea was concerning. Very concerning. That there are unsanctioned users of magic out there is not news. Part of the responsibility of the Tower is to track down those users and either invite them into the Tower, or otherwise ensure that they do not jeopardise the Silence."

"Why have we never been asked to do that?" Tabitha asked.

"Because you are too young."

Kimmy bristled, "Not too young to stop that creature from invading the Tower!"

Junie held up a hand. "You misunderstand me, Kimmy. I do not mean that you are not powerful enough. No, you are all growing into your strengths impressively. I mean precisely that you are too young. Think back to when I met you in your school. Timur and I displayed a certain level of gravitas. Yes, his Mind magic was helpful, but do you imagine you would have been as impressed by a pair of teenagers? Do you imagine that a group of mages in their forties would be?"

Zack pictured a reversal of the day they met Junie. Them trying to explain the Tower's role and the importance of the Silence and the Watch to a group of adults. Junie wasn't wrong about how absurd that would seem.

She continued, "There are those out there who have given their oath to the Tower and, while they do not seek knowledge from us, they learn a little by themselves. So long as they do not break the Silence in doing so, we allow it.

"Others still, by chance or determination, elude the Tower. These are the most dangerous, to the Silence and to our world. When we do find them, we give them a chance, when possible, to join us and to take the oath. But if they refuse? We end that danger. We must."

"You kill people?" Charlie asked, her voice soft across the sands.

"If they force our hand, yes. But we prefer to capture them, wipe their memory and return them to a normal life."

"How often do you get to do that second option?" Zack asked.

Junie was silent for a moment, before she answered, "Not as often as we'd like."

The desert was quiet for a time.

"So," Kimmy said, "does that mean you'll send out a group to deal with these people in Korea?"

"Yes. And no," Junie replied.

The dark night hid Zack's confusion and, he assumed, that of the others.

"The magic in the photos that Tabitha showed me is far too complex for a couple of people the Tower missed. They have been taught."

"And maybe by somebody in the Tower," Art added.

"What?" Bast turned, eyes wide.

"Think about it, Bast," Art said. "Why else would Junie drag us into the middle of the Sahara before talking to us about this?"

"You are correct, Art. I hope that I am being needlessly cautious. They were taught by someone, but that someone is not necessarily a member of Tower. But they may be." Junie clasped her hands together at her waist. "This is where you come in. You will help me investigate this."

"Why us?" Charlie asked.

Kimmy shot her a look, but Junie answered, "One, if a Tower member is responsible, I know it's not any of you; you haven't been trained in this magic. Two, you all trust each other, making it easier for you to work together on this where others would be trapped by suspicion. Three, others in the Tower underestimate you, because of your age. Few would ever believe I'd entrust something so important to children."

"What do you need us to do?" Tabitha asked.

"I'll find you a place to start your search. I can do that much without arousing suspicion. Then, you go in and see what you can hunt down. End the threat if possible. If not, gather information and return with it."

Zack nodded along with the others, trying to absorb the weight of their new responsibility.

"As full members of the Tower, my time as your exclusive liaison should be at an end and you would be expected to receive missions from any of the others, as well as from those who coordinate the specific functions of your Schools. However, I need you to continue to report directly to me, to prevent any interference with this task. I have sought special permission from the Tower's leaders, the Thirteen, claiming that your age qualifies you for more consistent supervision. They have agreed." Junie waved them back towards where the gate would soon reappear. "Come, it is time to return."

⸙———⸙———⸙

Zack picked the pieces of dried apple from his muesli bar and scattered them on the asphalt under the bench. Bast took a break from gnawing through his pear.

"So," he said, his mouth still full of fruit. "I have to be honest, I'm not wild about our new job description."

Kimmy raised her eyebrow at him.

"What do you mean? I don't love that Junie has apparently told the Thirteen that we're too young to hack it. But on the other hand, this special job sounds like a really good chance to prove ourselves."

Bast shook his head. "No, I get that. But I don't like the idea that we're up against other people. Zack, you're on the same page, right?"

Zack chewed his mouthful while he thought. "Actually, I think I'm up for this. Running down leads, putting clues together, trying to stop people from causing harm? Seems a lot better to me than going into other worlds and getting into fights."

"Yeah, until we need to fight these people. You going to be up for that?" Bast asked.

"Hell yeah, I am," Kimmy answered. "I won't be looking to hurt anybody, but if they try something-"

"Yeah, I don't know." Bast rubbed at his temple. "I don't know if I could do that."

"Me neither," Zack said. "But that's not the goal here. We just need to find out who is responsible for this dangerous magic getting out and get them to stop. It doesn't need to get violent."

Kimmy laughed. "Yeah, because everything the Tower has asked us to do has been violence free. What's the deal anyway? Bast, I've seen you stab about a thousand different things and even you, Zack, you've hit the stuffing out of plenty."

"Things being the operative word there, Kimmy," Zack said. "The creatures we fight aren't actually alive, they are a form that magic has taken. This is different. I'm not sure I could hurt an actual person."

Art hurled his schoolbag against the retaining wall and sat down next to Zack with a huff.

"I could definitely hurt a few right now."

"What's the matter?" Zack asked.

"Jackie."

"You want to hurt Jackie?" Bast's eyes were wide and confused.

"No," Zack guessed. "Jackie's bullies, yeah?"

"Yep, I found her in tears. Again."

"And you're going to let those girls keep doing that?" Kimmy's voice was tight.

"You think I don't want to stop it? I want to fill those girls' heads with so much fear they wet themselves in front of the whole school. Jackie's forbidden it. Said it's her problem to deal with."

Kimmy took a step back and looked down at her feet.

"Yeah, okay. That seems fair."

"But she's not dealing with it." Art ran his hands through his hair, pulling at it slightly. "I don't get it. You saw her in Korea. She's like a freakin' Viking spearmaiden. A pocket-sized one, but still."

"Girls are awful, man," Kimmy said, with more kindness in her voice than Zack had ever heard directed at Art. "Why do you think I'm friends with so few of them?"

"I thought that was because you made out with their boyfriends,"

Art replied, before his eyes went wide and he slammed his mouth closed.

Kimmy's mouth tightened.

"Kimmy, I didn't—" Art started, but it was too late. She scooped up her bag and stormed off across the quad.

Bast laughed into his hands. "She's going to make you pay for that one."

"I didn't mean anything by it! I've heard her say worse about herself."

"Yeah, but when she says it, it's not you saying it, is it?"

"I'm dead."

Zack clapped him on the back.

"Come on, let's hit up the weapons room this afternoon, work out some of the stress. You'll feel better."

"I'm in," Bast said with a grin.

"Yeah okay, one last training session before she uses me for firewood."

"That's the spirit."

CHAPTER 6

INVESTIGATION

"It's colder than I thought it would be," Bast said, crossing his arms in front of his body and rubbing them.

"It's like one o'clock in the morning," Tabitha replied.

"Yeah?"

"In Canada."

"Uh huh."

"And you're surprised that it's cold."

"I'm surprised that it's this cold, yeah," Bast said, with a slight sulk in his voice.

"Let's speed up then," Art said, glancing at his phone. "It's just a bit further down this way, I think."

"Did Junie say why she thought this shop was a good lead for us?" Charlie asked.

"Not really," Tabitha replied. "Apparently, it's kind of an unsanctioned magic shop. But I got the feeling it's more than a guess."

Jackie looked around at the street signs.

"Do they speak French in Montreal?"

"No, I don't think so," Bast said with a shiver. "I think Quebec is the French bit."

"Montreal is in Quebec, Bast," Charlie said.

"Okay, it's becoming clear to everybody I know nothing about Canada, so I'm just going to stand here and look pretty."

"Do any of us speak French?" Zack asked.

There were murmurs in the negative.

"No sweat," Art said, not looking up from the map on his screen. "I can cover us if it's a problem. Hey, we should get some poutine on the way back."

The streets became narrower and the buildings less well kept as Art led them through the dark streets of Montreal. He stopped under the awning of a boarded-up business.

"According to this, it should be right around the corner."

"What are we waiting for then?" Kimmy asked, taking a step forward.

"Hold on," Tabitha said. "We should be careful about this. We want to know what we're looking at before we go barging in."

"Barging?" Kimmy's eyebrows raised.

"I've got an idea," Charlie said. "Give me some space. Max, you stay with Jackie."

The large dog padded next to Jackie, who ruffled her fur with deep affection, while Charlie stepped towards a sewer grate. She knelt down next to it and concentrated, whispering. A russet-coloured light emanated from her hands for a brief moment before it was dark again and she stood. She returned to the others with careful steps, holding something in her hands. It was a rat.

"Ew." Kimmy screwed up her face.

"Ew?" Charlie stroked the back of the rodent's head. "This little one is just trying to live his life and he's going to help us out, so don't be so rude."

Charlie closed her eyes again and incanted, her fingers tracing in the air above the rat. As she finished, the rat's eyes flashed with a russet light, and when she opened her own eyes, they were the same colour. She staggered a step backwards.

"Oh wow, that's disorienting." She reached out with her free hand and knelt, feeling her way to the ground. "Okay, little friend. Off you go."

The rat bolted away from the group and down the street in the direction Art had indicated. Charlie stayed kneeling on the cold ground.

"Do you need a hand up?" Zack asked.

"No thanks. I'm looking through his eyes and if he's close to the ground, then it's safer for me if I stay down here. Okay, he's approaching the place. There's a light on. It's hard to see from this angle but it looks a bit like a cross between a pawn shop and a bookshop. Bars on the window." Charlie heaved, holding her hand to her mouth. "Oh hell, he climbed up the wall. Wasn't prepared for that. I can hear people inside, but I can't make out what they're saying. He can't see clearly from the window either, there's stuff in the way."

"Right, let's go," Kimmy said.

"Hang on." Tabitha held up her hand. "I don't think we should all go."

"Why not?"

"Seven of us and a dog, rocking up in the middle of the night? Stands out a bit."

"Who then?" Bast asked.

"I think maybe Art and Bast should go in," Zack said. "We know a Mind mage and a Movement mage were involved in Korea, so let's send in ours. Plus, Art might need to cover any language issues."

Tabitha nodded. "Good idea. You go too."

"What? Why?"

"Three is safer. Charlie will keep watch with her rat and we'll keep her safe until we need to come in with the cavalry." Tabitha tilted her head towards Kimmy.

Zack nodded. Charlie continued to stare into the night.

"Zack, why don't you pick up the rat and take him with you? That way I'll be able to see what's happening and you can call us if you need us."

Kimmy huffed. "If we were going to be stuck out here in case you boys needed rescuing, we should have brought weapons."

"As we agreed before," Tabitha said, "hanging around with swords and axes might have given off a more hostile vibe than we wanted."

"Fine." Kimmy crossed her arms. "Not like I exactly need an axe if it comes to that anyway."

"It's a recon mission, Kimmy," Charlie said.

"Yeah." Kimmy nodded. "Until it isn't. Then it's barbeque time."

"You are terrifying," Bast said.

"Thank you."

Art shook his head. "Let's go."

The three boys walked down the street towards the store. It was two storeys and older by a few decades than any of the other buildings around it. The dim glow emanating from the single window was the sole light in the street.

"Not exactly screaming out for business, are they?" Bast said under his breath as they approached. "No signs or anything."

"They probably don't depend on foot traffic," Art replied.

When they reached the door, Zack saw Charlie's rat clinging to one of the bars on the window. He took a deep breath and reached out for it.

"That thing doesn't look clean, man," Bast said.

"Yeah, I know." Zack allowed the rat to climb onto his hand before slipping it into his shirt's front pocket. "I'm going to get tetanus."

"Okay, let me do the talking." Art pushed open the front door and the clang of a metal bell heralded their entrance.

A middle-aged man with a patchy beard and glasses looked up from where he had been lounging behind the counter on the other side of the room. "Bonsoir."

Art strode towards the man with confident steps. "Hello, do you speak English?

The man rolled his eyes but nodded. "Yes, English, of course."

"Thank you. I've heard your store is the best place to buy that certain something special."

Zack looked around the room. It was filled with clutter. Shelves lined the walls and, while most were filled with books, others held a variety of goods. Candles sat next to small bones carved with runes, while woven bracelets hung from the same stands as rabbits' feet. Zack almost bumped into a second, much shorter man, who was eyeing the three of them with suspicion.

"You look a little young to be in this store," the short man said to the three of them.

"Thank you," Art replied. "I moisturise."

Zack watched Art trace the air behind his back, away from the sight of the two men.

"Now, now," the first man said, "a customer is a customer, especially one who has the currency to pay for the something special he is looking for."

"That I do," Art said, moving past the shorter man. "I might have a look around in a moment, see what else you have here, but in particular I was looking for some ink."

The shopkeeper took off his glasses and rubbed at his eyes.

"Ink? Let's see. Over there behind your handsome friend I have some vials of rose and pomegranate infused ink, perfect for love spells."

Art laughed and a faint purple glow appeared on his fingertips. "Um, not quite what I was looking for."

"Or perhaps some wishing ink? Harvested from a rare Mediterranean octopus?"

The shorter man in front of Zack had ceased his glaring and, instead, was leaning against the table behind him, humming softly to himself.

"No, my friend," Art said. "You misunderstand me. I'm looking for the real deal here. Some ink infused with something from another world. I heard from a friend that you had some in stock."

"Ah." The man tapped his nose and winked. "Apologies. I mishtook you for one of the tourishts. My father alwaysh had a nose for who was playin' around and who was for real. It was his shop, left it to me..." The man drifted off, staring into space.

"Art?" Zack asked.

"Looks like our friends may have had a little bit too much to drink." Art winked at Zack before turning back to the man. "That's okay, we'll be out of your hair soon. So, do you have any of that ink left?"

"What? Ink?" The man blinked at Art. "Oh, yes. Let me see."

He knelt down and fumbled through a cabinet below the counter before clambering back up. He held out a thimble-sized glass jar to Art. "Schorry, empty."

Art held up the glass close to his face. "There's a drop or two left. Can I buy this from you?"

"Sure thing. I'll take fifty for it."

Art held out a $50 Canadian note but pulled it back as the man reached for it.

"Do you know who bought the last of it?"

"No, no, no. Shales are shtrickly confidential."

"Of course, of course. But I simply want to see if he bought too much, perhaps he can sell me his leftovers. I'm sure he'd appreciate it. And there's a finder's fee in it for you." Art waved a few more notes towards the man, more purple light trailing from his hand.

The shopkeeper scratched his head.

"Well, that should be okay then." He turned and opened a drawer, making a mess of the well-ordered index cards. "Here, I only have his name and his number, but he asked me to call him if I got any more of the ink in."

Art handed over the cash and snapped a photo of the index card on his phone.

"Where did you get this ink from, anyway?"

The man shrugged. "People come in and sell me stuff. I try and work out if I'm getting fairy dust or if it's actually fairy dust, you know?" He giggled to himself. "This ink though, it was barely on my shelf a week before this guy came in."

Without warning, the rat darted out of Zack's pocket and up his shoulder, squeaking. Before Zack could react, it leapt across to a table and clambered up the window. Neither of the shopkeepers had noticed, but Bast looked over at Zack in alarm. Zack peered through the window and saw two figures moving through the darkness towards the store.

"We're about to have company. Let's get out of here."

Art pocketed the vial and raced towards the door. "Again, let me do the talking."

When the three boys exited the store, they found two men approaching. The two were dressed similarly in long-sleeved shirts and trousers, and they stopped walking as Zack and his friends turned to move past them.

"Hey," said one, a dark-haired man with a thin moustache, "what were you boys doing in there?"

"Just looking for pomegranate ink to write a love spell with," Art said, barely slowing.

"Wait up, I want to talk to you." The man stepped closer to them.

"My mum said not to talk to strangers."

"Heh, very funny. But seriously, what are kids like you up to in a place like this?"

"Nothing you'll remember to be worried about," Art replied, weaving his fingers towards the two men.

The second man blinked in confusion for a moment, but only a moment, because the first man's face broke into a smile.

"Oh, I don't think so, child."

He flicked the back of his hand towards Art and they glowed with their own purple light. Art's eyes went dull and he stared, dazed, around the street.

The second man made his own gestures before clenching his hands into fists. In the dim light, Zack watched as the skin on the man's hands hardened into stone.

"Zack, get him and run!" Bast shouted.

The men moved towards them but not before Bast incanted and gestured towards the ground at the men's feet. The asphalt turned slick and both men fell hard on their backs. Bast caught up with Zack and Art as they rounded the corner.

"We need to get out of here," Zack said as the girls stepped out of the shadows.

Tabitha nodded. "Kimmy?"

Kimmy chanted to herself and smoke billowed out from between her hands. Tabitha stood right behind her and traced a fast pattern into the air, causing a funnel of wind to carry the smoke back down the alleyway.

"Run," Tabitha hissed.

The seven teens and their dog charged through the night, taking corner after corner in an attempt to lose any tail they might have. Art, despite the confused look on his face, didn't hesitate to keep up with them. After ten minutes of solid running, they took refuge down the stairs of a closed metro station to catch their breaths.

"Jackie?" Tabitha asked.

Between pants, Jackie nodded and held her hand up towards the stairs.

"Nothing. They might still be out there looking for us, but they aren't close."

"Who's not close?" Art asked, with a concerned look.

"Those two guys we bumped into coming out of the shop," Zack replied.

Art nodded. "Oh, yeah, those guys." He scratched his head. "Um, what shop?"

Zack's eyes narrowed. "Art, what do you remember about tonight?"

"Well, it's funny you say that, because I was just about to ask why it's so late at night."

"Because of the time difference between Australia and Montreal," Kimmy answered.

"We're in Canada?" Art asked, his eyes wide.

"Oh, hell." Zack rubbed his face.

"What happened to him?" Jackie asked, worry in her voice.

"Everything went fine in the shop," Zack replied. "Art got some of the ink, and we—"

"I did?"

"Check your pocket," Bast said.

"Oh wow!" Art held up the vial. "Cool."

"Charlie's rat warned me to look out the window."

"That worked?" Charlie said, looking pleased. "We saw two guys walking your way and wanted to give you a heads up."

"It's good you did," Zack said. "They were asking us all these questions. Seemed really interested in why we were there. I think Art tried to memory wipe them, but one of them sent it back at him. That would explain things."

"So, he had Mind magic?" Kimmy asked. "Do you think they were the two we're looking for?"

"Maybe one of them," Bast replied. "But the second guy didn't have Movement magic. I think it was Earth or something."

"Let's unpack that later," Tabitha said. "The important thing is that we got the ink and we got away safe. We should get out of here and back to the Tower."

They all nodded and started up the stairs.

"Hey, if we're in Canada," Art said, "can we get some poutine?"

CHAPTER 7

BAIT

Zack eyed the school librarian as he palmed a pretzel from the 'pencil case' in the middle of the desk. Assured the coast was clear, he slid it into his mouth and turned his attention back to his Ancient History paper. The half yearly exams, the last set of tests before the finals, were only a few weeks away now and, to get the full advantage of Art's thefts, he had to nail this essay and commit it to memory.

The others were spaced around the 12-seater study table, focused on their own work, with the exception of Art who alternated between scrolling through videos on his phone and thrusting them in front of Zack's face. The alarm on Tabitha's phone vibrated against the wood of the table. She stilled it with a swipe across the screen.

"Okay, study over. Time to get to work."

Art pocketed his own phone. "Finally!"

Kimmy glanced over at Art but otherwise ignored him, closing her books and pushing them to the side.

"What are our next steps?" Tabitha asked them.

"We could take what we have to Junie," Bast said. "See if she has any ideas?"

Art and Kimmy both shook their heads. Kimmy scowled at Art before turning back to Bast.

"I don't want to go crawling back asking for help. She tasked us with this."

Tabitha nodded. "Let's call that 'Plan B'. But I agree with them, let's try to prove we can do this."

"But all we've got is a name and number," Charlie said. "What can we do with that?"

"We've got the ink too." Art held the vial up.

"You're carrying that around with you?" Kimmy's eyes were wide.

"No, Kimmy. I left magical gate creating ink in my house alone with my mum."

Zack attempted to head off the looming argument.

"What if we just called the number?"

Bast raised an eyebrow.

"Like 'Hi, have you been doing naughty magic and would now like to confess your sins?' Not sure that'll work."

Art snorted.

"No," Zack replied. "I was thinking more like. 'Hi, I got your details from a certain store in Montreal. The guy there said you were looking for more ink. I can sell to you direct if you want it'."

"That's really good, actually," Charlie said. "And then we meet up with him and demand some answers."

"Assuming he's not somebody who can turn the tables on Art like the other night," Kimmy said.

"That won't happen again," Art said, his lips tight.

"How won't it? You don't even remember it happening the first time."

Art ignored her. "I've looked up the number and it's in South Korea. Which makes sense. So, I say we go there, give them a call, and arrange a meet up."

"And then we convince them to join the Tower?" Bast asked.

"No," Tabitha said. "That's not our job here. Assuming these two aren't from the Tower, somebody has taught them complicated magic. That's the job Junie gave us, to work out who's out there teaching magic in a way that risks the Silence."

"We don't know it's two." Jackie's voice was almost inaudible.

"Sorry?" Tabitha asked.

"We don't know it's two mages," Jackie repeated.

"Well, there was Movement magic and Mind magic." Bast counted against his fingers. "That means two."

Zack shook his head. "No, she's right. It means at least two. There could be more."

Tabitha nodded. "Great point. So, we make sure we're ready for anything. We confront them, make it clear what they are doing is wrong and then find out as much as we can about who taught them."

"Okay," Art said. "I'll set up a meeting. I'm all over it."

Zack entered the Tower's main infirmary room, his heart thumping in his chest. Tom, a middle-aged Life mage with a ruddy-brown beard and a deep Scottish accent was reclining on a wooden chair, his feet up on a table.

"Steady on, pal." Tom pulled his legs back and sat up straight. "Ye look like ye about to face a dragon. It's just infirmary duty."

"I'm okay," Zack replied. "Just a little nervous about other Tower members depending on my healing."

Tom held up a pair of fingers.

"Two things. One, ye nay alone. Two, ye know how careful Sara is. She would nay have cleared ye for duty if ye weren't ready."

"Right." Zack took a deep breath. "So how does this work?"

Tom patted the chair next to him.

"It's a lot like guard duty. Mostly a lot of sitting around, with occasional excitement. Pays well though."

Zack claimed the offered seat.

"I'm not just doing it for the money, though. I want to help out."

"Nay, of course," Tom said. "Ye a good egg. But the money doesn't hurt. Our magical inclinations dinnae translate as easily into self-funded opportunities as others' do. I know Mind mages who cash in at high stakes poker, Movement mages who skim from bank vaults and even some Earth mages who discover gold deposits. Healing folk dinnae tend to pay as well, so it's nice to get it recognised by the Tower."

Zack thought about it for little while. "That seems fair."

Tom continued, "It's nay just the money, though. It's a way to prove ye commitment to the Tower. Things like guard and infirmary duty at first, later maybe a stint as a mentor or even liaison. They're all ways to show the Thirteen ye solid, ready and able."

"I think the simpler duties are more than enough for me at the moment," Zack replied.

"Fair. Still, ye started down this path a lot younger than most of us, ye got plenty of time to work ye way up. Who knows, I could be looking at a future member of the Thirteen." Tom slapped him over the shoulder with smile before standing up. "Come on, I'll show ye where we keep all the supplies."

※━━━━━━━※

"You set up the meeting yet?" Zack asked over his headset.

"Not yet," Art replied. "I'm looking into a few venues before I make the call. Behind you!"

"I see them." Zack whirled and clicked his mouse. His shotgun thundered in response and the mutants lay dead, loot icons shining above their bodies. "And how is that venue hunt going?"

"It's going. It's up on the other monitor. I'll make the call tomorrow."

"Okay, fair enough."

"I am taking this seriously, mate," Art added.

"Just checking," Zack replied. "I mean, you're like ten levels higher than me and this game came out like what, last week?"

"That's because I'm not taking high school seriously. And life would get a lot easier for you if you'd stop as well."

Zack scrolled through the list of scavenged items.

"Even if I didn't want to get into medicine, which I do, what about my mother makes you think that failing my final year of high school will make life easier for me?"

Art laughed. "Yeah, that's a non-zero factor."

Zack selected a flak jacket from the loot and equipped it.

"Hey, why don't we ever see anybody from the Tower wearing stuff like this? Ballistics vests and stuff?"

Art was silent for a few moments. Whether he was thinking, or whether he was concentrating on the creeper mutant who had ambushed them, Zack wasn't sure.

"Yeah, I don't know. Probably one of those things where you don't want to admit you need it if the others aren't wearing it either. Seen a couple of motorcycle jackets though. Still, the things we've been up against. Not sure I'd want something bulky slowing me down."

"Plus, we've got Jackie."

"Yeah," Art said, pride in his voice. "I'd take that shrimp over kevlar, any day."

Their two characters crossed the threshold of the safehouse, ending the level.

"Alright man," Art said. "I'd better finish up researching for this call. Gotta focus on getting the perfect location."

"Good luck, mate," Zack replied. "See you tomorrow."

A fluorescent light flickered its call for replacement, casting intermittent shadows against the concrete walls. A scattering of cars and other vehicles blocked some of the light and added to the gloom.

Tabitha's arms were crossed tightly around her chest. "An underground carpark, Art? Really?"

"Okay, you find a place to meet in a foreign country in the middle of the night, away from bystanders, that doesn't have cameras over the internet." Art waved his hand around the area. "Plus, we're supposed to be doing a shady deal. This is a perfect shady deal place."

"Assuming we don't interrupt some other kind of shady deal," Charlie said, her eyes flicking around the space.

"We'll be fine," Art said. "Anyway, all of you find somewhere to hide. We don't want to spook them."

Art reclined against a concrete pillar while the others, with the expectation that their contacts would come down the ramp from the ground level, took positions behind other columns and within alcoves. Several minutes later, the sound of footsteps tapping towards them echoed through the carpark. A young Korean woman, dressed for a night out, including high heels and a designer handbag, approached Art from the shadows. She stopped a few metres away, staring at him with a blank expression.

"Good evening," Art said in English.

"I am here to exchange money for your wares," the woman replied.

"Sorry," Art said. "I was expecting to meet with a man."

"I am here to exchange money for your wares," she repeated.

Art stared at the woman for a moment before closing his eyes and gesturing towards her in a gentle motion. When his eyes opened, he peered back through the carpark.

"She's under mind control. He's somewhere nearby."

Zack reached out with his senses in the direction Art had looked.

"There! He's crouched behind that van."

"On it." Charlie and Max raced out from behind a red hatchback.

The two rounded the front of the van when a motorcycle came flying sideways through the air, tumbling towards them from the direction of the up ramp. In a blur, Bast shot forward and pushed

Charlie out of the way. She bounced against a car and fell to her knees between it and the van, out of the motorcycle's path.

Bast was not so lucky. The back wheel of the motorcycle slammed into his shoulder and he shouted in pain as he fell to the ground. A second man stepped into the light, an orange glow around his hands. He tossed a knife up into the air in front of him and it zipped towards Charlie before bouncing off one of Jackie's shields.

Tabitha incanted and a burst of wind rushed towards the man, but he was too fast. He spun away from the gust and pulled a second knife from his pocket.

"Enough!" Kimmy shouted. Rich yellow light flooded the underground space as Kimmy stepped forward, two small bonfires filling her open hands. She yelled in, what Zack assumed was, Korean and the man paused for a moment before dropping his knife and placing his hands up. The orange light at his fingertips dissipated.

Charlie climbed to her feet and addressed the first man, a slightly overweight man with his hair pulled back in a ponytail.

"What about you? Are you going to play nice?" Max's growl punctuated the statement.

"Yes. Yes. I'll play nice," came the reply.

"Alright. Get off him, Max."

Bast groaned.

Zack ran forward and knelt beside him.

"Don't move. Let me work out what the problem is."

"The problem is, I got hit by a motorbike."

"If you broke him, you'll burn," Kimmy seethed, taking a step towards the second man, shorter and much slimmer than the first.

"Just a fractured shoulder blade, nothing to worry about," Zack said as he poured Life into the site of the injury.

Bast sat up and rotated his arm. "That definitely beats a bandage. Thanks, mate."

Zack nodded in reply.

"Kimmy, I'm fine, you can back off the poor guy." He levered himself up.

"You're lucky," she said to the man. "Now, go stand over with your friend."

He looked around at them. "You're... children."

Kimmy's eyes sparkled in the light of her flame. "Call me that again, see what happens."

He hurried past Kimmy to stand beside the other man.

"I thought you said you didn't speak much Korean," Tabitha whispered to Kimmy. "What did you say to them before?

"I'm not quite sure. It was whatever my grandmother used to say when she was telling me to behave."

Bast snorted.

Art sidled up to the others. "Time for the interrogation?"

"What happened to the woman?" Tabitha asked.

"I sent her to sleep and wiped her memory," Art replied. "She won't remember anything of this."

"Had a bit of practice at that kind of thing, huh?" Kimmy asked with acid in her voice.

"Excuse me?" Art asked.

Tabitha waved Kimmy off. "Focus. We need to find out what these two know."

Art's narrowed eyes lingered on Kimmy for a moment before he turned to look at the two men.

"Okay. Let's see." He stepped towards them. "You know Mind magic, right? And for you, it's Movement magic? That cabin in the mountains was yours?"

The two men looked at each other and then back at Art before nodding.

"How did you learn to do all that?"

"Why do you care?" the shorter man asked.

"Because what you did is dangerous," Art said, and Zack noticed his friend's hands twitch with a purple light behind his back.

"And we're the only ones between you and worse consequences for what you did."

The men looked at each other, before the first nodded for the other to speak.

"It started when we were boys," he said. "Our fathers were in the armed forces and we played together. One day, we were kicking a ball in the fields near our home when we came across some strange creatures. We hid until they were gone. A few days later, our fathers were redeployed and our families moved away from each other." He paused, and Art motioned for him to continue. "Over the years I forgot about that day in the fields. Or I thought it was a dream. But then I found I could do things. I could sense what people were feeling. Make them forget things. A year ago, I got back in touch with Min-Jung." He indicated the man beside him. "He could do things too. We started practising these things together. Making money together."

Tabitha stepped forward.

"It's fair enough to work a few things out by yourself, but—"

"Yeah," interrupted Kimmy. She gestured to Art. "Even this moron knows how to make people forget things."

"But," repeated Tabitha with an emphasised glare at Kimmy, "that magic in the cabin wasn't home research."

The man scratched his ear, avoiding eye contact.

"Uh, no. Earlier this year I got a phone call. They told me they knew what we could do. That we were special and that they wanted to help. The next day, there was a package on my doorstep. Instructions on how to do the ritual, as well as where to go to buy the ink we needed. Honestly, I thought you must have been with them when you called."

"I want to see those instructions," Art said.

"I, uh, have them here," the man said. He reached into his backpack.

"Slowly!" Kimmy hissed.

The man flinched. "Of course. Please don't hurt us." He thrust a bundle of paper at Art.

Art accepted the pages and flicked through them. Bast looked over his shoulder and spoke with a low voice, "This guy's being a little more helpful than I would have expected."

"I've been feeding him a steady stream of fear and friendship since he started talking," Art murmured back. "So, he's exactly as helpful as I expected. Does anybody else have any questions for them?"

"Do you have any way of contacting the people who sent you this?" Tabitha asked.

They both shook their heads.

"No," said the first. "Their number was blocked and they never called us again."

"That's fine," Art said. "I'm going to keep these. Now I want you to close your eyes and take slow, steady breaths, and this way, nobody has to get hurt."

They complied and Art incanted with more obvious gestures. The two men slumped to the ground, but Art continued, purple light from his fingertips bright in the gloom.

"Okay, they're not going to remember anything about tonight. Probably not even about the phone call, but I can't be sure."

Zack rifled through their pockets and found their wallets.

"Oh yeah, pay day," Art said.

"Zack!" Tabitha scolded.

"I'm not robbing them. I'm taking a photo of their I.D. so the Tower can find them later and offer them the oath."

"Good idea," Bast said.

"Yeah, fair enough," Art agreed, looking on with a sad face as Zack put the wallets back in their pockets.

"Did we actually get anything of value?" Kimmy asked.

"We won't know until we read through those notes," Tabitha said. "But either way, it doesn't sound like they knew any more about who sent it to them."

"Or why," Art said.

"Alright," said Tabitha, "let's get this woman somewhere safe and go home."

CHAPTER 8

AWRY

"That went alright, yesterday." Tabitha moved to sit next to Zack on the bus to the Tower.

Zack smiled. "Well, I was never really worried about maths. It helps to have the right kind of study materials."

Tabitha shared her own mischievous smile.

"Yeah, it does, doesn't it? But I've been thinking. This won't be an option for HSC exams. They turn up on the day in sealed envelopes."

The smile left Zack's face.

"That's been worrying me too. Art says he has a plan for it, though."

"He does have a plan for it." Art's voice came from the seat behind them.

"What is it?" Tabitha asked. "You're working out some way of finding the exams at the Department of Education or something?"

"Yeah, that's it," Art said. "I just need twelve other men and access to an industrial tunnel drilling machine."

Zack snorted.

Tabitha rolled her eyes. "Alright then, Clooney. What's the actual plan?"

"Clooney?" Art looked offended. "Surely, I'm more of a Brad Pitt."

"Matt Damon at best," Zack offered.

Art considered it. "Yeah, I'll take that."

"Are you both done?" Tabitha's hands were on her hips. "Are you going to share or not?"

"I'm working on it. Need to learn some new stuff. Timur says I'll be ready in time."

"Speaking of people who have been learning new tricks, does Bast really think he can open a gate to the same realm as in the cabin?" Zack asked.

"So he says. Between what he's been learning and the instructions we got in Korea, he's confident. Assuming he has access to the ink."

Art patted his breast pocket.

"Good."

"But then what's next?" Art asked. "We jump into the goblin ninja world and then what?"

"Bast said he'd explain once we got there."

Bast and the others were waiting in the training room when they arrived.

"Okay, what's the play?" Art asked.

"I've spent the last week going through the notes we got from our helpful Korean friends," Bast said. "They're intense. The basic principles are the same as the Movement magic I've been learning, but that's where the similarities end. My money is that this didn't come from a Tower mage."

"Well, that's a good thing," Art said.

"Yeah, but that's not important right now. The notes are crazy specific. Whoever wrote them was not trying to teach these guys magic. They were trying to teach them how to make a gate that would stay open and draw in magical creatures using imbued ink. And then the rest is what I assume to be Mind magic."

Art nodded. "From what I've skimmed of it, yeah."

"Well, I think the ink is the key here," Bast said. "It has to contain something from that realm. And whatever it is, would have taken time and effort to get. I say we go there and have a look around. Maybe, whoever made the ink left some kind of clue behind."

"That sounds like a bit of a longshot, Bast," Charlie said. "Don't get me wrong, it's amazing you've worked all that out, but this realm could be huge. How are we going to find this one spot?"

Bast held up his hands. "I agree, Charlie. There's a lot of maybes here. But I think I can get us close. The gate I make should hone in on where the ink was taken from."

"Um, if that's the case," Zack said. "Then it'll be honing in on where those dokkaebi came from."

"Dokkaebi?" Jackie asked.

"The creatures we fought in the cabin. I spent a little time on Google and Wikipedia. They have magical hats that can turn them invisible, and those clubs they had are supposed to be magical as well, otherwise they're basically Korean—"

"Ninja goblins," Art finished.

"Yeah. But my point is, they are probably nearby."

Kimmy pointed to the weapon racks. "Then let's arm up."

Zack ambled over to the rack of quarterstaves, running his fingers across them before selecting one. He whirled it around, testing the weight of it as the others did the same with their own choices. All except for Bast, who simply tightened his rapier around his waist.

They stowed the rest of their belongings in a nearby storeroom and climbed the stairs to the Gate Room. Once there, Bast approached the mage who was standing on duty and spoke to him in a quiet voice. The man nodded and gestured over to the three-foot high stone plinth in the centre of the room.

Bast moved next to it and called Art over. "I need the ink."

Art pulled it from his pocket and placed it on the plinth.

"Do you need to use it all? We might need this for something else."

Bast shook his head. "I won't be using it up. I just need it as an anchor."

"Awesome." Art stepped away, next to Zack.

Bast took a deep breath and closed his eyes. He held his hands above the ink and incanted in a low tone before making wide sweeping motions with his arms as if tracing an elaborate pattern in the air. He formed the shapes again and again, sweat gathering and then dripping down his face, until a spark of grey light appeared in the room. Despite his heavy breathing, Bast sped up his movements until Zack could no longer follow the pattern he was making. The gate grew and grew until, at last, it was big enough for them to walk through.

Bast finished his incantation and doubled over, hands on his knees.

"Are you okay, Bast?" Zack asked.

Bast sucked in a deep breath before standing back up, his hands shifting to his hips.

"Yeah, I'm good. That was…" He exhaled and inhaled again. "That was a lot. But yeah, I'm good to go. Let's get in there."

The other mage approached the gate and inspected it.

"It's respectable work, Bast. Not quite how I think Liam would have taught you, but it's functional."

"Thanks, Micah. We shouldn't be long."

"No problem. I'll be here."

One by one, the teens stepped through the shimmering grey oval. Zack's feet stepped down onto a dusty, dry hillside, populated by low lying scrub and the occasional kindling of tree. It could have been a dozen places on Earth, except the entire sky was a dull, burnt red colour. With no immediate threat visible, Zack followed his training and reached out to sample the Life of this realm. It was not hard to find. Abundant, but not overwhelming - again, this could have been many places on Earth. It was different, but only in that it felt unfamiliar, like the taste or smell of a meal he'd never had before. He opened his eyes.

"There's plenty of Life here, but it's a little different, like it has a different flavour, but not a different structure."

"Yeah, I think that's what I'm getting too," Bast said.

Tabitha and Jackie nodded.

Kimmy shook her head.

"I'm not so sure that's true for me. Fire here feels like it might behave differently. Nothing major, but like it would burn slower and for longer. Maybe it's nothing, if you guys aren't picking up anything."

"No, Kimmy," Charlie said. "Animal here is different. I'm getting the impression that most animals here are smart, a bit more like people maybe."

"Oh, that's what I'm getting," Art said, his eyes wide. "Normally I don't get too much from animals, but I'm getting background noise or feedback at the moment and I think it's because I'm almost picking up their minds."

"Okay, what now?" Kimmy asked.

"We look around," Bast said. "See if there's any sign of who came here and captured some of the essence of this place."

"What would that involve?" Jackie asked.

"No idea, little sis," Bast said. "Sorry. I was hoping we'd know it if we saw it."

"Well, can we make any assumptions, or even good guesses?" Tabitha asked.

"Could they have just picked up a rock? Or a branch or something?" Charlie asked.

"I don't think so," Zack said, hesitation in his voice. "We've been sent off-world a few times now and it's always been to take something significant for the Tower to do something with. It could be something like that."

"And if we're wrong and it's just some dirt, we won't find anything. So, let's assume for now it's something more obvious," Kimmy agreed.

"Whatever it is, it should be close," Bast said. "At least, according to the Korean guys' cheat sheet."

Charlie craned her neck and peered around. She looked down at Max, pointing into the distance. "That way, yeah?"

Max huffed in reply.

Charlie straightened and addressed the others. "There's something over that way. Looks like a rocky outcrop. It would make for a decent shelter and Max smells something normal over there."

"Normal doesn't sound very interesting," Art said with a raised eyebrow.

"Normal for us, I mean," Charlie said. "Abnormal for here."

"Well then, that's certainly worth investigating," Tabitha said, and moved to stride off.

"Hang on," Jackie called out to her.

"Yes, Jackie?" Tabitha turned around to face her.

"If we're leaving the gate alone, I want to set up some wards around it."

"Okay, good idea."

Jackie closed her eyes and stretched out her fingers in front of her, moving them as if she was typing in the air. As she finished, she extended her left arm in a broad sweeping motion. "Right, that's done."

The walk to the outcrop took a little more than ten minutes, but in that time, a wind picked up, carrying dust and other small debris over the hills. Zack spat the acrid taste out of his mouth before sealing his lips as tight as he could. Well before they reached their destination, it was clear that Charlie, and Max, had indeed found something important.

The first thing Zack noticed was the charred remains of a campfire almost large enough to be called a bonfire. It looked out of place, but perhaps could have been left behind by the local life. However, moving a little closer, a bag became visible. Canvas, or made of some other sturdy material, it looked like a backpacker or camping bag. Without speaking, they hastened their approach.

The impression Zack had was that of a campsite. The group spread out around the remains of the fire, looking for anything of value. Kimmy inspected the charred wood, Art and Tabitha crouched over the backpack and Charlie and Max ranged around the site. Jackie and Bast claimed their own space and closed their eyes, reaching out, Zack assumed, with their senses. Zack decided instead to look more closely at the rocky outcrop.

It was made of boulders, perhaps a single one that crested out of the earth. Too shallow to form any significant cave, the angle of the curve still produced a shadow in the centre, dark enough that Zack couldn't see through.

"Something was totally done here," Bast announced. "A ritual or something."

"Can you redo it?" Kimmy asked.

"What? Hell, no. No idea what it involved or what it did. It was definitely complicated though."

"Why are we even here then?" Kimmy scrunched up her face.

"To try and find something, anything, that might lead us to whoever sold the ink to

the magic shop," Art said.

"Well, the fire's a bust. It's hard to tell with the weird Fire thing going on in this realm, but I'm pretty sure it was left burning until it eventually went out on its own."

"Nothing here either," said Tabitha. "Nothing in the backpack has anything identifying in it. Some dried food, some water, a blanket, first aid kit."

"I found this." Charlie held up a metallic zippo lighter.

Max sniffed at her.

"Okay fine, we found this."

"This is a bit weird, isn't it?" Zack gestured around.

"What?" Art asked.

"This. Why leave all this stuff behind? Even if you're not worried about evidence, it's still expensive."

"Unless you were expecting to come back?" Bast suggested.

"Or, unless you had to—"

"Zack!" Jackie shouted, pointing behind him.

" — leave in a hurry," Zack finished with a tone of fatalistic resignation.

The look of horror that rippled through his friends' expressions was enough to chill his blood but the sound of skittering scratches on the stone behind him almost stopped his heart entirely. Zack whirled around, thrusting his staff out in front of him.

From the dark recess in the rockface, dozens of spider-like creatures swarmed out to cover the stone. The size of rats, they differed from Earth's arachnids in that they each had a separate head that craned up from their bodies. Red eyes stared at the teens, while small, teeth-filled maws screeched in rage, or perhaps hunger.

"None of that is okay," Art said.

Tabitha and Kimmy stepped forward to flank Zack. From the left, a gust of wind threw several of the creatures bouncing off the rock. From his right, a wave of flame flowed out, summoned by Kimmy. However, as she had predicted when they first entered this realm, the Fire was different here. What should have been a thin wall of flame instead dribbled out in a dark yellow spurt. Only three of the spiderlings were caught by it and they dropped to the floor, upturned and chittering in pain. The rest leapt from the rockface and scuttled forward.

The quarterstaff whirred in Zack's hand as he swung at the creatures, battering them away before they could close in on Tabitha and Kimmy. He slid his grip down to one end of the weapon, giving him the reach he needed to cover both girls. It was just coincidence it also gave him a foot or two more distance from the spiderlings.

Dozens more of the creatures swarmed out, with some moving around the three of them, towards the others behind.

"Drop back to the others," Tabitha said, as she released her spell and spun her flail in front of her.

Kimmy gripped her axe in frustration, backing up alongside Zack and they formed a line with the others.

"No, Max," Charlie shouted. "Get away, these things are probably venomous. It's too dangerous."

Max barked in objection but scampered back out of reach.

Zack noticed Charlie had a hunting knife in her hand rather than her bow. Not as practised at it as with arrows, she still wielded it with dangerous intent at the approaching creatures.

"Jackie!" Art screamed with fear in his voice. Two of the spiderlings had leapt onto her and one bit down on her exposed arm.

"I'm fine, Art," Jackie said calmly.

The spiderling let out a high pitched and pained shriek as it broke its fangs on Jackie's hardened skin. She knocked it and the other off with the flat of her spear and stomped on them.

"Bloody hell," Art said, his voice a mixture of relief and exasperation. The creatures stood little chance against him and his blade.

Bast darted back and forth, piercing several of them with precise blows to their thoraxes. The ground was littered with dead and dying spiderlings. Their numbers had lessened but there were still too many to count.

Tabitha stepped forward. Her spinning flail swept through the creatures with dark efficiency, but it did require a clear amount of space from any friendly torsos. Again and again, the metal head slammed through her opponents but, when the length of the chain had extended out, two of the spiderlings surged forward and leapt at her. Without a way to deflect them, and off balance from her recent lunge, she stumbled backwards.

Zack charged towards her. She fell to the ground, clearing the way for Zack to swing his staff like an extended baseball bat. The heavy wood crashed into both of the creatures and sent them sailing back towards the rockface, lifeless.

He heard a scream behind him.

When Zack had rushed to Tabitha's side, he had left Kimmy exposed and a spiderling flanked her from the left. She knocked it from her leg and crushed it under her boot, but not before it had bitten through her jeans and into her calf.

Art, Bast and Charlie surged forward, cutting down yet more creatures and herding the rest away, while Jackie planted herself between Tabitha and Kimmy, ready to ward off any that made it through. Kimmy hissed and collapsed to the ground, clutching at her leg. Zack dropped to his knees beside her and reached out to sense her Life.

"It freakin' hurts, Zack! Can you do something?" Kimmy grasped his wrist.

"No, I'm sorry. It's not really a poison, it's something else."

"Oh, hell!"

"But you can."

"What?"

"We don't have much time. Do you trust me?"

"Ah, yeah?"

"Use your magic. Burn your leg."

Tabitha climbed to her feet. "Are you serious, Zack?"

Zack looked Kimmy in the eyes. "There's no time. Do it!"

She gave him a sharp nod and then waved her hands towards her leg. The strange fire of this world poured out of her hands and landed on her thigh with a heat that forced Zack to recoil from beside her.

Kimmy screamed. Zack reached past her pain with his senses and focused on her leg. It was almost worse than her screams. Kimmy's Life was in overload.

Bast had moved to her side, his jacket in his hands. He stepped forward to smother the fire.

"No, not yet!" Zack held up his hand.

"Oh, come on, Zack!" Bast's grip tightened on his jacket.

The smell of her burning flesh filled Zack's nostrils. "Almost… Now!"

Bast knelt beside her, suffocating the fire with his jacket. Kimmy collapsed flat on the ground, whimpering. Art, Charlie and Max charged the remaining creatures as they scattered and fled. Zack poured life into Kimmy's leg. Veins, arteries, bone, muscle, fat, skin. And nerves. So many nerves, still sending messages of pain through her body. But, second by second, her breathing calmed. When Bast removed his jacket, her leg bore no evidence of the trauma. Zack fell backwards, exhausted.

"Is she okay?" Charlie asked.

"Yeah, she's okay," Kimmy answered without sitting back up.

Art kept his eyes on the rocks. "I think they've gone for now."

"What the absolute hell was that, Zack?" Bast's voice seethed.

"I'm sorry," Zack said. "It was all I could think of. I didn't know how to get rid of that toxin, but I knew I could heal burns."

"It's genius," Kimmy said, reaching out to pat his hand. "God, did it hurt though." She sniffed. "Is that me?"

"I think so." Zack grimaced.

"I smell frickin' delicious."

Art cackled.

"Far out, Kimmy." Tabitha shook her head.

Kimmy climbed to her feet and looked down at her leg. "An excuse to buy some new jeans, at least."

"How does it feel, now?" Zack asked.

She tested it with a step. "Yeah, weird. I mean, it's fine, good as new probably. But my brain isn't convinced it can be." She shuffled back and forth from foot to foot. "Yeah, it's good."

"What were those things?" Bast asked.

"I don't want to know," Tabitha said. "Nor do I want to hear what Art wants to c—"

"Arachnauts!" Art interrupted.

"Next time, you get to be the one who gets lit on fire," Kimmy said.

"Why does anybody have to get—" Art stopped talking when his sister's eyes widened with alarm. "What is it, Jackie?"

"My wards," she said. "Something is near the gate."

CHAPTER 9

CONSEQUENCES

"We have to get back there." Tabitha pointed towards the gate.

"We won't make it in time," Charlie said, snatching up her bow.

"Maybe I can." Bast incanted and orange light flowed from his fingertips to his legs. "Try and catch up to us as fast as you can, okay?"

"Us?" Tabitha asked.

"Yeah." He motioned for Jackie to jump onto his back.

She didn't hesitate, gripping her spear over his shoulder.

Art opened his mouth, but Bast sprinted away before he could speak. He threw his hands up in the direction of the gate. "Did that bastard just run with my sister towards unknown danger?"

"We'd better get after them then, yeah?" Charlie strode after Bast, Max loping along beside her.

The rest of them followed behind, but Zack had only taken a few strides of his own when he realised how tired he was.

"You guys go on without me," he puffed. "I'll be right behind."

Art gave a quick nod in recognition and sprinted away towards his sister, closing the distance between him and Charlie. Tabitha lingered.

"It's dangerous here, Zack. I don't think you… any of us… should be left alone."

Zack felt his cheeks burn. He struggled to imagine Tabitha worrying about any of the others being unable to defend themselves.

"I'll stay with him," Kimmy said. "That spider poison and, well, everything that came after it, kinda took it out of me too. Catch up to the others. We'll get there soon."

"Yeah, okay." Tabitha turned and ran towards the others.

"Thanks," Zack said.

"I'm not lying. I'm pretty tired." She hesitated. "And my leg feels a little funny."

"Oh damn, did I screw it up?" Zack reached out with his Life.

"No, I don't think so. There's no pain or anything, I think my brain's not ready to believe it's okay, though. C'mon, we need to get moving."

They jogged together towards the others, keeping a steady pace.

"I'm sorry about what happened," Zack said between breaths.

"Why?"

"Because you had to burn yourself."

"Yeah, that sucked. But why are you sorry about it?"

"Because I should have healed you without the fire."

"Could you have?"

"No."

"Should you have been able to?"

"Yes? I don't know. I'm barely getting basic regenerative stuff right. Toxins are really complicated."

"So, no then?"

"Sara could have."

"Yeah, so when you're a hundred-year-old shaman who lives in a magical tower, I'll be pissed off when you can't snap your fingers and cure me."

Zack grumbled.

"It's simple, Zack. If you think you need to be better at what you do, get better at what you do. If you can't, work with what you've got. But either way, I'd really like to stop talking about burning my own leg down to the bone."

Zack stopped grumbling. What was he doing? Going to the girl he'd caused so much pain to in the hopes that she'd make him feel better? How self-centred could somebody be?

They reached the crest of a hill and the others came into view. Art, Charlie and Tabitha hadn't reached the gate yet. Jackie was planted in front of the grey light, spear in hand. Bast, on the other hand, was a constant blur of movement, strafing to the left and right, never stopping. And then Zack saw why.

Creatures, like those from the cabin in the mountains, shimmered into view. They swung their heavy clubs at the two teenagers before disappearing again. Bast was too fast. He may not have been able to see where the attacks were coming from, but the dokkaebi couldn't predict where he was going to be either.

Jackie made a much easier target. The tiny blonde girl didn't dodge. She didn't parry, counterattack or even flinch. Club swing after club swing slammed at her, crashing at the last moment against the flash of a silver shield. Zack didn't need to feel her Life to know that she couldn't keep that up for long.

He lengthened his strides, ignoring the sharp pain that blossomed in his side and the fatigue in his legs. Kimmy matched his pace and they ran together towards the gate.

Ahead, Art had outpaced Tabitha and Charlie, and even Max trailed behind him. The sight of his sister in trouble had, without doubt, spurred him on. Jackie, exhausted from holding against a near constant onslaught, mistimed one of her shields. A dokkaebi's club glanced across her shoulder and she dropped to her knee from the force of the blow. Art screamed in a voice so loud it felt to Zack like he was standing beside him.

Bast's eyes widened and he took a few steps away from Art before he seemed to regain his composure. He looked from side to side, but the creatures remained lurking, holding off on their attacks.

Art skidded to a halt beside Jackie. His voice was muted to Zack, over the wind.

"Are you okay?"

"Yeah." She rolled her shoulder with a slight wince. "It's nothing."

Art spun towards Bast. "Are you out of your damn mind?"

"Art, not now!" Jackie snapped. "I don't know what you did, but they are still out there."

Art glared at Bast. "We aren't finished."

Tabitha, Charlie and Max joined them.

"How many are there?" Tabitha asked.

"At least six," Bast said.

"Maybe eight?" Jackie added.

"Okay, same plan as Korea," Tabitha said. "Back to back. Charlie, you're with Art. Bast, you with me."

"What about Jackie?" Art asked.

"Max has her covered," Charlie said.

The dokkaebi reappeared and attacked without warning. Art used his sword to bash away an incoming club, while Bast pulled Tabitha away from another. Jackie blocked a third and fourth attack with her magic.

The creatures vanished too quickly for much of a retaliation. Tabitha's flail found only empty air, as did one of Charlie's arrows. Max was fast enough to latch onto a dokkaebi's calf, but it shook her loose, leaving her with a well-earned mouthful of flesh.

Tabitha whirled her flail in a long, wild arc while Bast and Art tested the spaces in front of them with their blades. As Bast extended his rapier for a third time, a creature reappeared and swung its club under the thrust and into Bast's chest. His enhanced speed saved him from a direct impact and, instead, he took it against his ribs. The force lifted him off the ground and he struggled to find his feet as he landed.

A second dokkaebi appeared in front of Art and swung its own club at his head. Art twisted his blade to deflect the blow and did, but the force of it jarred the sword, knocking it from his hand. Charlie loosed an arrow at it, striking it in the shoulder. It staggered backwards and rippled out of sight.

Zack and Kimmy reached the others.

"Okay, we're good to get out of here, right?" Kimmy held her axe at the ready.

"Nope," said Bast, sucking in a breath through gritted teeth. "Not until we can be sure we aren't letting any of those things through."

"Well, damn," Charlie said. "Any ideas?"

A dokkaebi stepped into sight in front of Kimmy, slamming its club down at her in a vertical strike. She dived out of the way, skidding across the dusty ground on her side. Zack charged, swinging his quarterstaff. The creature raised its club to protect its face as it faded from view, but Zack's attack was aimed high. The dokkaebi reappeared, confusion on its face, and its dark blue cap fell to the floor.

"Magic hat!" Zack shouted.

"Oh!" said Tabitha. "I can do something about that. Hold onto your socks, everybody."

Tabitha dropped her flail and began her incantation, both hands moving in rapid and precise shapes. A gust of wind burst into movement, spiralling around her and growing in speed. Zack tightened his grip on his staff as he felt it being pulled away from him and he squinted to protect his eyes against the dust kicked up by the torrent of air spinning past him. He stumbled backwards as two dokkaebi appeared in front of him, their caps ripped away by the wind.

It was the first good look Zack had managed to get of the dokkaebi. Of living ones at least. They were a little taller than him, perhaps an inch or two shorter than an average human. Their faces and the exposed parts of their arms and legs were a dark, leathery green. They had oversized sharp teeth and long drooping ears and their too-large yellow eyes were wide in surprise. There were nine all up and they scrambled after their hats, which danced away on the last of Tabitha's wind.

Now was their chance.

"Everybody through the gate!" Tabitha shouted.

"Me last," Jackie said, stepping to the side and holding firm.

Charlie, Max and Bast ran past her.

"Not a chance, Jackie," Art said, pulling at his sister.

"It's okay, Jackie," Kimmy said. "I've got this. Better go through before your brother has a panic attack."

Kimmy whispered her words and waved her arm in a wide arc around her. Flames leapt from her fingertips, creating a curved wall of fire around the gate.

"Thanks, Kimmy." Jackie snatched her arm away from Art and stepped through the gate. Art followed.

Kimmy kept her attention on the flames.

"Ready, Kimmy?" Tabitha asked.

"Yep, right behind you," she said, stepping backwards towards them. Tabitha beckoned Zack through the gate before stepping after him, leading Kimmy through with a guiding arm on her shoulder.

No sooner was Kimmy through than Bast cast his own spell, slamming the gate shut. Zack closed his eyes, extending his senses through the Tower's Gate Room. Eight human lives and one canine. "We're good."

"Oh, we're a long way from good." Art pushed hard against Bast's chest.

"Excuse me?" Bast pushed back.

"Don't you ever pull Jackie into danger like that again," Art shouted. "She could have been seriously hurt."

"Seriously hurt?" Bast replied. "Like what your mate there did to Kimmy? Made her do to herself?"

Zack dropped his staff and tried to stand between them, wedging himself in with his arms. "I'm sorry, okay, Bast? You're right, I messed up."

Art yelled over the top of Zack's head. "I don't care what he did. That was my sister you ran off with."

"Where do you get off telling me what I can and can't do?" Bast snapped back.

"I'll do better, I promise," Zack said, while the taller boys pressed in against him.

"Are you all quite done?" Charlie's voice was sharp enough to cut through and silence them. "I don't know if you've noticed, but the four of us have accepted the same risks of this work the same as you boys and you have no right to lessen that choice with this white knight crap."

"That's my sister, Charlie."

Charlie's eyes widened in anger. "No, Art. That's Jackie. A Protection mage who stood like a wall against those monsters. Do you think any of the rest of us could have done that?"

Art opened his mouth to speak but Charlie pressed on, facing Bast.

"And you. You're really going to tell Kimmy that she didn't choose to do what she did? That she didn't accept the pain? That she didn't take that risk for herself when she stepped into that world? Or is she just poor little Kimmy who needs a big strong man to protect her and make sure she doesn't get into trouble?"

Bast studiously avoided meeting Kimmy's eyeline.

"And Zack." Charlie pointed a finger at him. "Get over yourself. You think you're the only one who struggles with their limitations out there? Or do you think that your limitations somehow matter more than ours? Do you know how patronising that is? Treating us like some kind of supporting act?"

Charlie stepped towards them, furious, with Max at her side.

The large dog wasn't exactly threatening the boys, but she had picked up on her human's mood and her ears were flat.

"You boys had better quit with this chauvinistic crap. We are all equal partners in this. Not lesser. Not damsels who need your permission before we pick up our weapons." She stormed towards the stairs. "You're embarrassing yourselves and us."

Jackie, Tabitha and Kimmy followed her down the stairs, each treating the boys to their own glare. The three boys exchanged looks in silence until a long whistled sigh came from the wall opposite the stairs. Micah, the Movement mage who had been standing guard, met them with a nervous smile.

"Maybe give them a few minutes to get away before you leave, hey? That was rough to watch."

⟡————◉————⟡

Zack collapsed into the canvas of a foldable chair in a secluded corner of Tabitha's backyard. He brought a bottle of beer to his lips and didn't pull it away until he'd emptied half of it.

"A bit like that, huh?" Art said, taking a swig from his own.

"Yeah. More than a bit, actually. But at least the exams are done. For now, at least."

"How do you think you went?"

"Alright. Even with the 'extra help', English was rough. But the rest should bring up the average pretty high."

"Not to mention two weeks of holidays."

"Do holidays mean anything when you don't care about studying?" Zack asked with a smile.

"Sure, they do. They mean two weeks without uniforms or getting up early. They also mean a two week break from getting dirty looks from Bast and the girls. I've had enough of that the last couple of weeks."

"We got invited tonight, so there's that."

"Well," Art paused to frame his words. "It's more like they didn't go out of their way to rescind the invitation."

Zack stared at him, eyes flat, before draining the rest of his bottle.

"What we need is some kind of lead on these dodgy mages," Art said, resting back in his chair and looking up at the night sky. "Get some kind of clue, find their home base, catch them in the act and reunite in our glory."

"So, Jackie hasn't forgiven you yet, either?"

"Um, no. She has used the word 'mortified' several times. You know, it wasn't that long ago that she was too young to know words like that."

"I think that's her point, mate."

"What, that she knows big words?"

Zack leant forward. "That we all know it wasn't that long ago that she was a little girl."

"She still is a little girl." Art crossed his arms with a frown.

"No. Charlie's right. And you agree. What was it you called her? A Viking shieldmaiden?"

"Spearmaiden," Art corrected through tight lips. "I suppose shieldmaiden kind of works too."

"And then her big brother treats her like a little kid in front of the rest of us."

"Yeah alright. I'll make it up to her. Tomorrow. For now, let's get ourselves another drink."

Zack climbed to his feet and followed Art around the corner. With the house no longer shielding them, the music flared up in volume and filled Zack's ears. A dozen teenagers sat in a ring around a metal firepit, drinking and talking. Kimmy had tucked herself in amongst them, a bottle of whiskey in her hands. She stared into the flames, her eyes lost to thought and sparkling in the orange light.

The fire flickered in a strange way and Zack realised it was moving in rhythm to the music. His eyes shot towards Kimmy's fingers, which were twitching as she held onto her drink.

He brushed past Art and crouched beside her.

"Hey, Kimmy."

She stared past him to the firepit.

He tried again. "Kimmy."

Nothing.

He reached out and held her fingers flat against the glass bottle. She flinched, pulling her hands away from him. The bottle tumbled to the ground.

"What the hell, Zack?"

"Are you alright?"

"Yeah, of course, I was just chilling."

"You looked a little…" He lowered his voice. "lost in the flames."

"I'm fine, Zack." Her eyes flickered to her thigh, then back to the pit, before returning to him. "I'm unwinding. Give me some space."

Several of the teens behind him snickered. One called out across the fire, "Oof, man. Shot down."

"Yeah, walk it off buddy, you'll be right."

Zack blushed despite himself. "Okay, Kimmy. As long as you're okay."

Art had lingered a few steps away from the ring of seats and Zack scurried back to him, eyes and whispers of laughter following him.

"What was all that about?" Art said.

He hadn't noticed. Maybe Zack had imagined it.

"Nothing. She just looked a bit out of it."

Art shrugged. "Who knows with her?"

Inside, Tabitha was playing at making cocktails to a small, if enthusiastic, audience. More than a dozen bottles, two blenders and a shaker were scattered in front of her and she danced around the kitchen, mixing drinks on advice from an app on her phone. She had finished pouring out a pink milky concoction when she saw them watching.

"Art! Zack! My boys!" She twirled over and threw her arms around them. "I love these boys."

Zack and Art exchanged confused looks. Tabitha ended the hug and squeezed their cheeks.

"You're such good eggs, both of you."

"You're, uh, not angry at us?" Zack asked.

"What? No. I mean, I think you both have some crap to work through. And Charlie definitely had a point, but no, I know your hearts are in the right place. Can I make you a drink?"

"No thanks, we're good with beers," Art said.

"What is it?" Her left eyebrow arced up. "Your fragile masculinity can't handle a pretty, fruity drink?"

"No, it's not that," Art said.

"We just prefer beer," Zack added.

"For the taste."

"We're not fragile."

Ten minutes later, they wandered back outside. Zack moved the two umbrellas in his drink away from the straw. Art sulked as he drank from his.

"You know…" Zack said.

"Don't say it."

"It's actually not bad."

"It's an image thing though," Art said. "It's not about masculinity or anything, I just think beer is a more mature drink."

Zack nodded in agreement as he slurped up what Tabitha had called a 'fruit tingle'.

The two paused as they rounded the corner to return to their seats and found them occupied. A couple, sharing the chair Art had vacated, were in an active and enthusiastic embrace. The girl, unmistakable from her messy, honey-coloured curls, was Charlie.

Art threw up his spare hand. "Oh whoa! Sorry to intrude!"

He and Zack retreated around the corner and to a pair of spare seats against the side fence. They sat in silence, drinking.

"You alright, mate?"

"Hmm," Zack replied, straw in between his lips.

"That can't be the first time you've seen Charlie and Dave making out."

Zack slid the straw from his mouth.

"That wasn't Dave."

CHAPTER 10

RESPITE

Zack was sitting in his grandmother's bedroom the next afternoon and feeling a little smug. Thirsty, but smug. Life magic was more or less the perfect cure for a hangover, except for the dehydration. Art had mentioned he could similarly wave away the fallout of a big night but Zack wondered how that could be true. A hangover wasn't mental; there were cells in stress, toxins to be cleansed. He dropped the thought and turned his attention back to the dog-eared textbook Sara had lent him. She wanted him to read the chapters on the role of proteins in the way diseases performed, before they met up again. He looked over at his grandmother. He didn't need extra motivation to learn about disease.

As if she sensed his thoughts, she opened her eyes. They were only unfocused for a moment before they settled on him.

"Hello, Zacharias."

"Hello, Babi. I'm sorry, I didn't mean to wake you."

"No? It seems you didn't. Strange though. I often find myself very awake when you are around these days." Her pupils twinkled.

He averted his own eyes away, almost feeling the weight of the Silence upon him. "You seemed like you could use the rest."

"But you wanted to sit with this sick old woman, anyway."

"Always," he said, and meant it. He'd been channelling Life into her since he arrived but had been aiming it at her lymph nodes and the cells that were fighting the cancer. Fighting and losing and there was nothing he'd been able to do about it.

His grandmother gestured towards the book.

"Your father mentioned you want to be a doctor."

Zack nodded. "I'm going to try."

"This is good. Your deda would be very proud to have a doctor as a grandson."

"Not you?" Zack said with a wry smile.

"No. I don't like doctors."

She turned her hand palm up and motioned him closer. He knelt beside the bed and placed his hand in hers.

"I am proud to have made a life here with him, in this strange, hot country. I'm proud of my three boys and the funny, noisy family they have grown. And I am proud of this boy who sits beside an old woman and worries about her." Zack blinked away some tears. "And if this boy wants to go and become something as silly as a doctor, then that is okay."

He smiled. "Thank you."

"But don't forget to do the living part as well. Especially while you are young. Don't just study, study, study. Go out, have fun, find that girl that makes you smile."

The previous night's image of Charlie flashed across his mind.

"There's plenty of time for that, Babi."

"No, there isn't. It seems like there is, but you use smaller and smaller words to describe how much time you have left. Starts with… what's that word? Not centuries, ten?"

"Decades?"

"Decades, yes. Starts with decades. Then it's years. Months. Weeks."

"Weeks?" Zack's eyes widened and he felt his heart drop.

"Maybe. The doctors don't know. They don't know anything. Are you sure you want to be one of them?"

He nodded, unable to find any more words.

"Well, be a better one than them. But yes, I'd like to talk to some of the others today, maybe see little Addison. Do you think I will be awake enough for that?"

It took him longer than it should have to realise what she was asking.

"Yes, yes, I think you will be."

He closed his eyes and poured Life into her. After the amount he'd been channelling in already, he could feel this extra pulling at his own Life. The edges of his hangover returned, but he kept going.

She squeezed his hand in a tight grip. Like warm soft paper over stone.

"Thank you, Zacharias."

He stopped, a headache burning at the very front of his skull.

"Of course, Babi." He leant over and kissed her cheek before leaving the room. He passed his cousin in the hallway. "She's awake if you want to go in."

"Thanks, I'll let Dad know."

Zack wandered outside and dropped himself onto the steps of the porch, looking out to their cramped, vegetable-garden filled backyard.

Weeks?

Zack sat backwards on a worn, splintery chair, resting his chin on the top of its back. Art lay stretched out on one of the old wooden cots along the wall while Tabitha and Jackie strolled back and forth across the room.

Every now and then, the Tower undertook powerful rituals and engaged teams, like Zack and his friends, to stand guard against any breaches drawn by the intense magic. They were among the least experienced in the Tower and were often guarding rooms furthest away from where the ritual was taking place, where breaches were less likely to form. The experience of their very first guard duty notwithstanding, Zack expected this one to be as uneventful and boring as all those that had come since.

What made this one different was they had been divided into two groups. For whatever reason, less mages had answered the call and they'd been allocated two rooms to guard instead of one.

"I'm not convinced we did the split right," Art said from the cot. He was balancing a coin on the flat of his elbow before snapping his forearm out and catching it.

Tabitha sighed. "State your case then."

"Okay. To start with, it's not all wrong. Splitting up Jackie and Bast is good."

Jackie raised a warning shot of an eyebrow at him.

Art threw up his hands and the coin bounced across the stone floor.

"No, not because of the other week. Because you are our two best chances of sensing a breach happen."

"So, there's no problem?" Tabitha asked.

"But." Art held up his index finger. "Jackie and Zack shouldn't be in the same group."

"Why?" Zack asked.

"Because you and Jackie are both supports. We've got shields and healing over here, over there they've got neither."

Tabitha's head bobbed in thought. "So, next time we swap Jackie and Bast around."

Art's eyes widened — he was about to get himself in trouble again. Zack spoke up instead.

"No good. Two swords in the same room."

Art nodded in eager agreement.

"How in hell does that matter?" Tabitha asked.

"It probably doesn't," Zack admitted. "I'm only saying if you are trying to balance the teams, one sword in each."

"So, that means Zack switches, not Jackie," Art said.

A smug smile grew on Tabitha's face.

"Well, if that's the case, then he can't swap with Bast."

"Nope," Art agreed.

"And he can't swap with Charlie," Tabitha continued. "Because she and Max are a package deal."

"Um, yeah."

"Which means…"

"I withdraw my objection. The teams are fine."

Tabitha laughed. "I thought you might."

Zack hauled himself off the seat and paced up and down the room. There were eight beds in total. The mattresses were old but clean, except perhaps for the one Art had been putting his shoes on. What did the Tower need with these bunk rooms? Was it an echo from the past, when it had been harder for Tower members to get home from their nearest Tower exit? Or was it a sign that the Tower's numbers were less than they were before?

Art sidled up beside him. "Sorry, man."

"For what? Trying to get rid of me?"

"What?" Art laughed. "No, for failing to get you in with Charlie."

Zack rolled his eyes.

"Seriously, what are you waiting for, man? She's back on the market."

"No, she's not," Tabitha said.

"It's rude to eavesdrop," Art responded.

"Then learn to whisper, dude."

"You didn't see what we saw that night at your party," Art said, eyebrows waggling.

"No, but I know what she told me yesterday. She's still with Dave. Things might be a bit tense there, but I'm not exactly a relationships expert, for obvious reasons."

"For obvious reasons?" Jackie asked.

"Well, yeah, because…" Tabitha looked towards the two boys.

They shook their heads.

"Oh, okay." Tabitha turned back to face Jackie. "I told the boys last year and I thought they may have said something. I'm ace. That means I'm—"

"No, I know what ace means." Jackie nodded in understanding.

"How do you know what ace is?" Art asked.

"Because I read," Jackie replied.

Zack and Tabitha laughed. Jackie sat; her face thoughtful.

"That must make things a bit simpler."

"Yes and no," Tabitha said.

"What do you mean?" Jackie asked. "If that's okay?"

"Yeah, it's okay." Tabitha sat down on the edge of a bed. "So, like, I'm ace. I'm not sexually attracted to anybody. And yeah, when looking around at other people, it does seem like life's a lot easier without all that, you're right. But where it gets confusing for me is that I'm not sure if I'm romantically attracted to people. Where's that line, you know? Am I just into surrounding myself with good people and connecting with them? Or is there something more there? I mean, maybe I'm biromantic? Or maybe it's that I like cuddling up with my friends and feeling close to them." She looked at Jackie and gasped. "Sorry. I can't believe I dumped all that. So um, yeah, maybe not simpler."

Jackie squeezed her hand. "Maybe not."

Tabitha looked over at the boys and blushed. "I'm so sorry for all that."

"If it makes you feel any better, Tabs," Art said. "I'm not sure I understood half of what you said. Who wants to go catch a movie tomorrow, or something?"

"I can't," Zack said. "I've got infirmary duty."

"How's that going?" Tabitha asked, with obvious relief that the conversation had moved on.

"It's good," Zack replied. "I've only done it a few times so far, and a lot of it is just sitting around, but each shift at least a couple of people come in looking for healing. Mostly, it's just patching up bruises or minor cuts, but I've seen some bigger wounds. Erik turned up once holding three of his fingers and six of his teeth."

Tabitha's jaw dropped. "And?"

"And now they are back where they're supposed to be," Zack said with a small amount of pride. "I got one of the other Lifers to check my work, though."

Tabitha laughed.

"That guy is full on. I trained with him a couple of times and it's clear he loves throwing himself into dangerous situations. Makes me feel lucky to have a Lifer with us when we go out."

"And our very own shieldmaiden." Zack nodded to Jackie. "Some teams have neither."

The two-hour alarm on Zack's phone vibrated in his pocket. "Guard duty's up."

Art swung his legs down and bounced up onto his feet.

"So, if tomorrow's out, how about we grab our pay and see a movie tonight?"

"Sounds good to me," said Zack.

They left the room and wandered down the hall.

"What's that, five guard duties in a row without so much as a peep?"

"Six," corrected Zack. "I don't mind, it's easy money."

"True," said Art. "But I could use a little bit of excitement from time to—"

He broke off as Bast, Kimmy, Charlie and Max appeared from around a corner. Each of them, Max included, was dripping from head to toe in some kind of dark green ichor.

"What in the world…?" Tabitha looked them up and down.

"Slime monster," Bast said, in a tired voice.

Kimmy pushed past him, her eyes scanning the other four. "Nothing?" Her voice raised to a higher, louder shrill. "NOTHING?"

"Yeah, it was a pretty boring couple of hours," Art said.

The look Kimmy shot him was dagger-filled and she stormed down the corridor muttering to herself. "Hair, ruined. Clothes, ruined. And he's bored."

Max gave a soft whine.

"I told you not to bite at it," Charlie said, combing the sludge out of Max's fur with her fingers. "Who knows what it's going to do to you?"

Zack moved beside Max and reached out with Life.

"I can't promise anything, but that stuff doesn't seem to be doing anything really bad. Her stomach probably won't like it, but it doesn't seem like it's particularly toxic or anything."

"Thanks, Zack." Charlie turned back to Max. "You're going to go and drink a lot of water, okay. We'll flush this junk out and then you can have some ribs."

Max barked.

"Shower first though."

Max sniffed at the mention of the shower and a stream of green slime shot out of her nose. She stared in surprise at where it struck the wall before lowering her head and following Charlie to go get cleaned up.

"So, what happened?" Tabitha asked Bast.

Bast blinked at her.

"It was the most disgusting thing I've ever seen in my life. I can't. I'm supposed to be going on a date tonight, but I don't think I'm going to leave my shower for a week." He strode after Charlie leaving the other four bewildered in the corridor.

"Just us for the movie, then?" Art asked.

Zack's eyes were on the open textbook in front of him but his mind had long wandered off into half-thought and distraction. A sharp jab in the arm brought his attention back to himself and he looked across to the source. Sara, sitting diagonal from him in her high-backed armchair, was holding a thin, twisted piece of wood, carved with strange symbols.

"Is that a wand?" Zack asked in surprise.

"A wand?" Sara looked down at it. "No. This is a stick. I use it for prodding students who slack off when they should be revising. What would I need a wand for?"

"They have them in the stories sometimes."

"In the stories I'd need to be white and have a beard to live in a Tower. Women like me are relegated to forests living in huts with chicken feet." She used her stick to tap the book in his lap. "Enough stories. These are the books you should be reading."

He nodded and turned his focus back to his book. It didn't last long.

"I don't think my friends trust me to be their healer," he blurted out.

She sat in silence for several long moments, observing him. His stomach sank. Why did he say anything? If this got back to Junie, she might look to replace him with somebody more competent and bounce him back down to a group of greener recruits.

Sara closed her own book and put it down on the table beside her chair before folding her hands onto her lap.

"Tell me what happened."

He described the 'arachnaut' attack and the strange feeling the toxin gave, moving through Kimmy's body. When he reached the part where he instructed Kimmy to burn herself, he looked down at his shoes, unwilling to see shock or disappointment on Sara's face. He explained the way he had healed Kimmy, but also the way things between him and some of the group had not been the same since. When he finished, he sat in silence, eyes remaining down.

It was eight long breaths before Sara spoke.

"The other Schools often think of Life as the easiest path. We linger towards the back of the fight, or perhaps even arrive after it has finished. We patch up those who do the real work, who master the real magic, so they can continue to do the real work and master the real magic."

Zack looked up and found her staring back at him, her eyes twinkling.

"Pah. They do not understand how hard it is to do what we do. I do not mean the difficulty of the magic. I mean the difficulty of the decisions we make. What do they choose between? Hit this in the face with fire or hit that in the face with fire?"

Zack laughed.

"And they cannot understand it, Zachary. All who serve the Tower will, from time to time, make decisions where they must weigh life and death. But these decisions are so much harder for those of us who can feel the weight of Life. I have made decisions that will sit with me forever. I have amputated limbs when I have needed to. I have cut out shrapnel and bone without anaesthetic. And I have, when all else failed, chosen who lived and who died. My friends looked at me differently after that too. And so did I."

Zack's mouth felt dry. "I don't think I'm ready for that."

"Of course you are not. I wouldn't want to meet someone who was. But that is why we are here. We work your magic so you are strong enough that you may not need to choose. We train your mind so that you can make the right decision when you do need to. And we try to ready your heart, for after that."

"I think I did some lasting harm to Kimmy."

Sara gave a slow nod. "It is possible. We can heal the flesh, regrow the tissue. But we cannot truly undo what has been done. For some, like Erik, as long as the wound has been mended, all is well. For others, the memory of the injury lingers. I reattached a man's arm once. Within a day, we had to stop him from cutting it off. He was convinced it wasn't his. Your friend will need time."

"I think she blames me. And some of the others do too, for not being able to heal her without harming her."

"Then you will be in good company, Zachary. The hospitals are filled with doctors and nurses who are blamed for what guns, cars and diseases have caused. I cannot teach you how to save the world, only to make a difference when you can."

CHAPTER 11

TROUBLES

The lunch bell rang and the room filled with the clatter of desks, chairs and backpacks as students scrambled to escape to the courtyard. Zack didn't move. He had barely heard the bell and sat, staring at the summary of topics on the whiteboard. With little over a week left to go before the Year 12 students finished their lessons in the lead up to the final exams, Zack was forced to acknowledge that he understood maybe half of what was on the board. And perhaps only half of that with any confidence. There would be no early copy of the exam this time to cheat off. Art had promised he would have a solution, but he had yet to deliver on it and the weeks before the first exam were slipping by.

Perhaps Art had decided not to bother, in an effort to convince the others that they didn't need to meet the mundane expectations of university admission or real world jobs. He hadn't even turned up to this lesson. Zack's mouth felt too dry.

The clearing of a throat snapped his attention back from his thoughts and he turned around. Tabitha stood there, holding her folder.

"C'mon buddy, let's get something to eat."

Zack nodded and hauled himself out of his seat. They walked

together down the hallway towards the double doors to the courtyard. Tabitha squeezed him on the shoulder.

"It's alright, dude. We've still got time before the exams."

"How could you tell?" he asked.

She laughed. "With the look you had on your face all class, you don't need to be a tall, blonde mind reader. Speaking of which, know where he is?"

"Nope. Since he worked out how to convince teachers they'd seen permission slips, he's been skipping classes pretty regularly."

"Figures."

"You seem pretty relaxed about the finals," he said.

"Nah, I'm like a duck."

Zack narrowed his eyes in confusion.

"You know, still and calm where you can see me, but under the water, paddling like mad?"

"Settled on a course you want?"

"Yeah, I think I'll go for environmental science. Feels like the right kind of mix for me. A bit political, bit sciencey. Still gonna do the gap year thing with you guys, though."

Zack nodded. They had all discussed it before and everybody had agreed to defer a year. Everybody except Art, who was adamant about not going to university at all.

"Your parents good with that?" he asked.

"Yeah. As long as I end up going. My parents are pretty relaxed about most things, but not going to university at all would have been a bridge too far, I think."

"Well, they're both professors, right?"

"Yeah. So, it's kind of always been assumed. And I want to go. For them and for me."

"I know what you mean."

"So, it sure would be nice to know that a certain Mind mage—"

"Psychomancer," Zack interrupted.

Tabitha rolled her eyes. "I'm not calling him that. But it sure would be nice to know he has a game plan for the exams."

They reached the end of the hall and walked down the steps towards their usual bench. The cold September air was sharp with the suggestion that winter wasn't quite done with them yet.

"Art has a plan. He always has a plan. Delivering on it is where he sometimes runs into trouble."

"Well then," Tabitha plonked down on the bench and flipped open her folder, "better shore up Plan B."

Zack reached into his own bag and drew out a sandwich and his chemistry notes. Bast, Charlie and Dave wandered over a few minutes later, and the five of them sat in relative silence as they focused on studying. In the corner of his eye, Zack noticed Charlie shrug off Dave's arm from around her shoulders. He tried to stay focused on his notes, but after reading the same paragraph half a dozen times, he slipped them back into his bag and stood up.

"My brain's full, I'm going to stretch my legs," he declared to nobody in particular. Tabitha, Bast and Charlie waved him off and Dave ignored his existence.

Leaving his bag behind, he decided to head towards the library to see if that's where Art was hiding away. The combination of wifi and couches made it seem like a decent bet. He strolled alongside some Year 8 boys playing handball and past the canteen before ducking in between two buildings.

At the other end of the passageway was Jackie. She had been cornered by four other girls and, as usual, 'Britney' was in the centre. Zack didn't know, or particularly care, what her actual name was. He'd thought of her as Britney for a while now. He couldn't hear what they were saying from this distance, but none of it was kind. Jackie had made it clear to Art that she didn't want him to step in, and Zack thought it likely that would extend to him as well, so he approached, but stopped a short distance away.

"Why are you like this? Why are you so cruel?" Jackie asked.

Closer now, Zack could see that her jumper was soaked. The water bottles in the other three girls' hands filled in the rest of the picture for him.

"Why are you like this?" Britney mimicked back. "Why are you so pathetic? And so wet? You're going to get sick or something."

The other girls laughed before the four of them turned and pranced away down the corridor. Jackie collapsed against the wall, sobbing. Zack sidled up and crouched beside her. She looked at him across the top of her cradled knees. Her eyes were red and damp.

"I don't want to hear it, Zack."

"Hear what?"

"That I should stand up for myself. That I shouldn't let those girls treat me like that."

"I wasn't going to say anything like that."

"No?" Her eyebrow arched up in suspicion.

"No." He shrugged out of his jumper and held it out to her. "But maybe you want something dry to keep you warm."

She sniffled but followed it with a small smile as she accepted the jumper from him. She peeled her own off and draped it over a nearby railing before slipping into Zack's. It was large enough to go down to her thighs, while the sleeves reached up to her knuckles.

Zack chuckled. "You're one of the few people that can make my clothes look big."

She folded the arms back over her wrists. "But what about you? It's so cold today."

"I'll be fine," he said. "If I really need to, I can give myself a mild fever for the afternoon, keep me nice and toasty on the inside."

"Really?"

"Well, yeah, I could. It would be a terrible idea, but I could. I'll be fine."

"See, that's what I don't get. You're so kind. How can other people be so cruel?"

"I don't know. Some people just are. Art and I had our fair share, or more, a few years ago. But we were lucky. We had each other. And Matt," he added in a wistful tone. "But you're not alone. You've got us. You've got Kimmy. One word to her and those girls will be history."

Jackie wiped the moisture from her cheeks. "I don't want them to be history. I want to know why they hate me and I want them to stop."

"It's not on you, Jackie," Zack said. "The guys who were picking on us didn't stop because they changed how they felt about us, they just moved on to other targets. There's nothing wrong with you, there's something wrong with them. There's something missing inside, and making you feel like crap distracts them from that hole. If it wasn't you, it would be somebody else."

Her lips tightened. "I don't want it to be somebody else. I don't want it to be anybody."

"I dunno. Somebody like Britney is always going to need a victim."

"Who's Britney?" Jackie asked, confused.

"Oh, sorry. That's what I call that queen-B."

"Her name's Clare."

Zack grimaced. "Clare? No, that won't do. It's definitely Britney."

Jackie giggled. "You're so weird."

"We're all weird. And you can always hang out with us."

"Two months is an awfully short 'always', Zack."

'What do you mean?'

'In a couple of months, your exams start. And after that, you're all done with this place. And I'll be here alone for another three years. And I can't make friends, not really. Leave alone the fact that Clare—"

"Britney," Zack interrupted, hoping for a smile.

Jackie rolled her eyes. "Clare has scared off anybody who'd want to be friends with me. Even if she hadn't, I can't exactly hang out with people on the weekend or after school. I'm busy."

"That sucks, Jackie. I'm sorry I hadn't thought of it like that. I just see you as one of us, it's too easy to forget the ways you aren't."

"And I love being part of the gang. But it's going to get really lonely here during the school day."

"You're a badass, and I'm sorry for the rest of the school never getting to find that out." Zack stood back up. "C'mon, grab your jumper and we'll go hang out at the bench with the others."

They walked back across the courtyard, and Zack did his best to pretend he wasn't freezing.

Zack stepped out of the Tower entrance and onto the streets of Montreal. Not too dissimilar from the Sydney entrance, here it was hidden as a side door to an independent real estate company that looked like it had seen better days.

Art strode out from the shadows of the doorway and looked up and down the street.

"You know, Montreal is really pretty. We should come back for a night out some time, like, just for fun. We should go more places for fun, really. I don't know why we aren't taking full advantage of the Tower."

"Because a bunch of seventeen-year-olds wandering the world without passports might draw the wrong kind of attention?"

"Oh, and it doesn't when we're hunting down ninja goblins or baby-stealing faeries?"

"That's different. That's legitimate Tower business."

Art groaned. "Why am I friends with such a square?"

"Because I've kept you out of trouble for a decade?"

"As if. But anyway, in six months we'll both be eighteen. Then we're travelling the world."

"Deal."

Art gave a satisfied nod. "Right, on to tonight's business."

The two of them walked through Montreal together. Ten minutes shy of midnight, the area near the Tower entrance was full of nightlife. Bars and clubs blared music out into the streets while locals and commuters loitered outside waiting for taxis or buses. Zack kept his head down and attempted a brisk pace, but Art waved, smiled and even chatted to those they passed.

"I'm still not sure about us doing this alone," Zack said.

"We don't need them for this, and you're the one who was worrying about a group of teenagers wandering the streets attracting attention."

"Yeah, okay."

"Plus, I'll be honest, I'm getting a little sick of the way the rest of them look at me when I'm using my magic. I can do without the judgement this time."

"They don't—"

Art silenced him with a look.

"Yeah okay, they do a bit."

"It sucks. Nobody else gets a hard time about the way they use their magic."

"I think it's that manipulating people's thoughts and feelings creeps people out a bit."

"That's the thing though, Zack. We all manipulate people's thoughts and feelings. We do it with our words, body language and actions."

They stopped at a street corner, waiting for the lights to change.

"That's not the same thing."

"Sure it is. Take Tabitha for example. She's super cool, everybody knows how kind she is, she's smart and funny. All of that impacts people and they feel friendly towards her."

The lights turned green and they walked as Art continued, "Now flip it to Kimmy. Horrible, simply horrible. And willing to get personal and even violent, if you cross her. Put it another way, she creates fear. I can just do all that with magic."

"That's different," Zack said.

"No, it isn't really. You can heal, but a decent doctor with the right set up can do the same. Kimmy can create fire, but I can do it too, with a lighter. Same for everybody else. Our magic makes us better at those things, but they're still things that can be done."

Zack was silent for a few moments, before a thought occurred to him.

"Bast creates portals into other realms."

"Yeah, okay, it falls down a little at some points."

Zack laughed. "Look mate, Mind magic just weirds people out a bit, okay? Our thoughts and feelings are what make us who we are, and even if they are manipulated by nice girls, scary girls and advertising, the fact that you can do it with precision takes it to another level. But I trust you with it."

"Thanks, man."

Zack led the two of them away from the centre of the city to the more derelict semi-industrial area that housed the magic store. They stopped around the corner.

"Okay, go over it again," Art said.

"There were two guys in there last time. You really only dealt with the main one. Old, beard, glasses. The other guy was little and bald. He had glasses too, reminded me of a mole. I think you did some magic to make them slowly get drunk or something."

"Yeah, brilliant," Art nodded.

"So, you got the ink and the phone number of the buyer."

"But I didn't get anything about the seller?"

"Nope. We got interrupted."

Art pulled a face. "By the creep who wiped my memory."

Zack chose not to remind Art it was he who had cast the spell; the other man had only reversed it. "So, you got a plan?"

"Yep. This time I'm after the seller."

"And what do you need from me?"

"You said these guys didn't seem to do any magic?"

"Not that we saw. They knew about it though."

"Yeah, that'll be fine. If you distract them for a few moments and then I can get to work. After that, watch my back. We should be in and out pretty quick. Ready?"

"Hang on, let me check the place."

Zack reached out with his senses and focused on the strange little shop at the end of the alleyway. He had reached out further, but the added challenge here was filtering out the rest of the life all around him. Montreal had a population of almost two million and that was just counting the humans. Narrowing in on the store was like trying to see a single candle amidst a house fire.

But he could do it. "Three people."

"Three?" Art asked.

"Yeah."

"Is one a customer, or are there three people working tonight?"

Zack squinted at him. "People don't give off different Life energy when they're shopping, Art."

"Heh, yeah, fair enough."

"Can you pick up anything?"

"Not from this distance."

"Right then, let's find somewhere to lurk while we wait to see if that person wants to leave."

"Lurk?" Art grimaced.

"It's absolutely what we're doing."

"See, this is what I was talking about before. Someone hears you saying that you're going to 'lurk' and you will make them think of you as a creepy weirdo, no Mind magic necessary."

Zack ignored him and crouched down between two dumpsters. Art slid in beside him.

A little over 10 minutes later, the door to the store opened and a woman exited. She looked to be in her 40s and was carrying a cloth shopping bag in each hand. She stopped for a moment and placed the bags down so she could adjust her scarf before she scooped them back up again and strode away down a side alley that took her away from where the boys were loitering.

Art stirred beside him, but Zack rested his hand on his friend's chest.

"Let's wait another minute."

Art nodded.

The street remained silent and, after the minute had passed, the boys stood up and entered the store. Inside seemed much as it had during their first visit, with the shelves and tables cluttered with candles, books and knickknacks. The two men were also the same as last time, and the shorter man gave Zack a familiar suspicious stare as they entered. He felt Art's hand on his back pushing him forward.

"Bonsoir," the bearded man said from the counter across the room.

"B- Bonsoir," Zack repeated, cringing at what his awkward Australian vowels did to the word. "I'm sorry, do you speak English?"

"Yes, yes of course," he replied.

The shorter man approached, looking the boys up and down. "You look familiar."

Art stepped past Zack, much to Zack's relief. "Yes. We visited some time ago. You don't mind getting back to your cleaning so I could speak with your friend, do you?"

There was something about the way 'cleaning' fell into Zack's ears that made it feel almost like a mosquito buzzed past his head, and a purple glow came from the hand behind Art's back. The man nodded and turned back around to the bookshelves behind him. Art stepped towards the counter and smiled at the bearded man.

"I've got a business proposition for you, but first I'd like you to listen to what I have to say."

Again, the word 'listen' vibrated on the edge of Zack's hearing, while the man stood still and nodded in silence as Art stood across from him. From that point, Art spoke in hushed tones, although his fingers did occasionally wiggle in gestures beneath the counter.

Zack turned his attention away from them and around to the rest of the store. The shorter man didn't stray from his tidying, lining up the books with an eye for detail that was missing in the mess that was the rest of the shelves. Whatever Art had done to him was holding. Zack cast his senses outside the store, feeling for any approaching Life.

A few minutes later, Art tapped him on the shoulder. "Time to go."

"Are we good?" Zack asked as they walked down the street.

"Yep. He has no way of contacting whoever sold him the ink, but next time he sees them, he'll pass on my phone number to them and say I'm a keen buyer. He won't quite know why he does it, but he'll do it."

Zack looked at him straight-faced. "Yeah, Mind magic is exactly the same as somebody being friendly."

"Hey, some people are really persuasive."

Zack arced an eyebrow.

"Yeah, okay. Hey, we should grab a beer before we head back."

"I have to go home and study in case my friend doesn't come through on his promise to help me on my exams."

Art clutched at his chest in mock pain. "How very dare you! It's all covered."

"Fine," Zack said. "One beer."

CHAPTER 12

FINAL EXAMS

It was the morning of the first of the final exams and Zack was freaking out. Bast, Kimmy, Tabitha and Charlie were sitting with him on their usual bench, but Art was nowhere to be seen.

"Where is he, Zack?" Tabitha's knee bounced with nervous energy.

"He'll be here," he replied with far more conviction than he felt. He hadn't seen Art for days.

"I am going to set him on fire," Kimmy said.

"You always said you didn't actually need his help," Bast said. "I thought you'd been studying."

"I've been studying what parts of a seventeen-year-old boy are the most flammable. I swear it, Zack. If he's not here..."

"If he's not here, what?" Art's voice came from behind them.

As one, they spun around.

"No, seriously," Art said. "I'd like to hear the end of that."

Zack moved up to him. "Cutting it a little fine, aren't we? The exam starts in five minutes."

"Yeah, I know. Sorry."

Zack took a closer look at him. Art's eyes were dry and red, sunken deep into dark purple bags. "You look like crap, man."

"Haven't slept in three days, running on fumes and guarana.

No time for that now, and no time for a test drive either. C'mon, grab your stuff, we've got to find Mr Hancock."

"Why?" Tabitha asked.

"No time, no time. You'll have to trust me to be awesome." Art turned and jogged towards the Humanities staff room.

"I hate him when he does that," Tabitha said.

"Just when he does that?" Kimmy asked, snatching up her bag and running after him.

The others followed suit and caught up with Art outside the staffroom.

"Okay. Ask for Hancock and then distract him for five seconds and I'll take care of the rest, okay?" Art said.

"Distract him?" Charlie asked.

Art knocked and then stepped to the side of the door. "Yeah, ask him something, whatever. Make him look at you."

Seconds later, the door opened. Zack had been preparing to ask for Mr Hancock and was momentarily stunned when it was Mr Hancock himself who answered. He stood there, mute.

Mr Hancock scanned the group of students in front of him before raising his arm to look at his watch. "What in the world are you all doing here? You should be at the hall! It's too late for any special consideration, so I don't want to hear the excuses!"

He continued his tirade while behind him, Art's face was tight with determination. His fingers moved in precise but fluid motions and a faint purple light flared before Art fell against the wall.

But Zack almost didn't notice, because in the same instant, he suddenly knew things. The poetry of Frost and Grey came first, then line after line of Shakespeare's Tempest and The Life of Pi. Every text, every stanza, every line he'd been struggling to remember for weeks was right there in his mind. And not just the raw text. He understood how they related to each other. How the themes were connected. How the metaphors of one drew on the allusions of another.

He looked at the others and found himself surrounded by bemused smiles.

"What on earth are you all standing there for?" Mr Hancock's exasperated voice cut through.

"Sorry to bother you, Sir," Tabitha said. "We just wanted to thank you for your help this year."

He looked at her in bafflement. "Thank me when you pass. Which you won't if you don't sit the exam."

"Yes, sir," Tabitha replied.

They scrambled away down the hall. Zack and Bast scooped up Art, and together the six of them ran to the hall. The exam supervisor scowled and closed the doors behind them, as they dropped their bags at the entrance and found their seats.

Two minutes later, Zack was smiling from ear to ear as he read the exam paper. Questions that would have taxed him half an hour ago seemed pedestrian at best. His mind formed arguments and examples with ease. He wondered what Art might have pushed out to make room for all this knowledge but now was not the time to pursue those thoughts.

The first hour of the exam flew by in a blur and Zack's pen didn't stop for more than a few seconds at any stage. He reached the end of the essay section and flicked back through the pages to review his answers. His smile returned. They were better than anything he had ever written. The words were still his. He could see arguments he'd attempted to make in the half-yearly exams but here they were refined, drawing on better examples and laid out with an elegance he knew would net him a great result.

Three rows down to the left, Kimmy's left hand shot up, while she continued to write with her other.

"I need another answer booklet," she said to the examiner without looking up.

Zack glanced at the empty space at the end of his own booklet and shrugged. He was satisfied with what he'd done. He scanned around the room for the others. Charlie was leaning back in her chair, pen down, and Bast, scoping the room like him, shot him a quick wave. Tabitha appeared to be editing her work, but otherwise seemed relaxed.

And then Zack saw Art. Two examiners were standing next to his desk whispering to each other in an attempt to determine what they should do. Because, in front of them, Art was fast asleep.

The exam finished and the hall full of students shuffled out, collected their bags and split off into small groups to compare notes or otherwise commiserate on the last two hours. Zack saw Charlie wander away with Dave, but Bast, Tabitha and Kimmy waited for him on a bench across from the exit.

Tabitha looked worried.

"Are you okay?" Zack asked. "Did it go okay for you?"

"What? Oh yeah, it was amazing. All that stuff in my head? No, it's Art. Did you see him?"

Zack nodded. "Yeah, looked like he was asleep."

"Do you think he did any of it?" Tabitha asked, looking past Zack.

Bast answered. "Yeah. He was only a few desks to the front of me. A bit after half an hour in, though, he just crashed. Those oldies they ship in to supervise us, had no idea what to do."

Kimmy laughed. "Loser."

Tabitha scowled at her, but Zack turned to face her.

"Kimmy, that's not fair. I get that you don't like him. I love him, but I know Art's not for everybody. Still, I'm like ninety-nine percent certain that he's been awake for days trying to learn the magic he used for us today. So, instead of giving him crap, it'd be nice if you just said thank you. Or nothing, that would be okay too. He put us all first today."

Kimmy gaped at him, her mouth only a little wider than Tabitha's and Bast's.

Zack looked back towards the hall and found Art heading towards them with long, lazy steps and longer, lazier blinks. He held up his hand in a slow wave as he approached. Before Zack could respond, Kimmy stood and took a few steps towards Art.

"Thanks for today, Art. That magic was really helpful. I appreciate it." Then she strode away towards the library.

Art stood still, confusion written on his face. After a few moments he patted at his chest and ribs. "Did… did I die back there in the hall?"

Bast laughed. "Nah, man. Come grab a seat and tell us about that magic."

Art accepted the offer and sank down onto the bench between Bast and Zack. He rifled through his bag and took a long drink from his water bottle.

"So?" Bast asked.

"Oh, you genuinely want to know?" Art asked.

"Yes!" Tabitha threw up her hands.

"Oh, okay. So yeah, this was my plan for months. But it turned out to be way harder than I'd first thought. It's the same basic principle as the way I learn languages when we go on a mission. Except it's not language, it's subject matter, which is different, and it's not a willing source, which is different and it's going into the heads of non-psychomancers, which is different, and it's going into a bunch of brains at once—"

"Which is different," Bast and Tabitha finished together.

Art gave a soft laugh. "So yeah, turns out it's kind of nothing like the language thing. But I didn't have a better plan. So Timur and I have been putting in overtime to land this thing. I'm cactus."

Zack placed his hand on Art's shoulder and poured Life into him.

Art sat straighter. "Thanks, man."

"I'm so sorry, mate. I should have done that before the exam, I wasn't thinking."

"Yeah, you were. You were thinking like a middle-aged English teacher. It's a side effect of the magic. But it's all good. I answered enough that I won't fail and that's enough for me."

"Why Hancock?" Bast asked.

Art yawned. "Out of all the English teachers, he's marked the most exams. I've got a list of teachers for all of our subjects, with backups in case they're away."

"How long is it going to last?" Tabitha asked, rubbing at her temple.

"It's probably already fading," Art said. "Which means we'll need to hit him up again tomorrow for the second half of the English exam. So before then, I think I'll go and sleep twenty hours and get ready for it."

⟩⟩⟩————⟩————⟩————⟨⟨⟨

"You look a bit dazed, dear. Are you okay?" Zack's mother reached across the family dinner table and squeezed his arm.

Zack shook his head to clear it. He'd had his Maths exam that morning and Art had poured in every bit of mathematics from Mr Ho's head, including what had obviously been university level three-dimensional calculus. It had made the exam a complete walkthrough, but it had lingered.

"I'm good, Mum. Maths was a bit full on this morning."

"How do you think you went?" she asked, failing her apparent attempt to make it sound like a casual question.

"Well, I hope. I think I peaked at the right time."

His father gave him a wink.

"That's great, Zacky. We're very proud. Of the effort," she hastened to add. "You've been putting in such a wonderful effort and we're excited to see it pay off for you."

Zack laughed and his father chuckled along. He finished his dinner and stood up to clear his plate.

"I don't have another exam until Thursday, so I was going to go hang out with some friends?"

"That's fine, dear. But don't stay out too late. A proper sleep routine is important to maintain. We wouldn't want you falling asleep on top of your exam."

Zack burst into renewed laughter and his parents looked at him in concern.

"Sorry, Mum. Just a funny thought, imagining somebody doing that."

He put his plate and cutlery into the dishwasher, grabbed his keys and wallet and headed out the door. Thanks to daylight savings it wasn't quite dark yet and warm November winds teased him with a summer soon to arrive.

Art pulled up in front of his house in a beaten up old car.

"Going my way, beautiful?"

Zack climbed into the passenger seat. The air inside the car was thick and muggy and he fanned at himself in an attempt to stave off the heat.

"Yeah, sorry about that. The AC is busted. Wind down your window."

"That's okay. But can I ask, why is your car such a piece of crap? Like, it's better than my non-existent car, but I'd expected you to just put the whammy on the dealer and get a good one."

"The whammy?" Art asked.

"Yeah, you know." Zack did an impression of mind rays by wiggling his fingertips.

Art laughed. "Yeah, and that would be fine until my parents asked me how I was affording a sweet set of wheels. I've got a plan, though. Next year when we're working for that 'promotions company,' I'm going to get to borrow a 'company car' a lot. Until then, this crapbox is what we've got. The radio works though."

Winding the window down made all the difference and, with his best friend beside him driving his first car and music blaring on the radio, Zack lost himself in a moment of simple, teenage joy. He held his hand out the window and felt the oncoming air against his fingers.

Before too long, the smell of salt flavoured the air and Art pulled up at a beachside car park. Charlie, Bast, Kimmy and Tabitha were staking out a sheltered picnic table looking out at the surf.

"There's the man of the hour!" Charlie shouted when she saw the boys approaching.

"Man of the month, more like it," Tabitha cheered.

Zack looked up at Art and saw him blushing.

"Come dance with us, Psychomancer," Tabitha said, using her phone to start music playing on her bluetooth speaker.

"I don't da—" Art's face lit up in realisation. "You used the word!"

"You deserve it, now get over here."

Zack gave him a good-natured shove towards the girl and Art threw up his hands before joining the girls down on the sand.

Zack sat down next to Bast. "How's things?"

Bast shrugged. "Yeah, alright." His flat tone suggested otherwise.

"What's the matter?" Zack asked.

"I got approached by an athletics club today. They offered to train and manage me, fly me around to competitions, all free of charge. Hell, it even has a small allowance attached to it."

Zack's eyes narrowed. "That's great, isn't it?"

Bast turned to face him. "Is it? It's a lot of eyes on somebody who isn't training hard enough to be making the times I've been making. Not to mention the commitment that I can't really make. Two years ago, this would have been a dream. But that's not even the worst bit."

"What's the worst bit?"

"They approached my dad. So now I have to come up with some reason why I don't want my dream anymore."

"Yeah, okay. I get it now. Lying to family is tricky."

"No, Zack. It's not. It's freakin' easy and I hate it. I say anything to my dad and he'll believe me, because he doesn't expect me to lie. Do you know how many years I hid being gay from him and my brothers?"

Zack stayed silent.

"Zero years, Zack. Zero months, zero weeks. I just talked to them about it while I was figuring it out and they supported me without hesitating. And now I lie to them every damn day. I've never been in the closet and then the Tower has come along and forced me into a different kind of one. I hate it."

Zack squeezed his shoulder. "I'm sorry, mate. I didn't know."

"I listen to the way you guys talk about your families. I mean, Kimmy's got a weird thing going, I'm not going to touch that, but the rest of you…" He paused in thought for a moment. "Your parents seem great, but it's almost like there's two teams: parents on one, kids on the other. You're not against each other, but you're not on the same team."

Zack thought about it. "Yeah, that seems fair."

"I've never had that. I don't know if it's just because I'm a blackfulla, family's important to all of us. But it might be more than that. My mum died and all of a sudden, my dad had four boys to look after on his own and we've always been like the one team. He's our captain, but it's like he's the first among equals."

"I'm sorry, mate. I didn't get how hard this has been on you."

Bast ran his fingers through his hair. "There's a bit more to it too, I think. This stuff we're doing, magic, and strange creatures, and other worlds, it sounds a lot like the stories my uncles and aunties taught me my whole life. Most of us, we don't think they're real. Like, the stories are important, they're our truth, but they probably didn't happen. Except now I'm thinking maybe they did. So, I'm not just lying about myself. I'm keeping stuff about our culture, something my mob were this close to losing when you lot invaded, to myself. It's a bit much sometimes."

"I don't know what to say."

"Nothing to say. I gave my oath and that was the price. I just have to make sure that price is worth it. I'm protecting my mob as much as I'm protecting the rest of the world. I have to do good things with this opportunity. Now c'mon, I can't stand watching somebody as straight and white as Art dancing without joining in."

Zack and Bast headed down to the others on the beach.

It was the last week of the finals and, more importantly, it was the morning of Zack's final exam. On paper, Zack was still in school until the end of the year, but in practice, today was the end of high school. He rolled out of bed and put on his uniform for the last time before heading downstairs.

His mother was waiting for him in the kitchen.

"What can I get you for breakfast?"

"It's okay, I can get it myself," he answered.

"I know you can, I raised a very competent young man. But it's my baby boy's last exam today and I'm going to make him breakfast."

Zack laughed. "Toast then, please."

"Toast it is. Go pack your bag and I'll bring it to the table."

Zack slid his notes, water bottle and a few snacks into his backpack and returned to his mother in the kitchen. He was so distracted by his thoughts that he didn't see it until he was a few steps away from the table.

"Oh, god."

The tabletop was covered in photo albums. His mother patted the empty seat next to her. Zack's shoulders dropped and he collapsed into the chair.

"Humour me," she said, pulling across an album open to his first day of kindergarten.

Ellen walked into the kitchen to make a coffee and laughed.

It was half an hour before Zack could get away, so he was later than he had intended getting to school. The other five had all finished their exams, but Art was waiting for him. He had a worried look on his face.

"We have a problem."

Zack dropped his bag beside him. "What is it?"

"I can't find Mr Gordon or Ms Tolino," he said, listing the school's two senior biology teachers.

Zack took a moment to think. "Okay, maybe we can find Mr—"

"I can't find anybody, Zack. I've asked around. My way. The entire science room is out of commission. Two of them are in the city with the Year Nines, going to the Powerhouse Museum, the rest are down with food poisoning. Apparently, Mr Cole brought in a cake for his birthday yesterday and he's wiped them all out."

"Oh," said Zack, staring towards the hall and his impending exam. "So, it's just me and what I've got in my brain already then."

CHAPTER 13

SETTING A TRAP

Zack made the long walk to the hall and waited for the doors to open. Other students were there, either clutching at notes for some last minute cramming, or chatting to distract each other from their nerves. Zack stood aside. Instead of biology notes, his mind was spinning with different thoughts. He'd taken for granted that Art would be able to help with this test the same way he'd done with all the others. Zack's other good exam results wouldn't be enough, not with his poor assignment scores weighing down his averages. He had been counting on a strong result in biology.

The exam supervisors opened the doors and the other students shuffled in while Zack stood, staring. His thoughts looped through images of poor test results, hard conversations and all the other consequences of failing this exam, while he trudged his way to his assigned desk and dropped into the chair. The supervisors walked up and down the rows, handing out the tests and then the timer started. Using his basic magical training, Zack steadied his mind and found calm. He exhaled and opened the booklet, expecting the worst.

The first section's questions were similar to those asked in the half-yearly exams. So far, so good, but he doubted his luck would hold out. The second section started with a complex question related to cellular biology that he did not remember learning in class.

But he did remember discussing it with Sara. One component in particular pulled him right from his seat in the hall and straight to the Tower, sitting in the cozy windowless room accompanied by dozens of books and a patient, knowledgeable woman. He smiled to himself as he worked through the answer.

Question after question called more on his study of Life than any token effort he'd put in at school. But he knew the answers. He knew it all. Zack raced through the exam with a confidence that surprised and delighted him. He put his pen down and looked at the clock; more than an hour was still to go and he'd finished. He spent another ten minutes checking his answers and made a few edits to his long form answers, before raising his hand to call over one of the supervisors.

High school was over.

He was almost dancing as he exited the hall and scooped up his bag. Art and Jackie were waiting outside in the shade. Art looked worried, checking the time on his phone.

"You're out early. Was it that bad?"

Zack beamed at him. "Nah, mate. I rocked it."

Art let out a loud whoop of excitement and hugged him. After a tight squeeze he let go and stepped back. "Okay, mate. Time to go, we're on the clock."

"What?" Zack was confused.

Art held up his phone.

"Half an hour ago I got a message. The ink sellers are willing to meet with us. The others are on their way to the Tower. I pulled Jackie out of class and I've just sent for an Uber. It's game time."

Zack changed into spare clothes he had stashed in the Tower before he joined the others in the Training Room. Art was pacing back and forth.

"Why are we rushing this?" Charlie asked. "Wouldn't it be safer to set up a meeting for a few days from now so we can scope it out?"

"Yeah," Art said, "and I was worried it would sound exactly like we were planning to do that. I wanted him to think I was so keen on buying from him that I wasn't thinking of anything else. I tried to sound desperate."

Kimmy opened her mouth to make the obvious comment.

Tabitha cut her off. "Leave it."

Kimmy pouted.

Bast looked over at the racks. "Do we arm up?"

"We're walking through the middle of Montreal," Tabitha said. "I don't want to get caught with weapons."

"I can deal with any cop that busts us," Art said. "But if we turn up armed to the teeth, we'll definitely spook the seller."

"What if we stuff them all into one bag?" Zack asked. "That shouldn't attract too much attention."

"Okay," Tabitha said. "But everybody pick something light. All of them in the one bag is going to be heavy."

A few moments later, a duffel bag had been filled with weapons and placed at Zack's feet.

"Why me?"

Kimmy shrugged. "It was your idea."

Zack peered in at the heavy metal weapons nestled in against his short wooden staff. "But I only ordered the side salad."

"What?" Kimmy asked, confused.

"Never mind." He took off his jacket and stuffed it in and around the weapons in the hopes it would muffle the inevitable clattering, before pulling the straps onto his shoulder.

"Alright, let's go."

It was evening as they exited the Tower's Montreal entrance

and the city was bustling with more life than Zack had seen on either of his last visits combined.

"So, what's the plan?" Bast asked as they waited at a crossing for the lights to change.

"Same plan as the first time?" Tabitha asked. "Charlie finds a little friend to check out the area, then we send in the boys while the rest of us lurk."

"Maybe I should hang back too, this time," Zack said. He patted the bag.

Tabitha looked ready to object but Art nodded.

"The fewer with me when I meet them, the better the odds they'll trust us."

"Okay, but then what?" Kimmy asked, crossing the street as the light changed.

"Plan A is, I get them talking and we find out what they know," Art said. "Plan B is that Bast and I stun them long enough for the rest of you to charge on in and we force them to give up."

Tabitha nodded. "We need information. Junie wants to know who they are and she's getting impatient."

"I thought she wanted to know who gave those two guys the ritual instructions," Charlie said.

"They could be the same people," Bast said.

Kimmy scrunched up her face. "That doesn't make any sense. Why not give them the ritual and the ink at the same time?"

"You mean, why give them the ritual and then sell them the ink they need to do the ritual?" Art asked. "That sounds like a strong business model to me."

"Yeah, you would think like that." Kimmy turned her nose up at him.

"We don't know any of this," Tabitha said, "which is why we need to question them."

They walked through the city towards the magic shop, but when they were a few blocks away, Art gathered them in an alleyway.

"We're a little bit earlier than I told them; we might want to hang back for a bit."

"Why?" Kimmy asked. "Early is good, we can scope it out."

"Unless they are early too. Then we look suspicious," Art replied.

"Charlie? Can you find a rat and help us out?" Tabitha asked.

"Help, yes. But not a rat." Charlie closed her eyes. "I've been practising."

The rest of the group quietened as Charlie twitched her fingers and made soft, strange noises. The dark reddish telltale of her magic filtered out through her fingers and faded into the air. Less than a minute later, accompanied by an awkward flutter, a pigeon landed on the footpath. It cooed and then seemed to notice Max and scrambled closer to Charlie.

"It's okay, little friend," Charlie said. "She won't hurt you."

Max looked at the pigeon with undisguised disdain.

"I'm sorry, Max, but they're going to notice a giant dog like you skulking around."

Max whined.

"Yes, because you're pretty. They'll say, 'what a pretty dog, she doesn't belong here'."

Max sniffed, seemingly satisfied and settled down on her haunches. Tabitha crouched beside her and scratched behind her ears. Charlie turned to the pigeon.

"Now, you hold still, okay? I need to borrow a ride."

The pigeon cooed, while Charlie incanted again. When she finished, her eyes were alight with the rusty red of her magic, staring blindly into the space in front of her.

"Okay. Let's go check out the meet."

The pigeon flapped its wings and leapt into the air.

"Oh, god." Charlie heaved and reached out to steady herself on the wall. The pigeon lurched in the same direction and crashed into the side of the building. Charlie squealed as it fluttered to the ground, where it wandered around in circles.

"I thought you said you had been practising," Kimmy said, surveying the scene.

Charlie smoothed out her clothes. "Oh, I'm sorry, Kimmy. Do you have much experience with flying?"

Kimmy gave a curt shake of her head, but Bast's eyes were alight with excitement at the comment.

"It's very disorienting." Charlie steadied her breathing. "Particularly with the size difference and the fact his eyes are on the sides of his head."

"It's okay, Charlie," Zack said. "Take your time. Are you okay?"

"Thanks, and yeah, I'm fine."

"Is the bird?"

Charlie nodded. "Yeah, just a little dazed. Okay. Take two."

This time, Charlie started against the wall and, although she still clutched at her stomach as the pigeon took flight, she guided it over the rooftops of the nearby buildings and towards the alley in front of the magic shop.

"Right, I'm there."

"Can you see anybody?" Bast asked.

"No, not yet. Hang on, I'm going to find somewhere to land. Oh, wait. There is somebody there. They're leaning against the dumpster we hid behind when we were here. I can try and get in closer."

"No," said Tabitha, "just find a spot to watch the area. Don't do anything a pigeon wouldn't do."

Charlie smirked. "Sure thing, boss. Okay, I'm sitting on a fire escape. I can't see them well from here but if they step out into the middle of the alley to talk, I'll see everything. Probably hear it too."

"Right. Watch them for a while, see if they do anything dodgy."

"Will do." Charlie saluted with unfocused eyes.

Zack watched her from the edge of the alley.

Art sidled up beside him and spoke to him in a soft whisper. "Just curious…"

"Yeah?"

"Do the dark red eyes make her more or less attractive to you?"

Zack answered him with a narrowed stare.

"More? You're such a freak," Art teased.

"Shut up. Shouldn't you be getting your own game face on?"

"Oh, I'm ready." Art bounced from side to side. "This is our break, man. I can feel it."

Charlie held up her hand and Art settled.

"They're stepping out into the centre of the alley. It's a woman. I don't recognise her."

"I didn't talk to a woman," Art said.

"Well, we didn't expect this to be one person," Tabitha said.

"True, but then why is she alone?" Bast asked.

"She might not be," Zack said.

"She just checked her phone," Charlie relayed.

"That's because it's time for the meet," Art said, looking at his watch.

"Okay, you two head around and we'll be right behind you. Charlie will let us know if anything goes sideways and we'll be there right away."

Bast nodded, but Art was too eager and strode off. Zack shouldered the bag, while Kimmy and Tabitha slipped Charlie's arms around their shoulders and helped her follow Jackie and Max down the street. They stopped at the mouth of the side street that Art and Bast had entered and slid in between a parked car and a large air conditioning unit.

"Right," Charlie said, settling down to a crouch, "Art and Bast have seen her and she's waved them over."

"What's she look like?" Tabitha asked.

"Late twenties maybe?" Charlie answered. "Jeans, brown leather jacket. She's platinum blonde, with that hairstyle that's shaved on one side, long on the other. Always wondered if I could pull that off."

"You couldn't," Kimmy answered without hesitation.

"Focus," Tabitha said. "Anything else, any weapons?"

"Not that I can see."

Zack eased the duffel onto the ground and removed the girls' weapons, placing them within reach beside it, just in case. Tabitha saw him and nodded, while Jackie picked up her shortspear, her eyes never straying from her brother's direction.

"They're talking," Charlie relayed. "Says her name's Nicole. She's commenting on their ages. Art's trying to be cute."

Kimmy rolled her eyes.

"She's cut right to it. Wants to know how they heard about the ink. Art said he heard about it from some guys he met online, came to the shop to check it out. Now she's pointing out their accents, wants to know how they got to Canada so fast. Oh, nice. Art says the fact they could shows they'll know what to do with the ink."

"She's got him talking, it needs to be the other way around," Kimmy said.

"Give him a chance, Kimmy," Zack said. "He's probably working magic on her while they talk."

"Ugh, what's this chick's deal?" Charlie asked. "Now she wants to know how they are so capable, so young. Art's played the internet card again. Well, that and a comment about being handsome and talented. Okay, Art's flipped the question. He's asked her how she knows magic. She says she and her brothers had a teacher for a little while, but he's gone now and so they've taught themselves."

Charlie watched on in silence for a few moments.

"I think Art's hit her with Mind magic. This is like those two guys in the carpark, she's talking a lot, offering up a lot."

"We need more than stories," Tabitha said. "We need names, places. Something that either points the finger at somebody within the Tower or away from it."

Charlie waved her away to silence.

"Art's asking her about the ink, about how she learned how to make it. She's giving a long answer but it's all over the place. Is she drunk?"

"Um, that may be one of the ways Art's getting her to talk so much," Zack said.

"Smart move," Kimmy said.

Zack was surprised at the compliment. "What?"

"I hate being sober and talking to him. Probably the same for her."

Charlie kept up her relay. "She's talking about travelling to another realm, about her brother opening up a passageway. Art is confirming with her that her brother is Movement School."

Charlie's mouth dropped open.

"Oh, no. Her entire body language changed when he said that. She's stopped slurring. So you are from the Tower, are you? She's looking at me. She's casting!"

Charlie screamed and clutched at her face.

CHAPTER 14

CLOSING THE TRAP

Jackie and Kimmy were running before Charlie's scream stopped echoing around the alley's entrance. Max gave a low growl, her ears flat as she crouched beside her human. Zack started to reach out with his senses, but Charlie opened her eyes.

"I'm okay." She snatched her shortbow and quiver as she stood. "Bitch hit the bird with something. Killed it. It was... awful. C'mon, the boys need us."

They raced after Jackie, and Kimmy and caught up to them around the second corner. A wall of complete, black darkness stood in front of them, blocking all sight of the alley beyond.

Jackie was shaking. "Art! Are you in there?"

"Yeah, I'm okay. We're okay," Art called back.

"We can't see you," Tabitha shouted. "The alley is all dark."

Zack looked around. It was surreal. Everywhere else in the alley was early twilight, even the sky above the block of darkness. But in that one spot it was darker than midnight.

"Oh, thank god. I thought we'd gone blind!" Bast called out.

"Come towards my voice," Tabitha said.

"No," Art said. "If the darkness stops over there then it probably stops somewhere on the other side too. We need to get after her."

"She could be in there with you." Charlie knocked an arrow.

"Nope, it's just Bast and me. No other minds."

"He's right," Zack said. "No Life but theirs."

"Okay. Pair up," Tabitha said, clutching Zack's empty hand within her own. "We're coming through."

"We'll meet you on the other side," Art said from the dark.

If the darkness was strange from the outside, it was terrifying from the inside. Bast was right, this is how Zack imagined what being blind was like. He wished he had his staff out, but it was still in the bag with the two swords. Twice, his knee slammed into whatever large painful objects loitered in the middle of the alley. The others seemed to be having a better time of it. Jackie whispered last-second instructions to Kimmy that were undoubtedly saving her from bruises, while Max loudly sniffed her and Charlie safely through the magic night.

They might have been in there for half a minute or ten, but in the space of another step, they were out. Zack's eyes watered in the bright dusk light. Art and Bast were waiting for them.

"Come!" Art waved as he started running. "If she didn't come past you, she had to have gone this way."

"What School of magic can do that?" Charlie pointed back down the alley.

"We can work that out when we catch her," Art said. "Let's go."

Art and Bast sprinted away towards another side street and the others followed. Zack and the others caught up to them as they exited the alley on the other side of the block. A dozen cars were banked up at a set of lights.

"We've lost her," Kimmy said.

"No, we haven't. There!" Bast pointed across the street to a figure who crossed the footpath and bolted down another alley.

"Get her!" Art called as he ran across the road, weaving between cars.

The others plunged into the traffic, following behind. The

light ahead remained red, but a few horn blasts still heralded the commuters' displeasure at having a group of teenagers slide alongside their bonnets and doors.

They charged into the alley. The woman was nowhere to be seen but, up ahead, a plastic bin rolled along the ground from where it had likely just been disturbed. Bast outpaced the others. Whether or not he was using his magic, he was still a better runner than any of them and, fit as they all were, there was no contest.

He skidded to a halt at a corner and pointed down it.

"There she is!" He took a stride in that direction, but Tabitha called out to him.

"Wait up. We have to stick together."

"We're losing her," Bast said.

"Better than losing you," she replied.

Bast groaned in frustration. "Okay, hang on."

He murmured and wove his hands and orange light flowed from them and swirled around the floor before it streaked off towards their feet. Zack felt a tingling that started in his toes and rippled up to his thighs.

"Now you should be able to keep up." Bast turned and zoomed around the corner.

Art followed behind but skidded sideways and crashed into some wooden pallets leaning against the wall. He gave a nervous chuckle.

"Gotta learn how to drive these things."

His next strides were shorter and he picked up pace as he set off after Bast. Zack and the others learned from Art's mistake and took care as they ran. Zack's feet were lighter, but they also felt like they were on some kind of track, a bit like on a treadmill where the ground propels the feet forward. It was fast, but the amount of control he had was questionable.

The alley turned another corner before ending in half a block of open space. It appeared to be a combination of loading dock and staff car park for some of the nearby businesses.

"I can't see her anywhere." Art paced around the mouth of the alley, looking in each direction.

"Nope," Charlie said. "Maxie, where did she go?"

Max's nose dropped to the ground and she sniffed her way across the asphalt. After a few moments, she retraced their steps back into the alley.

"Your dog's broken, Charlie," Bast said. "She definitely went this way."

Charlie stared at him with narrowed eyes.

"Max knows that. She's trying to isolate the smell. There's been a lot of foot traffic here."

"Oh, okay," Bast said, before adding, "sorry."

Max gave a soft yap of excitement before making her way past them again and toward a three-storey customer parking structure. When they were about halfway toward it, they could see the side door had been forced open and they could hear running footsteps inside.

"Why is she going in there?" Zack asked as they sprinted to the door.

"Who cares?" said Kimmy. "Maybe she's hiding."

"Or maybe she has a car," said Art.

They hurtled through the open door and peered around the car park. Thanks to the fluorescent lights, the area was at least as bright as outside and their eyes needed no time to adjust. The car park was almost empty and their footsteps made echoing squeaks on the shiny concrete floor.

"There." Kimmy pointed across the building towards the ramp where a figure ran down to the floor below.

"We've got her." Art whooped with excitement. "We'll have her cornered down there."

"Just stick together," Tabitha said.

The teens raced down the ramp, urged on by Bast's enchantment. They rounded the corner at the bottom of the ramp and saw the woman duck through an open door to the fire stairwell.

"So much for cornered," Kimmy said.

"It doesn't matter," Art replied. "She can't outrun us."

They closed the distance to the stairwell.

Three metres away from the door Bast gasped in surprise. "Guys, wait up, something's wrong. I can feel—"

Bast slid to a halt, but the others had less control over their magically hastened feet and crashed into him. Zack fell against Tabitha, who in turn, tripped over Charlie, while Art bumped against Kimmy and collected Jackie as they all tumbled up with Bast. The bundle of teens continued on through the door and into somewhere else.

Still they fell, further than the floor of the stairwell should have been, before crashing into hard concrete amidst a chorus of screams and grunts. Zack forced himself to his feet, feeling the bruises forming on his knees where he hit the ground. It was colder here and dark, with no clear source of light. He could make out the others in the dim, but nothing else about the room.

"Is everybody okay?" he asked.

"What happened?" Charlie asked, kneeling next to an agitated Max.

"It was a gate," Bast said. "I don't know why we couldn't see it, but at the last second I could feel it."

"Does that mean we're in another realm?" Jackie asked.

"No, I don't think so," Bast replied. "It felt more like the Tower's front door."

"That confirms it then," a voice said from the darkness. It was male, deep and gravelly. "You are from the Tower."

"Show yourself, cowards," Kimmy shouted.

"Why would we do that?" the voice returned.

Zack closed his eyes. Life lit up around the room in his mind.

"There's eight of them, spaced around the room, some of them are up high."

"That's cheating," the voice said.

A heavy clunk echoed through the dark and lights flickered on, illuminating the room. They were in the centre of a large concrete chamber, like a warehouse or bunker. Wooden crates lined one of the walls and a pair of metal double doors were on the opposite side. A steel grill platform, two or so metres above the ground, ran around the edges of all the walls. They were surrounded, with four people on the ground floor with them and four others watching from above.

"Shit, you're just children," the speaker said.

The man who had been speaking appeared to be in his late thirties, perhaps as old as forty. He looked to be the oldest in the room, while the woman from the alley, Nicole, seemed to be one of the youngest. She stood against the crates, smirking at the teens.

"Let's start again," the man in the centre said. "You can call me Connor, what are your names?"

"No dice, old man," Bast said.

"Fine, then answer this," Connor said. "Why is the Tower sending children against us?"

"Don't call us children," Kimmy said, her voice dripping with venom.

"Why wouldn't I? And answer me, why did they put you in this position?"

"We found you, didn't we?" Tabitha said.

"You found us? My dear, look around. We found you. Do you think the enchantment you left in Patrice's mind would go unnoticed?"

"Who?" Bast asked.

"The man who runs the store in Montreal. And so, we wanted to know who was after us and why. That is why you are here. Now tell me, why is the Tower looking for us?"

"The ink you made," Zack answered.

"What about it?" Connor's brow furrowed in confusion. "We've heard of the Tower's rules. If you keep your head down and keep the magic a secret, they don't come knocking."

"Except it was used in a ritual that risked that secret," Tabitha said, "and somebody taught the two guys responsible exactly how to use your ink."

Connor hesitated. "We just make the ink. I don't know anything about any ritual."

"Well, that's a lie," Art said with a snort. He turned to Nicole. "I don't get it, I thought I had you happy and drunk."

She sneered at him. "That's what we wanted you to think. Nathan was with me." She pointed to the man against the side wall to her left. "He was shielding me from your little mental tricks."

"Is he why we couldn't see the gate?" Bast asked.

"No, that was—"

"Enough!" Connor shouted. "Drop your weapons and stand down while we work out what to do with you."

Zack glanced around. The girls were all gripping their weapons but the bag with his, Art's and Bast's was still over his shoulder. On the other hand, two of the figures on the platform pointed modern crossbows at them, while the other two watched with close intensity. On the ground floor with them, Nicole drew a long knife while Nathan and the other man held metal bats. Connor was unarmed, watching them. All of them were wearing jeans and heavy jackets.

"Why don't you drop yours?" Kimmy asked.

"This is not a negotiation. Drop your weapons or we will take them by force."

"I don't respond well to threats," Kimmy said.

"I don't make threats," Connor said. He gestured to one of the men on the ground floor. "Oscar, take their weapons."

Oscar held his bat loose in his right hand. He took steady

steps towards the group, his empty left hand palm up. Charlie was closest and he reached for her bow. Max leapt in between her and the man, teeth bared and growling. Oscar stepped back, both hands on the handle of his bat.

"Call off your dog," Connor shouted.

"Call off yours!" Kimmy spat back.

"Back it off me," Oscar screamed.

"Everybody calm down," Tabitha said. "We can work this out."

"If that thing bites him, it's on!" Nicole pointed her knife towards the group.

Voices bounced and crashed against each other and the room groaned with noise and tension. Zack could feel the stress and confusion building up. Something was about to go wrong and he couldn't think of anything to stop it. Kimmy moved to stand beside Charlie and Oscar flinched, taking half a step towards them. Max barked and shifted to meet his step.

Oscar, his eyes wide with panic, swung his bat. It slammed against the side of Max's skull with a loud crack. She made a soft whine and collapsed to the ground. Blood pooled on the concrete floor. The room fell silent. For one second.

"No!" Charlie screamed and raised her bow. "You bastard!"

She released the arrow and at this distance she couldn't miss. It pierced Oscar through the left side of his chest and he fell to the floor beside Max.

The room erupted into chaos.

CHAPTER 15

RENEGADES

Nicole screamed, "Tilverson!"

She charged towards Charlie, but Kimmy intervened, knocking aside the woman's hunting knife with the blade of her axe. From above, two loud thrums heralded the crossbows firing. Jackie threw up shields, but one bolt scraped past the edge and hit Bast. Off course, thanks to the shield, it missed his chest but tore a gash across his upper left arm before clattering along the floor. He cried out in pain and clutched at the wound.

Realising he still held the weapons bag, Zack wrenched out his staff and slid the bag along the ground to Bast. The duffel stopped against Bast's feet, but he ignored it, orange light collecting around his fingers. Before he could finish the incantation, one of the men from the walkway jumped down behind him, landing nimbly on his feet. Zack charged past Bast and forced the man backwards with the centre of his staff. The movement distracted Bast, who lost his spell with a frustrated string of swear words. He snatched his rapier out of the bag and kicked it towards Art before starting to cast again.

Charlie, her eyes still filled with rage and her cheeks wet with tears, pulled another arrow from her quiver and fired towards

Connor. It was a clear shot and the arrow flew straight at her target, but at the last instant he stepped to the side, faint orange light in his wake.

Bast finished his second attempt at the spell and flung the scabbard from his blade. "He's mine."

Art bent down over the bag, struggling to find the angle needed to pull his sword free. Tabitha screamed, her eyes wide with horror. Her flail clattered to the ground as she slapped and scratched at the skin on her arms and legs.

Zack glanced around, finding the man called Nathan, standing still against the wall, looking towards Tabitha.

"Art!" he shouted.

Before he could say more, the man in front of him finished his own spell. Deep pink light flared inside the man's chest and he grew. Within half a second, he was close to seven feet tall with the thickest arms and legs Zack had ever seen.

"Looks like you made him angry," Art said, tugging his sword free at last.

"Don't worry about me," Zack said, ducking under a punch. He pointed to the other man, "I think he's hit Tabs with a fear spell."

"The hell he gets to do that." Art stalked towards Nathan, his sword in his right hand with his left stretched out.

Tabitha's screams stopped and Nathan's attention snapped to Art.

"Game on, then," he said to Art, their eyes locking.

A boulder flew down from the platform at the teens and shattered on one of Jackie's shields. She grunted from the effort as pebbles and dust rained down on them all.

"Watch out!" Jackie pointed at a weaponless woman, brown light gathering in her hands. "Stay close, so I can cover us."

Charlie hadn't heard or hadn't listened. Instead of moving in, she crouched over Max's still body and fired an arrow at the woman above.

A gust of wind shot out from the hands of another man on

the platform, blowing the arrow off course. Charlie screamed in frustration and nocked another arrow.

Kimmy and Nicole continued to trade blows, sparks flying as knife blade struck axe again and again. Kimmy swung her axe at the woman's neck and she leaped back to avoid it. She scrambled along the crates that lined the wall and her hands glowed with deep blue light. Ice crept from her fingertips and up the dagger until the sharp ice covered the blade almost doubling its length. Kimmy roared and charged after her.

Bast ran towards Connor who drew his own long bladed knife as he approached. The two were a blur of motion. Bast flicked the point of his rapier at Connor's face, who parried it, running his knife down the length of the blade, stopping only when it clanged against the wrist guard.

The enlarged mage kicked towards Zack with the sole of his foot, but Zack slid past it, swinging his staff hard at the back of the man's other ankle. It connected with a loud thwack and the man fell, landing hard on his back. Zack's weapons training urged him to complete the staff's rotation and bring it down on the vulnerable target, but he hesitated, reluctant even now to truly harm another person. The man glared at him and swung wildly at him from the ground as he shifted back to his feet. Zack dodged his arm and prepared to hit the man in his side, hoping that a broken rib or two might keep him out of the fight, but he was struck from behind. He staggered forward, only just avoiding the grasping hand of the man on the ground. Zack spun around, holding his staff in front of him, and saw that the other man with the crossbow had discarded it and swung down from the walkway on some kind of vine. The larger man clambered back to his feet and Zack prepared to defend himself.

Past them, Art and Nathan fought in a manner that was the opposite of Bast and Connor's fight. While the latter pair were fast and fluid, Art and Nathan attacked each other in halting lurches. Purple flashes from their free hands suggested their battle was not reserved for the physical realm. Art shook his head as if to clear it and raised his sword in just enough time to block a bat swung at his head.

Jackie's shields deflected boulder after boulder as the woman on the platform hurled them down from above. "Someone needs to do something about her," she said between gritted teeth. "I can't do this forever."

Charlie's cheek and left arm were bleeding from where the stone debris had bounced off Jackie's shield and torn at her skin. Unwilling to leave Max's side, she fired yet another arrow at the woman, only to have the magical breeze knock it aside.

Tabitha stepped up beside Jackie, her eyes red and raw. "Let's see what I can do about that wind." Her fingers moved in sharp, precise shapes and light blue energy gathered in front of her hand. She pushed out towards the ceiling and the gusts of air sputtered and stopped. The man on the platform yelled in response and his hands moved to rework his magic.

Kimmy pursued her foe along the row of crates. Nicole dodged the wide swing of Kimmy's axe before lunging in with a thrust of her icy knife. Avoiding the attack, Kimmy reversed her swing to bring the axe back towards Nicole, who retreated again. Kimmy was forcing her back towards the corner, when the woman murmured and flicked her free hand towards the ground. Midstep, her axe half an inch from Nicole's face, Kimmy's foot came down hard on a magical ice slick. Her front foot slid forward and her back knee slammed hard on the ground. Nicole dodged the wild axe swing and leapt at Kimmy with a savage slash of her knife. Kimmy let go of her weapon and tried to roll away but was not quite fast enough. The edge of the blade sliced into her cheek. She hissed in pain.

Sparks flashed in the dark corner into which Bast and Connor's duel had taken them. The advantage the length of his rapier should have given Bast, was completely negated by the fact that Connor was, simply, faster than him. Bast gave a desperate swing on his sword that would have taken the throat of a slower opponent, but Connor dropped to his knees and slid underneath it. His momentum took him right to Bast's feet and he lashed out with his knife, cutting into Bast's thigh.

"Surrender!" Connor shouted. "Tell your friends to drop their weapons."

"I don't really speak for the group," Bast said with a groan as he punched down with the guard of his rapier. He struck Connor across his jaw and stumbled back clutching his leg.

Zack saw both Bast and Kimmy get hurt but there was nothing he could do for them, let alone for Max who lay still on the ground in the centre of the room. He didn't like his odds against two opponents, particularly when one of them was the size of an ogre, but if he could occupy two of them for as long as possible, then that might give the others a chance.

The two men nodded to each other and stepped apart, circling Zack. He held his staff in a guard position, and moved from side to side, attempting the impossible task of tracking both men. The huge brute clenched his fists, the crack of his knuckles echoing in the room, while the other man incanted in a soft voice. Dark green energy gathered on the back of his hands and coalesced into sharp thorns at least two inches long.

The larger man stepped towards Zack and swung a right hook towards his head. Zack dodged to the side and knocked the massive fist away with the top of his staff. The second man leapt forward to rake at him with his thorned knuckles and Zack thrust the bottom end of his quarterstaff at him, forcing him back.

In the centre of the room, Jackie shattered more of the magically hurled boulders against her shield and the rubble from one rained down over the enlarged man. He looked away for a moment and Zack sprang into action. He swung his staff at the man's neck, but the brute turned away, blocking it on his shoulder with a loud grunt. Zack didn't stop; he spun back, keeping the staff moving, and snapped the other end of it against the side of the thorned man's knee. The man's legs went out from underneath him and he crashed to the ground.

Zack caught a glimpse of Art, who was still locked in his mental duel with Nathan. Both men's eyes were wide and twitching as they fought against the magical attacks the other forced upon them. Zack turned towards a noise from behind him to find the large man swinging down at him, both hands clasped together in a huge, doubled fist. He brought his staff up to block the blow and braced his feet to meet it. The powerful attack slammed down against the wooden staff and snapped it in half with a loud crack.

Zack didn't hesitate. He spun the two pieces of his broken weapon around and hammered them against the man's ears. His large foe moaned in pain and clutched at his head, taking a few steps back. Zack spun, expecting the other man to seek the advantage, but found him incanting again. He gestured towards Zack and, without warning, the two pieces of quarterstaff writhed in his hands as thin strands of growth sprouted out of it in all directions. The tendrils moved to wrap themselves around his fingers and hands, and Zack threw the pieces to the floor, shuddering.

Distracted, he was slow to react as the man launched towards him, swinging at Zack's face with his thorned knuckles. He fended off both punches, knocking them aside with his forearms, but his delay cost him and one of the thorns bit into the side of his neck. Zack pushed the man away with the sole of his foot and strafed to the side, getting his back to a wall.

His eyes flicked to Tabitha standing in the middle of the room, her hands raised above her head as she hurled wind towards the other Air mage. The two of them were locked in a duel of currents and streams, and from the way Tabitha's knees were bending, it was clear she was tiring. But her job had been done. Charlie fired her arrow up at the other mage and without the interfering gusts, it flew true, taking the woman in the ribs. She gasped in pain and fell to the ground, clattering onto the metal walkway.

The enlarged man returned, his eyes alight with anger and he threw a punch to Zack's face. Zack dodged it, rather than trusting himself to block a fist that size barehanded, and threw himself towards the other man, kicking out at his leg. The man skirted away from the attack, but it gave Zack the opening he wanted to keep moving, staying out of reach of both of his opponents.

Behind him, Art and Nathan's battle continued until Nathan's backswing was interrupted by his sudden outburst of laughter. Zack spun, fearing the laugh was a sign he'd got the better of Art, but then he heard the hysterical edge in his voice. Twitching, Nathan launched himself at Art. He swung his bat, but it was off target and clumsy. His strange cackling continued as Art stood firm, holding his blade against the charge. Nathan ran straight into the point of the sword, and it cut deep into his sternum. He collapsed to the floor at Art's feet, pulling the sword from his grasp.

Nicole had been facing in that direction and threw herself onto Kimmy, pushing the tip of her icy blade against the centre of Kimmy's throat. Kimmy's hands locked around hers, trying to force the knife back, but the woman had gravity on her side and blood welled at the knife's point.

Nicole spat as she screamed at Kimmy. "You'll pay for their lives with yours."

Kimmy's lips moved, but no sound came out.

"Sorry?" Nicole taunted. "I couldn't hear you."

"I said," Kimmy rasped. "Your shoe's on fire."

Nicole's eyes flickered down to her foot where a small blaze had sprung to life. Kimmy used the distraction to knee the woman in her stomach and twist her wrists. The blade spun around and, as Kimmy rolled on top of her, she forced the knife into the woman's chest.

"No!" Connor shouted. He feinted towards Bast with his knife but, in the last instant, struck out and kicked Bast in his wounded leg. Bast fell backwards, scrambling to keep his rapier pointed towards Connor.

But Connor didn't press the attack. He incanted and disappeared, reappearing near Zack. There, he grabbed onto each of Zack's attackers and the three disappeared, to once again reappear on the walkway above. Jackie held a broad shield up and Charlie loosed another arrow at the group but it pinged off the walkway's rails. Tabitha dropped her spell and pointed to the ladder. She and Art ran towards it.

The men above ignored them all. The enlarged man scooped up the woman Charlie had shot while Connor incanted again and a gate opened in the wall. The four ran through it, carrying the wounded woman with them.

The gate closed behind them and the room fell silent.

CHAPTER 16

RECOVERY

With a cry of anguish, Charlie hurled her bow in the direction of the closed portal. She dropped to her knees beside Max and cradled the dog's head in her lap.

"I'm so sorry, girl. I'm so, so sorry." Tears fell to the floor.

Bast hissed in pain from where he lay on the floor, clutching his leg and arm, while Kimmy paced, wide-eyed, back and forth beside Nicole's body. The cut on her cheek dripped blood down her neck and chest. Art stood quietly in the corner; his eyes fixed on Nathan who stared lifelessly at the ceiling. Tabitha and Jackie looked around and then to Zack, clearly unsure of what to do next.

Zack took a breath.

"Bast, I'll be over in one second." He knelt beside Charlie, who took no notice of him and felt towards Max's life. "She's still with us."

Charlie looked at him, eyes wide and mouth trembling. He wasn't sure she'd heard or understood him.

"It's faint. I'm not promising anything." He closed his eyes to focus but felt Charlie's hand squeeze his wrist.

"Please, Zack." Her voice wavered.

"I'll try."

He gathered Life to him. There was some in the room, but he added his own to it and fed it into Max. He followed the flow of it and found the areas of harm. His hours of study and practice had been on human bodies, not canine, but he told himself the principles would be the same. She had a heart, a brain, bones, blood and muscle. He narrowed down on the point of impact. The blow had been brutal. Max's skull was cracked and the blood vessels all around it showed signs of trauma. Signs of concussion. Max had been knocked out, but there was more. Fragments of the skull bone had cut into the brain tissue and blood had been seeping into the brain from the fracture site.

Zack took a deep breath and focused the streams of Life down to specific tasks: reverse the bleed, repair the skull, repair the nerves and flesh and skin. As always, Life knew what to do, he just needed to feed and urge it into action. He felt the sweat drip down his neck as he channelled. A good amount of Life needed to be poured into Max, she had so little of her own and it was also intense work. The familiar buzz of distractions whispered in his mind, but they were nothing more than part of the process to him now. He listened to them, turned them into reasons, into needs and he continued. Zack left the brain until last. It was delicate work and he allowed Max's own Life to lead him, depending on its enduring need to heal her. He threaded the stream of Life, wisp thin, around it.

Max turned her head and licked dazedly at Charlie's face. Charlie squeezed her tight.

"My good girl. My good girl." Her tears hadn't stopped.

Zack staggered to his feet, lightheaded and tired.

"Okay, Bast next. Then Kimmy."

He made his way towards Bast and knelt down beside him.

"Sorry man, I had to at least try and help Max first."

Bast narrowed his eyes. "Damn right you did."

Blood had drenched Bast's shirt around his arm from where

the crossbow bolt had sliced him, but the cut on his leg looked to be the more dangerous of the two.

"Right, steady on." Zack fed Life into Bast, repairing his wounds. After Max, this was basic work, but he kept an eye out for any sign of infection that might have crept in along the way. A few moments later the work was done and he limped over to Kimmy.

The nick on her neck wasn't deep enough to have bled much, but the cut on her cheek was something else. Unlike the knife underneath it, the ice had been jagged and torn at Kimmy's face as much as it had sliced. Blood had oozed from the wound and around half an inch of skin hung loose below the cut, exposing the tissue underneath. Despite all this, Kimmy stood calmly as he inspected the damage.

"Maybe I should ask you to leave me a scar," she mused aloud. "It would look badass."

"It would," Zack replied. "I won't do it, though."

"But—"

"I'm not going to argue with you, Kimmy. I'm too tired to work out how to do it even if you did decide to permanently mark up your face."

She eyed him up and down. He knew he didn't look steady on his feet.

Kimmy relaxed. "Yeah, okay."

He streamed Life once again, knitting up the cheek wound and closing the smaller cut on her neck. Kimmy explored her cheek with her hand and smiled as Zack shuffled over to one of the crates and slid down to sit against it.

Art stared at Nathan's body before wrenching himself away and facing the others.

"We need to get out of here. Now."

"We won, man," Bast said. "They ran off with their tails between their legs."

"We don't know that," Art said. "They could be pulling together some friends right now. Or they could be calling the cops on us. We're down here covered in blood with a bunch of dead people."

"They wouldn't," Kimmy said, "would they?"

"They aren't the Tower," Art replied. "They didn't swear to keep the Silence."

Zack hauled himself back to his feet. "Art's right. We should get moving."

"Not yet," Tabitha said.

"What?" Art replied.

"I agree we need to get out of here, but not before we turn this place over. We have had no real leads for months, and after this," She gestured around the room. "After what we did here. This can't have been for nothing."

Art nodded. "Okay, but we've got to be quick."

Tabitha pointed at the crates. "Let's have a look through those and then we'll check out the rest of the place while we look for an exit."

"Maybe keep an eye out for a change of clothes or two?" Bast suggested.

Tabitha looked back and forth between Kimmy and him. "Yeah, that's a good point."

Zack slid the top off the crate nearest him and peered inside. "No clothes here. And nothing that looks like a clue. It looks like camping equipment. Maybe you could wear a tarp, Bast?"

"You know, maybe?" Bast said, delving into his own crate. "Nope, I've got a better offer, blankets. I could throw together a couple of nice little ponchos with this. Like the sound of that, Kimmy?"

She stared at him with a silence that disagreed.

"Will these do?" Jackie asked, drawing a heavy overcoat out of her crate like a rope. "There's a bunch of them in here."

"Life saver, little sis," Bast said, stripping out of his blood-soaked shirt.

Jackie blushed and averted her eyes, holding out the coat. Kimmy pulled her own from the crate and changed out of her shirt with only marginally more discretion.

They rifled through the remaining crates.

"Nothing." Tabitha slammed the lid down on the last.

"I think this is their 'go stash'," Zack said.

"What do you mean?" she asked.

"Camping equipment, blankets, heavy coats, ropes, tupperware, backpacks. I think this is where they keep the gear for their missions. For when they do things like go to that world with the dokkaebi."

"Yeah, okay," Tabitha said. "But that doesn't tell us anything we don't know."

Zack nodded. "Not much more, no. But I think we can guess it's not a one off. That they prepare for this and do it often."

"Doesn't help us find them."

Zack shook his head. "No, it doesn't."

Tabitha threw up her hands, deflated. "Well, let's clear out then. Art's right, we should get a move on."

Charlie held up her hand. "Hang on, everybody shush for a sec."

They stood in silence. Bast's and Kimmy's hands moved to the hilts of their weapons.

"There's something behind these two crates," Charlie said, pointing. She looked around. "I don't think it's dangerous or anything, but there's something there."

Art and Bast dragged the crates aside. Zack wanted to help, or rather didn't want to be seen not helping, but he was swaying on his feet as it was. The crates had been hiding a vent in the wall, about a metre in length and half as high.

"It was probably a rat or something," Kimmy said.

"It isn't. But I don't know what it is." She stepped past the boys and ran her fingers along the top of the panel. "This is really scuffed, and these screws are worn. I don't suppose anybody has a screwdriver?"

Zack didn't, and he reached for his keys, hoping they might

work. But Bast stepped forward, pointing his finger at Charlie like a pistol.

"Watch this." Bast incanted in a short, sharp tone and pointed at the nearest screw. It spun backwards and flew into his hand. One by one the others did the same until the panel crashed to the ground with a booming clatter. He winced at the noise. "Sorry."

Nobody responded. They were all staring at what the panel had fallen to reveal. There were four thick mason jars, sitting on a shelf. Inside each was some kind of glowing fluid that swirled around like a cross between a snow globe and a lava lamp. All four had different consistencies and colours.

"That'll do," Tabitha said, her eyes alight with excitement.

"Is that the ink?" Kimmy asked.

"No," Bast answered. "I don't think so, anyway. I think it's more. It's what they make the ink from. This is what they've taken from those other realms."

"How did you sense this?" Zack asked Charlie.

"I didn't. I sensed that." Charlie pointed to a metal case about the size of a lunch box. If a lunch box was metal and was secured by a length of steel chain wrapped multiple times around it and fixed with a padlock.

"Oh," Zack said. "Well, that's not at all unsettling."

"Let's grab the jars and get out of here," Tabitha said.

"We can't leave that behind," Charlie said.

"Is there an animal trapped in there?" Jackie asked.

Charlie's brow furrowed as she concentrated. "Well, not quite an animal. But it's something."

"Great," Art said. "There's a thing in there that isn't quite an animal, and that other mages have felt the need to lock up and hide and you want to carry it along with us?"

"No, I don't want us to carry it with us," Charlie said.

"Thank heavens," Art said.

"I want us to open it and let it out," she finished.

"What?" Art and Tabitha said at once.

"We are not leaving it trapped inside that tiny box," Charlie said. "If it's evil, we kill it. If not, we let it free."

"Absolutely not." Tabitha crossed her arms.

The sound of chains unravelling to the ground echoed around the room. Bast finished incanting and faced Tabitha without apology.

"Look, I agree with Charlie," Bast said. "Leaving anything locked in that tiny space is monstrous and we didn't have time to argue. So there, it's done."

Tabitha and Art gripped their weapons. Zack felt exposed without his.

The case shifted, then stopped. It shifted again. Then it rattled. It bounced from side to side and fell from the shelf onto the ground. It flung open on impact and an ornate dagger clattered out of it along the floor. It was a piece of art, with a gleaming blade, a detailed, wiry pommel and a leatherbound handle.

"That's pretty," Kimmy said.

The dagger leapt up into the air and zipped around the room. The teens scattered in shock and Zack tried to track it as it whirred in the air. Art held his sword at the ready and it surged towards him, bouncing off a metre or so away against Jackie's shield. It wobbled from side to side and then retreated, slamming against the closed door several times before turning again, pointed blade first towards them.

Zack stepped closer to Art, in the hopes that Jackie's shield would cover him too, while Bast held his rapier forward. Max, her ears flat against her head, growled in a deep rumble as she tracked the dagger's movements.

Kimmy walked in calm, certain steps towards the hovering weapon. She held up her open palm to it and simply said, "Stop."

The dagger seemed to give an uncertain flutter at its hilt end, but otherwise stayed where it was in the air.

She took another step. "It's okay. We're not going to put you back inside that box. We got rid of the people who trapped you in there."

The dagger moved but, instead of attacking, it made small U-shaped dips to the left and the right and returned to float in front of Kimmy's face, the blade now pointing up at the ceiling.

"That's right," Kimmy said. "They're all gone. If you stay calm, maybe we can help you out of here."

The dagger did a tight loop-de-loop in front of her.

She laughed. "You're very clever."

"So, what?" Art asked. "This thing is not going to stab our eyes out the second we drop our guard?"

"No, it's not," Kimmy said between gritted teeth. "Because we are going to put down our weapons and show it that we're not its enemy."

With some reluctance, Bast, Tabitha, Art and Jackie lowered their weapons.

"Is that what you sensed behind the wall, Charlie?" Tabitha asked.

"Yeah, definitely."

"So, it's an animal somehow?" Bast asked.

Charlie scratched at her cheek. "No, it's definitely not an animal, but at the same time I'm picking up an Animal vibe. A dog vibe, in particular. It thinks like a dog."

Max whined.

"No, it doesn't think like you. You're brilliant and special and I love you." Charlie dropped to her knees and hugged her close again.

"Hold on." Bast held up his hands. "It thinks? It's alive?"

"It's not alive," Zack said.

"I didn't say it was alive," Charlie said, disentangling herself from her cuddle and standing back up. "Look, I don't know, but my guess is that somebody made this thing and modelled it on a dog. It's hard to describe, but it's like looking at a cartoon drawing of a dog. You know it's not the real thing, but you also know what it's supposed to be. That's what Animal is telling me."

"We're supposed to destroy magical creatures," Tabitha said in hushed tones.

"But it's not alive," Charlie said. "Zack can sense the Life in magical creatures. This isn't one of them. It's just an enchanted object or something."

"So what, we let it go now?" Art asked.

"But what about the Silence?" Tabitha's voice held a note of frustration. "If it goes zipping around living its best not-life, it's not going to do much for keeping magic a secret."

"Okay, new plan." Kimmy turned back to the dagger. "Would you like to come with us? That way, I can keep you safe from any other people that want to lock you up or hurt you."

The dagger fluttered again and then bobbed towards her.

She opened one of the deepest pockets in the massive overcoat she was now wearing. "If you pop in here, you'll be out of sight. Just don't poke me, okay?"

The dagger bobbed its way through the air and sunk down into Kimmy's open pocket.

"There, it's settled," she said. "Let's get out of here."

Art and Zack placed the three mason jars into his duffel bag, protecting them as much as possible with the clothes inside.

A heavy steel bar held the double doors closed and lifting it tore rust free from its brackets. The doors' hinges objected to being opened with a loud squeal and let the teens out into a long dark hallway with dim, flickering lights.

"Where do you think we are?" Art asked.

"No idea," Tabitha answered. "By the look of that door, they don't actually use it to come and go from their little hideout, so we could be anywhere."

They walked down the hallway and passed three single doors, but each of those had been welded shut and the dust and grime that caked the base of them, indicated they hadn't been used for a long time. The hallway continued on for 50 or 60 metres before turning to the right. There was another double door at the end of this length of the hallway. As they approached, they could hear a loud rushing noise.

"Is that a—?" Bast started.

"Train?" Kimmy finished.

The teens reached the doors and attempted to force them open. They cracked open just enough for them to see and hear the chain that prevented them from opening any further.

"Can you unlock it, Bast?" Art asked. "Like you unlocked the box?"

"Not if I can't see the lock," Bast replied.

"I got it," Kimmy said. "Hold my axe."

"Actually," Tabitha said, "if we're about to head back out into the real world, time to stash the weapons again."

Zack opened his duffel bag and everybody slid their weapons in beside the jars. He eased the bag back over his shoulder and tried to hold it still against his body. Meanwhile, Kimmy reached through the gap in the door and grabbed hold of the chain. After a couple of whispered words, the air grew warm and, a few moments later, the chain crashed to the ground with a rattle. Bast and Art forced the doors open and the group stepped out into an underground subway system.

Several notices were taped on the outside of the walls. Zack peered close to one and tried to read it in the dark. He skimmed it aloud.

"Safety concerns related to mould and structural… blah blah blah… closed to all personnel and the public… blah blah blah… Ah, order of City of New York."

"We're in New York?" Tabitha asked.

Zack shrugged. "I guess so. We'll have to try to get out of here and up to the surface and then find the local Tower entrance. I assume there's one in the city somewhere."

"There is," Charlie said with confidence. "It's in what looks like a closed laundromat. New York is on my travel list, so I looked it up. I've got the address in my phone."

"Brilliant, Charlie," Art said. "Lead on then, I've had enough of today's little adventure and I want to get home."

Kimmy looked over at him. "Me too."

Art nodded at her in shared understanding. Charlie and Max took point and the group made their way along the access path and, eventually, back home.

CHAPTER 17

BLOWING OFF STEAM

The group returned their weapons and left the Tower without saying a word about the ambush or the jars and magic knife tucked about their persons. It felt absurd to Zack that it wasn't even night yet; it seemed like they'd been gone for days. And while he had recovered from the worst of the exhaustion, he still craved the comfort of bed. The bus took them north across the harbour and Zack gazed out the window. The buildings, the people, the water, it all looked the same.

He turned and looked at his friends. Nothing was the same. Five hours ago, they were a group of teens staring down the end of high school. No more classes, no more exams. And now, three people were dead, by their hands.

Kimmy was hard to read, as usual, but Charlie hadn't taken her arms from around Max since she sat down on the bus. Art appeared lost in thought, Jackie beside him, squeezing onto his hand. Bast and Tabitha noticed him watching the others and nodded at him. Zack returned a nod and stared back out of the window.

One by one, the others exited the bus until it was just Zack, Art and Jackie left and, a couple of stops later, they stepped down onto the street themselves. When they reached Art and Jackie's street, Art asked her to head on without him.

"Remember," he called out, "you were in school the full day."

Jackie's mouth tightened. "Yeah, I'll remember. Don't be long, it'll be time for dinner soon."

Art nodded and watched as she crossed the road and made her way towards their house. Zack waited patiently, leaning against the tall rendered-stone fence of the corner house.

Silence settled in for a few minutes before Art spoke again. "You're probably going to tell me I had no choice, right?"

"No," Zack answered. "You probably had a choice."

Art arched an eyebrow at him; he didn't seem to expect that response.

Zack continued, "You could have let him kill you. You could have left him alone to use his Mind magic on one of us. How long would Bast have lasted with a fear spell distracting him? How long would any of us have lasted with Jackie too drunk to deflect those rocks?"

Art spoke in one long exhale. "I don't know that I needed to kill him, though."

Zack reached out and squeezed his friend's shoulder.

"I'm not sure anybody ever needs to kill anybody. But maybe, sometimes, it's the least terrible option. I don't know what you're going through, but I also don't know what would have happened if you hadn't done it, or if Kimmy and Charlie hadn't."

Art pointed his fingers at his forehead. "His face is, like, right there."

Zack nodded.

"I could make that go away, you know. There's parts of it I could switch off. I could forget him, forget what I did, maybe even switch off caring about it. Just for a little bit."

"I'm not sure, mate. I think you'd be better off letting it sit with you. I don't think we want it to be easy, do we?"

"Yeah, maybe. My parents are going to be the tough part."

"What do you mean?"

"Well, when you and Jackie look at me, you see who I am. They're going to look at me like I didn't do what I just did. Like I'm still 'normal old me'."

"You still are 'normal old you', Art. Well, maybe not normal, that ship sailed a long time ago. But they see who you are and so do Jackie and me. You're a good guy who protected his friends and protects this world."

"Yeah, yeah okay." Art stood up from the wall. "Thanks, mate. I better get home. I'll call you tomorrow, okay? We'll work out our next steps."

"Sure thing," Zack said. "You need anything though, I'm two streets away, okay?"

"I'm good. Have a good night, mate."

Zack waited a few more moments, watching his friend meander down the footpath towards his house, before he headed off for his own. It was early enough that his father wasn't home yet and Zack cut across the driveway on his way to the front door. He dropped his bag in the hallway and wandered into the kitchen to get some water for his dry throat.

"You survived!" his mother exclaimed from her desk in the corner of the room, eyes locked on her laptop screen.

His heart stopped beating as he stared at her. When he didn't respond she looked up at him.

"Your final exam? All of high school really. You survived."

Relief crashed down on him. Of course that's what she meant.

"Uh, yeah. I'm done."

"Honey, I love you, I'm proud of you, we're getting your choice of take-away tonight, but I've got to knock out a few emails before I can wrap up for the day."

"Yeah, that's okay. I'm going to chill out in my room for a bit."

"Come over here first," she said, beckoning with her hand.

He complied and she reached out to hug him, squeezing him tight.

"I'm super-proud of you, whatever the results."

"Thanks, Mum." He hugged her back, just as tight.

"Now off you go. You deserve to relax."

He grabbed a bottle of water and retreated to his room. He closed his doors, then his curtains and turned off the light before collapsing onto his bed. After drawing so much of his Life today, particularly when saving Max, he was bone tired. More than that though, what they had done today weighed on him. Whether it was Art, Charlie or Kimmy who had held the weapons, they'd worked together to take three human lives. Maybe four, if the Earth mage Charlie had shot didn't survive. He thought back to what Bast had said about the way the Silence bore down on him. The price it demanded from him on his relationship with his family. Right now, Zack felt that more than ever. He wanted to tell them and have his mother tell him it was all okay. To have his father give him a piece of advice that would seem obvious after he said it. Even for Ellen to make fun of it the way only a big sister could and help him realise it wasn't such a big deal. But he couldn't.

So, he laid there in the dark. Alone with his thoughts.

The next morning his phone buzzed with a group message from Tabitha.

We need to blow off some steam after yesterday. There's a party on around the block from my house tonight. We can crash at mine afterwards.

Art and Kimmy's replies came through on top of each other's.

Awesome. I'm in.

PARTY!

Zack was mulling over his reply when a direct message came through from Art.

Don't even think about bailing. You're coming.

Yeah, I was about to reply.

Good. I'll pick you up at 1. We'll get some lunch and buy you some decent clothes.

I don't need new clothes.

I wasn't asking your opinion. C U at 1.

Bast and Charlie had replied before Zack tapped back to the group thread.

I'm in too. See you all there. He put his phone down and sat in front of his computer. He still had a few hours before Art came over and he had some ideas he wanted to look into.

Time flew by as he tapped and clicked away and, before he knew it, he heard Art downstairs.

"Hey Mrs M. I'm just here to pick up your baby boy."

He saved his work and thrust his phone, wallet and keys into his pockets before heading downstairs.

"How did your exams go, Art? All done?"

"Yeah, alright, I think. I didn't study as hard as him," he said, pointing to Zack as he stepped into the room. "But I'm not planning on university. At least not straight away."

"Oh really?" She sounded a mixture of curious and amused. "What's the plan, then?"

"Work a lot. I've got a job for next year and a few side hustles ready to go. Millionaire by 25, retired by 35."

"That'll be nice, Art."

Zack smiled. She'd used the same tone with him when he'd told her he wanted to be an astronaut. He'd been six years old.

Art studied Zack from head to toe as he approached.

"Yes. I need to take you shopping."

"My clothes are fine."

His mother ignored him and spoke to Art instead.

"Make sure that he buys a nice shirt or two."

"Full makeover, Mrs M. By the time I'm done, he'll be prom queen."

"Very good, Art. Zack, I'll get you some money." She left to get her purse from the kitchen.

"No need, Mum. I've been saving the tutoring money. Plus, I'm not going to spend that much."

She returned with some cash in her hand and narrowed her eyes at him before looking at Art.

"I'll give it to you then. You make him buy something."

Art held up his hands. "I can't take money from you, Mrs M. I owe you too much from the food I eat alone."

"We're good, Mum." Zack strode towards the front door, towing Art behind him. "I'll buy something, I promise."

He climbed into the passenger seat of Art's car. Art started the engine and smiled at him.

"Let's hit up Pitt Street."

"The city? Parking is pretty expensive; we should take a…" His voice trailed off as Art shot him a look.

"Free parking, man. For life."

"Yeah, alright. But we're getting slurpees on the way."

"Damn right we are."

Late spring sunshine lanced the car and the boys wound down the windows to let in the cool air.

"You seem good today, mate," Zack said.

"I am, I am," Art said, skipping through radio station presets with his free hand. "Dinner with the family was good. Weird, but settling at the same time."

"I think I know what you mean. So, do you want to talk about yesterday?"

"Not even a little bit. Plenty of time for that later. Today's about fun."

"And tonight." Zack nodded along.

Art shook his head. "No. Tonight's about more than that. Tonight's about girls."

"I'll leave that to you, man. I'm good."

"First of all, no, you're not. Second of all, I'm talking about you and Charlie, Zack."

"She's still with Dave. Tabitha said—"

Art cut him off. "I don't care what Tabitha said. We know what we saw. I also know you saved Max's life yesterday. That's a pretty big deal."

Zack scrunched up his face. "Yuck, Art. She doesn't owe me anything for that."

"Whoa whoa whoa! Who said anything about owing you? I'm not even talking about her; I'm talking about you. You had a chance to show her what a hero you are. And more importantly, to show yourself that too. You keep that in mind, keep your confidence high and I think you're in with a shot tonight."

The sides of Zack's stomach clenched and his heart tightened. "You really think so?"

Art pulled up at a red light and turned to look at him. He chewed his lip. "Honestly? No."

"What?"

"Not in a shirt like that."

Zack threw his head back into the headrest. "Fine, I'll buy a new shirt."

"Good." Art turned back and accelerated as the light turned green. "And pants, belt and shoes."

"Ugh!"

"We've probably got time for a haircut too."

"My hair's fine."

Tabitha's face lit up as she opened the door. "Look at you, Zack! Nice haircut."

Zack rubbed at his forehead. Without the tuft of hair hovering above his eyeline he felt exposed. Naked, almost. "Thanks."

Beside him, Art puffed up like a proud mother hen. "You're looking gorgeous, Tabs."

"Thank you, Art." She spun around in a circle, showing off her top and slinky skirt.

"The others here yet?" Zack asked.

Tabitha waved them inside. "Nope. Bast should be here any minute, Kimmy is running late and Charlie is going to meet us there."

"Is Dave coming?" Art asked with a melodramatic air of forced innocence.

"I don't think so. Why?" Tabitha's eyes narrowed as she caught on. "Oh." She looked Zack up and down again. "Ooooh. Good on you for going for it."

Zack blushed. "It's not like that."

"It's not like what?" Bast jogged up the front steps behind them before they made it into the house. He caught sight of Zack. "Oh, nice shirt, man. Wait, did you get a haircut?"

Zack walked away into the living room looking for a cushion to scream into.

"My parents are out for the night," Tabitha said, "so, if you want to, work out where you're going to crash and I'll go make us some pre-game drinks. Oh, and Kimmy has claimed Victor's room."

"How can you claim a room before you get here?" Art raised his voice in outrage.

"Because I don't want to argue with Kimmy. And because boys are smelly when they get drunk."

"I'm a god damn bed of roses, twenty-four seven," Art huffed before eyeing the chair in the corner. "Bags the recliner to sleep in."

Forty-five minutes later, Kimmy showed up but, even though Art was already two beers into the evening, he wisely held his tongue. It was a short walk to the party, two blocks down and to the end of a cul-de-sac. The house itself sat on the edge of a nature reserve and the party had bled into the shadows amongst the trees. Kimmy and Bast entered the backyard a few steps ahead of the others and, seeming to recognise a few faces, split off in opposite directions. Tabitha said she was going to find the host and left them as well.

"Where do you want to set up?" Zack asked.

Art didn't answer. He was scanning the party.

"Art." Zack tapped the backpack full of bottles. "Where do you want to put these?"

"Actually mate, can you look after them for us? There's a girl over there who's just dying to meet me."

"Um, yeah, okay."

"Great, great." Art pulled two bottles from the bag and walked away. He spun back for a moment. "You go settle in somewhere, I'll come find you in a bit."

Zack looked around at a sea of faces he'd never seen before. "Awesome."

Zack sat down on the sloping hill of the nature reserve. A couple of hours had passed and Art had not come and found him, but that was okay because he'd been steadily working his way through the backpack. He emptied his most recent bottle and laid back. The music from the party poured into the parkland and the grass under his body was still warm from the heat of the day.

He closed his eyes and sank into the moment. This was nice. After the stress of the final exams and the intensity of their Tower mission, here was a single point in time to forget it all and just be a teenager. The music filled his ears and he slipped into his senses. The Life from the party-goers around him rippled with energy and excitement, juxtaposed by the serene and steady life of the trees, grass and the small number of animals who dared linger close to watch the strange humans. The music, Life and alcohol swirled in his senses and he lost himself inside it. He wished, at that moment, that he knew how to paint, or write music, or something, so he could try and capture this feeling.

He felt, before he heard, a person approach and sidle down beside him and recognised the unique signature of Life.

"Hey Charlie," he said without opening his eyes.

She giggled. "How did you know it was me?"

"I'd know your Life anywhere." The words tumbled from his mouth before he could stop them.

"Really?"

He scuttled up into a seated position and opened his eyes. He hoped it was dark enough that she wouldn't see how red his cheeks were. "Well, any of the group."

"Oh, of course." She took a sip from a bottle of raspberry schnapps. "I've been looking everywhere for you."

His heart skittered around in his ribcage so violently he thought it might knock him over. Say something smooth, he thought to himself.

"Yeah?" Ugh.

"Yeah. I got here a while ago. Found the others, but none of them seemed to know where you had gone off to."

Zack chuckled. "Oh yeah, that's definitely me. Heading off and leaving people in the dust to wonder where I went. They just do parties very differently from me."

"I should have thought to look for you out here. On the edge of things. Close enough, but not in the middle of it all."

"Is that what you think of me? An outsider?" he asked, the words sticking to the edges of his throat as he said them.

She moved closer to him, lowering her voice. "I think you are more comfortable on the fringe than in the centre. Where you can watch, waiting to see if anybody needs your help. Like with Max yesterday. I can't even begin to thank you for that."

"You don't need to," he said, aware of how close she had moved. "I would have done that for anybody."

"I know," she breathed more than whispered. "That's who you are."

He felt her words land on his lips and then she leant forward and he felt her lips as well.

CHAPTER 18

BREAKDOWN

The warmth of Charlie's mouth pressed against his own and Zack's mind emptied of anything resembling thought. She leant against him, touching his cheek with her hand and he kissed back. His brain finished its reboot and he tried to process what was happening. After all these years she was here, in his arms, kissing him. This was what he'd always wanted.

Or was it?

He leant back, breaking the kiss. She moved to follow him, but he turned his head to the side.

"Is everything okay?" she asked.

"Y- yeah." He tried to wrestle his thoughts into place, but they danced away in his mind.

"What's the matter?" Charlie bit her lip and tucked a stray curl behind her ear.

"Nothing, it's just… Maybe we shouldn't do this when you've been drinking."

"I'm no drunker than you. It's okay."

"And this isn't your way of thanking me for Max?"

"Um, no, Zack, I'm not paying for your healing by making out with you. What's going on? I thought this is what you wanted. I thought you wanted me."

Zack struggled to put his thoughts into words. "I want you to want me."

Charlie leant back, her eyes flickering back and forth across his face. "What?"

"I said, I want you to want me."

Charlie winced and crossed her arms tight around her waist. "No."

Zack's heart sank. "You don't want me?"

"No, not 'No, I don't want you.' 'No, you don't get to know that.'"

Zack stared at her confused, blood and alcohol sloshing about in his mind.

"You get how messed up that is, right Zack?"

He could see from the expression on her face that he'd hurt her. "I'm sorry? I don't—"

"My feelings are for me." She touched her chest, above her heart. "You don't get to have them. To claim some kind of right to access them."

Charlie had misunderstood what he meant. He tried to explain, "It's just that—"

She barrelled on, her voice growing tighter.

"Is that what you mean? You don't actually want to kiss me? You just want me to want to kiss you? Are my feelings just a test you're trying to pass?"

Zack realised he'd ruined this and his mind whirred trying to find the words to fix it, but the alcohol sloshed against his thoughts.

Charlie stared into his eyes. "Zack?"

A dozen thoughts came to mind, but they were jumbled and Zack was worried he'd make it worse. Charlie's lips tightened and her back straightened. "Is that what I am in this? Validation? Something to measure yourself against? Dave was a jerk who was so worried about losing me that he tried to control everything I did. But at least he did that because he actually wanted me. You only want my seal of approval."

"It's not like that!" he blurted.

"No? Then tell me, Zack. Do you even know why you want me?" Anger was creeping into her voice and she sat further back. The distance between them seemed more than she could have moved in the last few moments.

"Yes. Of course."

"Really?" Her left eyebrow leapt up into a sharp point. "Just what about me?"

"You're smart, and nice—"

She didn't look impressed. "Those aren't reasons to want to kiss me."

"You're beautiful."

"Lots of girls are beautiful. I've seen hot girls checking you out at school and at parties all the time. Try again."

Zack was struggling and he knew it. He'd fantasised about this moment for years. Sometimes it had gone well, sometimes badly, but it had never gone like this.

"I don't know, but I have. For years!"

Charlie took a deep breath and the sadness shone through again.

"That's what I thought, Zack. You don't want me. I'm just some thing you've made up in your head to work out if you're good enough. That's a pretty crappy way to treat somebody, you know?"

Charlie stood up to leave and Zack scrambled to his feet beside her.

"Charlie, it's not like that. Look, I think we've both had too much to drink and it's all got messed up. Give me a second and I can sober us up and we can talk about it."

"Damn it, Zack. Not everything that's messy needs to be fixed. I'm drunk because I want to be. I broke up with Dave because I wanted to. I looked for you for an hour at this freakin' party because I wanted to find you. And I kissed you because I wanted you." Charlie ran her hands along the sides of her head, collecting her errant curls. "Zack, stop trying to manage the world and rating yourself against it. Work out what you want. Not what you think you should want. Not what you think other people think you should want. What you actually want."

Charlie turned and stormed away. Zack collapsed back down to sit on the grass. A figure stepped out from between the trees and Zack's body jolted before he recognised it was Bast.

"I don't know what I walked in on, mate. Are you okay?"

Zack blinked, long and slow. "Um, yeah, I think so."

"Good, because you need to come with me."

Bast stepped closer and Zack could see he looked worried.

"Why, what's the matter?"

"I'll explain on the way. C'mon." Bast strode off towards the house and Zack almost had to jog to keep up.

"So?"

"It's Kimmy. Sis is about to lose it at Art and she's too drunk for me to trust that she's not going to go full Lavagirl while she's doing it. Tabitha is trying to calm her down, but that's not going to work, just slow her down if we're lucky."

Bast's speech was rapid-fire and Zack had begun this conversation with a head full of confusion.

"Wait, what's happened. What did Art do?"

"That's the thing man. I'm not even sure she's in the wrong here. But none of that is going to matter if we don't stop her from breaking the Silence."

"Just tell me what's going on," Zack insisted as they entered the backyard.

"I think Art's been—"

Kimmy's voice ripped through the party music and the background noise.

"Get the hell out of there, scumbag. Before I drag you out!"

Bast's eyes widened and he dragged Zack inside the house.

Kimmy was banging against a closed door at the end of the hallway. Tabitha stood to the side of the door, talking to Kimmy, when she saw the boys as they entered the house. She waved them over with frantic gestures.

"Kimmy," she said in low tones between the other girl's hammer strikes against the door. "The boys are here. Let's give them a chance to handle it."

Kimmy spun around and bore down on Zack. She jabbed her index finger hard into his chest.

"Are you going to do something about this for once? I've had it. It's disgusting!"

"Can somebody please tell me what is going on?" Zack said, his back flat against the hallway as Kimmy pressed on.

The door opened and Art peered out. His hair was mussed and he was no longer wearing his shirt. Behind him, on the bed, two female figures clutched at blankets.

Kimmy turned and lunged at him, but Bast was faster and interposed himself between the two of them. With his back to Kimmy, he looked Art straight in the face.

"We all need to get out of here."

Art looked confused. "What? Why? I'm having a great time."

Kimmy screamed over Bast's shoulder. "You sick arsehole! Using your M—"

Tabitha stopped her by clamping her hand over her mouth. "Stop it."

Zack slipped past and whispered to Art. "We've got to go, mate. She's going to break the Silence and then we're all in it."

Art looked around at them and his mouth tightened. He snatched his shirt off the ground and turned back to the bed.

"I'm really sorry, ladies. This was just about the best night ever, but I have to go deal with this situation."

"What?" one of them called out. "Is she like your girlfriend or something?"

"God, no," he said, stepping past Kimmy and marching out of the house.

Tabitha hurried after him. "Look, let's head back to my place and we can work this out."

"Whatever," he said, wrenching his arms into his sleeves. "Not like I really have a choice here."

"Are you serious?" Kimmy screamed behind him. "You're going to complain about not having a choice?"

"Kimmy, cool it," Bast said. "He's coming."

"Cool it? You can't tell me you're okay with this."

"We hear him out first, right? And to do that without breaking a certain unbreakable rule, we have to leave."

"Fine." Kimmy strode down the hallway, pushing past Zack hard enough that he bounced against the wall.

Zack and Bast followed behind.

"You don't actually believe he used his 'advantages' to get those girls, do you?" Zack asked Bast in hushed tones.

"Don't you?" Bast asked, holding the front door open for him. "Look, I know he's your best friend. But last year he couldn't get a girl to talk to him for ten minutes, let alone get their phone number. And now?"

Zack glanced back into the party. The music was still playing but everybody had stopped what they were doing and all eyes were fixed on him and Bast. They may have kept the Silence, but they'd been loud while doing it.

When they left the house, Bast jogged to catch up with Kimmy and, further ahead, Art stomped alongside Tabitha. Left alone at the back of the loose, stretched column, Zack paused and turned back to the party. Small pockets of teenagers milled around drinking, laughing and talking. He didn't see Charlie amongst any of them and wondered where she had gone after she left him. After he'd screwed it all up. It was probably better that she wasn't here. He needed to focus on Art.

Was it possible that he'd used his Mind magic on those two girls tonight? Zack thought he recognised them. Seniors from a nearby private school, they'd been at the same parties that Art had dragged Zack to for a few years. And Bast was right, they'd never given Art the time of day before. He wished he could talk to Art alone, but that wasn't going to be an option. He sped up to catch up to the others.

He was on Bast's and Kimmy's heels as they entered through Tabitha's front door and he closed it behind him.

Art stood in the centre of the living room.

"Do you want to tell me what the hell your problem is, Kimmy?"

"My problem?" She didn't so much as raise her voice as just start at a screaming pitch. "My problem, Art, is what you did to get those girls into bed with you."

"Okay, first of all, Chloe and Michelle are both eighteen, so it's women, not girls. Second," he counted off his fingers. "Just come out and say it, Kimmy."

"You mind controlled them, didn't you?"

Art stood still, wide eyed and fuming.

'C'mon Art, set the record straight. We're listening.' Tabitha stood to the side, her arms crossed loosely at the forearms.

'You know what?' Art's face grew red with anger. 'No. You're a hypocrite. You all are.'

'What?' Kimmy seethed back at him.

'You heard me. Hypocrite. I don't hear any complaints when I mess with a security guard or cop's mind to get us out of trouble. I don't hear any when I use my magic to get us free tickets or sell things to a pawnbroker. I don't hear a thing when I jump into a teacher's head and get them to change test scores, forget they've seen me stealing answers or push their knowledge out of their brains and into yours. And what did I hear when I worked my way into a stranger's mind yesterday, to make him laugh while I slid my sword through his heart? Not a damn word from any of you.' Art barged past them and tore open the front door. 'I've done all of that for us. All of us. And all it's done is make you look at me like I'm a monster. Go to hell.'

He stormed past them, slamming the door behind him.

Silence filled the room until Tabitha ended it with a loud exhale.

"He's not wrong about the way we look at him, sometimes."

"We look at him that way for a good reason," Kimmy said, pointing out to the front yard. "And I didn't hear a denial in all that. I'm going to drag him back in here."

Bast moved between her and the door. "Just hang on a second."

"Don't tell me you fell for that sob story?"

"No. Well, maybe a little, but it doesn't change anything. If he forced those girls, whether or not they realise it, we have a problem. And we'll deal with it. But not tonight."

"But—"

"You stopped him, right? There's nothing more we can do when everybody has their backs up. Cooler heads and all that."

"I'll go talk to him," Zack said. "He'll talk to me."

"That's probably a good idea," Tabitha said.

"Is it?" Kimmy asked. "He'll take his side."

"His side?" Zack replied. "If he's done what you think he has, he's no longer my friend. But maybe he'll talk to me alone."

"Fine." Kimmy turned and sat down on the reclining chair, avoiding eye contact with the others.

Zack nodded to the other two and hurried from the house. Art was in his car with the radio blaring, but the engine was off. Zack moved to the passenger side and tapped on the window. Art looked up from where his head was slumped against the steering wheel and beckoned him inside.

Zack claimed the seat and shut the door. "Are you alright?"

Art gave a bitter laugh. "Yeah, I'm peachy."

"Mate, you didn't exactly help yourself in there."

"With them? Fuck what they think, Zack. I want to know what you think."

"Me?"

"Yeah. Do you think I'm capable of using my magic to force women into bed with me?"

"No."

Relief flooded Art's eyes.

"But," Zack continued, "I need to ask. Did you do something less than that? Talk yourself into some kind of line in the sand where it was okay to, maybe, make them think you're the funniest, coolest guy they've ever met?"

"Are you saying I'm not?"

"Art."

He gripped the steering wheel tight in both hands.

"No, Zack. I did nothing to them. I've never used my magic on another person like that. Not to get a date, a kiss, a smile, anything."

His shoulders slumped and he let go of the wheel.

"Okay then," Zack said.

"I could have, though. Just like you said. I could make them laugh and smile and be a bit drunker than they were. I could put them in the mood for anything I wanted them to be in the mood for. I could make them happy to be near me or to crave my touch. None of that is particularly tricky magic, especially when people are already drinking and already kind of in the mood." He leant forward and gazed out the front windscreen. "But I would never do anything like that, mate. It's wrong and it's yuck and it makes my skin crawl to think about doing it."

"Right. I believe you. So, let's go back in there and tell them that."

Art shook his head in silence.

"Why not?"

"Because do you know what else I can do? I can make people forget they were angry at me and what they were angry about. I can make them like me and trust every word I'm saying. Hell,

Zack, in a few years, I'm going to be able to drop thoughts and memories into people's heads."

"What's your point?"

"My point is that nothing I do or say matters. You either trust me, or you don't. If they don't trust me at a high school party, why would they with anything else? I go in there, I open my heart and tell them that I've never, and would never, misuse my magic in that way. And they see I'm sincere." He paused, pointing to his watering eyes. "Hell, they see me tearing up, and they believe me."

"Yeah? That's good."

"Until I leave. And then they start wondering. Was Art actually sincere, or did he make me think that? Did I accuse him with no actual evidence, or did I see him casting a spell on those women, but he's removed it from my memory? Am I actually his friend or has he implanted that in my brain?"

Zack sat in silence.

"Well, are you going to say anything?"

"You're not wrong."

Art thumped the back of his head against the headrest. "Damn, I was hoping I was."

"No, I'm pretty sure that's solid. Nobody can trust you because we can't trust where that trust is coming from."

"Shit."

"But I do trust you. Completely."

"For how long though, mate?"

"Until the end. No hesitation."

Art wiped at his eyes. "You mean that, don't you?"

"Yeah. Look, I get you don't want to go back in there. But I'm going to go have a word with them, okay? Tell them you didn't use magic to get laid."

Art sucked air in between his teeth.

"What?" Zack asked.

"That's not technically true."

"What?" Zack repeated, louder.

"I said I didn't use magic on them."

"Who did you use magic on, then?"

Art pointed a finger at his own head.

"You used magic on yourself?"

Art nodded.

"To do what?"

"I turned off all sense of fear."

Zack stared at him for a moment before bursting into laughter. "That's it?"

"Yeah, honestly. I've been doing it since the middle of last year. I switch it off and suddenly I'm not worried about striking out, I'm not worried about embarrassing myself, it's just fun."

Zack continued to chuckle. "Yeah, alright. You good to drive?"

"Yep. I was sobering myself up before you tapped on the window."

"How does that work?" Zack asked. "You've still got alcohol in your blood."

Art shrugged. "Yeah, but I just tell my mind to ignore it."

"Oh," Zack nodded. "But wait, if you get pulled over, it'll still be on your breath."

"And then I wish the officer a lovely evening."

"Of course. Yeah, okay. Drive safe." Zack opened the door to climb out.

"Zack?" Art reached over and grabbed his arm. "Thanks, man."

"All good, mate."

Zack closed the door behind him and tapped twice on the roof. He waited until Art had driven down the street before he went back inside the house.

Tabitha, Bast and Kimmy were waiting for him.

"He's gone?" Tabitha asked.

"Yeah, headed home."

"That's what he told you anyway," Kimmy grumbled from her chair.

"Okay, this is the deal." Zack looked at them each in turn. "You don't have to trust him. I understand if you can't. He understands if you can't. So, trust me. I vouch for him. And if you can't accept that, then there's no way we can work as a team."

"And that's that?" Bast asked.

"Yep, it can't work any other way."

Tabitha nodded after a moment. "Yeah, okay. I can work with that."

"Me too," Bast said.

"What about what he did tonight?" Kimmy said.

"He didn't use magic on them, Kimmy. I promise you."

"What, I'm supposed to believe he won them over with his personality?"

"Well, that and whatever they were drinking?" Zack said.

"His abs probably helped too," Bast added. "Seriously, the man got shredded this year."

"So, you believe him now?" Kimmy asked Bast.

"No, I believe Zack. That's the deal and I'm taking it."

Kimmy shook her head.

"Look, no offence Zack. I do trust you, it's just not enough to make me trust him. But, I'll play along for now and keep the team together."

Zack collapsed onto the lounge in relief. "I'll take it."

CHAPTER 19

RECONNAISSANCE

"Are you sure we shouldn't have brought the others?" Bast looked down at his shoes as he spoke, allowing the brim of his cap to shield most of his face.

Tabitha shook her head, her own face concealed behind oversized sunglasses.

"No, this job is better with just the three of us. Art and Kimmy need some time apart and I'm not going to pick one over the other. And Charlie has been a bit hot tempered, too."

Zack pulled his heavy coat around him, hiding his face from the other two as much as anybody else. Bast looked along the bench at Zack anyway.

"Yeah, I think I saw some of that, too. Do you think it's because all three of them...?" Bast slid his thumb across his neck.

"Yes, Bast," Tabitha replied flatly, "I think maybe they are processing having killed people."

"Charlie, in particular, would have a rough time here today," Zack said, gesturing down from the hilltop, toward the headstones. A small canopy had been set up over an empty grave with a dozen folding chairs placed to the side.

It was Zack who had reached out to Tabitha with the idea. Of the three men who had died that day in the tunnels under New York, one of them had been identified. Oscar Tilverson. With half an idea in his head, Zack had searched for him online. Nothing came up, but Zack kept looking and started to hunt through obituaries. He focused on New York first and then the rest of the United States. Still nothing. Then he remembered Oscar's accent and switched to British sites. It took him hours, but he found it. A funeral notice with a time and location. Tabitha suggested they keep the group small and just bring Bast along.

Bast crushed a clump of dirty snow under his boot. "I hate the hemisphere jump. I can't wait to get back to the warmth. And I'm still worried this is a trap."

"It was bloody hard work to find for a trap. And even if it is one, they'll be looking for more than three of us," Zack said. "Plus, we're out in the public. Even if they don't care about the Silence, they aren't going to want to attack people in broad daylight."

"And if they do, you'll speed us out of here," Tabitha added.

Bast shook his head. "That guy, Connor. He's faster than me."

"I think we'll be okay," Tabitha said. "We just need to keep our eyes open and not draw attention to ourselves."

"Well, here we go." Bast tilted his head towards a car pulling up near the gravesite. A middle-aged couple stepped out of the vehicle and loitered underneath the tent. The woman clutched at the man, clearly distraught even from this distance.

"Oh god, this is going to be rough," Tabitha said.

"They ambushed us, remember?" Bast said. "They lured us into a room and threatened us. This guy nearly killed Max."

"I get all that, but that couple down there didn't," Tabitha replied. "They just lost somebody they loved. Their son, probably."

More mourners arrived at the site. Some lingered by their cars, but others approached the first couple and exchanged handshakes, hugs and kisses. Five minutes later, a hearse rolled down the neat cemetery road and parked next to the gravesite. Zack, Tabitha and

Bast held their breaths in shared silence as six of the mourners gathered around the back of the hearse and carried the coffin from the curb to the grave. They eased it onto the raised frame and rejoined the others for the service to start. A priest began the service, but his voice didn't carry to the three on the hill.

"I don't see anybody from the fight," Tabitha said.

Zack had been scoping out the people as they arrived. "Me neither. I can't be sure at this distance, but nobody really fits the bill."

"What do we do if we do see them?" Bast asked. "Like, what's the plan? You never said, beyond coming and having a look."

"Honestly, I'm not sure exactly," Zack answered. "But we need intel and this is one of the few leads we've got left."

"Connor clearly has connections to some other group," Tabitha said. "Probably the ones that gave out that ritual magic. Junie's happy with our progress, but she still needs us to follow the clues all the way to the end, to make sure nobody from the Tower is involved."

"Or to find who in the Tower is," Zack added. "So yeah, if they turn up today, then we see if we can follow them. See if they go to a particular place or meet with somebody. Whatever they are doing, they manage to avoid the Tower's wards somehow."

Music wafted up from the ceremony below. The wind stole away any lyrics it may have had, but the melody was soft and sad.

"I wonder what School of magic this guy knew," Bast said, staring down at the service.

"Creation," Zack answered without hesitation.

Tabitha turned to him in surprise. "What? How do you figure?"

Zack shrugged. "Somebody hid the Mind mage from us in the alley and somebody hid the gate in the car park. That's Creation magic from what I understand. They can create solid things, but they can also create light and make us see things that aren't there or hide things that are."

"Okay," Bast said, "but how do you know that was him?"

"Process of elimination. Connor is Movement, like you, Nicole was Water, like Erik. Art was fighting the Mind mage. And upstairs were Plant, Body, Earth and Air mages."

"Or the Creation mage was somewhere else," Tabitha said.

Zack nodded. "Yep, that's possible."

"Hey, I think that's them." Bast nudged Tabitha.

"Okay, don't all look at once," Tabitha said, pretending to play with her phone. "Where abouts are they, Bast?"

"They're walking in from deeper in the cemetery. Five of them, can't miss them."

"Right. Look away now and I'll have a peek." Tabitha continued to fidget with her phone as she glanced up. "Oh yeah, that's them. Definitely Connor and that Air mage, I got a good look at him. I think it's all five of them. Your turn, Zack."

He counted to ten before looking over. Even at this distance he was confident it was the five from the Underground. "That's interesting."

"What?" Tabitha asked.

"Well, Charlie didn't kill that Earth mage. But she's limping. The Body mage is supporting her."

"Makes sense, she took an arrow to the side," Bast said.

"Yeah," Zack agreed. "Just like you took a deep cut to your leg. How's your limp going?"

"Oh, they don't know a Lifer," Bast said.

"At least not one they can reach out to in a few days," Tabitha said. "Good intel, though."

The ceremony continued and soon the mourners lined up to toss handfuls of soil into the grave. The five mages hadn't approached. Dressed in blacks and greys, they stood watching from a few rows of plots away.

The ceremony ended and people filtered away, some stopping by the first couple to offer a few words or a squeeze of a hand or arm. When they had all gone, the couple sat in silence, holding each other as they stared at the grave. Tabitha sniffled back a tear and Bast gripped her hand. The couple rose, made their way back to their car and left.

Connor and the others waited until the car was out of sight before they approached the grave.

"What if they see us?" Bast asked in a whisper.

"Then we run," Tabitha said. "But they won't. There's enough people wandering around the cemetery. We're blending in fine."

The group of five stood around the open grave. Connor himself had his back to the bench, so Zack was not sure if he was speaking, or if they were all standing in silence. Zack closed his eyes and stretched out with his sense. They were not so far away that it was difficult to sense their Life, but he wanted more than that. He focused on Connor and, blocking the others from his mind, attempted to become familiar with the unique pattern of his Life, so that he could, hopefully, recognise it later. It was challenging from this distance, but Zack was hopeful he could remember it.

A quarter of an hour or so later, the group moved away from the grave, retracing their steps deeper into the cemetery.

"Where are they going?" Bast asked. "Is there an exit over that side?"

"Not according to the map," Tabitha said, pulling it up on her phone.

"Which means they're probably leaving the same way they left the Subway," Zack said.

"Right," Bast said. "So, if I'm going to be of any use, I need to get close enough to the gate to read it before the Movement energy fades."

"How long after it closes does that happen?" Tabitha asked.

"Maybe a minute? If we're lucky."

"Let them go a little further away, then we'll start following. I should be able to track Connor's Life."

Tabitha pointed to a memorial plinth on the hill. "Let's go after them in a bit of a circle."

Zack nodded. "Good idea."

The three teens made their way across the cemetery. They were halfway up the hill when Tabitha stopped.

"Did either of you see where they went?"

Bast pointed off to the right. "That way, I think."

Zack closed his eyes. "Yeah. I think they are behind that mausoleum over there."

"Okay, let's try and get closer," Tabitha said.

They made their way towards their targets, winding between the graves and headstones. Zack's eyes were drawn to the inscriptions on the stones, and he found himself working out the maths with the etched dates. Most of the departed in these rows had been in their sixties or older when they died. He hadn't passed any as young as Oscar Tilverson would have been.

Did the number of years make a difference to the grief though? His grandmother was in her late 80s. Would that make it 'okay' when she died? He didn't have long to stop that from happening.

Wait — something was wrong. He grasped Bast's arm and pulled him to a stop.

"What?" Bast's voice halted Tabitha as well.

"I'm not sure," Zack said. "Wait, there's only four of them behind the crypt. Hide!"

Bast threw himself to the ground, rolling behind a larger headstone. Tabitha looked side to side and darted away to crouch behind another. Zack himself struggled to pick one before he jumped behind a couple's joint headstone.

They stayed on the ground, waiting; the icy, muddy soil seeping cold up their legs. Bast made eye contact with him and raised his hands in a silent, 'What do we do?'

Zack wasn't sure. Maybe he'd been wrong. At this distance, counting individual Life signatures was always a challenge. He was about to stand up when he heard the crunch of a heavy boot against a nearby clump of snow. Zack reached out.

He couldn't be sure, but he thought it might have been the Body mage he had fought under New York. He gestured to the others to stay down and held his breath. The footsteps retreated and Zack tracked the Life back to behind the mausoleum. He counted to ten and then stood up.

"What was that?" Tabitha asked, dusting the dirt and snow off her jeans.

"One of them circled back," Zack said.

"Does that mean they saw us before?" Bast asked.

"I doubt it," Zack said. "Or they would have come at us harder. Maybe they are just being careful."

"Then we need to be twice as careful," Tabitha said.

Bast twitched and looked towards the dark stone mausoleum. "They're opening a gate."

The three hurried towards it and, as they approached, Tabitha glanced at Zack with a questioning look. He closed his eyes.

"They're gone. All five of them," he said.

"And the gate has closed," Bast said, running forward.

Zack and Tabitha followed behind and made their way around the stone building. Once on the other side, Bast pressed his palms against the wall with his eyes closed.

"Getting anything?" Tabitha asked.

"Shhh," Bast responded.

Tabitha pressed her lips closed and stood beside Zack. His eyes still closed, Bast's head twitched from side to side, as if he was hearing or smelling something faint. After a few moments he stepped back from the wall.

"Get anything?" Tabitha asked again.

"Yeah. Yeah, I think so," he answered. "For one thing, that was a gate to another realm, I'm sure of it. And I'm pretty sure I recognise it. I need to get back to those jars we found in New York."

"Why?" Tabitha asked.

"Because, if I'm right, this gate shared an energy signature with one of those jars. And you know what that means."

"You can follow them," Zack said, excitement in his voice.

"That's right," Bast said.

"Well." Tabitha looked back and forth between the boys. "That means we need to prepare to go wherever they did."

Sara tapped away at the blackboard in her study with a piece of chalk. The diagrams were a combination of scientific models, arcane script and shorthand she had developed to explain the shape and direction of Life flows. A couple of years ago it would have looked like gibberish, but to Zack it was a clear guide on how to magically cure an established bacterial infection.

Sara pointed to the chalk flows.

"Here is where it differs from the treatment of viral infections. The underlying principles are the same, but the flows should be split to allow more and finer targeting. Do you understand?"

Zack nodded along. "I think so."

"Good. I'll keep an eye out for anybody with a cold or running nose so that we can have a practical lesson if possible."

Zack was quiet for a moment. His time in the cemetery the day before, and thoughts about his grandmother, had reinforced the consequences of not learning everything he could about healing. He needed Sara to teach him more. "Can these principles be used to cure other diseases and illnesses? Like degenerative illnesses or cancers?"

"It depends on the illness," Sara answered, as she sat down facing him. "Some illnesses are caused by either too much of a substance somewhere it should not be, such as plaque or calcium, and other times by the absence of a substance from where it should be, such as insulin or hormones. In either of those cases, it is possible that magic can be used to guide the patient's Life into correcting those imbalances. Other diseases are much more difficult. Cancer, for example, is the patient's own cells. Life is as likely to protect those cells as to want to remove them."

Zack tried to stay calm, but the words pummelled into him.

"It is possible though. If you are interested, and if you master the comparatively simpler magic, I will teach you."

Zack nodded eagerly. Perhaps too eagerly. Sara's eyes narrowed.

"I know you wish to be a doctor, and likely use your skill with Life alongside your medical practice. And that is okay. The Tower permits us to use our magic so long as we keep the Silence. But there is the challenge. A patient here or there, the balance tipped gently in favour of recovery, few are likely to notice. But Dr Zack, striding through his oncology ward with record breaking remission rates? This will draw attention."

"But that would mean letting people die that you know you can save," Zack said, shaking his head.

"Yes, it does," Sara replied. "It is why so few from our School enter the health system. Never forget, Zack, that the purpose of the Tower and the training it provides is to defend our world from magic. It is a far greater danger than all the diseases put together and the Silence is one of our greatest protections. It cannot be jeopardised."

Zack's heart sank.

"Still, if you are willing and able, I will teach you. And then perhaps you will be able to do a little extra good in the world. Quietly, around the edges."

Zack sat up straighter. "I will. Please continue with the lesson."

He had to try.

CHAPTER 20

ON THE SCENT

Art groaned as they stepped out of the Tower and into the streets of Brisbane. Zack sympathised. It was at least eight degrees hotter than it had been in Sydney and triple the humidity. Zack's t-shirt was stuck to his skin and they'd only been outside for a minute.

"This is a terrible idea." Art fluttered the front of his own shirt in a vain attempt to stimulate some airflow.

"No, it's not," Tabitha said. "We can assume they know we're Australian, but they won't know where we live, yeah? So, operating through other cities will keep them off our trail."

"Do we really think they'll be trying to find us?" Charlie asked.

"Well, we're trying to find them," Bast said. "Makes sense for them to be looking for us."

"And they didn't even kill any of us," Kimmy added. "Which means a few of them couldn't go behind their friends' backs and scope out our funeral alone."

"Oh, come on Kimmy." Tabitha wiped the sweat from her forehead. "It made sense to go there in a smaller group and not attract attention."

"Did it also make sense to not tell us?" Kimmy tightened her arms across her chest.

"What are you all talking about?" Art asked. "I'm not complaining about the plan or the funeral recon, I'm just saying why Brisbane in December? Why not somewhere cooler, like Melbourne?"

"There's no Tower entrance in Melbourne," Bast answered.

"Really?" Art asked, surprise in his voice.

"Yeah, I know, right?" Bast said. "Closest one is in Bendigo. We can go there, but figured a busier city would hide us better."

"Fair enough. But can we at least get somewhere with aircon soon? I'm literally going to die."

"Yep," Tabitha said. "We've booked a hotel room a couple of blocks away."

Tabitha led the group on a 10-minute walk down the street before stopping outside a budget hotel.

Art looked in at the lobby and made a face like he'd smelled something rancid.

"Here? Really?"

"We're not actually staying here, dude." Tabitha stared at him. "You get that, right? I'll go check in and then Art, can you distract the staff so the others can all get in, with Max?"

"So, this is one of those situations where you want me to interfere with somebody's mind and take away their will?" Art asked, his voice dripping with false sincerity. "I wouldn't want anybody to be upset by the way I use my magic."

"Are you serious?" Kimmy's eyes widened. "This is nothing like—"

Bast stepped in between her and Art.

"You're right, mate. I'm sorry about the other night. We were worried you'd done something really wrong, but we didn't handle it properly. We should have given you a fairer go at explaining it."

Kimmy fumed behind Bast, but Tabitha whispered to her and she settled, turning her glare away from Art.

Art appeared unsure of how to respond to Bast and Zack took the opportunity to pull him aside.

"C'mon mate. Give them a chance to show they're willing to trust you. We need you."

"Yeah, it's not when they need me that I'm worried about the trust. But fine, I'll be a team player."

"Okay," Tabitha said. "Kimmy, you come check in with me. Then Art clears the way for the rest of us."

Art nodded. "Whatever gets us out of this heat."

A few minutes later, the seven teens and Max were crammed into a small hotel room.

Bast scanned the room. "He's not wrong, Tabs. This place is hideous."

Kimmy scrunched her nose. "Definitely not the kind of place to turn on a black-light."

Art scratched his head. "Zack, would your Life-sense work like one? You know, because—"

Zack held himself back from heaving at the thought. "I am not going to find out the answer to that question."

"Would everybody focus, please?" Tabitha said with her voice raised. Zack noted, however, she had stepped away from all the surfaces and was standing in the centre of the room. "Bast, do you have enough space to do your thing?"

"Yep. I'm going to use the bathroom door; it'll help me centre it. You all might as well get comfortable. This would be tricky in the Gate room; it'll be even harder here. Honestly, I'm not even certain I can, but I'll try."

"Should we be doing this in the Tower then?" Charlie asked.

"Not an option," Bast said. "We can't risk any of these people getting into the Tower, which means I'm going to have to close the gate behind us. And I definitely don't have the skills to open a gate from another realm through the Tower's wards."

"When we get there, will you be able to open one back?" Jackie asked.

"Definitely. But only if I get a bit of space and silence so I can concentrate." Bast shooed them away with his hands.

They stood in cramped and awkward silence, nobody wanting to touch the bed or the two-seater couch and watched Bast work. For several minutes, he didn't appear to be doing anything at all, but then he began to move. He pulled one of the mason jars from his backpack and, as he incanted, drew orange light from it. He wove the light between his fingers and traced shapes in the open doorway to the bathroom. The light trailed behind his fingers like a sparkler in the dark, fading only as Bast wrote more symbols over the tops of them.

On and on, Bast wove the light. His movements slowed and his incantations began to sound breathless. Zack thought about sharing some Life with him, but they hadn't discussed it and he was worried he would distract him and disrupt the magic. Tabitha and Jackie looked worried and Kimmy opened her mouth to say something, but then a familiar grey light shone in the doorway.

The light was small at first. Bast continued with renewed effort and the light grew until it all but blocked the bathroom. He staggered backwards to lean against the door out to the hallway.

"Okay, wow, that was rough." Bast wiped sweat from his face and neck.

"Are you okay?" Kimmy asked.

"He will be." Zack stepped forward and poured Life into him.

Bast's breathing slowed and he stood up straight. "Okay. Thanks, man."

Tabitha reached into her backpack and drew her flail. "Weapons out, everybody. We don't know what we're about to walk into. If it's dangerous, we jump right back through the gate and Bast closes it. Otherwise, he shuts it behind us and we see if we can learn anything about who these people are."

Kimmy twirled her axe in her hand. "Me first."

"I'll go with you," said Jackie, clutching her spear.

Kimmy held out a fist. "Definitely. Shields and firepower all the way."

Jackie blushed and bumped her fist.

To his credit, Art didn't say anything and elected instead to stand with his lips tightened as the two stepped through the gate. A second later, Jackie's head popped back through the grey light.

"It's safe. Dark, but safe."

Zack followed the others through the gate and into a darkness broken only by the light of a flame Kimmy was holding aloft in her hand. They appeared to be in some kind of cave or tunnel, with craggy, sharp stones on the roof and ceiling. The ground was made of the same stone but worn smooth.

Bast closed the gate with far more ease than he'd opened it, but remained in place, concentrating for a few moments after he had finished.

"Right, this spot has had a lot of Movement magic poured into it in the past, so I'm pretty sure I can open a gate back to the hotel from here without any trouble."

"Does that mean this is the same spot they would have entered this realm?" Zack asked.

"That would explain these," Charlie said, pointing to where Max was sniffing at a dozen cigarette butts scattered on the ground.

"Yeah, I wasn't sure, but this is what I was hoping for," Bast said. "Without focusing on anything specific in this realm, my magic found the path of least resistance."

"So, where to from here?" Art asked.

"What do you think, Maxie?" Charlie asked. "Can you smell out any more of those yucky cigarettes?"

"Hey!" Kimmy said.

"Smoke as much as you want," Charlie replied, "doesn't stop them from being disgusting."

"My arm is getting tired holding this flame up. I'm going to try something," Kimmy said.

The tunnel fell dark as her fire disappeared and Kimmy whispered to herself. After a few moments, Zack's eyes adjusted and he noted a faint luminescence coming from the rocks. Too faint to see anything but at least enough to show where the tunnel walls were.

Kimmy's whispers grew before another light flared into life and she gave a whoop of excitement. Zack blinked away the tears caused by the brightness and realised that this time, the flames were coming from the head of Kimmy's axe.

"That's pretty cool, Kimmy," Tabitha said. "But maybe give us more of a heads up before plunging us into darkness in a strange realm?"

Kimmy rolled her eyes. "Whatever, fine."

Max sniffed her way past Jackie and Kimmy and further up the tunnel. The group followed and they slowly made their way deeper into the cave system. From the corner of his eye, Zack thought he saw Charlie looking at him as they walked, but when he turned toward her, she was looking the other way. They hadn't really spoken since the night of the party and she had avoided standing too close to him all day. Now, even in the confines of the tunnel, she seemed to hug the opposite wall.

Between Bast dragging him off to deal with Art and his online pursuit of the other mages, Zack had successfully avoided thinking about that night by filling his head with other things. Now, with her so close, it was all he could think about. He wanted to apologise to her but wasn't sure what he would be apologising for. He wanted to tell her that she was wrong, but he wasn't quite sure that she was.

Something flared in his mind. "Hang on, something is up ahead."

The sounds of skittering echoed down the tunnel with deep clack-clacking. Weird shapes loomed into the range of Kimmy's flaming axe, splashing weirder shadows across the walls.

"Yeah, I think we picked that up too, Zack," Bast said.

The figures inched towards the light and revealed themselves as crab-like creatures, with a tall torso and four limbs, each ending in massive claws. Three of the creatures were visible in the light, but from the sound of things, more hid behind them in the shadows.

"Ideas?" Kimmy asked, gripping her axe in two hands, readying herself for their approach.

But the creatures didn't move. Instead, they remained a few metres away, clicking their claws together.

"What are they doing? Why aren't they attacking?" Bast asked.

"None of them wants to be first," Kimmy said, feinting her axehead towards them.

"I don't know," Tabitha said. "It's like they are waiting for something."

"I can't read them," Art said. "Not sentient enough."

"I'm getting something," Charlie said. "It's hard, their minds are strange."

The creatures crept forward, clicking their claws. Another two stepped out of the shadows behind them.

"Any time now, Charlie," Kimmy said.

"Tab is right, they are waiting for something. I'm trying to understand what. Give me a second."

One of the creatures loomed over Kimmy, the bulk of its body casting a wide shadow and plunging the others behind it into darkness again. It clicked its claws a few inches from Kimmy's head.

"I don't have a second." Kimmy tightened the grip on her axe. "Hell with it. Lobster for dinner it is."

"Kimmy, no!" Charlie shouted, but it was too late.

Kimmy's axe sliced through the creature's closest arm, severing the claw from its body. It screamed in a high-pitched chittering sound, and the others behind it took up the call. Max barked and nipped at their legs, but their hard exoskeletons gave her little in the way of targets.

"Max, back to me," Charlie called.

The dog bounded back down the cave to Charlie's side and Art moved forward to stand behind his sister, sword ready.

A second creature scurried forward beside the first and snapped towards Art. One of Jackie's shields held the claw back and Art slashed at it with his blade. Unlike Kimmy, his attack missed the thinner joint of the limb and instead left a large crack in the claw itself.

Kimmy pulled the left leg of her jeans up. "Out you come, Mr Shanks. Time to get to work."

"What?" Art's face was wide with shock and confusion as an ornate blade rose out of a sheath at Kimmy's ankle and zipped towards the creatures, point first.

"You brought that thing with you?" Art ducked under a claw the size of his head. "What's to stop it stabbing at us if it feels like it?"

Kimmy blocked a claw with the flat of her axe and forced the creature back a step. "He won't. I've been training him."

"Him?" Art turned to face Kimmy.

Another claw snapped at his neck, only to crash against the steely light of Jackie's shield. "Concentrate, Art."

Beside him, at the back, Charlie held an arrow to her bow, the string half drawn.

"I can't get a clear shot with us grouped together like this," she said, as much to herself as anybody else. Max whined at her side.

Bast incanted and his shoes flared with orange light. He bounded forward, stepping up onto the wall and around until he was running along the roof. He ran towards the creatures but ducked away as Kimmy attacked one of them with a wild overhead swing. "Look out!"

Without a way to follow, Zack, Charlie and Tabitha were stuck behind, watching. Zack could see Jackie was already tiring. She could probably have held a single shield the size of the tunnel with relative ease, but that would have prevented Art and Kimmy, and now Bast, from attacking as much as it would have protected them. Instead, she needed to fire off smaller, rapid-fire shields to block the half dozen remaining claws from crushing them.

The creatures were faster than things that size should have been, too. Art and Kimmy had both landed strong first blows on them, but now the two creatures were focused on them, both sword and axe were batted away to land harmlessly on their hard shell.

The dagger was zooming around in the background, similarly scraping against the creatures' armoured hides. But at least, Zack thought, it seemed to be distracting the second row of creatures, who snapped at it as it flitted around them.

Zack crept forward. "Fresh pot of coffee incoming, Jacks."

"Oh god, thanks," she replied, not looking back.

Zack streamed Life towards her and her own Life thirstily drank it up. He cut the flow off well short of what she needed, as he was already aching from what he had given Bast. And he was worried he'd need to repair what those claws might do.

The cave's ceiling was at least a foot or two lower than the halls of the Tower, where Zack had last seen Bast use this spell, and that extra height made all the difference. Here, Bast was stuck in a crouch to avoid any errant sword or axe blows from down below. And his rapier was not particularly effective at piercing the creature's hide or parrying their bulky claws.

Tabitha sucked air between her teeth in frustration as her flail's chain dangled at her side. The enchanted dagger soared back through the two front creatures towards Art. He flinched with a yelp, bringing up his broadsword to deflect it. The dagger stopped short of him and turned on a sharp angle towards the creature attacking Kimmy, but Art's reaction left him wide open and a claw thrust in around his guard. The pincers latched onto the flesh and bone on his hip and hauled him forward.

Art yelped in pain and Jackie screamed, thrusting at the creature with her spear. The point of the spear did little but scratch the carapace, but the noise and movement distracted the creature long enough for Bast to leap down from the ceiling. With his full weight behind his rapier, and his aim true, his blade slid in the gap between the claw and the torso and severed it.

The creature reared back, and the claw, separated from the body, opened and fell to the floor. A spray of blood shot out from Art's hip. He collapsed in a crouch against the wall and clamped his left hand over the wound.

Meanwhile, the flying dagger hovered over the head of the other creature. Kimmy feinted again and, as the creature moved to block the flaming axe with two of its three claws, the dagger streaked forward. The creature raised its third claw to deflect the dagger, but it was too slow and the enchanted weapon sliced into one of the tiny eyestalks at the top of the torso. The creature shuddered backwards and bumped into another one. They crashed together and Kimmy stepped forward to press the advantage.

"Retreat!" Tabitha called from behind.

"What?" Kimmy shouted. "We have them!"

"We don't," Tabitha replied. "It's taken everything just to wound them and who knows how many there are behind them. Art's injured and the rest of us will be soon too. Bast, can you get us out of here?"

Bast glanced at Kimmy before looking over at the blood seeping out of Art.

"Yeah, it should only take me a moment. Hold them off."

He ran past them down the tunnel.

"Charlie," Tabitha said pointing. "You go with him and get ready to fire down the right side of the tunnel. We'll run down the left, so you'll have a clear shot."

"Don't know how good these will be against those things, but I'll give it a crack." Charlie chased down the tunnel after Bast.

"Zack, you—"

"On it." Zack stepped forward and sent a thin stream of life into Art. Just enough to close the wound and get him on the move. Any more would have to wait.

"Get him out of here," Tabitha said. "Jackie, you go with them and get ready to plug the hole. Kimmy and I will try to slow them down."

Zack slipped his shoulders under Art's arm and half helped, half dragged his friend down the tunnel, Jackie at their side. Over Art's hisses and grunts, Zack heard Tabitha speaking with Kimmy.

"Ready to throw up a wall of fire for me to blow at them?"

"Fine." Kimmy's voice was tight.

The tunnel lit up behind him.

When they reached the others, Bast's gate was just wide enough for them to step through.

"Get him through, Zack," Jackie said. "I've got to stay."

"No!" Art said, but Zack nodded and dragged him through. Charlie sent Max through and Bast followed right behind.

Art dropped to the floor, clutching at his side. Zack knew there was torn muscle and chipped bone in there, but it wasn't life-threatening and he didn't know what state the others would be in when they made it through. Bast had already begun the work to close the gate when Charlie jumped through, followed by Tabitha.

"Where's Jackie?" Art shouted.

"She's coming," Tabitha said, sucking in air. "She's holding them back. You're ready to close it, yeah?"

Bast nodded, his face strained with concentration. Kimmy was next through. And then, finally, Jackie. Bast's hands flurried into action and the gate began to shrink.

"Wait!" Kimmy yelled with a look of shock on her face. "Don't close it yet."

"We can't leave it open, Kimmy," Tabitha said. "Shut it now, Bast."

"No!" Kimmy ran back to the gate and stuck her arm through it.

Tabitha grabbed her other arm and tried to pull her back. "What are you doing, Kimmy? Those things are in there."

The gate was already shrinking in size under Bast's direction. "Don't be stupid." Tabitha tugged with her full weight.

Kimmy's feet slid a few inches, but her hand stayed inside the gate up to the wrist. The gate was closing fast, now only the size of a dinner plate.

"Come… on…" Kimmy strained to reach out into the gate.

"I can't stop it!" Bast screamed, as it shrunk to the size of a saucer.

"Yes!" Kimmy relaxed against Tabitha's strain and fell to the ground with her as the gate slammed shut.

Kimmy held the magic dagger tight in her hand.

CHAPTER 21

MISALIGNMENT

'Are you out of your bloody mind?' Art pulled himself to his feet but still leant against the hotel room's built-in closet.

Zack kept his head down, and since nobody else seemed to be injured, he began to knit together the muscles and bone around Art's hip.

"What? I'm supposed to have left him in there?" Kimmy hauled herself up.

"You weren't supposed to have brought it at all," Art said, standing up straight.

"And since when do you get to tell me what I can and can't do?"

Tabitha stood up beside her. "You could have at least given us a heads up you were bringing that thing along."

"Oh, you're taking his side, are you? I didn't see you up there stopping a giant crab from snapping my face off."

"The tunnel was too tight," Tabitha said.

"We shouldn't have been attacking them at all," Charlie said. "I told you to wait."

"It was about to rip my face off. Wasn't it, Jackie?"

Jackie looked down at her feet.

"Well," Kimmy continued, "if Tab's great plan was supposed

to work, we needed to stay and force our way through them. You shouldn't have called us off them."

"We were barely making a dent and Art got hurt."

"Well, no offence," Bast interrupted, "but if Zack could get more healing magic flowing during the fights instead of after them, maybe we could stand our ground longer."

Zack felt that like a blow to the chest, but before he could respond, Art leapt in, bristling.

"Mate, between her possessed knife flying at my face and you crawling around on the ceiling, I had no idea what was going on. What were you doing up there?"

"You three were hogging the front line, I was trying to help," Bast replied.

"And you couldn't throw one of your spells from behind them?" Tabitha asked. "Trip those things up?"

"Yeah, Bast," Kimmy spat. "Don't you know you have to run all your plans past Tabitha?"

"Just having a plan at all would be nice, Kimmy," Tabitha replied. "As opposed to starting something and leaving it to somebody else to finish it."

"Well then, I'll save you the trouble. I'm finished with this." Kimmy stalked through the group, wrenched the door open and left. Bast shook his head and followed behind.

Tabitha doubled over, holding her face in her hands. "I can't keep doing this. I can't keep forcing this group together. I don't know, now that we've all finished high school, maybe this is it?"

A strangled squeal came from Jackie and she bolted from the room.

"Really, Tabitha?" Art scowled. "We've 'all' finished high school? Way to punch her in the guts."

Tabitha frowned with genuine concern.

"Oh god, I'm sorry, Art. I wasn't thinking of her when I said it."

"Yeah. Kinda the point, I think." Art shook his head and chased Jackie out the door.

Tabitha hammered the doorframe with her fist. "Dammit." She hurried after them.

Zack surveyed the room. Their weapons lay scattered on the patterned carpet where they had dropped them as they poured through Bast's gate. He grabbed one of the duffels and started loading it up. Charlie knelt down beside him and passed him Art's sword.

"Thanks for hanging back to help," he said, avoiding eye contact.

"Well actually, I'm hanging back because the guy who was supposed to help me smuggle out my she-wolf left."

"Ah." Zack zipped up the bag and hoisted it over his shoulder.

"But since you're here. About the other night…"

"No, it's okay." Zack moved to the door. "I'll distract the desk staff for you. Wait a couple of minutes and then make a break for it."

"Oh, okay."

He fled down the hallway before she could say any more.

Zack had taken his time replacing all the weapons back onto their racks and it was late afternoon by the time he stepped back onto the streets of Sydney. Summer was in full swing, but the city's wall of apartment blocks and office buildings cast deep shadows on the streets and brought them a premature dusk. He fished his headphones out of his pocket and was looking forward to a long bus ride in which to fade into his jumbled playlist. His phone buzzed in his hand; Charlie had sent a message to the group chat.

I'm being followed.

And then another.

I'm pretty sure it's that chick I stuck an arrow into in London. She's on the bus with me home from Sydney.

And another.

I don't know what to do.

Zack checked the time they were sent - one minute ago.

Kimmy replied before he could. *Damn. Bast and I are still in Brisbane. We're on our way.*

Zack tapped away. *Get off the bus as soon as you can so they can't follow you home.*

Art messaged as well. *Jackie and I are on a bus too. We're jumping off to come back.*

A long minute later, Charlie messaged again. *I'm off the bus. I'm going to hide in the alley behind this church.*

Which church? Art typed.

I don't know. It's Baptist. Near the cinemas.

I know the one. I'm coming. Zack wrote.

I've sent Max away. I'm going to try something crazy. I won't be able to message. Please find me.

Zack pulled up directions to the church. It was less than two kilometres away and the app said he could get there in 18 minutes by foot. He started running.

His phone kept buzzing in his hand, but he didn't stop to look at it, hoping it was just the others saying how far away they were. It didn't take long for his legs to tire, but he kept sucking in air and focused on getting to her. The phone, the pain, the shocked pedestrians scattering out of the way, they all faded as his mind bent toward the only thing that mattered in the moment. As had happened before when he lost himself in something important, he felt himself reaching out to Life. He pulled it in towards him, filling his lungs with it as much as oxygen. The heat in his chest and the strain in his legs faded and he ran on. He ducked between cars, jumped over fences and on one occasion slid under a ladder before pulling himself up in front of the church. He checked his phone. He'd run it in less than six minutes.

Zack scanned the street looking for Charlie or the woman

she'd said was following her. His attention had been elsewhere during that fight, so he wasn't even sure he would recognise her if he saw her. Still, none of the passers-by seemed likely candidates and certainly nobody appeared to be actively searching.

He checked the group chat. Art and Jackie were on their way, but Bast and Kimmy were still rushing through Brisbane and Tabitha hadn't answered the group chat at all. He hoped she hadn't left the Tower yet, rather than any other worrying possibilities.

Charlie first. She had said the alleyway. He walked around the front of the church and saw the narrow gap between it and the next building. It was not particularly deep and he couldn't see anybody at first glance.

"Charlie? Are you there?" he whispered.

A fluffy cat leapt down from a window ledge to a dumpster and meowed at him.

"Sorry, kitty. I was looking for my..." He realised the cat was looking at him a little more intently than a random cat should. "Charlie? Are you looking through its eyes?"

The cat waved its head side to side.

Zack looked more closely at it and noticed the colour of its fur - a familiar shade of honey. His eyes widened in surprise. "Charlie?"

The cat meowed in response.

"And you can understand me?" he asked.

Meow.

"Yeah, okay, that doesn't help. One for yes, two for no. Are you okay?"

Meow.

"Is that woman still around?"

Meow-meow.

"Okay. Art and Jackie are on their way. Ready to change back and we can go meet them?"

Meow-meow.

"Um, okay. I guess we'll stay here and wait for them."

Meow.

Zack leant against the dumpster looking out on the street before taking his phone out and messaging the group.

I've found Charlie. She's safe. Art and Jackie, come find us and we'll head home together. I think we need to be careful going home from now on, make sure we aren't being followed.

Bast replied. *Thanks, mate. We're on our way back and we'll take a few different buses to be sure. Let us know if you need us.*

Zack idly scratched Cat-Charlie's head as he kept watch on the street. When he realised what he was doing he snatched his hand back and his mouth went dry at the thought of facing her when she changed back. But then he felt a tiny paw on his arm and glanced over to see the cat tilting the top of her head towards him.

"Yeah, alright then," he said and returned to scratching between her ears.

Several minutes later, Art and Jackie came jogging into the alley.

"You okay, Zack?" Art asked, scanning around. "Where is she?"

Zack indicated the cat with a tilt of his head.

Jackie's eyes lit up to twice their normal size. "She's a kitty?"

"Sure is," Zack said, turning back to Cat-Charlie. "Ready to change back yet?"

With a single meow, she dropped off the dumpster and padded towards the back of the alley to where a tall brick wall blocked them off from the buildings behind. The cat closed her eyes and, after a moment, deep rust light blurred her shape and when the light faded, Charlie lay on the asphalt. But something wasn't right.

Charlie gasped with pain. "It hurts!"

Zack had barely reached out with his Life before he could see what was wrong. Everything. Externally, Charlie seemed fine, but inside her organs, bones, nerves, everything was misplaced, unaligned or even misshapen.

"Oh hell, Charlie."

"What's going on?" Art asked.

Zack didn't take his eyes off her. "She hasn't turned herself back properly."

Charlie reached out for him, but her arm only twitched. When she spoke, the words seemed forced from disobedient lips. "I've never done this before. Only… ah… only talked about it. Theory."

"Can you change her back?" Jackie asked.

"No," Zack replied. "She's not injured, I can't… No. Charlie, you need to fix this, you're the only one who can."

She groaned. "I can't even think straight. The pain."

"Maybe I can help with that. But I'm not going to be able to do much more." Zack summoned Life from all around him and wove it into dozens of thin threads. Every organ, every muscle, every cluster of nerves or arteries. Wherever Charlie's body suffered as a result of a jumbled shape, Zack directed the flows of Life to ease it. Her body relaxed, her breathing slowed, and her voice steadied.

"Thank you, Zack."

He nodded, already feeling the strain. This magic was both complex and involved a lot of Life in a constant stream. The damage was still there and he could only ease the trauma from it.

"Okay, Charlie," Art said. "You heard the man, your turn."

She closed her eyes and concentrated. But after a moment she opened them again, fear in her eyes. "I can't. I've spent hundreds of hours studying every kind of animal you can think of. Except this one. I don't have a sense of what a human body should be. I thought separating the clothes back out would be the hard part, not changing myself back!" She started to cry.

"No, no." Art paced. "It's okay. Maybe we can just get you back to the Tower."

Zack shook his head. "I can't keep this up for much longer, and she won't make it long after that."

"Damn." Art rubbed his chin in thought. "Okay. That's fine. You might not know the human body, but this guy does. I'll just do what I did for our exams, I'll push that knowledge into you. You might end up with a lot of comic book knowledge as well, but—"

"No," Zack pushed out the words, trying to maintain focus. "I don't know enough about the human body to shape it in three dimensions."

"What?" Art asked. "Then how do you heal it and regrow bones and muscles?"

"I don't do any of that," Zack said. "Life does."

"Oh," Art said. Then his eyes lit up. "Oh! Okay. So, I have an idea. And it's either a great one or a—"

"Do it, Art. Please," Charlie cried.

"Right." He turned to Jackie. "The three of us are going to be out of commission. You got our back?"

Jackie's lips tightened. "Nothing gets past me." She turned and faced towards the street.

"Alrighty then," Art said. "Look, I don't know how to explain what I'm about to do, but just roll with it, yeah?"

Zack nodded, steadying his breathing against the effort of holding all the strands of Life in place.

Art knelt down beside him and began to incant, but straight away something was different. The words and rhythm of the incantation, murmured though they were, sounded strange in Zack's ear.

He looked across at Art. "Are you singing Poker Face?"

"Shhh," Art replied.

He placed his hand on Zack's forehead and the world fell away. The graffitied walls of the alley, the dumpster, the hard asphalt floor, even Jackie faded from view as if dark purple clouds of smoke had rolled in, and all that was left was Zack, Art, and Charlie. No, that was not all. Zack could see the turquoise ribbons of light that were his Life weaves, reaching out from him to the multitude of targets in Charlie's body. He was so shocked he lost his hold on the magic and the lines strayed for a moment, and Charlie gasped in pain before he pulled them back in line.

"Sorry!" he said, and noticed his voice had a strange distant quality to it, like it was echoing from the depth of a tunnel. "A little warning would have been nice, Art."

"Look, this is new to me too, right? But it's working. Is that what your magic looks like?"

"You can see it?" Zack said.

"Yeah. Well, that's the idea. Charlie can see it too. And you can see hers." Art pointed past Zack's weaves. Underneath, a deep rust coloured light was pooling throughout her body.

Zack understood what Art meant.

"Okay, Charlie, we can do this. You're going to use your magic to reshape your body."

"I'm trying, Zack, but I don't know where it needs to go." Despair was thick in her voice.

"I know, Charlie and I don't either. But Life does. Reach out with Animal and follow the Life. We'll start from the top and we can work our way down from there. Okay?"

"Yeah. Yeah, okay."

"Um, I'd hurry if I could, guys," Art said. "No idea how long I can hold this for. I've already got a blindingly painful headache."

Zack pushed through the strain of maintaining his existing network of Life and reached out with another single strand. He guided it towards Charlie's brain and began to investigate it. The brain itself was in relatively good shape, but the blood vessels and the nerves connecting it to the eyes and spine were a mess. Life was undeterred, it flowed on, mapping out how it should be.

A thick column of Animal poured in behind it. In the dark of wherever Art had taken them, it shone like smokey-topaz and all but extinguished the string of turquoise that had guided its path. As it flowed, the structures in Charlie's head reshaped to their proper form.

She sighed in relief. "I can feel it working."

Under Zack's direction, Life flowed on down her body, throat and collar bone, then lungs, heart, and ribs. The wave of Charlie's Animal magic came behind, following the turquoise blueprint that Life left in its wake. The more Charlie reformed, the fewer other strands Zack needed to hold in place, and he gladly let them fall, easing the strain of his own workings. But he couldn't pause to appreciate it.

"Get a move on. I'm losing grip of this thing." Art's rasps bounced and echoed off the now swirling black clouds.

"Charlie, I'm going to go faster. Are you ready?" Zack asked.

"Floor it," she answered.

Zack's guiding strand of Life sped through her body, and Animal was no longer merely following behind. They bounded along together, like a farm dog racing beside a horse, or perhaps more like a dolphin and whale, twisting around each other under the water before rising together to crest the waves. Where they moved, Charlie used Animal to remake her body and now there were only her limbs to go.

The dark clouds wavered, as if being blown away and Art groaned through his teeth.

"We're almost there," Zack said, forcing Life onward faster and faster. One leg, then the other; nerves corrected, arteries and veins lengthened, bones and muscles reshaped.

Zack felt himself fading away from the clouds, but he pushed on, Charlie urging her magic to follow. Left arm, then the right. He could barely see the strands anymore but, just as daylight poured in and the blaring sound of Sydney traffic returned, they finished.

CHAPTER 22

INSIGHT

The three of them lay breathless on the hard alley ground, squinting against the harshness of the sun, despite the shade.

"Um, are you all okay?" Jackie asked, still with her face to the street.

Art clambered to his feet. "Yeah, I think so." He rubbed his temples. "Wowzer, that hurts though."

Zack eased himself up onto his elbows and leant towards Charlie. He didn't have much left in the tank, but it was enough to confirm they'd got the job done.

"Well done, Charlie. Everything back in its place."

Charlie sat up; her eyes glossy with tears.

"Thank you so much, both of you. And you, Jackie, for watching over us." She rubbed her eyes dry. "Oh wow. I am not doing that again any time soon."

"You were a very cute kitty, though." Jackie looked over her shoulder with a smile.

Zack climbed to his feet and helped Charlie up. She stepped in close to him.

"I mean it, Zack. Thank you so much. And about the other night, I'm—"

Zack squeezed her arm. "It's okay, it's what I'm here for. But we need to get you home safe. I kept everything running as best I could, but your immune system wasn't on my priority list and would have been weakened. You need to get some rest and let it fight off whatever germs you almost certainly picked up."

Charlie's brow furrowed. "Okay."

"What happened with the woman who was following you?" Art asked.

"I knew I had to hide," Charlie said. "Max and I can't really stand toe to toe with somebody who can hurl boulders. I sent Max away to keep her safe and I turned myself into a cat. Sadie has been teaching me the basic theory behind shape changing. It was stupid to try it, but I was desperate. I'd only just changed and climbed up onto the window ledge when she came jogging around the corner. She searched the whole alley before she left and headed back down the street. And she was pissed. She called somebody as she was leaving and I could hear her screaming at them."

Charlie stumbled and braced herself against the wall.

"We need to get you home," Zack said. "Jackie, if we get you two a taxi, can you go with her?"

"Yeah." Jackie turned around. "But what about you two?"

"We'll make sure you aren't being followed, and then let the others know what happened," Zack replied. "You got enough juice left for that, Art?"

"Yeah, probably. Hostility is a pretty loud emotion."

"Okay, that sounds like a good idea," Charlie said. "I feel like I need to sleep for a week."

Art flagged down a taxi and opened the door for them. He handed Jackie some cash and spoke softly to her. "Pay extra and take a long way home. Reckon you'd feel it if anybody was following you?"

Jackie took the money and nodded. "If they mean us harm, definitely. If they don't, then still, maybe."

Zack realised he'd missed something. "What about Max?"

"She'll find me at home," Charlie said with confidence. "She knows I'm safe now through our bond, just like I know she's safe and brimming with attitude for sending her away while I was in danger. I'm going to be hearing about it for weeks."

The girls climbed into the back of the taxi and pulled the door closed. Zack and Art waved to them as it drove away.

"Anybody nearby following them? Or us for that matter?" Zack asked.

Art released a soft sigh. He closed his eyes and rubbed at his temples while he concentrated. "Nah, we're clear. A bunch of road rage and people angry at their bosses, but nothing coming in at us or heading after the girls."

Zack's tension faded and he pulled out his phone. "That's a relief. I'll message the others."

The chat had dozens of new messages in it. Most from Tabitha, who indeed had only now left the Tower. Charlie had just responded to her.

I'm ok now. Thanks to Zack, Art and Jackie. Heading home safe. No sign of anybody following us.

Tabitha responded. *Thank heavens. What happened????*

Charlie wrote back. *Sorry. Too tired. I'll talk soon.*

That didn't seem to satisfy Tabitha. *WHAT???*

Zack started tapping away, filling in what he hoped was sufficient detail to satisfy her.

Tabitha replied. *Okay. I'm so sorry I wasn't there to help.*

Art had been reading along on his own phone. *Everything worked out. I guess we just need to be careful about being followed from now on. You know, unless you can wipe someone's memories.*

Kimmy's response came in fast. *It's also hard to follow somebody when your face is on fire.*

The chat filled with a series of wide-eyed emojis from the rest of the group.

The boys slipped their phones away.

"Ready to head home?" Zack asked.

"Not really," Art answered. "Kind of feel like a beer or five."

Zack thought about it. "Yeah, that sounds good. But can we drink a little closer to home? So, it's not as far to go after?"

Art smiled. "That's a plan I can get behind."

Art sat down and slid a replacement beer across the table to Zack, who couldn't help but glance nervously at the staff behind the bar before claiming it. Art saw the look and pulled a face somewhere between disappointment and disgust.

"C'mon man," Zack said in defence, "we're both underage and this place is way too close to school."

Art shook his head. "It's like you go out of your way to insult me."

"Oh, no." Zack's tone was dry. "Beware the wrath of the great psychomancer."

"Damn right, beware." Art took a long draught from his glass. "Man, beer really hits the spot after heavy magic use. Or is that just me?"

"Nope. It's not just you. Alcohol excites the neuro inhibitors in the brain, which helps reduce the stress from magic use."

Art squinted at him through the side of his eyes. "How much of that is true?"

Zack only smiled in reply.

"Stay away from the brain, Lifer. The mind is my stomping ground."

"It's all cells, man," Zack replied. "I could reach out and sober you up right now."

"Don't you dare."

Zack held up his hands. "I won't. As long as you tell me more about that magic you did earlier."

"Yeah, cool, wasn't it? I definitely need to keep working on it, but I think I've got something there."

"What's it supposed to do?"

"Mostly what it did, I reckon. More stable though."

"No, I mean like, when your mentor does it."

"Oh," Art said. "No, that was an Art original."

Zack choked on air. "You invented a spell?"

"Um, yeah. I got the idea a while ago and hinted around it with Timur during our lessons but got no bites. So, I let it rest and focused on what he wanted to teach me. It kept lingering in the back of my head, though, so I started to play around with it. Seems like I was on to something though."

"And the Lady Gaga?"

Art rubbed the side of his neck. "Um yeah, well I was going to make up some kind of incantation, but Charlie's thing kind of put me on the spot so I grabbed at something that would hold my thoughts in one place."

"It's impressive."

"Thanks. I guess I was really curious about how we couldn't see the way each other used our magic. Like, there's that turquoise flare that lights up your hand when you're about to heal one of us, but it's nothing like the purple streams of light I can see when I'm casting a spell. But then I thought, maybe if I brought you into my head, you could see those streams and vice versa." Art set down his glass. "Now, you answer me. What's the deal with you and Charlie? She wanted to talk to you, but you made up some rubbish about immune systems and pushed her into a taxi."

Zack sat up straight on his stool. "Infections can be serious."

'Yep,' Art said, undeterred, "'and if you thought it was an actual risk you would have dragged her back to the Tower, not sent her home."

Zack shrank back down and attempted to hide behind his beer. "Yep."

"So, what is it?"

Zack took a deep breath and then told Art about the night at the party.

Art's eyes widened. "That was like a month ago! Why didn't you tell me?"

"I don't know," Zack shrugged. "You had your own crap to deal with from that night. And it's pretty embarrassing. The girl of my dreams kisses me and I still managed to screw it up."

"Okay then." Art slid his beer to the side and leant in. "What's next then? She still seems to want to talk to you."

Zack shook his head. "Nope, not yet. I need to work out how I can prove to her that I actually like her."

"Which you couldn't do when she was literally throwing herself at you."

"I wasn't expecting it, you know?" Zack stared down into his beer. "And I got stuck in my own head and everything I said came out wrong."

"But you still can't do it after weeks of thinking about it."

"I don't know. I've planned out the next conversation a thousand times and every time, imaginary Charlie pulls apart my arguments."

"Uh huh." Art took another long pull from his beer.

"What?"

Art rested his empty glass on the table. "Mate, are you sure she's the one you need to prove it to?"

Zack stared back at him in confusion and Art shook his head in disbelief.

"Seriously, you're the smartest guy I know, and you're telling me that in the past, what, five weeks, you haven't been able to think of a single reason that you want this girl?"

"It's not as simple as that."

"It should be," Art replied. "I mean, be honest with yourself for a second. I know how long you've been keen on her, but Tower aside, do you even have anything in common?"

Zack's mind whirled, along with a rush of frustration that Art seemed to be taking Charlie's side in this. "Since when do you care about that? Do you have anything in common with the girls you hit on?"

"Yep, the one thing I need. We both want the other one to touch the fun parts of our bodies." Art smirked at his own humour. "But I'm not looking for a relationship with them. Come on, finish your beer and let's get moving."

Zack pushed away the sullen feeling that had crept up on him and drained his glass before the two of them shuffled outside. It wasn't even 10 yet and the night air was still warm from the heat of the day. They walked in the direction of Art's car.

"I'm sorry, mate," Art said. "She's right."

Zack's only reply was a long exhale.

"So, whatcha gonna do about it?"

"I don't know," Zack said. "I need to have a think."

Art laughed. "Or maybe don't? I'm not sure that's worked out for you so far. Might be better to think less and just talk to her."

Zack's stomach lurched at the thought. "Sounds scary."

"Scary? I've seen you take on three statues at a time, let alone going toe to toe with the Hulk and Groot in New York. And you're scared of a cute blonde?"

"Groot? That's good, I was going with 'Poison Ivan'."

"Poison Ivan? Damn. No, that's better. But seriously, you've got nothing to be scared of here. I think part of the issue here is that you think she's better than you. She's not. Don't get me wrong, Charlie's great. But you're a badass."

Art's words triggered a memory in Zack's mind and he groaned.

"What?" Art asked.

Zack frowned. "I've got an idea for something to help bring us all back together."

"And I'm not going to like it?"

"Worse," Zack replied, "you're going to love it."

CHAPTER 23

REALIGNMENT

Zack leant against the edge of the slide at Tatters Park, waiting as the others arrived and claimed their own makeshift seats on the equipment.

"Where's Jackie?" Bast asked, his feet dangling from a swing.

"At school," Zack answered.

"Oh, yeah," Bast said. "I keep forgetting."

"That's item two on the agenda," Art said from the climbing frame.

"Oh, so you two have this whole little meeting planned out, do you?" Kimmy hadn't claimed a seat and stood with her arms crossed.

"Yep." Zack stood up and stepped away from the slide. "We need to get our crap together."

Kimmy scoffed and Tabitha rolled her eyes. "Easier said than done, Zack. Especially after yesterday."

"Yesterday is what I'm talking about," Zack replied. "It was one thing for us to screw this up and even fall apart as a team when this was just about helping the Tower or impressing Junie. But it's not about that anymore. They are coming for us, after—"

"We killed their friends," Bast finished.

"You didn't kill anybody," Charlie said, stroking Max's muzzle. "Kimmy, Art and I did."

"Does that make a difference?" Tabitha asked.

Kimmy opened her mouth to speak but Zack interrupted. "I think it does, Tabs. I can't know what it feels like to do what you three did. You did it after that guy nearly killed Max, and Art and Kimmy did it to protect the rest of us, and all I can do is thank you for that, but I can't pretend to know what it is like."

Charlie and Art stared down at their feet while Kimmy looked slightly mollified.

Zack continued, "But Tabitha is right in that I don't think it matters to them. And I think there's another thing that won't matter to them that might be worse."

"What's that?" Kimmy asked.

"The Silence," Tabitha answered.

Zack nodded. "So, we need each other. This isn't about proving ourselves in the Tower, this is about our families. We need to find them before they find out where we live."

"Well, if we're going to get through those crab things, you all need to step up," Kimmy said.

"No," Charlie said, "we didn't need to fight them. You didn't let me explain yesterday. They've been taught to let people through who know the command."

"So? We didn't know it," Kimmy replied.

"I would have, if I was just given five more seconds."

"Kimmy," Tabitha said, "you've always been brave and tough and you amaze me sometimes. But lately, you've been looking for fights and you've been reckless once we get in them. I don't know where that has come from, but it's there."

"It's been happening since Zack made her set herself on fire," Bast said. "I'm sorry, but it's true. How could somebody be the same after that? It's honestly terrifying to get into fights knowing that getting healed could be more traumatic than getting hurt in the first place."

"Whoa!" Art stood up. "That's not fair. We've all got limitations to our magic. Zack is no different from the danger we're in when it takes you as long as it does to open gates, or the fact that I can't put thoughts into people's minds yet."

"Or so you say," Kimmy said. "We don't actually know what you can do or have done to any of us."

"This isn't working," Tabitha said to herself.

"Stop it," Charlie shouted at them. "If it wasn't for Art, I'd be dead in an alley from organ failure."

"Nobody is saying that all of his magic is bad," Kimmy said.

"No, but it's at the end of that train of thought," Charlie said. "Art can do bad stuff with his magic, so we can't trust him. We can't trust him so we can't keep him with us. We can't keep him with us so he's not there to help us. Well, we need him. So, we trust him. And Bast, same for Zack. Again, organ failure death without him. He held my entire body together with his magic while he showed me how to rebuild it. And Tabitha?"

"What?" Tabitha looked up at her.

Charlie walked over and put her hand on her shoulder. "Get your shit together. If we're going to get this done, we need you leading us."

"Why me?"

Art laughed. "You're the only one who ever has, Tabs. If the five of us agree to play nice and to listen to you, you'll stop freaking out and step up, yeah?"

Tabitha nodded.

"Well, I'm in," Art said.

"Me too," Zack added.

And me," Charlie said.

Bast looked at the three of them. "Yep, me as well."

Kimmy chewed on her lip, eyeing Art. She threw her hands down. "Fine, me too."

Tabitha stood up. "Alright, I'll lead. For as long as we agree that I should. But that means that you follow my calls, right?"

"Absolutely," Bast replied and the others nodded.

Tabitha locked eyes with Kimmy. "Right?"

"Yes, agreed. Okay," Kimmy replied.

Tabitha nodded. "Okay, I lead. Assuming Jackie is okay with that too."

"Well, that's the other thing," Zack said.

"What?" Tabitha asked.

"Jackie's having a rough time," Art answered. "She's feeling left behind and left out. She's worried about us falling apart, but even without that, she doesn't feel quite a part of us, not an equal part. I can feel the loneliness radiating off her."

"But she's not alone, she's one of us, like anybody else?"

"Is she, though?" Charlie asked. The others looked at her and she held up her hands. "Don't get me wrong, I feel the same way as Bast, but we don't treat her that way. We've finished school and she hasn't, we have parties and go out and we don't bring her along. We treat her as an equal when it suits us and forget about it the rest of the time."

Tabitha nodded. "We need to do better."

"About that," Zack said. "Art and I have a plan."

The burr of the electronic bell rang in the end of the school year, echoing around the playgrounds and students poured out of the buildings. The beginning of the summer holidays arced like electricity between the children as they jostled through the gates towards waiting buses or parents, or to make their own path home. Zack and the others stood just outside the gates, looking for Jackie.

Five, then 10 minutes passed and the waves of students were replaced by the stragglers before Jackie appeared. Her head down, she shuffled through the courtyard towards the exit. She was only 10 or so metres away but hadn't seen them yet and Zack almost called out when he noticed she was about to walk past a cluster of students sitting on picnic tables. And of course, there in the centre, was Britney.

"Have a good Christmas, loser," she called out to Jackie. "Hope the soup kitchen has the nice gravy this year."

Jackie flinched at the chorus of cruel laughter that followed but, when her eyes lifted from the ground, she saw Art and the others. Her lips tightened and her shoulders broadened. She stepped back towards Britney's gaggle.

"Clare, I think I've had enough of the way you talk to me and treat me. It ends, now."

Zack shook his head. Clare just sounded wrong. Even if that was her actual name, she'd remain Britney in his mind, and Britney seemed surprised by Jackie's reaction. She looked around at her friends before her face twisted into a sneer at Jackie.

"Well, then move schools, or kill yourself, because you get the treatment I decide you deserve."

Art surged forward, but Kimmy put her hand on his shoulder and whispered, "Wait."

"I'm sorry, Clare." Jackie spoke with calm.

"Yeah, you are sorry. And pathetic," Britney snapped back.

"No. I'm sorry that you're a sad, empty little girl. I'm sorry you are so terrified inside that if you don't stay the little queen of the playground, keeping all your so-called friends in line with fear, you'll be all alone. And I'm sorry that you're right to be terrified of that, and you would be alone. And," Jackie paused, looking straight into her eyes, "I'm sorry that I took your crap for so long."

Britney's eyes widened and, as she looked back and forth between the other students, she saw Zack and the others by the gates.

"Oh, your brother has come to pick up his little baby sister from school. Is that why you're feeling so brave?"

"No, my friends have come to pick me up from school. Because they care about me and they want to see me. Look around. Would anybody here go out of their way to see you, or are they all just scared of being your next victim? Have the Christmas you deserve, Clare."

Britney spluttered as Jackie turned and walked to the gate with a giant grin on her face.

"I would have punched her," Kimmy murmured, "but that wasn't bad either."

Britney leapt forward, her face a bright livid red and snatched a basketball from one of the boys at the edge of her cluster. With a violent one-armed throw, she launched the ball at the back of Jackie's head. Zack tried to call out a warning, but it was happening too fast and the words tumbled around in his mouth.

Jackie spoke a single word and a brief flare of grey light flickered in the palm of her right hand. Still walking towards the gate, her arm snapped back and, with a closed fist, she knocked the ball away. Except that the ball didn't bounce away. Instead, it ricocheted off Jackie's hand, flew directly back at Britney and struck her in the face.

Jackie still didn't turn around and headed right up to the others by the gate. Behind her, Britney had fallen into a sprawled sit, blood streaming from what Zack diagnosed as a well-deserved broken nose. Nobody moved to help her.

"That is the best thing I've ever seen in my life," Kimmy said.

Jackie smiled. "Part of me feels bad. But it's a really small part and the rest feels amazing. Can we go now?"

"Oh no, not yet," Art said.

"Why not?" Jackie asked.

"Because a cake like this demands icing." Art waved a signal down the street.

Jackie looked in that direction. "Are you kidding me?"

Art winked as a stretched limousine pulled up in front of the school. He held the door open for Jackie who climbed in, followed by the others. Zack's last view as the car drove off was of Britney's face, bloodstained and stunned.

⟫———————————⟪

"This was an excellent idea," Art said. "I'm glad I thought of it."

Zack looked around the tattoo parlour where the other five were laying down on benches or sitting in chairs getting inked. Jackie, Bast and Tabitha were nearly finished, while Charlie and Kimmy had taken longer with their artists designing their tattoos and still had a while to go.

"Um, it was my idea," Zack said, "to seal the whole 'exclusive club' vibe."

"Well, last night it was. But I think you'll find I was the one who came up with all this months ago." Art pulled open his shirt and looked in the mirror, staring at the all-seeing-eye on his chest. "Man, I am in love with this."

"It looks really good," Zack said.

"Well, show me yours again."

Zack undid the buttons on his own shirt, revealing his tattoo, an intricate design of angles and triangles.

Art nodded in appreciation. "I've never seen that before. What is it?"

"It's Živa, the Slavic symbol for 'She who Lives'." Zack rebuttoned his shirt.

Jackie joined them, followed by her artist.

"All done." Jackie beamed.

"I'm so sorry, ma'am," the artist said. "I've never, ever had that many needles break on me. It must have been a bad batch."

"It's okay," Jackie replied, looking sheepish. "I guess I have tougher skin than most. It looks great though, thank you."

The artist smiled and headed back to her table to clean up.

"Ma'am?" Zack asked.

"They kind of see us as a lot older than we are," Art said.

"I thought you said you couldn't implant thoughts." Zack narrowed his eyes.

"And I can't. This is different and complicated. They all currently have a blindspot for ages. Something that Timur taught me early on. I've needed it sometimes when being a kid gets in the way." He turned to Jackie and rolled his eyes. "Let's see it."

She blushed, but rolled down the waistband of her jeans, revealing a small shield shape at the front of her hip, covered in plastic wrap.

"You are going to be begging me to use Mind magic on our folks if either of them catch you with that."

Jackie shook her head. "No. But I am worried about that. I figured I'd be able to just keep it covered up in that spot, but apparently, I need to keep it uncovered as much as possible to heal."

Zack waved his hand over the area and fed in a thin stream of Life. "Good to go."

"Thank you." Jackie peered around behind her. "Should I keep the wrap on, to pretend?"

"That depends." Zack turned to Art. "You're wiping memories before we leave, right?"

"Yep, and I'll get them to wipe the security cameras. Full 'Men In Black' protocol."

Jackie clapped excitedly and peeled off the plastic.

"Oh, I love this! Thank you so much for letting me do this."

Art hugged her in a tight embrace. "I didn't let you do anything. You're one of us."

Jackie hugged back, muting a sniffle against her brother's shirt. Zack looked away and noticed Bast strutting toward them, his shirt still off. His own artist had stayed behind to clean up, and when he reached them, Bast spun dramatically to show off his tattoo.

A palm sized alchemical Mercury symbol had been tattooed over his right shoulder blade.

"That looks awesome, man." Zack waved his hand over it. "And it should be easier to hide now."

"Thanks," Bast said, "but my dad and half my brothers are already inked, plus it's not like I'm underage like you two. I didn't really need the special access to this, but I love that we're doing it together. And not having to worry about peeling, that's sweet."

Tabitha joined them. "Speak for yourself, Bast. Eighteen or not, I would much rather my parents not know about this. They gave Victor such a hard time about his septum piercing. So, if you would be so kind, Zack?"

"Of course," he replied, waving his hand over the stylised whirlwind covering half of her left shoulder. "It looks great, by the way."

"Thanks." Tabitha turned around and rolled the back of her t-shirt down. "This was the best idea, boys."

It was another half an hour before Kimmy strutted towards them, topless except for a bra and a look of daring defiance on her face. Tabitha shook her head before burying her own face in her hands. The outline of flames wound from her right shoulder blade halfway up her neck.

"What? I said what I was getting."

"Kimmy, what is your mum going to say?" Tabitha asked, her head still shaking.

"I know what she'll say. Doesn't matter, I've decided I'm moving out as soon as I can anyway. Thanks, Zack," Kimmy said as he healed her tattooed skin.

"I want in on that!" Charlie said, joining the rest of them. "What do you say, Tabitha? We're easily pulling in enough for a nice three-bedroom place."

"Four bedrooms," Tabitha answered. "Jackie gets her own room for whenever she's allowed to crash. And in the meantime, she can keep her Tower gear there."

Jackie's eyes glistened under the fluorescent lights. "You mean it?"

"Definitely," Charlie said. "You're fifteen next year. We'll come around and pick you up more from your place, let your parents get to know us a bit better. Hopefully, they'll get a good impression of us and you can stay over a lot."

"Sounds like a plan," Kimmy said.

"Well, maybe just Charlie and me, Miss Neck-Tat."

Kimmy rolled her eyes and was about to retort when the three of them were tackled into a hug by Jackie. Zack turned his head to blink away some tears and caught Art doing the same.

Art cleared his throat. "Alright, break it up. Out to the limo, we've got one more stop tonight, but first I have to pay up and tidy up in here."

"One more stop?" Jackie asked, disentangling herself.

"Frozen custard," Art replied.

"With mix-ins?"

"With mix-ins."

"Best. Night. Ever!" Jackie ran outside to the waiting limousine.

CHAPTER 24

BACK ON THE SCENT

Zack sat next to Art on the desk in the Brisbane hotel room, watching Bast work his gate magic. He looked over at where Jackie held her spear, ready for the unexpected. She seemed taller. For Jackie, at least.

"She was pumped up all weekend," Art whispered. "Honestly, I almost pity the other girls when she goes back to school next year. Almost. Then I remember how they treated her for the last few years and I want to show up and take pictures."

"I don't reckon she'll go out of her way to be harsh to them," Zack said.

"Shame. Anyway, you got out of doing your family dinner today?"

Zack nodded. "It's become a bit less of a set thing since my grandmother has been so unwell. I went and visited her yesterday, though."

"How's she doing?"

Zack shook his head. "Not good. Doctors are surprised she's made it this far. I'm doing what I can, but it's not enough. I'm spending every spare second Sara has, trying to learn more, but you know how strict she is with making sure I'm ready before moving on to the next thing. I'm just not learning enough, fast enough."

Art looked confused. "But I've seen you close massive wounds and you basically brought Max back from the dead."

"No," Zack said. "Cancer is a totally different thing. It's kind of part of her, her own cells doing the wrong thing. It has its own Life."

"Can't you just suck the Life out of it, then?"

Zack's eyes widened. "That's a big no-no. Life is different from all the other magic. When it's in something, it belongs to that thing and it can only be given willingly. If you use magic to force it out, it resists and then it changes."

"Into what?" Art said, leaning in.

"Something else. Something bad." Zack shrugged. "I've never done it. Sara's never been as strict on anything as that. And the more I get to know Life, the more true it feels."

The grey light from Bast's gate radiated through the room and the other two boys hopped down off the desk and gathered with the other five. Charlie and Max approached the gate.

"Okay, the two of us go in first this time. At least, until we get past those crab creatures."

"Crustacanoids," Art offered.

She ignored him and stepped through the gate. The others followed, Bast entering last and closing the gate behind him.

Once again in the dark, smooth cave, Kimmy ignited her axe into flame and held it aloft like a torch. The group made their way along the tunnel, following their previous path and, before too long, they heard the familiar skittering approach from up ahead. Weapons shifted in hands and Charlie shot a stern look back at the group.

"Don't provoke them. I've got this." She sounded confident, but Max's ears and tail were low and flat.

The sounds increased and then the looming figures of several crustacanoids emerged from the shadows. As they had before, they moved no closer and instead stood in place, clicking their claws together. Charlie took a deep breath and cupped her hands over her mouth, producing a warbling-whistling sound. The strange noise bounced around the smooth tunnel walls and the creatures clicked their claws twice more before scurrying away, disappearing into holes and crevices in the cave walls.

"Wait. That's it?" Kimmy stepped up beside Charlie.

"Yes. That's it," Charlie replied.

"Well, how was I supposed to know?"

"You weren't," Tabitha answered. "That's the point. But somebody else did. Now that we're past them, you and Bast take the lead."

Kimmy grumbled. "Yeah, fine."

Charlie slipped to the back of the group, next to Zack and, as the others moved forwards, she slid in closer to him.

"You've been avoiding me."

"No, I ha…," his voice trailed off as she stared through him, her blue eyes shimmering in the flickering light of Kimmy's flaming axe. "Yeah, I have."

"That's okay," she said. "I'm sorry for what I said at the party. Or at least for the way I said it. I didn't mean it to come out like that."

Zack scuffed his feet across the rocky ground.

"It's alright. I've thought a lot about what you said, along with a couple of hundred more answers to why I… why you're special. But I've also realised that I think you're right."

"I know I'm right." Charlie smiled at him. "I've seen the way you look at me, like I'm some ideal girl. But that's not me, Zack."

He nodded. "It's not. You're more than that."

Charlie's eyes widened in a mixture of confusion and worry. He held up his free hand.

"No, I'm not saying… I just mean that you do deserve more than being treated as a stand-in for some fantasy in my head. I'm sorry."

"I think that's why I got angry," Charlie said. "I ignored my judgement and decided to kiss the cute boy, anyway. And I was angry that I might have… or we might have screwed up a really good friendship."

"That's what I've been worried about too."

Charlie smirked. "And you thought that never talking to me again was going to help with that?"

"When I talk, I tend to screw things up," Zack said.

"No. When you try to say the 'right thing,' you screw up." Charlie wiggled her fingers in air-quotes. "So, when you work out what kind of girl you're looking for, rather than one you think you should be looking for, just talk to her. Okay?"

"Deal."

Charlie reached out and squeezed his hand. "Good talk."

"Great talk," Kimmy called out from the front. "A bit hard to follow with all the echoing off the walls, but overall, very sweet. If you're done, though, we've hit a dead end."

Tabitha covered her face with her hand. "Seriously, Kimmy? You can be such a cow. Anyway, should we look around for a clue or double back?"

"Neither," Bast answered. "This is the right place. I can feel gate energy. Traces of it, at least. Give me a second to test the jars and I'll work out how to open it."

While Bast dropped to his knees and sorted through his backpack, the others relaxed against the stone walls. Art looked across at where Zack was standing next to Charlie and shot him a combination of shrug and thumbs up. Zack smiled in reply. He wasn't quite sure what he had been hoping for between him and Charlie since the party, but this felt good. Bast had pulled one of the mason jars from his bag when Max sniffed her way to one of the corners at the end of the tunnel and pawed with obvious intent.

"What have you found, Maxie?" Charlie asked stepping past Bast to stand beside her.

She reached down and picked up the end of a metre-high sack, stone-dust cascading off the heavy cloth as she held it up.

"Careful," Tabitha said.

"Anything in it?" Kimmy asked.

Charlie widened the opening of the sack, her body poised to jump back if she needed to. But instead, her face scrunched with confusion and she reached inside before dropping the sack to the ground and revealing a long coil of blue plastic rope.

"Rope?" Kimmy asked.

Charlie nodded. "Ah huh. And there's like half a dozen more bundles of it in there."

"Should we take some?" Tabitha asked.

"Definitely," Art replied. "This is what we fantasy experts refer to as a quest item. We take two."

Kimmy snorted. "Such a loser."

"I'm serious, though," Art said, reaching out to take the coil from Charlie. "This is nylon, or something, and that means it almost certainly came from our world. Which means it almost certainly was put here by these mages we're hunting. So, either it's in that sack because they need it to get from here to back down the tunnel, which doesn't seem to be true, or they need it for whatever happens on the other side of the gate Bast is opening. We take two."

Charlie nodded and drew a second one from the sack. A moment later, Bast's gate illuminated the tunnel.

"Time to find out," Tabitha said and stepped through.

"What the hell is this place?" Kimmy shrieked as they entered the second realm.

Her voice, while loud, did not seem to carry far or echo. Which was not the strangest aspect of their current experience.

They had exited Bast's gate and stepped down onto a bright green platform that was, perhaps, three metres wide and a dozen or so long. The platform seemed to be suspended in an off-white sky that extended in every direction, including down, for as far as Zack could see. Other objects also hung in the air. Almost touching the green platform, an orange zig-zag created a staircase upward for several metres, but only half as wide as the platform. Further away, a red circular disk floated perpendicular to the platform, along with dozens of other coloured shapes that were either much further away or far smaller.

Max whined in distress. Charlie comforted her with a scratch behind the ears.

"I know, girl. It's like Escher and Malevich had a weird and scary baby."

The others looked at her confused.

"Oh yeah, none of you took art as a subject," Charlie said. "Never mind, I just mean it's weird."

Bast laughed. "Thank heavens you took that subject; I wouldn't have understood this place was weird, otherwise."

Charlie stuck her tongue out at him but smiled around it.

"Why would they want to come here?" Kimmy asked. "In fact, why travel through the realms at all?"

"I think they are avoiding the wards," Jackie said.

"Sorry?" Tabitha leant in closer to hear Jackie's voice.

She cleared her throat and spoke up, "Junie said the Tower normally finds mages who do serious magic, right? That's how we found the two in the cabin. But they haven't found these ones. They didn't even know they existed. Maybe they are doing whatever they are doing in the actual realms."

Art nodded along. "I reckon you're right, Jacks."

"Fair enough," Kimmy said, "but what's the deal with this realm?"

"Well," Zack mused aloud, "using Jackie's theory, this realm is either another checkpoint in the path through to their base, like the last one, to try and prevent unwanted visitors. Or..."

"Or it is their base," Tabitha finished.

"How are we supposed to know which?" Bast asked.

Tabitha pointed to the top of the orange zig-zag. "How about you boys climb up there and see if the view is any better?"

Art shrugged and threw his coil of rope over his shoulder before stepping across to the base of the orange staircase. Bast was next and as Zack followed behind, he looked down at the gap between the two platforms. Even though they were only a few inches apart, the fact that both were simply floating in air made his stomach twitch. But it didn't seem to bother the other guys, so he swallowed hard and followed.

Before he was halfway up, Art had made the top.

"I don't know, Tabs," he shouted down, pointing away from the gate. "Maybe there's a few more platforms that way?"

Zack craned his neck around the side of the orange steps and looked in that direction.

And then the girls started screaming.

Zack spun around to see the green platform floating away. No, not just away, tilting upwards as it moved.

"Quick!" he called, shuffling down the steps. "Jump over to us."

"What are you talking about?" Tabitha shouted over the other girls. "The steps are going to throw you off!"

Zack didn't understand. The green platform was moving slowly but soon the girls were going to start sliding off. Except that they weren't. Even at the gentle angle the platform had turned on, they should have been leaning against it, but they weren't.

"C'mon girls, jump!" Bast called behind him.

"No," Zack said. "We need to get back to them. Now."

Zack didn't wait. He bounced as carefully as he could down the orange steps and he threw himself as hard as he could from the base up and toward the green platform. It wasn't enough. Zack reached up in the air towards the platform, but he was falling short. However, before he fell back towards the orange steps, he felt a tumbling sensation in his ears and stomach. His body lurched towards the green platform and he crashed down beside the girls. Kimmy grabbed hold of him to stop from sliding towards the edge.

Bast looked towards him in confusion. "What the hell was that?"

"We don't have time," Zack replied. "You're getting further away."

Bast crouched, chanting quietly to himself, before orange light gathered at his feet and he leapt towards the others. His magical jump hurled him towards the green platform and, as his personal centre of gravity flipped, he slammed hard into it.

"Okay, now your turn, Art," Zack shouted.

But the slow turn of the platforms had taken the orange zig-zag all the way up and over the green, and six teens stood looking almost directly up at Art. The platform seemed to come to a rest there.

"So, uh, what are you guys doing all the way up there?" Art asked.

"Seriously, dude?" Tabitha said.

"Hang on," Art replied. "If the gravity switches over in the middle, I just need to jump that far, and then I'll fall up... or down... to you. Okay, get ready to catch me."

The others shuffled in anticipation, but as Art jumped, he fell right back to the orange steps. He was at least five metres away. There was no way he was making half the distance.

"Okay, that didn't help," Art said, his voice light and casual.

Jackie bit her lip as she looked up at her stranded brother.

"Ooh, I know," Art said. "I'll throw my rope down to you and then you can all pull me towards you."

"Will that work?" Charlie asked.

"I don't know," Tabitha replied. "Zack?"

"No idea, but why wait to find out?" Zack answered. "Throw it."

The others stared directly up at Art as he whirled the coil of rope before flinging it towards them. It travelled a metre or so in their direction but then it turned and, as the coil unravelled, it snaked out almost at a right angle, towards neither Art nor the others and fluttered there.

"What the crap was that?" Kimmy said.

"Um, any other ideas?" Art called down.

"Maybe I can pull the rope down towards us," Bast said. "I haven't moved something that far away before, but I can try."

Bast incanted, his fingers traced lines and shapes in the air. Orange light collected at his fingertips but, as he reached out towards the rope, he groaned and the light disappeared. He rubbed his eyes.

"Sorry, I can't do it. Movement here is out of whack. There's either no ground or a couple of thousand different grounds and I can't move the rope in relation to anything."

"Right, so maybe I just sit here until the platform spins back?" Art asked.

"Or it floats further away," Tabitha replied. "We have no idea how things work here."

"I've got an idea," Kimmy said.

"I can't really see her face from here," Art called down. "On a scale of one to gremlin, what does her smile look like?"

"You don't have any other options," she replied, her evil grin in full glory. "Pass me that rope, Charlie."

Charlie handed her the coil and Kimmy opened up one side of her jacket. "Out you come, Mr Shanks."

"No, I don't like this idea," Art shouted.

The ornate dagger rose out of the makeshift pocket Kimmy had sewn inside and hovered in front of her.

"Okay, I've got a job for you. I need you to help somebody," she said to it.

"Nope," Art murmured from above.

"He's probably not worth the effort, but other people seem to think so, so we're going to sort him out, okay?"

"Nope, nope, nope." Art had crossed his arms tightly.

"I'm going to tie this rope to you." Kimmy held up one end of the coil and looped it around the dagger's hilt. "And then

I need you to take it up there to that idiot who's making all the noise."

"No thank you, next idea, please."

Kimmy ignored Art as she finished the knot. "I wish I could tell if he understood me."

"He did," Charlie answered. "That little shimmy movement he does with his hilt, that's his body language for liking an idea. When he sways the blade back and forth, that's the opposite."

Kimmy's evil grin broke into a genuinely radiant smile. "How do you know that?"

Charlie shrugged. "I told you, it's Animal. At least Animal enough."

"Alright," Kimmy said, focusing back on the knife. "Ready? Up you go."

"I refuse to be harpooned by Kimmy's pet dagger," Art screamed.

"Calm down, Art. This might work," Jackie replied, her voice wavering.

The knife launched up into the sky towards Art, the uncoiling rope trailing behind it. About a third of the way there, it faltered and drifted to the side. It turned back, but seemed to over-correct and moved another way, and then another. It was like it was fighting against currents. But it persisted and, inch by inch, it made its way to Art.

The tall, stranded boy flinched back, but the knife hovered in front of him.

"Hurry up, Art," Kimmy shouted. "Take the rope and tie it around yourself."

"And what kind of guarantee do I have that this magical entity isn't going to stab me full of holes if I touch it?"

"None," she replied. "But hurry up anyway."

Art took a deep breath and gingerly reached out to the rope. Avoiding the knife where he could, he unfastened the cord and tied it around his waist.

Bast and Zack joined Kimmy at their end of the rope.

"Alright," Kimmy said, "on the count of three, you jump and we'll pull you towards us."

"Yeah, okay," Art replied.

"1…" Kimmy counted. "2… 3."

Art jumped as high as he could, his fists tight around the rope. The three on the other end pulled hard and, as Art reached the peak of his leap, the rope pulled taut and held him up. Together with Kimmy and Bast, Zack reeled in the rope, pulling Art closer. Once he reached the space between the two platforms, Art drifted, or even fell, in random directions, the same as the rope had. His knuckles turned white on the rope, and his lips pursed tight together, but the others reeled him closer and closer until, with about two metres to go, he crashed down onto the green platform.

Art rolled over onto his back and sighed with relief.

"Thanks guys."

"Ahem," Kimmy said. "We're not the only ones you need to thank."

The knife floated next to her.

"Really?" Art asked.

"Would you rather be on his bad side?" Kimmy asked in response.

"Fine." Art sat up and faced the dagger. "Thank you, Mr…"

"Shanks," Kimmy supplied.

"Mr Shanks. That was very kind."

The knife flitted from the hilt end.

"See," Charlie said. "He liked that."

Art groaned and rolled his eyes.

"Good boy," Kimmy said, and opened her jacket again. "Back you go."

The knife flew into her pocket and disappeared.

"So, what do we do now?" Charlie asked.

Zack looked around. "I just can't see how anybody could dependably get anywhere in this place. You can't rely on the platforms to be where you want. You can't even rely on what's up and down."

Tabitha's eyes lit up. "I think you're right. Pass me one of the ropes."

Art handed her his first rope and, while he worked at untying the second, Tabitha tied it tightly around her own waist.

"What are you doing?" Charlie asked.

"Testing a theory. Like Zack said, they can't depend on anything, except this platform. And they can't depend on up and down. But they did make sure these ropes were available." Tabitha handed the other end of the rope to Bast. "Hold tight for me, okay?"

"Sure," he said, taking hold of it and winding it around his wrist. "But why?"

"Testing a theory," she said again, and stepped off the side of the platform.

The others cried out or lurched forward in shock but, with her leg outstretched, Tabitha didn't fall down. She fell around. Her back foot had barely lifted when the front landed solidly on the underside of the green platform.

She laughed with excitement.

"It worked. Bast, you come next. I need you to confirm my theory.

Bast handed his end of the rope to Zack, who promptly waved Art over to help him hold it. Bast knelt on the edge of the platform, the middle of the rope tight in his hand. He took a deep breath and rolled over the side, and the line went taut as he used it to guide him.

A second later he whooped in triumph. "That was deadly!"

"Okay," Tabitha said, "now, can you sense a gate on this side?"

"Oh, yeah, okay," Bast replied. And a few seconds later, "Yes. Definitely. And it's to somewhere else. That's brilliant."

"Right, everybody else, come on over," Tabitha called. "It's time to leave this trippy place behind."

CHAPTER 25

CHRISTMAS

Zack stepped out of Bast's next gate and icy air stung at his skin through his clothes. He gasped, sucking in a frigid breath that fared him no better on the inside. None of the others were coping particularly well either, with the exception of Kimmy who seemed fine despite her skinny jeans, singlet top and light jacket. An ice and snow covered tundra stretched out all around, but it was hard to concentrate on anything with the cold biting at them.

"Okay," Tabitha said, "we're not dressed for this, so let's be quick. Everybody have a look around."

"This looks like a pretty clear path." Bast pointed at where the ice and snow had been broken into a muddy line, possibly from heavy use.

"And there's a metal chest here with the same kind of rope we have," Charlie added.

"See. Told you it was a quest item," Art said.

"Actually, this whole setup here is different," Zack said, his face scrunched in thought.

"What do you mean?" Tabitha asked.

"Well, there's the clear path away from, or towards this point. There's the obvious chest, rather than a hidden bag." He stomped hard on the ground. "The ground has been flattened to lay this stone."

"And?" Kimmy asked.

"They aren't hiding this spot," Zack replied. "Work has been done to set this up, not hide it."

"He's right," Bast added. "And the gate magic here is prepped, I can feel it. I bet there's runes or enchantments laid into the stone beneath us. Nothing like the Gate Room, but it would help somebody open one."

"That means this probably isn't another checkpoint," Tabitha said. "We might have found them."

"What now, then?" Charlie asked. "Do we follow the path?"

Jackie pointed to the right of the muddy trail. "What if we head uphill, that way? We might be able to get a view of where it goes."

"That sounds good to me," Bast said and trotted out ahead of the others.

The icy snow crunched under Zack's feet as he made his way up along the ridge. Their footprints didn't seem particularly deep or obvious, but Tabitha walked at the back, using gentle jets of wind to mask their path. By the time they made it to the crest, Zack was panting, along with the others, and the cold air he was inhaling brought a chill deep inside him.

They clustered behind a line of windblown boulders and looked down across an icy valley. Four stone mountains broke through the snow across the valley from them and a fifth stood alone to their right.

Art wore a thoughtful look on his face.

"Zack, does that mountain structure remind you of something?"

Before Zack could answer, Tabitha interrupted, "Forget the mountains. Look down there."

In the centre of the valley, maybe 20 minutes' walk from where the gate had opened, was a strange stone building. Neither a house nor a castle, it instead looked like it had been carved out of a single massive piece of stone, with no visible windows and a single chimney that pumped smoke out into the sky. The distance made it hard to judge, but Zack thought it could easily be 10 times the size of his family home.

"I reckon that's them, then," Bast said. "So, what do we do now?"

"We go back and tell Junie," Tabitha said.

"We came all this way and we're not going to go check it out?" Kimmy asked.

"There are people at home. But I can't tell how many are in there from this distance," Zack said.

"And they'll see us coming long before we get close," Art added.

"We'll tell Junie we found them and then she can send more people to shut it down," Tabitha said, more firmly than before. "This is good. We've succeeded."

"Yeah," Kimmy huffed, "and maybe, if we're lucky, Junie's group will let us tag along and hold their bags while they do all the real stuff."

Tabitha shook her head. "Alright, so back through the gate?"

"Actually," Bast said. "I think I can try and open one from here all the way back to Brisbane. And then, if we do need to bring Junie's group through, we can be more useful than holding their bags. Yeah, sis?"

Kimmy smiled. "Awesome."

"Right, well this is going to take me some time." Bast traced shapes into the snow.

"Want access to a bit more Life while you cast?" Zack asked.

"That would be deadly, yeah," Bast replied. "I shouldn't need too much, but a little more would mean I wasn't pushing so hard."

Zack nodded. "Just let me know when you need it."

While Bast got to work, the others sat down against the cold rocks, the icy wet snow seeping into their jeans.

"I hope we've got a few hours of daylight left when we get back," Charlie said. "Max and I will need to thaw out."

Max whined in agreement.

"What were you saying before?" Zack asked Art.

"Those mountains." Art shuffled closer and kept his voice soft.

"What about them?" Zack asked, matching his volume.

Art held out his right hand with his fingers sticking up and rotated them to match the position of the mountains. Zack knelt up and looked back around the boulders.

"No… You think?"

Art nodded. "More than that, I reckon this could be Jotunheim. Or at least, whatever inspired those stories."

"And our friendly rogue mages over there have set up shop in the palm of a frost giant?"

Art shrugged. "I might not go prodding around for a mind deep in the ground to find out. I think I'm more comfortable with this as a theory."

"Zack," Bast called out in the midst of his incantation.

"Got you," Zack replied and poured Life towards him.

Bast's face expressed the strain of his efforts and sweat rolled down his skin despite the chill in the air. The gate grew slowly. At first the size of a coin, it took another full minute for it to reach a size they could step through. Bast doubled over with his hands on his knees.

"Good work, man," Tabitha said. "Let's get out of here and get warm."

Nobody argued and they filed through the gate, back to their hotel room.

After a hurried journey through Brisbane and back to the Tower, an hour later, they were in the Sahara with Junie, walking with her in a meandering circle through the sand.

"You've all done very well," she said. "It appears this group of renegades has taken great efforts to hide themselves from us."

"So, what's next?" Tabitha asked. "Will the Tower send in a group to question them?"

"And can we be part of it?" Kimmy added.

Tabitha scowled at her, but Junie shook her head.

"Unfortunately, I still cannot inform the rest of the Tower."

"Why not?" Tabitha asked.

"I need more information. We don't know that there isn't another gate point inside leading to yet another realm. I agree with your logic, that the building you saw is likely their refuge, but that needs to be confirmed. But more, I remain concerned that this group may have Tower members in their ranks. Perhaps more so, given the way they have evaded our wards. I can't even risk running it up the line to those above me."

"What about taking it directly to the Thirteen?" Art asked.

"That's not a simple task, I'm afraid. The steps I would have to take would draw the very kind of attention I'm trying to avoid. I'm afraid, I need you to go back to that realm and investigate further."

Kimmy clenched her fist in victory.

"I acknowledge that this will be dangerous," Junie continued. "And I don't enjoy the idea of sending you in when you could very likely be outnumbered. But it would be more dangerous to expand our circle of trust without knowing more. So, take the time to prepare and train. It is better to do this right than to do it quickly. It's Christmas next week, so perhaps go after that. And when you do, be careful. If you need to retreat, do so, but I must know more before I can risk telling others. Understood?"

They nodded before following her back out through the gate to the Tower where they collected their things and exited back to Sydney.

"Art and Jackie, any problems?" Tabitha asked.

The blonde siblings closed their eyes and a moment later shook their heads.

"I'm not getting anybody paying us any attention," Art said.

"And nobody who wants to harm us either," Jackie added.

"Great," Tabitha said, "but let's walk a bit and catch a bus from a different line."

"We should have checked out the building," Kimmy said, as they moved together down the street.

"Kimmy," Charlie replied, "we weren't dressed for the cold, we weren't ready to deal with whoever was in there and we had no way out if we needed to run."

Kimmy threw her hands up, flustered.

"Well then, we need to be ready in the future. Or they'll never take us seriously."

"Like 'assign us a secret mission that nobody else in the Tower gets to know about' serious?" Bast asked, his face deadpan.

Kimmy opened her mouth to respond, but Tabitha interrupted, "You're right, Kimmy. We need to get ready. We've got nine days. Practise our magic, train with our weapons and enjoy the heck out of Christmas. Boxing Day we go back."

If Zack had a favourite week of the year when he was growing up, it was the lead up to Christmas Day. Carols and music pumping out of every public audio system, an eternal war between tasteful and kitschy decorations, crowded chaotic shopping centres and the almost tangible atmosphere of shared anticipation; all finally culminating in a double feature of European Christmas Eve and Australian Christmas Day through which he was invariably spoiled with food, presents and family.

This year felt different. The looming reconnaissance of the renegades' hideout played a large role. In Zack's opinion, they had been lucky to come out of the Montreal trap as well as they had and the worry that their good fortune would not hold, hung like a cloud in his mind. But it was more than that. His grandmother's health had waned in these past few months; months he had spent chasing clues around the world instead of dedicating it to mastering the magic needed to save her and it was written on his father's face: it was expected to be her last Christmas.

Only if he failed.

He had skipped the shops and decorations this year and the festive music had to come from his headphones, because he had spent the last week bouncing between Sara's study and his grandmother's bedside. With the occasional detour to the Training Room to take out his frustrations on as many statues as the Commander would allow, leaving only when the blows of their wooden weapons rendered him too injured to continue.

Now, while his uncles, aunties and cousins passed gifts around in subdued celebration, he sat on the edge. His mind was lost in the sense of his grandmother's dwindling Life in the next room. Lost in the knowledge that he'd healed six bruises, four cuts and a fractured rib on himself this morning, but could do nothing for her, beyond buying small portions of time.

He couldn't ask Sara, or any of the other Life mages, for help here; there was too much of a risk that it would be flagged as a danger to the Silence. That a woman with such a bleak prognosis would make the kind of strong recovery Zack needed her to make. So, it was up to him and him alone. He was close, but the magic involved was intimidating in its complexity and the consequences of screwing it up were terrifying. He needed more time. She needed more time. No, she needed him to stop being distracted and learn what he needed to learn.

Zack turned his attention back to the room and was surprised to find the last of the gifts were unwrapped. Distracted was right. His cousin, Luke, moved to his side and punched him jokingly in the arm.

"Thanks a lot for those exam results, Zack. Mum's only brought mine up 18 or 19 times in comparison since she found out you aced yours."

Zack found a smile. "Sorry. I'll be more considerate next time. But does anybody really care about your high school results when you've got a degree?"

His cousin pointed at where Zack's aunty was playing with her granddaughter on the floor. "Just one person. So, were they good enough to get into medicine?"

"Into medical science at least, which is the first step towards post grad medicine."

Luke slapped him on the shoulder. "Congrats, man! You should be celebrating."

As a reflex, Zack glanced out to the closed door in the hallway. "Not really feeling it at the moment."

Luke looked him in the eyes, his ever-present smirk now absent from his face.

"Yeah, I know. It's rough."

"The two things aren't entirely unrelated though, are they?" Zack's father sat down opposite them and it seemed he had been listening in. He offered beers to both of them, which they accepted. "Your drive these past two years, your focus on getting into medicine. I can't help but think it's to try and find an answer for what's happening to her. To stop what's happening to her."

His father was wrong, of course. It was Life that had turned him towards medicine. But then again, his father wasn't actually wrong. It's just that the drive he'd seen hadn't been towards school and Zack's exams, it had been towards magic. And there Zack had found plenty of answers. But no way of curing her yet.

"It's okay, Zack. It's understandable and it's wonderful and she's so proud of you. But it's not the kind of thing that there are answers to. Half a dozen specialists can't stop it. Neither can the rest of us. And neither can you. All we can do is be there for her. And for Deda. And for each other."

Luke seemed to accept that as a makeshift toast and clinked the neck of his bottle against Zack's father's and Zack followed suit. Except his father was wrong, of course. Zack could stop it. Unless, then again, his father wasn't actually wrong.

CHAPTER 26

TRESPASS

Zack dropped to his knees behind an outcrop of rocks and trees, taking in frigid air in ragged breaths and trying to ignore the sweat beneath his insulated layers that was turning icy. It had been a hard and hurried slog through the snow from Bast's portal and they weren't at the strange, stone building yet.

Art leant on the trunk of a tree next to him, wheezing. "A day late, but I'll take it."

"What?" Zack asked.

Art gestured around the frozen tundra. "Like, technically it's Boxing Day, but this still counts as my first White Christmas. Actually, what time is it? It could still be Christmas Day somewhere. I don't suppose Jotunheim is in a timezone, though, or that a Norse realm recognises Christmas."

"Do you ever shut up?" Kimmy's glare had enough heat to melt the ice.

"She's got a point," Tabitha said. "We don't want to be heard approaching the building."

Art scoffed, "It's all the way over there and on top of this wind, they aren't going to hear us."

"What did you mean, Yotten-ham?" Charlie asked.

257

"Jotunheim," Zack answered before Art could. "One of the nine realms in Norse mythology. We think this place looks a bit like it."

Art opened his mouth to say more, but Zack shook his head. He didn't think this was the best time to introduce Art's idea of buried mountain-sized giants.

"Before we make the last dash, are you three able to sense anything in the building?" Tabitha asked.

Zack peered through the leafless branches and reached out to the building with his mind. "Maybe ten people in there? Pretty sure they are human, but beyond that, it's still too far. They seem to be at the very back of the building though."

"Ten?" Tabitha's eyes were wide with worry.

"I can't do much more than confirm. Too far to pick up emotions or thoughts, but ten feels about right. I don't think they are alert to us though, that would feel different, louder."

"Jackie?" Tabitha asked.

"Sorry. The whole building is a big ball of dangerous probability. But nothing immediate."

"What's the play, Cap?" Bast asked.

"Cap?" Tabitha asked with a smirk. "Yeah, okay. I can't see any windows, so the front door looks like the only approach. We go inside, stay together. If they're all at the back, then we should be able to check out the front couple of rooms and try to find enough intel. Jackie, you'll be our lookout. If we get busted, we throw something flashy at them and get out. Bast runs ahead, gets the gate open and we get out."

"And if we can't get away?" Kimmy asked.

"We do whatever it takes to get away," Tabitha answered. "They outnumber us and we're on their turf. Alright, let's go."

The group bolted the remaining distance to the front of the building. Zack found himself bending over as he ran, as if a shorter, crooked boy would be less visible against the ice and snow. Shaking his head at himself, he straightened up and picked up speed.

After a few minutes of running, the group made it to the door. Tabitha held a finger to her lips and, in silence, they attempted to catch their breaths. Unlike the unnatural shape of the building, the door looked normal. Heavy, but no different from one Zack expected to find on the shelf of a hardware store. Kimmy shrugged at the others, approached the door and turned the handle. Zack's entire body tightened in anticipation. Kimmy turned back.

"Locked," Kimmy mouthed more than said.

Bast nodded and stepped past her. A few murmured syllables later and the door swung open. The group moved inside and Zack eased the door closed behind them.

It was warm inside. Enough to want to take off their jackets, but not enough to be stifling. The walls of the entry room were lined with stone shelves. Not only were there no seams in the walls, there were none between the wall and the shelves. Zack now suspected they, and the whole building, had not been carved, but rather moulded by magic. The shelves were filled with heavy coats, boots, bags and weapons.

Art pointed at a pair of swords. "Hopefully they're all unarmed in here, then," he whispered.

Kimmy's eyes flared at him and she held a particular finger to her lips. Tabitha gestured deeper into the building and tapped the side of her head.

The first room was small and opened into a much larger room, around the size of a classroom. Benches, chairs and tables, made from the same stone as the building, furnished the room. The seats were adorned by blankets and cushions, while the tables were covered in papers, boxes and unlit candles. Four shadowed doorways led deeper into the building.

When he entered the room, Zack's attention was pulled away from the furniture and down to his feet. His steps sounded differently because, unlike the entry room, the floor was wooden. Why would they bother with floorboards when they were satisfied with sitting on stone chairs? Maybe it kept the room warmer?

He was about to draw attention to it when Bast waved from the centre table. Twice the size of the other tables, it was covered by a single map of Earth. Tabitha stepped in beside Zack, snapping dozens of photos on her phone.

"What do you think these pins mean?" she whispered, gesturing above a cluster of them across Asia.

"There's numbers written next to them as well," Bast said.

"And the whole thing is covered in lines and other markings," Art said from the opposite side of the table. "Who knows what any of it means?"

"Hopefully, Junie will," Tabitha said, slipping her phone away.

"I think they are Tower entrances." Charlie slipped in beside Zack with Max on her heels.

"Are you sure?" Tabitha asked.

"Let's see." Charlie's fingers bounced across the map from pin to pin. "Yeah, I think so. I've made a similar map for my travel plans next year. And my bet is that these numbers are coordinates."

"Reckon this is enough for Junie?" Bast asked.

Tabitha shook her head. "No, this just poses more questions. Do they have a person on the inside who showed them where all the entrances are? Or have they worked it out themselves? And why?"

"To avoid the Towers?" Bast said.

"Or to target them," Zack replied. "Remember, they've scoped out the Sydney one looking for us." He offered Charlie a sympathetic smile at the memory.

"See, we don't know enough," Tabitha said, frustration evident on her face. "Has anybody else found anything?"

"I've got copies of those rituals we found in Korea," Kimmy whispered from another table. "And maybe a list of names and addresses."

"Tower members?" Tabitha asked with hope in her voice.

"I hope not. There's dozens of names here."

"What about you, Jackie?" Tabitha turned to where the younger girl was standing at another table.

She didn't answer.

"Jackie?"

Something was wrong with the way she was standing. Her arms were rigid and her neck had an awkward tilt.

Zack felt out with his mind, but it was too late. "We're—"

"Unwelcome guests who didn't even care to knock?" a deep voice finished from a doorway. "Yes, I agree."

Max howled a warning and Zack discovered why wood had been laid into the floor.

A flood of liquid amber poured out of the knots and cracks, oozing upward and over their feet. Zack leapt onto the nearest stone bench, wrenching himself out of the hardening goo. Across the room, Tabitha and Bast had also managed to jump onto furniture, but the others tugged their encased legs in vain.

"Now, now. This will go much easier for us if you give up." A man emerged from the shadows. Zack recognised him, with his dark hair and pencil thin moustache, from the first night in Montreal. And there were more lurking in the other doorways.

"Don't you mean easier for us?" Tabitha replied, rising into a crouch on the table.

"Oh no." The man's smile held no pretence of kindness. "You lost that chance when you played Scooby-Doo all over our business."

"Kinda telling on yourself there, gubba," Bast said. "'Cause that makes you an old whitefulla with a real estate scam."

"Art, he's the guy who wiped your mind in Canada." Zack kept his eyes on the other doorways. "And he's not alone."

Ignoring the now hardened amber encasing his feet, Art stretched out his hand toward the man, his face contorted in rage. "Get out of my sister's head."

A faint purple light illuminated Art's hand but, with his own hand glowing the same colour, the man brushed it away with a look of contempt.

"Really? Did you actually expect that to work?"

The rage dropped from Art's face, replaced by a smirk. "Nope."

A torrent of wind erupted from Tabitha's palm. It scattered paper and trinkets into the air and slammed the man up against the wall. Art craned towards Jackie, tracing frantically in the air.

"Snap out of it."

Her body relaxed down to an awkward squat and she exhaled with a sob.

"That was awful."

"We need to get out of here!" Tabitha shouted.

"Maybe if I…" Kimmy focused down at her feet and incanted.

"I wouldn't do that if I was you." Another man stepped into the room from the opposite doorway.

Zack recognised him too; the Plant mage he'd fought under New York. Kimmy screamed. Her magic had softened the amber around her ankles, but it now bubbled against her.

"I warned you." The man sauntered forward. "Amber can be quite dangerous when it's hot. But that's only the beginning of you paying for killing Nicole."

"Let us out of this, now." Charlie eyed the man down the knocked length of an arrow.

The man smirked and the bow jerked downward. The arrow slipped loose and skidded along the amber, slicing small gouges out of it. Connor, the Movement mage from the fight under New York, raced into the room with his outstretched arm pointing at Charlie. Several others ran in behind him.

Connor pointed towards Jackie.

"Phet and Kaylani, occupy the little one. The rest of you, spread out."

Art screamed in frustration and, his sword in both hands, dug down at the amber in a frenzy. Kimmy tried the same with her axe, while Bast drew his rapier and chanted.

A man and woman approached Jackie, who saw them and readied her spear. The man flicked his fingers toward her and colourful lights flashed around her eyes. Jackie flinched and covered her eyes with her left forearm. The woman waved her hand and the glass candleholders from the nearby table launched toward Jackie, crashing against the light of Jackie's shield an inch from her body.

"Leave her alone!" Tabitha shouted.

"Worried you can't hide behind her now?" the Plant mage taunted and a spray of thorns shot out from his hands towards Tabitha.

With rapid precision, Tabitha cast her own spell and a gust of wind sent most of the thorns astray. One made it through and cut a chunk of skin from her cheek.

Another mage raced past Zack's bench toward Bast, who charged forward to meet him. The man held machetes in his hands and Bast ducked and weaved around his slashes, rather than risking his lighter blade in a parry.

Zack recognised the face and form of the mage who strode towards him and looked in distress at his staff, stuck where he had left it in the amber.

The hulking shape of the Body mage charged forward and threw a violent punch at him with a sneer.

"Not so tough without your stick, huh?"

Zack ducked under the blow.

"Not so tough without your sight, huh?"

"What?" the man replied, confused.

Zack snatched up the thin, woollen blanket from the bench and flung it over the brute's head. The man stumbled back, grabbing at the wool, but Zack launched himself forward. Putting all of his weight into his forearm, Zack rammed his elbow into the man's face and felt the crunch of bones as he connected with the man's nose.

Kimmy finished her own incantation, and a white-hot beam of fire lanced out from her right hand toward the mages. One of them responded with his own gesture and a cloud with a rich, brown glow gathered at his hands. The beam of heat fizzled a few feet away, with small wisps of red light fluttering into the cloud.

He laughed. "Is that all you've got?"

"No," Kimmy said, biting off the word and she launched a second beam of fire with her left hand.

The Air mage from New York stepped forward and, with a flick of his hand, a similar but light blue cloud appeared. Kimmy's new beam of fire failed in the same way, drawn off into the second cloud. She screamed in frustration.

The Mind mage staggered back into the room, bracing himself against the wall as he scanned the combat. Art saw him first and ceased his futile attacks against the amber to throw a mental attack at the man. The man flinched but then turned to face Art, whose eyes widened in alarm. The two were locked in an invisible battle and, at least, comparing Art's stretched expression to the still one of his opponent, the older man held the upper hand.

Charlie glanced over at Zack and their eyes met.

"I need to try," she mouthed, and he knew what she meant.

He nodded, hoping she understood he'd be there to help her find her way back to human form if she needed it. Charlie dropped her bow and traced patterns in the air. Rust coloured light travelled down her fingertips over her hands and along her forearms.

Before she could finish, a chunk of stone the size of a bowling ball flew across the room and slammed into her side. Her incantations turned into a cry of pain before her eyes rolled up into the back of her head and she fell to the ground beside a distressed and whining Max.

"Charlie!" Tabitha screamed. But then Connor flicked his hand and objects that had been scattered on the table flew sideways, knocking Tabitha's feet out from under her. She landed hard on her back.

Zack realised, with a sharp knot of terror in his stomach, that they'd lost.

"Bast!" Zack shouted and saw the other boy's eyes flick to him for a brief second as he ducked away from the pair of knives. "We're not all getting out of here today. Run for the Tower!"

Bast nodded and made a wild slash at his opponent's throat, forcing him back. The opening was all he needed and he turned to make a dash for the exit. But the doorway rippled and the stone flowed down like it was melting, closing off the exit.

A massive hand grabbed Zack by the back of the neck. He had taken his eyes off the brute for too long. He willed Bast faster as his friend raced to the shrinking doorway. The Body mage picked Zack up one handed and slammed him down towards the stone bench. He struggled, but it didn't help. The last thing he saw before his head crashed against the stone was Bast colliding into the wall.

CHAPTER 27

INTERROGATION

Pain came back first. Or maybe it had never left. Instinctively, Zack reached out for Life, but the ache in his head flared bright and nausea joined it until Zack let go. As he struggled to catch his breath, hearing returned. Muffled at first, or perhaps muddled by his likely concussion, he couldn't be sure. But he knew the word concussion and that was a small ray of optimism in the dark of his mind.

"...to not bite me, or I'll kill it instead of just muzzling it, okay?" A male voice, perhaps the Plant mage.

"Okay, okay." Charlie's voice trembled with fear and her breaths sounded uneasy and pained. "Max darling, don't hurt them, alright? Be a good girl and it'll all be okay."

Max whined.

Even through Zack's mental fog, he could tell Charlie sounded injured. He tried to speak up and ask to heal her, but no sound came out. He could feel it now, tightness around his face and something jammed in the edge of his mouth; he'd been gagged. And blindfolded, which explained why his sight hadn't returned. He focused on the rest of his body and found that his wrists were tied behind his back.

This was bad.

He tried to find his calm centre, as Sara had taught him, but between the concussion and the fear of impending execution, it wasn't easy. A sense of panic lurked in the shallows, waiting for the slimmest of excuses to emerge. Zack pushed it away and took stock.

He was sightless, voiceless and restrained and he assumed the others were too. That all the others were too, he emphasised, refusing to even consider that any had not survived the fight. Without their hands and speech, magic was very hard. Throw in the blindfolds and the beating they'd taken and it was all but impossible. Which, Zack supposed, was the point.

HEY, ZACK!

Art's voice blared inside Zack's mind like a church bell in a cupboard and he bit down into both the gag and his lips to stifle the scream. He could taste blood in his mouth and by the time his head had calmed down, the voice was gone.

"Alright boss, what's the plan?" The Plant mage again, but further away this time. Zack couldn't be sure whether they intended for him and the others to hear, or whether they didn't care.

"We can't wait any longer," said the voice of the Mind mage. "The fact that these children found us means the Tower is almost certainly close behind. Connor, you start calling together your people. You have three days."

"You told me I had a month," Connor's voice replied. "They aren't ready."

"Seventy-two hours." The Mind mage's tone was immovable. "Pawel, see what you can get out of our guests. Assumptions aside, we need to find out how much the Tower knows. I'll leave Phet and Kaylani here with you. The others will come help me with the rest of our preparations."

"And if they aren't willing to talk?" the Plant mage, Pawel, asked.

"Make them." The Mind mage's voice was firm and icy. "Even if you need to make an example out of one or two of them."

"Armand, these are the kids the Traveller spoke about," Connor said. "He said they were not to be harmed."

"We don't know these are those children," the Mind mage, Armand, replied. "And they won't be harmed, if they cooperate. But I don't really give a damn what the Traveller wants. He ceased to be of any help to our undertaking a long time ago."

"We owe him—" Connor began.

"Nothing," Armand interrupted. "We owe him nothing. Any debt from the early days has been repaid. Many times over. Am I understood?"

"Hey, no complaints from me," Pawel said.

The silence lingered.

"Agreed." Connor's voice was soft and subdued.

"Good. You have your tasks. We're at the final stage now, it will all be worth it."

The conversation ended and footsteps took at least some of them away.

Zack.

Art's voice was softer this time, but it still made Zack's temples ache. He tried to think back but wasn't quite sure how.

Art. Can you hear me?

Yeah. Kind of. Bloody hell this is tough without the incantations. Are you okay?

Yeah, Zack replied. *Well, apart from having my head bashed in, being tied up, gagged and blindfolded.*

What do we do?

I don't know. Wait? Tell the others to wait until we have some kind of chance to get out of here.

Okay. I'll try.

Art's thoughts faded from Zack's head and the pain lessened back to a dull throb.

"Okay, listen up, children." Pawel was back in front of them. "You're going to tell me what I want to know. And while I'm talking to each of you, the rest of you are going to stay here and behave. I don't particularly want to kill you, but I don't always get what I want. If we see even the hint of magic from any of you, down to the twitch of a single finger behind your backs, you will die. Connor underestimated you once and you killed three of my friends. I won't repeat his mistake. Let's start with him."

There was a shuffle and a muffled grown as one of them, Art or Bast, by Zack's assumption, was led away.

Zack? Art entered his mind again.

That wasn't me. He thought back. *Bast then?*

I guess so. What are they going to do to him?

Whatever they do, we need to be ready. Talk to the others. I think they are only leaving three of them here to watch us.

Three's enough if they've got a crossbow or something pointed at us. Art's thoughts were filled with nervous energy.

So, we wait until we have a chance, Zack replied.

Okay. I'll talk to the others.

When Art left his mind, Zack focused on calming his breathing. His head still ached and he couldn't risk trying to heal it. Beyond the dangers of trying to control streams of Life around his brain in his current state, it would also likely be seen by whoever was watching them. He reached out with his senses, but the pain doubled and the nausea returned. Too bad. He took a long, deep breath and pushed with his mind. His head swam, but he gritted his teeth and persisted. They were all still there: Art, the girls, Max, and one guard. He didn't linger to check their injuries, and instead stretched further out. There was Bast, with two others. And at least four others more still in the building. Acid was creeping up his throat and he let his senses relax to avoid vomiting into his gagged mouth.

He spent the next few minutes steadying his breathing, before Art returned.

His voice was faint. *It's hard work, getting a bit woozy. They are okay. Hurt, but okay. I think Charlie is the worst, her mind was pretty shaky. I couldn't reach Bast, he's too far away.*

Zack thought back. *I found him. He's with two of them in another room. I think it's Poison Ivan and someone else. But there's still others around, they haven't left yet.*

Okay. Everybody is willing to wait until we have a chance. Do we have a chance, Zack?

Yeah, we do, but not before the others have left. I'll keep checking on them. Does anybody have any ideas?

Maybe. Kimmy suggested… Art's voice grew distorted. *Hard to tell with her. I gotta go…*

Art's voice slipped away.

Zack, left alone in his mind, forced himself to think through the options. Not for the first time, he lamented that his magic couldn't be used offensively. All the others, if given half the chance, could turn the tables on their captors, but not him. Well, then maybe it was up to him to give them that chance, whatever the cost.

Maybe he could rush the guard. He'd never make it, not if they were armed, but that might be enough to buy the others their escape. Not Bast though. Alone with two of them, there was a real risk that Pawel would use him as a hostage or even kill him. Chances were, they were already torturing him.

Zack stretched out with his senses towards the guard. They were four or five metres away and closer to his friends than him. Life didn't show him the exact shape of their body, but he guessed they were sitting down and was almost certain it was a woman. What was the name Armand had said? Kaylani? That didn't provide him with any answers, but it felt good to be gaining information. With the pain rising, he gave up his investigation and returned to his slow and steady breathing.

The headache was beginning to soften around the edges when he heard movement. He reached out again. It was the two men returning with Bast. Reaching out further, he found at least three others in the building. He turned his attention to Bast. He was alive but injured and his body lay limp on the floor. Zack felt the signs of fresh bruises and welts all over Bast's body.

Zack? Now? Art's voice returned.

No! There's still too many here.

"This one," Pawel's voice ordered and a pair of hands grabbed Zack by his wrist and neck, forcing him up.

Who is he——? Art began.

Me, Zack replied, forcing his mind calm against a threatening wave of fear. *You might need to try without me.*

Not a chance, mate. We'll be ready when you get back.

Art's voice faded away as Zack was dragged down a corridor, around a corner and pushed into a hard stone seat. His gag was torn away from his mouth and he coughed at the resulting rush of saliva. His blindfold and the bindings on his wrists were left in place.

Pawel's voice came from above him. "That gag can go back on just as easily. You answer our questions, and you'll be okay. I even think you're using whatever magic you've got and you'll regret it. Understood?"

"Yes," Zack replied, but his mind was racing. Whatever magic. They had never seen him use any magic so they didn't know what he could do. It was a slim advantage, but it sparked an idea. What School of magic could he pretend to be?

"What do the others in the Tower know about us?" Pawel asked.

"Everything," Zack said, letting the spark ignite something in his head.

"Your friend said the opposite." Pawel's voice did not seem impressed.

If Zack knew Bast, he wouldn't have said anything at all, which seemed all the more likely given the injuries he'd received in this room. He decided to risk it.

"No, he didn't." Zack spoke with a confidence he did not feel.

"He said nothing at all. The Tower is aware of your plans, your movements and this location. And they are coming."

Pawel snorted. "I'm sure you hope they are. But let's pretend you're telling the truth. What have you told them about us?"

Zack ignored the question that could reveal his bluff and pushed on. "I don't hope, I know, because I can see them approaching. Just as I can see you, Pawel, and you Phet." He turned his head to where the second man's Life was. "Just as I saw you beat my friend for not talking. Did it make you feel tough?"

Phet gasped but Pawel jabbed at Zack's chest with his finger.

"Hang on, if your magic lets you see things so clearly, how come you fell into our trap in Montreal?"

"Who fell into whose trap?" Zack replied, scrambling for an answer. "How many of my side walked away compared to yours?"

Pain exploded against Zack's left cheek and the ache in his skull flared back to join it.

"Didn't see that coming, did you?" Pawel screeched.

Zack realised he might have pushed things a little too far, but it was too late now.

"No, but I do see what will happen to you when the Tower arrives. There are consequences for what you have done, but they are nothing compared to what will happen if you are responsible for our deaths."

Both the men were silent and Zack wondered if he'd allowed himself to get a little carried away.

"This is bullshit!" Pawel shouted, pacing back and forth across the room with heavy steps. "Bring him back to the others. If the Tower is coming, we're going to be ready."

The gag was forced back into Zack's mouth and he was pulled onto his feet. As he was steered down the corridor, he stretched out with his senses. Phet was behind him and Pawel a few steps back from that. Apart from his friends and their one guard, the building seemed empty. Against the throbbing ache, he held onto his sense of Life.

When he was a few steps away from the main room, Art's voice entered his mind.

Zack?

Are you guys ready? Zack asked. *This could be our only chance.*

Yeah… we might have something. When?

Now! Zack shouted into his mind.

Zack feigned a stumble and dropped into a half-crouch. Phet followed behind, his grip tightening on Zack's shoulder and wrist. Even with the beatings he had taken, Zack knew exactly where his target was. At this close range, the cluster of bone, nerves, blood and grey matter was unmistakable when sensed through Life. Zack bounced as forcefully as he could off his front foot and slammed the back of his head straight into Phet's face. He felt the small bones in Phet's nose shatter, and the man released his grip. The blow had also loosened the blindfold around Zack's head and he shook it free with frantic twists of his head. The cloth fell down over his nose and, as his eyes attempted to adjust from the darkness of the blindfold to the dull light of the corridor, a blinding burst of flame flared from the main room.

Blinking back the tears, he caught a glimpse of Kimmy exhaling a torrent of flame towards the ceiling. The fire had consumed her gag, but it had badly charred her lips and cheeks.

Kimmy hissed from the pain as she shouted. "Shanks! Cut us free!"

The enchanted blade struggled its way loose from inside her jacket but, once free, it flipped over her body and wasted no time in sawing through her bonds.

A noise from behind him prompted Zack to turn to find Phet clutching his bloodied face and, further down the corridor, Pawel incanting. Still bound and gagged, Zack charged towards him, hoping to at least to interrupt the spell. Green light had collected around Pawel's fingertips before Zack's shoulder crashed into his chest. A heavy breath of air wooshed out of him and the two tumbled to the ground in a tangle.

With his hands still tied behind him, Zack struggled on the ground and had only just managed to roll onto his back when Pawel loomed over him. The Plant mage began to incant again and Zack lashed out with his legs. Pawel sidestepped the kick as he finished his spell and familiar clusters of thorns grew from his knuckles. Zack scampered backwards and worked his way into a sitting position against the wall, but Pawel pursued him, murder in his eyes. He punched down at Zack's face but Zack ducked to the side, swinging his legs around behind Pawel's ankles. This time the blow connected and, off balance from throwing the punch, Pawel fell backwards onto the ground.

Zack was beyond exhausted but the thought of the thorny growths tearing into his body triggered a rush of adrenaline. He found the wall again and scrambled up it, ignoring the scrapes and bruises it caused. Zack pushed his cheek against the stone and the gag came free. The two of them found their feet at the same time and they sized each other up. Pawel, armed with rage and barbed fists, stared back at Zack, beaten and with his arms tied behind his back. Zack didn't feel like he had much in the way of any advantages.

Except for the one he'd been playing so far.

Just as Pawel seemed about to charge toward him, Zack looked past him towards the main room. He feigned an expression of exhausted relief.

"Master Gygax, I knew you'd find us!"

Pawel spun around to look down the corridor and Zack bolted towards him. As Pawel turned back with a sneer, Zack launched himself forward, feet first. Pawel swung his fist in a hook towards Zack's exposed stomach, but Zack twisted in the air and the thorns tore into the flesh around his hip. With no gag to muffle his voice, he screamed in pain, but his body continued on its path and his foot landed hard on the side of Pawel's knee. Accompanied by the sound of bones cracking and by Pawel's shout, the knee joint collapsed into an unnatural angle and Pawel dropped to the floor, holding his chest up with his hands.

The addition of the sharp sting in Zack's side to the rest of his collected injuries made him dizzy, but he knew he couldn't stop. Pawel manoeuvred his weight to his undamaged leg and thrust himself upwards, swinging a wild punch. Zack sidestepped the thorny fist and kicked at Pawel's head with the rest of his strength. His foot connected and he saw Pawel's eyes roll back in his head before he fell limp.

Zack leant panting against the wall, fearful that if he fell down, he wouldn't get back up. At some stage during his brawl with Pawel, Phet had left the corridor, most likely to enter the main room with the others.

The others!

Loud voices and clanging echoed down the corridor, and Zack levered himself along the wall towards them. Every step made the wound on his side flare up in pain but he kept moving. The clamour from the main room was suddenly overwhelmed by a pair of terrified screams and Phet and Kaylani bolted past the entrance to Zack's corridor and down another, their howls of fear trailing behind them. Art ran into view and stopped when he saw Zack.

"Oh, thank Odin," Art said and hurried to his side.

"Odin?" Zack asked with a wince.

"Well, if this is Jotunheim… I mean, it always pays to be courteous. C'mon, we've gotta get out of here."

"Before those two recover and come back?" Zack slipped his arm around Art's shoulder to move faster down the hall.

"No," replied Art as they entered the main room, "because of that."

The room was ablaze. While the structure and most of the

furniture was stone, there had been enough flammable material for Kimmy's flames to feed and grow and now the fire had spread to the wooden floor.

The others were clustered towards the exit. Bast, barely conscious, was held upright between Tabitha and Kimmy, while Charlie rested heavily against the entryway. Zack and Art stepped around the growing flames to join them.

"It's great to see you, Zack," Tabitha said, "but I don't suppose you've got any healing in you?"

Zack shook his head. "Sorry, I wouldn't trust it at the moment."

"Then we'll have to do without." Tabitha moved towards the door.

Zack nodded towards Charlie.

"Art, help her out, I reckon she's got at least one broken rib, maybe more and that trumps a scratch."

Charlie looked like she was about to object, but her face was pale and her body trembled as she leant on Art. Zack and Jackie followed behind with a nervous Max shadowing Charlie's steps. Tabitha pushed the doors open and a burst of frigid air rushed past them into the building.

Kimmy turned back into the building.

"Mr Shanks, time to go!"

The enchanted dagger zipped from inside the building past the others, including within millimetres of Art's left ear and hovered in front of Kimmy.

"You were exceptional, Mr Shanks," Kimmy said and the dagger wiggled with pleasure. "Time for a rest."

The knife floated into Kimmy's open jacket and disappeared inside. Tabitha looked at each of them in open assessment.

"We need to lay low. Bast is in no condition to open a gate and Zack isn't in one to fix that. And I think going to either their gate location or ours is too risky. I say we head the opposite way and find somewhere to hide and rest."

Nobody objected and the teens staggered out into the cold. The smell of smoke, so strong from the building, was soon carried away by the freezing winds. Zack lost track of time as they trudged uphill, winding their way around clumps of ice and snow. The pain in his side had faded, but he worried it was simply being numbed by the cold invading his body. Over his shoulder, he saw a snowstorm rolling towards them over the building.

"Tabitha!" he shouted over the wind.

Wearily, she turned around but her eyes went wide when she saw the storm.

"We need to find shelter now!"

Jackie pointed toward a dark outcrop of rock jutting out from the ice. "Over there. See how it's leaning? I should be able to use my magic to seal us in."

Tabitha nodded and the group picked up their pace. They trudged on another five, then 10 minutes, but the potential shelter must have been further away than they thought, because it did not seem to get closer. The storm caught up to them, hurling wind and snow at their backs and removing the rocks from sight.

"Not much further, we can make it!" Tabitha yelled, but Zack wasn't sure even she believed it.

Art stumbled first, bringing Charlie down to the ground with him. Zack had fallen behind and struggled through a snowdrift towards them. By the time he got there, Jackie had fallen beside Art and Max was laying beside Charlie, licking her face.

Tabitha and Kimmy were up ahead, struggling to keep Bast upright.

"Can you help them, Zack?" Tabitha called.

"I can try," he said, although he wasn't sure his voice could be heard over the storm. He knew he didn't have enough in him for the three of them, but he could try.

"What's that?" Kimmy's voice cut through the wind.

Zack looked to where she was pointing and there seemed to

be a tall figure standing in the distance, but when he blinked the snow out of his eyes it was gone.

"No!" Kimmy shouted. "I saw it. Hey, come back! Help us!"

Zack knelt down beside his fallen friends and called Life in towards him, but his mind was clumsy. And cold. And tired.

Kimmy wrenched Bast and Tabitha along with him, as she staggered towards where the figure had been, but Tabitha had been caught flat footed and slipped, letting go of Bast as she did. The sudden shift of weight pulled the other two down as well.

Zack pulled harder at Life, binding it to the last of his own, but his mind felt so slow and fuzzy and it slipped away. And, after a moment, so did Zack.

CHAPTER 28
CABIN OF A MOUNTAIN GOD

The first thing Zack noticed was the smell of stew. Which was a strange thing to smell when you were dying of hypothermia.

The second thing Zack noticed was that he wasn't dying of hypothermia. Instead, he was warm. Sore, bruised and with a stinging pain in his side, but warm. He levered himself onto his side, resting his elbow on the wooden floor. Wooden floor? Fearful they'd been recaptured and returned, he bolted forward onto his knees, grunting as his body protested with a chorus of aches. He did his best to ignore the pain and look around.

It was a different building. Smaller, with wooden walls and a sunken fire pit on one side. Tabitha and Jackie were sitting nearby, eating from clay bowls, while Kimmy leaned by a window, a bowl in her hand while she peered outside. The others were sleeping on the floor around him.

Tabitha had seen the look of alarm on his face. "It's okay, we're safe."

"But how?" Zack took a closer look around.

They appeared to be in a cabin with a single door and a pair of windows on the opposite wall, each with a hide covering, rather than glass, to keep out the wind and snow. Apart from a blackened pot suspended over the fire, a straw mattress and a wooden table were the only items in the room.

"I don't know," Tabitha answered. "The last thing I remember was Kimmy shouting about somebody in the storm."

"Shouting at somebody in the storm," Kimmy corrected through a mouthful.

"And then we woke up here. But there was some man here at first, standing over the pot. When he saw me getting up, he turned and walked out."

"Was he one of the mages from before?" Zack asked.

"Nope. Older. Maybe in his sixties but fit. Had a missing eye."

"Bullshit!" Art lurched upright.

"I know what I saw," Tabitha replied.

"No, I believe you." Art turned to Zack. "But mate. Old guy. One eye. Wandering around an ice realm. It's got to be, right?"

"Google, please translate idiot to English," Kimmy said.

"Odin," Zack answered. "Art is suggesting that we just had our lives saved by the Allfather of the Norse gods."

"And you disagree?" Art asked.

"Is that bad?" Tabitha spoke before Zack could reply, gesturing at her bowl. "Is this like in the fae realm? Should we not have eaten this?"

Zack sifted through his memory for what he might have read about Norse mythology. His head was better than before but still a little cloudy. "I'm not sure, but I think you're okay. There's something about hospitality rites and feeding us, suggests we're guests."

"Good." Tabitha looked relieved.

"Why would he have saved us?" Jackie asked. "Will he want something in return?"

"We can't worry about that now. We need to get back to the Tower," Tabitha replied, handing full bowls to Zack and Art. "Eat up, it's really good."

Tabitha was right. The stew was rich and had a warmth that spread deep into Zack, melting away both the chill and the memory of the trek through the storm.

Kimmy finished hers first and gestured to where Bast and Charlie lay sleeping, with Max tucked up beside her mistress. "The storm is gone, but neither of them look like they're going to wake up any time soon."

"We came close to none of us waking up again, but they were hurt the most," Tabitha said. "How are you going, Zack?"

He knew what she was asking. "Yeah, I think I'm up to it."

Zack moved between the two of them but turned towards Bast. He'd heal Charlie too if he could, but Bast was the most practical choice; he was their only way home. Zack closed his eyes and reached out. It was a struggle, but nothing like before and he coaxed Life towards Bast. His body was a tapestry of cuts, bruises and fractures, not to mention what the stress, exhaustion and exposure had done to him.

"Art, if you're up to it, I need to borrow some energy."

"Yeah, okay. What do you need me to do?" Art asked.

"Just be willing," Zack replied and opened a channel between them.

Art's Life flowed freely down the connection, and Zack poured it through Bast. Knitting the bones, cleansing the blood and easing the tensions. It was barely a minute before Bast opened his eyes, but Zack felt drained and Art was laying back with his knees bent, panting.

Bast groaned in pain and rolled over onto his elbows and knees before craning his head around the room.

"Where are we? Are we safe?"

Zack patted him on the shoulder.

"Yeah, we're okay, I think. We're going to need an exit, though."

Bast knelt, leaning back on his calves.

"Alright. At least I can reopen the gate from before. Makes it a bit easier."

"Sorry, sweety." Tabitha gave him a sympathetic smile. "I don't think we're anywhere close to where we came in."

"What? Bloody hell." He eased himself up onto his feet. "Where do we want it, then? Inside or out?"

"Definitely out," Tabitha answered.

"Not too close to this building either," Zack added. "Assuming it's safe."

"It's clear out there, as far as I can see," Kimmy said.

Bast stretched with a groan. "It's going to take me a while and, since I'd like to get the hell out of this place, I'd better get started. Kims, can you come watch my back?"

"I'll come too," Jackie said, standing up with Kimmy and following Bast outside.

Zack turned his attention back to Charlie and assessed her injuries. Tabitha knelt down beside him.

"Take what you need."

He nodded. "It shouldn't be too much. If I fix her ribs, she should breathe easier and be able to support herself. I just have to hold it together."

Zack focused and opened a channel to Tabitha. Her Life flowed through with strength, but the connection itself was made with his Life and was fading fast. Well then, he had to be twice as fast. It helped that Life had so recently mapped out her body to him, almost cell by cell, when he had helped her in the alley. He unleashed Tabitha's Life into Charlie, directing some of it to the fractures but allowing the rest to spray out and join with her depleted reserves. His thoughts grew hazy and, realising the danger just in time, he snapped off the channel. Tabitha slumped forward across Charlie's legs, her head landing on Max.

"Is she okay?" Art's voice held a note of alarm.

"Yeah, yeah. I cut the flow in time. She just needs a breather."

Charlie's eyes opened and she looked down her body. "Why is Tabitha laying on me?"

Art smiled. "Good to have you back with us, Charlie. It's time to go home."

Zack had only managed to clean up their superficial wounds by the time they hobbled through the doors to the Tower. After a short detour past the School of Life quarters, Tabitha led them to where Junie was speaking with a pair of Air mages.

Junie's expression betrayed no emotion when she saw them, but she broke off the conversation almost immediately and walked the group into her study, closing the door behind her. There were not enough seats for all of them and Junie elected to stand as well.

"How did you go?"

"Not well," Tabitha replied, before launching into a detailed report that was only occasionally interrupted by Kimmy.

Junie listened without asking questions until Tabitha had finished.

"You've all done well and against the odds. It is clear this group poses not only a risk to the Silence, but to the Tower and our world." She rubbed her temples between her thumb and forefinger. "The Tower needs to respond to this, but I wish we knew if any of us are involved."

"We did find a list of names," Tabitha said, "but then we were attacked and after that there, um, was a fire."

"I don't think anybody from the Tower is involved," Zack said in a murmur.

"I don't want to think it either," Junie said, "but that doesn't mean it's not a possibility."

"No, I know. But I've been thinking this through. Most Tower members know about the seven of us, don't they? You've said we're a large group to all be Awakened at once and we're young to be let in. And then there was the attack at the beginning of the year."

"I don't quite follow where you're going, but yes, I'd say you're well known within the Tower."

"But these people didn't know us."

"They knew me well enough to negate my fire magic with their stupid elemental clouds," Kimmy said.

"Yes, but they'd seen you do Fire magic before," Zack said. "But not me. I've done enough shifts in the infirmary that anybody who wanted to know, would. But they had no idea what School I was. I got them thinking I was Knowledge."

Junie was silent for a few moments.

"It's not proof, but it's very clever and it'll have to be enough. Okay, I'll start readying the Tower. Given the rituals you keep finding, I think there's a very good chance it involves gates. I'll call in as many teams as I can and when our wards detect these gates, I'll start sending out response squads. We won't give these renegades a chance to finish before we stop them."

She walked around her desk and pulled a notebook from a drawer.

"Now, first, I need a full description of every one of the renegades that you've encountered, including names and Schools if you know. Then, get home and rest. You've done amazing work, but we may need you again before this is over."

It was late morning on the day after Boxing Day when Zack walked through the front door of his home in a stupor. He'd refreshed his phone four times on the bus ride from the city, unable to fully accept that only a day had passed since they'd left on their mission.

He dropped his bag in the corner near the door and remembered what Art had said on the way home from their last ambush.

Depending on whether Pawel had survived the head trauma, the burning building and being stranded in another realm, it might be Zack's turn to see his parents look at him and not know that he'd ended a life.

He entered the kitchen and found his father at the counter, throwing together a container of cold cuts and cheeses. He looked up at Zack and his eyes were raw.

"What's the matter, Dad?" Zack asked.

"Is that Zack?" His mother rushed into the room and threw her arms around him. "I'm so glad you're home."

He hugged her back, his heart thumping its way up towards his throat.

"What's happened?"

When neither of them responded, he knew. "Babi?"

His mother stepped back and his father answered, "Not yet, but very soon. Between her exhaustion and the painkillers, she hasn't woken up since the day before yesterday and the doctor doesn't think she will." His father paused for a moment and drew a long steadying breath through his lips. His chest shuddered at the effort. "He says that's probably for the best, because she'd likely be in a lot of pain."

Zack moved around the counter and squeezed his father tight.

"Now that you're home, we're heading over there. To support Deda and…" His mother's voice trailed off.

"And to say goodbye," Zack finished.

CHAPTER 29

GOODBYES

One of Zack's aunties greeted them at the front door. Ellen hugged her before taking the container of food through to the kitchen and his parents stopped in the hallway to talk with his aunty in hushed voices. Zack moved through into the living room and found his other aunty, his uncles and his cousins all there. The little two-bedroom house was as crowded as on Christmas Eve and the two-foot tall tree was still in the corner, but nothing else was the same. He was greeted by red eyes, wet cheeks and tightly controlled lips, so he sat down quietly in the corner.

Unlike everybody else in the room, Zack was not there to say goodbye. From the moment he got in the car, he had been running through the magic in his head. He wanted more time to practise and be sure, but time had run out. His parents had migrated into the kitchen and the smell of coffee being brewed wafted into the room. Now was his chance.

He slipped across the hall and gently opened the door to his grandparents' room. His grandmother was lying on the bed, intermittently inhaling long ragged breaths, not quite asleep but not conscious either. Beside the metal stand that held her drip bag, his grandfather sat hunched over, staring at her. He hadn't heard Zack enter and took a few moments to react when Zack touched his shoulder.

"Oh, hi Zacharias." He reached up and squeezed Zack's wrist. The hand that had regularly crushed walnuts as a party trick was now weak and shaking.

"Hi Deda." Zack wrapped his arms around him in a hug. "You look like you could use a coffee and a sandwich. Dad's getting it ready in the kitchen."

"No. I'm alright," he replied, turning back to the bed.

"It's okay, Deda. I'll stay here and I'll get you if anything changes."

His grandfather closed his eyes and took a deep breath.

"Yes, okay. I should go and make sure everybody has something to eat."

Zack followed him to the door and eased it shut behind him before racing back to kneel beside his grandmother. He wouldn't have much time alone with her before his grandfather came back or somebody else popped in. He reached out with his mind and his heart fell into his stomach. The doctor was right, there was very little Life left within her and her body was prioritising only the most basic of functions.

He needed to wake her for this to stand any chance of working, but before he did that, he shut down the pain receptors with a thin stream of Life along the nerves and into the brain. This was normally a dangerous thing to do, since pain was there to keep a person safe, but she was past the need for it. After this, he channelled a swell of Life towards her and waited.

His grandmother's breathing steadied and her eyes crept open. She gave him a soft, tired smile, but her voice was dry and scratchy.

"I expected to see you again, Zacharias, before this was all over."

"Hi, Baba. It's not going to be over; I can help." Zack heard how rapidly he was speaking and he tried to slow himself down. "It might feel a bit strange, and I can't explain much more about it, but I can—"

She reached out and held his hand. "No, Zacharias."

"No, you don't understand, and that's okay, but I can make you better."

"I understand. And I said 'no'. I am too tired for this."

"I can fix that too." His voice took on a pleading tone.

"No." His grandmother's eyes locked with his. "I have earned this, my boy. I have paid with every ache, every weakening, every lessening of who I was. I won't have gone through all of this only to pay it all over again when the next thing comes along. I can't."

No, no, no. This was not how it was supposed to go. "You won't have to. I can keep you well."

"And what will that do to him?" There was no doubt who she meant when she said 'him' that way; his grandfather. "You have all been looking at me, but I have been looking at him. This is draining him away. And he won't understand what you've done; he'll keep worrying and draining himself."

"I can keep Deda well too," Zack said.

"And how many more, for how long, Zacharias? No, it is my time to be at peace and his time to rest."

"But he'll miss you."

His grandmother released his hand and gestured at her body. "He already misses me. He worries and he tires himself and he misses me."

Tears welled in Zack's eyes. "I'll miss you."

She reclaimed his hand. "Of course you will. Good boys are supposed to miss their grandmothers and you have always been a very good boy."

"Are you sure? It could be just the fatigue making you feel this way."

"I am sure. I decided months ago to say no if you offered."

"You thought I'd be able to cure you?" Zack asked, finding that he wasn't as surprised as he might have been.

"I thought you'd try. Your Deda might be very proud to have

a doctor for a grandson one day, but I am already very proud to have a witch for one. I've always liked witches." Her eyes twinkled along with the twist in her smile.

"Is there anything I can do?" A few stray tears had made their way down his cheeks.

"Could I maybe stay awake long enough to say goodbye to everyone?"

Zack nodded, not trusting himself to speak.

"I love you, Zacharias. Keep this boy safe as he becomes the man, yes?"

"Yes. I love you, Babi."

"Now, go get him. I'll need to set him straight before he gets his silly hopes up."

Zack nodded and stood up to leave.

"And Zacharias?"

"Yes, Babi?"

"Maybe, it will not hurt too much at the end?"

"No, Babi. I promise. It won't hurt."

She relaxed her grip and let him slip out the door to send his grandfather in.

Zack sat on the back porch, looking out at the garden through blurry eyes while his family took turns to share their goodbyes with her. And, as he sobbed, he admitted to himself that his last words to her had been a lie. He could only stop it from hurting her.

It was well towards noon the next day and Zack hadn't left his bed, lost in thoughts of the day before. After all the goodbyes, his grandfather had sat with his grandmother as she slipped away while the rest of them comforted each other and waited. More than once, he heard a cousin, or an aunty, speak of how blessed they were, or what a miracle it was, that they had those final moments with her.

He didn't think they'd feel so blessed if they knew what he should have been able to do months ago.

His phone vibrated on his bedside table, but he ignored it. It had buzzed on and off all morning. He'd messaged Art when he got home about what had happened, but he couldn't face any of his friends right now. He wasn't certain he could even face his reflection.

The bedroom door squeaked open. His father entered and sat on the end of the bed. He had been the one to make all the necessary phone calls after his grandmother had passed away in the late afternoon and had held it together until he had sat down in the front passenger seat of their car. Then he had wept the whole way home and retreated to the bedroom. And now he was showered, shaved and patting Zack's knee through the bedsheets.

"How are you doing, mate?"

"Yeah, okay. Just laying here thinking about it all," Zack replied.

"Thinking is good. But get up, get changed and have some breakfast. Then I'll leave you alone to do some more thinking." His father sniffed the air and then took a more deliberate sniff over Zack. He scrunched up his face and walked towards the door. "Actually, shower, get changed and have some breakfast. Dear lord!"

Zack took his own investigative inhale and his nose wrinkled. His father had a point and, now that he thought about it, he hadn't showered since before he had left for the last mission. Turned out that fighting, getting interrogated and trekking across a tundra in a snowstorm could really build up a funk. He hauled himself out of bed and lumbered to the bathroom.

The warm comfort of the shower lulled him back into his thoughts and he lost himself in them until he was snapped back by a loud thudding against the door. He hopped out and threw a towel around him before opening it. Ellen was there, fist poised for another round of battering.

"Finally."

"What?" Zack asked, with perhaps more attitude than he intended.

"Well, for one, don't use all the hot water. And two, there's some girl sitting on the front fence."

"What does she look like?" Zack asked.

"I don't know. I'm not going to go perv on her for you." Ellen strode away down the hall.

Zack hurried back to his room and peered out of his window. Their front yard had a two-foot high brick wall, separating the yard from the footpath and nature strip, and sitting on the corner of it, next to the driveway, was Tabitha.

Zack found some clean clothes to wear and shuffled outside to meet her.

Tabitha gave him a soft smile as he approached and pushed a white paper box into his hands.

"I know the traditional thing is to give a casserole or something, but I can't cook."

Zack looked through the clear plastic lid. "Donuts?"

"Well, I also can't bake." She wrapped her arms around him. "Art told us. I'm so sorry, Zack. I know you probably wanted to be left alone, but I had to check on you."

"Thanks."

Tabitha released the hug and sat back down, patting the spot next to her.

"How are you going?"

Zack sat beside her, resting the box on his lap. "Okay, I guess. It's just hard. The rest of the family were consoling each other by saying that it had been coming for a while, that they'd had more time with her than they could have hoped, that now the pain was gone and maybe this was best for her."

Tabitha nodded along.

"But they don't know that I should have been able to help her. This wasn't the best we could have hoped for. This was a failure. My failure. She's gone because I'm not the Lifer I should be." He heard the self-loathing in his voice as he spoke and lowered his head.

"Oh, Zack." Tabitha hugged him again, resting her forehead on his shoulder. "It doesn't matter how powerful we get; we all have limits. You can't stop the world from dying."

"I'm not talking about the world, Tabs. One person. Her. If I couldn't save her…" he struggled to find the words. "If I couldn't save her, when that's all I've wanted from this magic, what I've been working so hard for, then how can I be trusted with anything else? What else am I going to fail at, when somebody else could have worked harder or learned it faster?"

Tabitha sat back up but left a hand on his leg as the pent-up words continued to tumble out of Zack.

"You know, my parents were so proud of my results this year and proud of the work I did to earn them. And the only thing that stopped me from being sick with guilt was telling myself that I had been working hard and I had been getting results, just not in a way I could show them. But those real results came in yesterday. I failed."

"Zack—"

He kept going. "How can I be trusted with any of this? Trusted with any of you? I mean it, Tabs, I really think we should talk to Junie about making sure you have a real Lifer in the team."

"Zack." The sharpness in Tabitha's voice snapped him out of his vocalised thoughts. She lifted the box of donuts off his lap and placed it on the fence beside her before taking his hands in hers. "I could tell you that we are all still learning our magic."

"Not like—" he started, but she cut him off.

"And it would be true. And I could point to dozens of examples, some very, very recent, of your magic saving our lives. And they would also be true. But honestly, that's not the point."

He blinked at her; confusion clear on his face.

"Even if you were the worst the School of Life had to offer, I wouldn't want anybody else on our team."

"What? Why? Tabitha, you need somebody there who can save you."

"I need somebody there I can rely on. You all picked me to lead and that's amazing. And I'm willing, but I can't do it without you."

"We all support you, Tabitha."

"I'm not talking about the others." She held up a hand and started counting off her fingers. "Bast likes to be given a task so he can deliver it. Charlie likes to hang back and not make waves. Jackie has great ideas if we could only get her to say them out loud. Art's always lost in some kind of angle to prove how clever he is. And Kimmy is, well, she's Kimmy. But then there's you. You speak up without trying to take control, you offer ideas without any ego and you notice things when everybody else is too caught up in what they expect to see. I mean it, Zack. I can't do this without you."

Zack's mouth dropped open.

"I'm sorry that you lost somebody special to you. And if you want, I'll go, and you can go back inside and grieve with your family. But stop doubting yourself. You're our Lifer and you're my First Mate and there's no getting out of either."

Tabitha squeezed his hands and they sat in silence. Zack felt the sunshine on his skin and allowed Tabitha's words to sink in along with the warmth. He thought of his grandmother and, setting aside his feelings of failure, he considered what she had seen in him. The boy she had been so proud of. It might not have been so distant from how Tabitha saw him.

Well then, fine, he thought. He may never be the Lifer that either of them needed, but he could do his best to be the man they asked him to be.

"Thank you, Tabitha." Zack smiled. "I don't suppose there's any news?"

"From the Tower? No. But Bast has been looking more closely at some of the rituals I took photos of and he thinks there is something different about these gate rituals. He says it's got something to do with how the ink was made."

Zack squinted. "Does he have any ideas how that could be used?"

"No. But the rest of us are going to head into the Tower this afternoon and run it past Junie. Bast has spent more time working with those rituals compared to the rest of his School, so maybe he's picked up something they've missed. We'll let you know if it leads to anything."

"I'll come."

"You don't have to, if you need more time."

"No, I'll come. Give me the rest of the morning and I'll be ready."

"Okay then." Tabitha stood up and handed him back the donuts. "I am really sorry. Wish your family the best from me, okay?"

"I will. Thanks, Tabs. For everything." Zack shook the box. "Including the baked goods."

CHAPTER 30

LOCKED OUT

Art picked him up at three in his dinged up, second hand car. Zack's parents, assuming he was heading out to blow off steam, hugged him on his way out the door. As he approached the car, Jackie unbuckled her seatbelt, but Zack motioned for her to stay in the front seat and slid into the back.

"How are you doing, mate?" Art asked from the driver's seat.

"Yeah, mostly keen to be thinking about something else."

"I hear that. So, I reckon I'm about two months away from being able to upgrade this piece of crap to a nice big seven-seater. Got my eye on this Audi. Room for all of us, weapons, and even Max in the back."

Art droned on for a few minutes about different models of SUVs and Zack's mind slipped back to his morbid thoughts.

"Hey," he said, interrupting Art's sound system comparison. "How does the Tower handle it if somebody dies in service? I mean, there's all this stuff that goes on, like getting someone declared dead and all that would risk the Silence, wouldn't it?"

Jackie shifted uncomfortably in her seat, but Art's tone was relaxed as he answered.

"That's psychomancer territory. It's mostly a lot of paperwork and it changes from country to country, but you get the right officials to sign the right documents and you're sorted. Where possible, you plant a few memories in the next of kin's minds as well, so they remember getting the news and asking all their questions."

"Oh my god, Art," Jackie gasped. "You mean their memory of their loved one's death isn't going to be real?"

"No memories are real," Art replied. "Our minds alter them all the time and sometimes make up entirely new ones. But yeah, to keep the Silence safe, and to keep those people safe, you have to edit out the magic bits. But you can also help them along with their shock and give them a story about the person they can hold on to."

They lapsed into an uncomfortable silence and, after a few minutes, Art turned on the radio for the rest of the drive. Twenty minutes later, they parked and met with the others around the corner from the Tower entrance.

Charlie rushed to his side and threw her arms around him. "I'm so sorry, Zack."

Bast and Kimmy echoed the sentiment while he returned Charlie's hug.

"Thanks," he said to all of them, stepping back from Charlie. "I'm still kind of processing it and, in the meantime, I'd like to focus on Tower stuff instead."

"Let's go talk to Junie, then," Kimmy said. "Make sure we're not getting cut out of this."

"That is not what we're here for." Tabitha followed her across the road to the entrance. "Bast is just going to share what he's worked out about the rituals."

"Yeah," Kimmy said in a tone that seemed to agree with Tabitha, "and then we go with the rest of them and get some payback for Yacht-hammer."

"Jotunheim!" Art said. "I've said it how many times?"

"You're assuming I listen to you at… hang on, what the hell?"

Kimmy had been mid-sentence as she stepped into the shadows of the Tower entrance, except that she didn't disappear through the shadow. None of them had. Instead, they were in what appeared to be the three-by-three metre vestibule at the front of a mid-renovation accountant's office.

"I've always wondered what was actually here," Bast said, craning his neck to see above the newspaper stuck over most of the glass.

"Why didn't it let us in?" Charlie asked.

"Let's try again," Tabitha said and herded them all back onto the footpath.

They stepped through the shadowed entrance and once more found themselves in the vestibule.

"I don't get it," Kimmy said. "Has Junie blocked us out to keep us from the action?"

"She can't," Bast replied. "The entrance magic is part of the Tower and it accepts all Tower members. We'd have to be formally kicked out for it to not work for us."

"I think we can assume we weren't," Tabitha said. "Which suggests that nobody can use this entrance."

"It's worse than that," Bast said. "The magic that runs the entrances comes from the Tower's side. If it was only this entrance out of play, there would have to be a block of some kind here and I'd be able to feel it. And there isn't, which means…"

"It's all entrances," Art finished.

"It's happening right now, then," Zack said.

"We're too late?" Jackie asked.

"Maybe not." Tabitha paced back and forward rubbing her chin. "I mean, the first thing you'd do is block off the Tower and then you'd kick off with whatever you're going to do."

Bast laughed. "Tabs, that makes it sound like they pushed some furniture in front of the door. They aren't like any old gate opened up for a quick trip. They're part of a complex network of Movement magic. The sheer amount of energy needed to close down the Tower entrances would be crazy, I don't know how they'd have anything left in the tank to do anything worth pissing the Tower off."

"Hang on," Zack said, "what if they aren't spending the energy to close down the entrances?"

"What, like they found a switch or something, and turned it off?" Kimmy shook her head.

"No, it's what Bast said. The entrances are maintained by the Tower. Maybe shutting down the entrances is just a happy side effect." Zack's mind was racing. "This has all been about Movement magic. That stack of rituals that Kimmy found means that guy in Korea was probably only one of many. Armand told Connor to get his people together. That's what those rituals and the ink were all about, training up Movement mages. I think they're tapping into the Tower's entrance magic to fuel whatever they are doing."

"The map!" Charlie turned to Tabitha. "Pull it up on your phone."

Tabitha opened the photo she'd taken of the map and they crowded around her to look at it.

"I'm sure those are all Tower entrances," Charlie said. "But it's not all of them. The New York one isn't there and neither is Brisbane."

"Zoom in on Brisbane, Tabs." Art squeezed in to peer closer.

Tabitha pushed his head out of the way and stretched her fingers across the image.

"There!" Art pointed at the numbers written onto the map. "There's no pin, but they do have the coordinates."

"Then what's the deal with the pinned ones?" Jackie asked.

Tabitha flicked the map down to Sydney. "Look at this one. They haven't just pinned it; they've drawn a line through it."

They followed the line south-east, where it stopped at a pin in New Zealand, but to the north-west it passed through pins in Indonesia and India before it hit a junction point with several other lines. Each of the other lines passed through multiple pins and there was only one place they all met: north Iran, close to the border with Turkmenistan. There was no pin at the junction but there was tiny writing that Tabitha had to zoom in very close to see. Coordinates.

"So, they're there?" Kimmy asked.

"We don't know that," Tabitha replied, pulling back her phone.

"Well, I think something is there," Zack said.

"We don't even know what those lines mean," Tabitha said.

"Ley lines?" Art looked at Zack.

Kimmy rolled her eyes. "I swear you just make up crap sometimes."

"No, it's a thing," Zack said to Kimmy before turning back to Art. "I don't know, I've never heard Sara or anybody in the Tower mention them."

Bast's eyes narrowed in thought. "What are ley lines?"

"I don't really know," Zack replied. "But it's the idea that magic travels in lines across the land, so that some places are more magical than others, or at least more connected to it."

Bast nodded. "I think there might be something to that. I've never heard my dickhead mentor use the phrase 'ley lines', but the idea of connections and flows to certain places is definitely in the ballpark."

That seemed to bring Tabitha around. "Okay, okay. So, we're saying that whatever has shut down the entrances could be there. How does that help us?"

"Well," Bast said. "I think I can get us there."

"Really?" Tabitha asked.

"I think so," Bast replied. "Bring me up a good satellite photo of the coordinates to help, but yeah."

"Should we, though?" Charlie asked.

"Hell yeah." Kimmy slapped her palm against her fist. "I want payback."

"Payback for when they handed our arses to us," Charlie replied.

"I'm not sure we have any other good options," Zack said. "Based on our info, Junie and whatever squads she could pull together, were waiting inside the Tower to respond to this. If they're trapped in there, we're the only ones who can do anything about this. Maybe we can disrupt it long enough for the entrances to open up."

"So, we're doing this, then?" Bast asked, looking around the group.

Tabitha presented a satellite image on her phone. "Zack's right. We swore the oaths. We have to do this."

Everybody else nodded.

"If the coordinates are there." Zack pointed at the image. "Bast, can you open up a gate about a kilometre or two away, maybe around there?"

"Good idea. Let's not appear in the middle of what they're doing. Okay then, give me some space." Bast knelt at the far end of the vestibule and began his incantations.

Art sighed melodramatically.

"What?" Tabitha asked.

"Well, apart from Bast's sword and the floating nightmare I assume is in Kimmy's pocket, we don't have our weapons."

Kimmy patted her jacket.

"I hadn't thought of that," Tabitha said. "I guess we're going to have to be smart about this, then."

The teens shivered as they hid behind a snow-covered mound. The clouds above the mountain, Bast had deposited them on, covered the sky but were thin enough to allow weak beams of sunlight through.

"Well, I guess we know why they were practising in frost giant country," Art said through chattering teeth.

"Are you sure they're up there?" Tabitha asked Bast.

Bast nodded. "The amount of Movement magic up there is almost making me dizzy. We need to hurry." Without waiting, he paced his way up towards the peak and the others scrambled after him.

It was a gentle climb, even if unpleasant in the cold and within 10 minutes, they were close enough to the top to hear them. The swirling wind carried a chorus of incantations, but other voices could be heard in between. They stopped their climb just short of the relatively flat plateau at the peak of the mountain, crouching just beneath it to observe the scene.

"Bloody hell," Charlie whispered in a hiss. "There's so many of them."

Zack counted 15 mages on the snow dusted mountaintop and hoped that no more were hidden nearby. They seemed to be in four groups, with three pairs surrounding the remaining nine. It was the pairs that were incanting.

"The ones on the outside are all Movement mages," whispered Bast. "They're dealing with a crazy amount of mojo."

Zack looked closer and could see Connor paired up with the Korean Movement mage, Kaylani with another and the other Movement mage from Jotunheim with a sixth one. In the centre was Armand, the Body mage in his normal size, Phet, and a few others, but Pawel did not appear to be there.

"We were right," he said. "I don't recognise anybody from the Tower."

"So, what's the plan?" Charlie asked.

"If we disrupt the Movement mages, that should unlock the Tower, right?" Tabitha asked.

"In theory," Bast replied. "No idea what the delay would be, though. They've been banking up some magic here."

"So, no cavalry coming to the rescue any time soon then," Tabitha said.

"And we've got to stay alive long enough to stop them from starting it back up again," Zack said.

"If somebody can give me a distraction," Bast said, "then I can get close to the pairs and maybe throw a spanner into whatever they're doing. The feedback could knock them around enough that they won't be ready to try again for a while."

"Is that safe?" Charlie asked.

"No, that's kind of the point. Hopefully I can make it unsafe for them."

"I can do the distraction," Kimmy said.

"What about after that?" Art asked. "We're outnumbered, just like last time."

"That's not why we lost last time," Zack said.

Tabitha raised an eyebrow. "What do you mean?"

"We've been outnumbered before and won. We lost last time because they knew what to expect from us." Zack looked around at his friends. "But now we know two things."

"Which are?" Kimmy asked with impatience.

"We know what to expect from them. And we know what they expect from us."

Art nodded. "Yeah, alright. I can work with that."

"Okay, let's break up into teams then," Tabitha said. "Jackie, you—"

A groaning sound that was felt, as much as it was heard, tore through the air and a half metre wide circle of grey light opened near each of the pairs. As each circle of light opened, another groan, like an echo of the first, rippled out and a second circular gate grew behind each of the first ones. The sound tolled again and a third trio of circles appeared.

"Oh, crap!" Bast's eyes were wide.

"What?" Tabitha asked.

"Those aren't gates."

CHAPTER 31

RITUAL

"What do you mean they aren't gates?" Art asked.

"I get it now," Bast replied. "Why I couldn't understand the rituals scrawled on the side of the map. Gates are two directional. These aren't, these are more like… like valves. They are sucking parts of other realms into this one."

"Why would they do that?" Jackie asked.

"I think we're about to see," Charlie said, pointing towards the group in the centre.

Armand spoke to one of the people that Zack didn't recognise; a tall man who appeared to be in his late 30s. The man stepped forward to stand in the centre of the triangle created by the three pairs of Movement mages. He was there for only a second before he grunted and some kind of force lifted him half a metre off the ground, where he stayed, hovering.

"Deadly," Bast whispered.

"What's happening to him?" Kimmy asked.

Bast's voice was filled with awe. "Movement magic. More of it than I can keep track of. It's sucking some kind of energy out of a bunch of realms and pouring it into old mate floating over there."

"We need to stop this now," Tabitha said. "Let's go!"

Art ran forward. He closed the distance quickly and was only a few metres away from the edge of the triangle when the group in the centre saw him.

"Haven't you learnt your lesson yet, child?" Armand smirked and stepped towards Art. "How many times must I teach you that you don't have the power to face me?"

"Nah, I picked that up already, thanks," Art said with a sly smile, and Zack and Charlie caught up with him.

Armand's smirk widened into a sneer and he gestured towards Art, purple magic collecting around his hand. "A beastmaster and a seer? How will they help you?"

Art's fingertips glowed purple. "Well, that's the thing. My buddy here told a fib; he's not a seer."

Zack took that as his signal and, taking the connection of Life he'd established with Charlie, he extended it to Art. Life rushed through the channel and Art unleashed his magic into Armand's mind. The man's face froze in confusion and shock before his eyes glazed over, his mouth fell loose and he collapsed limp to the ground.

"Is he dead?" Charlie asked.

"Nope, I've just stunned him as hard as I could," Art replied.

The other mages looked at the dazed form of Armand in shock, but a few stepped forward.

"Hey, losers." Kimmy had crept closer while they were distracted by Art. "Ready for a barbeque?"

She incanted and a swirling globe of fire formed in between her hands. It grew from the size of a golf ball until it was a little larger than a basketball, spurts of flame licking out from the surface.

Three of the mages lined up and made their own gestures, forming the brown and bright blue clouds that had countered Kimmy's flames before. Three lines of red Fire drained off the flaming orb towards the clouds and Kimmy strained in effort as it began to shrink. The others from the centre group murmured their own incantations and Kimmy cackled.

"Everyone's so focused clearly on sunshine…"

"… they never see the storm coming," Tabitha finished from behind her and completed her own incantation. The clouds above the mountain rippled and a bolt of lightning shot downwards, striking amidst the centre group. Their bodies scattered, while their shouts and screams were lost amid the deafening boom of thunder.

Bast raced towards the closest pair of Movement mages and made frantic gestures toward the trio of shimmering grey discs. Whatever he did, worked. There was a pulsing, almost subsonic boom that knocked the two Movement mages to the ground where they lay motionless. Bast, himself, was caught in the blast, but was able to stagger back to his feet, rubbing his temples.

The Body mage was the first from the centre group to regain his feet and, as he did, he grew larger than he had before until he was more than twice Zack's size. He scooped up a metal baseball bat and lumbered forward.

Zack sighed. "Round three, I guess." He paced towards the brute, trying to gauge the man's reach.

A woman they hadn't met before was next up off the ground, but as she stood, her body shimmered behind a russet glow and a grizzly bear emerged.

"Oh, we call dibs," Charlie said before looking down at Max. "Let's get her."

She worked an incantation and emerged from her own russet shimmer as a grey wolf, almost half again as large as Max. The two canines sprinted towards the bear, circling around it.

"Oh, Mr Shanks," Kimmy called out and the ornate dagger floated out of her jacket. She pointed at the Earth mage who had broken Charlie's ribs with a boulder last time they met. "Put some holes in her for me, please."

The knife wiggled its hilt before zipping toward the woman who had just regained her feet. With a hasty gesture, her hands and wrists formed a rocky hide and she parried the thrusts of the animated blade an inch from her throat.

"I'm taking the other Earth mage," Kimmy said, running at the man still recovering from the lightning blast.

"Suits me fine." Tabitha ran beside her towards the Air mage.

Bast appeared to have cleared his head and turned his attention to the three valves pouring magical energy into the man in the centre.

"Do you know how to close them?" Art called out to him.

"Nope," Bast answered, "but I think I'll pretend that I do, hey?" He incanted, tracing shapes and symbols into the air in front of him and the three grey circles began to shrink.

The brute launched a massive swing at Zack, who ducked it just in time. The bat, looking undersized inside the man's overgrown fist, sailed above him and Zack bolted forward. He kicked hard at his opponent's knee and forced it sideways. The hulking mage grunted in pain and stumbled, dropping to his other knee to stop from falling over. Zack leapt backwards to avoid an elbow to the chest and noticed a man, he recognised as the Mind mage from Korea, gesturing towards him.

"Um, Art! Little help!"

Art spun away from watching Bast and looked towards Zack. "Oh no you don't, tiger!"

The Mind mage's eyes snapped wide and he wrenched his body around to face Art, the two now locked in a mental duel.

The bear roared and the Charlie-Wolf responded with a howl, echoed by Max. The two canines had flanked the bear, who circled backwards, her head turning from side to side in an effort to keep both enemies in sight. Charlie darted forward, snapping her teeth, and the bear responded, raking out with an enormous and sharp set of claws. But Charlie's attack had been a feint, and the bear had now lost sight of Max. She took advantage of the opening and bit deep into the bear's hamstring. With a roar of pain, the bear kicked out and Max was thrown across the snow and gravel, but not without taking a chunk of fur and flesh between her teeth.

The animated dagger slashed and lunged away at its target but was deflected each time against the woman's stone-covered parries. On one thrust, it went high, skating over the forearm and cutting deep into the woman's shoulder. She hissed in pain and tried to grab for the hilt, but it weaved away through the air and readied for another attack.

The other Earth mage was still on his back as Kimmy advanced towards him, but when she was only a few steps from his side, he flicked his hands and a spray of gravel and dirt shot out of the thin snow cover and engulfed Kimmy. She turned her back to protect her face, but the sharp stones tore through her jacket and into her skin. She staggered on her feet while the man pushed himself onto his.

A few metres away, Tabitha and the Air mage met each other with torrents of wind. Snow and mud splashed out from each side as the two streams of air crashed against each other. Tabitha gritted her teeth and planted her legs to stop from sliding backwards, but the two were otherwise in a stalemate.

Bast shouted in celebration. "I've got this, they're almost shut!"

The three valves had shrunk to the size of coins and Bast pushed on, forcing them towards closure. As the discs disappeared, there was a deafening crack, louder than Tabitha's lightning bolt. The flow of energy towards the man in the centre faltered and he wavered in the air, still kept aloft by the remaining two streams. However, closer to the site of the valves, the effects were more intense. The cracking sound was accompanied by a violent ripple of orange energy. Bast, fatigued and distracted from closing the valves, was unprepared and could only flinch and wait for the orange bubble to ripple over him. But instead, it crashed against a barrier of Jackie's steely grey magic. The other two Movement mages had no such protection and the orange energy passed over them. Wild kinetic energy snaked through their bodies, fracturing bones and joints, before dissipating.

"Okay," Bast said in a stunned voice. "So, it's a little different from closing a gate. Thanks, for the shield Jackie!" He ran towards the next pair of mages and trio of valves.

Zack charged back towards the brute, hoping that if he made it inside his reach, he might negate some of the size advantage. The man swung down at him with the bat, but Zack had anticipated it and darted to the side, straight into the man's left foot which kicked Zack square in his chest. The air rushed out of him and he sailed several metres backwards. He didn't even need to reach out with his Life; at least four ribs were broken.

"Are. You. All. Right. Zack?" Art forced out while locked in his psychic battle.

Zack didn't trust himself to speak, but forced his hand up from the ground and gave a raised thumb.

"Good." Art inched towards the other mage. Both their faces were tight with the effort of their control, but the wideness of their eyes revealed the horrors they were inflicting upon one another. The other man's lips trembled as Art crept ever closer, but neither of them gave in.

The bear snapped her sharp teeth at Charlie, who skittered back to avoid the bite. But as soon as she did, the bear sprinted on all fours towards where Max was recovering from her slide across the ground. The bear was fast, but Charlie was faster. She raced alongside the large ursine creature and leapt at its head, raking her jaw with her wolf-form's short claws. The weight of Charlie's body knocked the bear off target and by the time it had turned back to Max, Charlie crouched in between them, snarling.

The animated dagger continued its assault and the Earth mage was slowing down. Twice more the blade found a way past the woman's rocky carapace and drew blood. Gritting her teeth against the pain, she incanted and the hardened earth that encased her arms melted into mud. The next time the dagger soared forward, she fended it away with her forearm. Some of the thick, clayish mud clung to blade and hilt as the dagger emerged and it bobbed clumsily against the added weight. Undeterred, it whipped forward again.

Kimmy waved her fingers through the air and murmured some words under her breath before sprinting at the second Earth mage. The man began his own incantation, but his eyes widened in shock as fire engulfed Kimmy's right hand past her wrist.

She launched herself toward him and slammed her fist into his chest. "Syphon off these flames, arsehole," she said, raising her fist to punch him a second time.

The man dodged to the side and kicked out at her with the flat of his boot. Kimmy thrust her fiery hand against his leg and the Earth mage grunted in pain as the impact of his kick pushed the two of them away. Before Kimmy could close back in on him, the man whispered his own incantation and a stone club grew in his hand.

He gripped it with both hands and, although his movements were visibly pained from the burns to his chest and leg, he readied for Kimmy's next attack.

Nearby, Tabitha and the Air mage were still struggling against each other's jets of wind, but Tabitha was faltering. She had dropped to one knee and the strength of her torrent had lessened against his, forcing her back across the ground.

The Air mage gave a mocking laugh.

"That lightning show was very impressive, but it seems it didn't really leave you much in the tank." He moved towards her, pushing her further back and the rocky ground tore at her knee. "Wielding the wind requires strength and endurance, which you clearly lack, little girl."

Tabitha glared at him, but the jets from her hands wavered. The man's cruel smile widened to show his teeth and his own streams of air picked up in strength.

Tabitha dropped to both knees in an effort to plant herself on the ground, but she still slid. She hissed through the pain of her knees and shins being cut up by the ground and forced out another incantation. The man's eyes widened in fear and his smile disappeared as he realised what she was doing. Before he could react, Tabitha finished her spell and reversed the direction of her own streams of wind.

With both jets now forcing the air in the same direction, the torrent was violent. Tabitha used the last of her strength to throw herself to the side, out of the brutal corridor of wind. But the doubling of the wind jets forced more air forward from behind the Air mage, snatching him up and pushing him into the streams. Caught up in the small, but chaotically strong, windstorm, the man was lifted into the air and propelled past Tabitha and hundreds of metres down the mountainside. Tabitha watched him sail away before she collapsed on her back, trying to catch her breath.

Bast raced around the fighting to reach the second of the Movement mage pairs. He skidded to a halt further away than last time and traced his hands through the air. Movement magic poured in amongst the valves and disrupted the pair's efforts. Kaylani looked towards him in alarm and took a few steps away from the other mage, but it was too late. She and the other mage were knocked to the ground by the magic released from their disrupted spell. Bast, on the other hand, had dropped into a crouch to brace himself against the wave of force. The moment it had passed, he began the ritual to close the three valves.

Zack tried to get back onto his feet, but the pain in his chest barely allowed him to lift his head off the ground. He drew Life into himself and directed it towards the fractured ribs and the small lacerations the breaks had done to his muscles and flesh. He could hear the brute charging towards him but was in no state to get up or even roll out of the way until his bones were healed. The pain and his growing fatigue made it hard to concentrate so the flows of Life were not as efficient as they should have been and before he was finished, the Body mage loomed over him, his metal bat raised high above his head, ready to strike down.

Zack abandoned the streams and prepared to throw himself to the side, waiting at the last moment to do so. The bat came crashing down towards him but, an instant before Zack dodged, the bat struck a shimmer of steel light and bounced back, striking the man in the face. His partially healed ribs protesting, Zack leaped up and wrenched the bat from the dazed brute's hand before dropping low and swinging it into the side of his knee. The kneecap crunched under and the man fell to the ground.

Zack looked over to where Jackie was facing him and he waved a thanks towards her. She smiled and returned the wave but, over her shoulder, Zack saw Phet had recovered from the lightning blast and was incanting. A small axe coalesced in the man's hand and he hurled it at Jackie's exposed back. Zack tried to scream a warning, but Jackie didn't turn.

Instead, when the axe was half an inch from hitting her, she spoke a single word and her right arm snapped back over her shoulder and snatched the axe from the air. The weapon twirled in her hand and traces of steely energy followed its path as she spun around on her left foot and launched it straight back at Phet. The head of the axe struck him in the centre of his body and he stumbled backwards, but Jackie didn't wait. She charged at him while he fumbled at the weapon, trying to dislodge it from his body. Jackie's small frame slammed into him and, when he fell to the ground, she landed on top of him. She raised her fist to hit him, but he had struck the back of his head against the earth when he fell and was lying still.

Art and the Mind mage were less than a metre apart now and the other man's eyes were wide with terror. His body shook and Art pushed forward, his face tightening with increased concentration. In the last moment, the Mind mage broke away and snatched up a large stone from the ground. He threw himself at Art, screaming in fear and madness and slammed the stone against Art's upper arm. Art gritted his teeth and blinked against the pain but held his focus and the man dropped the rock and sprinted away, still screaming. He ran with such recklessness that, as he reached the top of the slope, he tripped and tumbled down the mountain. Art dropped his mental assault and fell into a sit, clutching his arm.

The bear faced off against the Charlie-wolf and Max, holding her arms out ready to swipe at either canine if they tried to flank her. Charlie darted forward, snapping her muzzle at the bear's wounded leg. The bear retaliated, slashing down at Charlie's head and cutting deep along her snout. But Max saw an opening and charged. She bounded up along Charlie's back and leapt off her shoulders, her mouth wide open. The bear reared back in surprise, but this only left her more vulnerable and Max bit down, latching onto the bear's throat. The bear thrashed and clawed at Max's body, but between the pain and awkward angle, there was not much strength in the attacks. Stumbling on her feet, Charlie slipped around behind the bear and bit down on the bear's injured calf. The bear roared in fear and agony and collapsed to the ground, where it shimmered with russet light and returned to the form of the Animal mage. Charlie and Max circled away and the woman, covered in blood, held up a hand in submission before passing into unconsciousness. Charlie and Max licked each other's wounds and looked around the mountain top.

The animated dagger was now covered in mud and even when its slowed strikes found their mark, the edges of its blade were so encased that they could no longer break the skin. The Earth mage murmured an incantation and the mud around the dagger expanded and hardened. The extra weight was too much for the knife and it crashed down to the ground, where it could do little but shake back and forth in the snow and grit. The Earth mage looked towards Kimmy and her fingers traced out shapes and symbols. Kimmy moved toward the other Earth mage but found her feet and ankles had been encased in thick clay, binding her to the spot. The male Earth mage laughed and limped toward her, his stone club ready.

Kimmy abandoned her flaming fist and worked a new spell, building another ball of fire between her twirling hands. Both Earth mages responded with their countering brown energy clouds, and streams of Fire were syphoned from the sphere. Kimmy hissed through the exertion and pulled more Fire into her incantation when there was a thunderous cracking sound behind the two mages. They flinched and looked aside, but there was no lightning bolt. However, their break in concentration was enough for Kimmy to hurl the ball of fire between them. It struck the ground and a wave of flame rippled over them both, setting them alight. Tabitha flicked Kimmy a weak salute from where she cast the air vacuum that had caused the bang. Both girls dropped to their hands and knees in exhaustion.

Bast was already halfway toward the last of the Movement mages when the second set of valves closed and detonated in a wave of brutal orange energy. The last two were Connor and the Korean Movement mage. Connor turned to Bast as he approached. He dropped the spell that was maintaining the valves and began to cast another, but in his haste to prepare for Bast's approach, he must have misjudged the effects of being so close to the valves. The Movement magic he drew crashed against the valve ritual and both spells fractured. The pulses that Bast had managed to effect against the other pairs were nothing compared with this burst of energy that launched both men four metres into the air. The Korean mage landed hard onto the ground and did not stir, but Connor fumbled as he fell and, dazed as he was, completed a spell that left him hovering in the air above the valves.

Rather than attack him, Bast turned his attention to the valves, working the spell to close them for the third time. Connor drew a knife from his belt and flew towards Bast, blade first. Bast's hands blurred as he worked his magic with dangerous speed but, an instant before Connor's knife tip reached him, the valves slammed closed. Bast jumped backwards and kicked out at Connor with the flats of his feet. Connor slashed at Bast's leg, cutting deep into his thigh, but Bast's kick landed on Connor's shoulders and pushed him backwards into the oncoming wave of orange violence. Connor's body was cracked and broken as Bast's, propelled by the impact, slid through the snow and gravel to safety.

With the final valves closed, the man in the centre of the ritual fell to the ground. Zack looked around at where his friends were standing victorious, but not without injuries. Injuries that needed their Lifer's aid now. He sidestepped the brute's clumsy grab at his leg and swung the bat against the side of the man's head. The brute twisted at the blow before collapsing limply to the ground. Zack hoped he would live, but some of his friends might not if he wasted any more time with him. He ran towards Bast, who was clutching at his blood-soaked leg. Before he could channel any Life, Armand and the tall man who had been at the centre of the ritual stumbled to their feet.

CHAPTER 32

REVELATIONS

"How dare you!" Armand shouted at them, his face red with rage. "Pathetic little pawns of the Tower. Your masters keep all the power to themselves and send you out to prevent any of us from gathering more than crumbs."

"I don't know about that, mate," Art replied. He braced his injured arm with his other and eased himself back up. "The Tower sends us out to protect the world, including from textbook psychos who want to rip the world apart by opening a bunch of gates."

"Protect the world?" Armand's laugh was full of derision. "Is that what they tell you? You are fools."

"If we're fools, then how did we stop you?" Kimmy replied.

"Did you?" The other man spoke in a deep voice and looked toward Kimmy with a singular intensity.

"C'mon, man," Tabitha spoke past the man to Armand. "Just surrender. The Tower will be here soon. We don't want to hurt either of you and you're totally outnumbered."

"You're right. Let's rectify that." Armand incanted with rapid precision and his fingers flicked back and forth across him.

Art's face went slack with shock and, at Zack's side, Bast swore. "What the shit?"

Orange light collected at the supposed Mind mage's fingertips and, a few metres to his left, a gate opened.

"How is that possible?" Tabitha wondered aloud.

"Simple. I haven't been brainwashed," Armand answered.

His next words were interrupted by a chorus of skittering and clacking as a swarm of creatures emerged from the gate. About a foot in diameter, they had the appearance of spiders except their bodies were entirely made of bone. As they scuttled forward, similarly sized creatures flew out above them, their wings sharp and skeletal and, within seconds, there were dozens of them.

"I believe that rebalances the numbers," Armand said, before directing the creatures. "Kill them!"

Charlie-Wolf and Max didn't hesitate and barrelled into the swarm of crawling bones. They each crushed one between their jaws and kicked out at others with their paws, snapping off their thin limbs and sending them bouncing away. But for every one that they removed, several more took its place.

"I need to close that portal," Bast said, trying to stand.

Zack put a firm hand on his chest. "Not before I fix this leg."

He channelled Life into Bast's wound, repairing the damage done to the vein and muscle and closing the wound. Bast had lost a fair bit of blood, and he tried to stimulate more from his marrow, but there wasn't much that could be done without some water and a lot more energy. And the latter would take Zack out of play.

"Go easy, mate," Zack said, releasing his hold on Bast.

"No worries, Zack. Cheers, I've got this." Bast whispered his own incantation and his movements accelerated. He drew his rapier. "We need to clear a spot safe from those things if I'm going to close this gate."

Zack stood up and tested the weight of the baseball bat. "Right behind you."

The tall mage who had been in the centre of the ritual snapped his fingers, and a three-foot wide ball of fire appeared in his hand.

He laughed in exaltation and reached into it before hurling a piece of it toward Kimmy. The flaming orb crashed against one of Jackie's shields, inches from Kimmy.

"Two can play that game," Kimmy shouted and launched a thin jet of fire at the man.

With a casual ease, the Fire mage blocked the incoming jet with his ball of fire, which grew in size. Kimmy snapped off the stream and looked to Tabitha for help.

Tabitha was struggling to stay upright, but she signalled to Kimmy and Jackie. "Circle around him to take him off guard." The other two girls nodded and spread out.

Zack and Bast made their way towards the wolves, lashing out at both the crawling and the flying creatures as they moved. Zack's baseball bat wasn't as balanced or versatile as his preferred weapon, but it was ideal for smashing tiny critters made of bone and he destroyed one with every swing. Bast's rapier was less suited, but while the thin blade wasn't very effective against bone, its length did help deflect the creatures' attacks. Bast kicked and stomped at the crawlers instead.

Charlie and Max fought in unspoken tandem and, with each protecting the other's flank, the crawlers could not get close enough to strike. But they were far more exposed to the flyers. The bat-like bone clusters swooped and raked at their backs, splashing blood as they circled back around.

Zack and Bast were not as unified as the canines and both crawlers and flyers crept inside their defences. Bast smashed one flyer in half with the wristguard of his sword, but another slashed across the back of his neck. Next to him, Zack warded off two flyers and shattered a third, but two crawlers leapt onto his thighs, piercing into them with their sharp legs. Zack screamed in pain and knocked them off with his club. This close to them, he saw their bodies consisted of just their bony limbs with no recognisable head or torso.

Bast must have noticed the same.

'These things are weird. I mean, how do they even eat?'

Zack's mind latched onto the question and, by reflex, he reached out with his mind to sense the nearest crawler's Life. What he found was not Life. Rather than the warming coolness of Life, it was, instead, both freezing and sweltering, like a fever. It was darkness, without being black or colourless. It was rapid and shallow while also being drawn out and rasping. And, whatever it was, crept back up his sense towards him. Zack retched and tore his mind away. His vision blurred as he stepped away from Bast and lashed out in broad wild circles around him. He felt the bat slam into several of the creatures, but others slipped past it and slashed into his body. Art and Armand were locked once more in a mental duel and Art's face was sweat drenched and strained.

Armand laughed. "Without your friends, you're no match for me and you know it."

"Not normally," Art replied through clenched teeth. "But you're not exactly coming to this fight fresh."

"Neither are you, boy. Tell me, how painful is that broken arm? Do you think you're doing more damage to it, holding it like that?"

Art's eyes flicked down to where he was bracing the break with his other hand and then hissed in pain. He refocused on Armand.

"Oh, nice try, but I'm not going to let you borrow this pain."

Armand shrugged. "No matter, some of my little friends seem to be coming over this way to give you some more."

He wasn't lying. Four of the crawlers made their way in a wide circle around Armand and scuttled towards Art.

"I need a little help over here!" Art's shout had a high-pitched edge to it.

The Fire mage hurled bolt after bolt of flame at Kimmy, Tabitha and Jackie as they circled around him. Most crashed against Jackie's shields or were narrowly avoided by a quick duck or sidestep, but twice Tabitha was struck by a glancing blow on her leg and arm and the burns were slowing her down.

"Now!" Kimmy shouted, and the three of them charged forward.

Despite having no weapons, they each dropped their shoulders as they sprinted towards the man. He craned his neck left and right in an effort to keep them in sight and, when they were only a metre away, he stomped and a wall of flame sprung up from the ground. The snow sizzled as it melted and evaporated and the burst of heat pushed the girls back. Tabitha fell over backwards while Kimmy and Jackie scampered back from the fire.

The man laughed and, as he waved his fingers amongst the flames, they swept outwards away from him.

"Get your shit together, man," Bast yelled as he hammered one of the crawlers off Zack's back.

Zack sucked in a long breath of air and pushed down the feeling of deep nausea that had enveloped him. He blinked his eyes clear while he shifted his grip on the bat.

"Right, sorry. I'm with you."

"Good. Because they need us." Bast didn't point to Charlie and Max so much as he charged towards them, rapier first.

Zack followed, smashing apart the bone creatures as he ran. The flyers had discovered that the two canines were particularly vulnerable to the swooping rakes and both Charlie and Max's fur bore the bloodstained evidence of their attacks. Still, neither of them had stopped their relentless assault against the crawlers and countless broken bones littered the snow all around them. Zack and Bast swept past them, knocking a pair of flyers out of the air.

Zack pointed at where Art was struggling against Armand.

"Ladies, if you can help out Art, we'll keep the creatures off you."

Charlie-wolf answered with a short bark and the two canines bolted away towards the two Mind mages, with Bast at their heels. Zack's limbs burned with fatigue, but he batted another flyer out of the air and followed the others.

The group of crawlers had already made their way to Art and he attempted to kick them away, but his movements were distracted and sluggish. The closest skittered away from his kick and launched itself onto his other leg and, when he put his other foot down to brace against that pain, a second crawler climbed up that leg.

"Help!" Art screamed, his eyes flickering between the creatures and Armand's smug smile.

Charlie and Max bounded forward, each crushing a crawler beneath the weight of their front paws before tearing another off Art's legs. The sharp bone legs cut deeper into his flesh as they were removed, but at least Art could return his focus to the duel.

Tabitha crawled backwards, away from the wall of fire, but it was expanding out faster than she could move. She stopped her futile retreat and incanted, pushing out with her right hand. Accompanied by a scream of effort, a torrent of wind burst from her hand and pushed the flames back towards the man. Kimmy took her lead from Tabitha and cast her own spell, wresting control of the fire and tightening the circle around the Fire mage.

"It's no good," Tabitha cried. "We're going to be exhausted long before he is."

Jackie's eyes lit up.

"Exhausted!" she squealed. "Hold on as long as you can, I've got an idea."

She whispered her incantation to herself and moved her hands in wide horizontal circles in front of her until, just as Tabitha's wind was starting to fade, Jackie pushed her hands forward. The effect of Jackie's magic was not immediately noticeable, but then the Fire mage gestured for the flames to sweep out again. The fire's movement crashed against a telltale flash of steely light, revealing the magical dome Jackie had placed over the Fire mage.

His smug smile turned to anger and he poured more magic into the flames. The flames grew and whirled around inside the dome.

Tabitha pulled herself up and moved next to Jackie. "Well done."

Jackie nodded without looking at her. "It's so hot in there, though."

"You can feel it?" Tabitha asked.

"Kind of, in here." Jackie tapped the side of her head. "It doesn't hurt or anything, but it's uncomfortable."

"Will it hold?" Kimmy asked, her eyes locked onto the dome.

"He's giving it a beating," Jackie replied. "But I've got it for now."

Away from the dome, Charlie and Max had turned their attention onto Armand. He waved at them with his left hand and the bone creatures surged towards them. Max whined in pain as a crawler slashed down the length of her hind leg and Charlie turned from her approach on Armand to crunch it between her jaws.

Armand returned his full focus to the mental duel and seemed to be winning. Art's eyes widened and lost their focus and his lip trembled. Bast and Zack raced to Max and Charlie's sides and knocked away the flyers bearing down on them.

"Focus on Armand," Zack shouted. "We've got you."

Max tried to lunge forward, but the cuts in her leg were deep and she struggled to keep the weight off it. Charlie moved herself in front of Max and a dark, deep growl rumbled from her chest. A crawler slipped past the boys and latched onto Charlie's shoulder with its sharp legs, but she ignored it and barrelled forward towards Armand. The blood from her dozens of wounds had stained her fur and the footprints she left in the snow were painted red, but she leaped through the air and sunk her teeth into his thigh.

Armand shouted in pain, but not half as loud, or as crazed, as Art did. Zack spun around to find his friend with a wide smile on his face.

"Got it!" Art yelled. "Back away from him, quick!"

"Are you okay, Art?" Zack asked.

But before Art could answer, Zack saw the creatures change course. The flyers broke off their diving assaults, the crawlers disengaged and, as one, they moved towards Armand.

"Charlie, let go!" Bast called out and Charlie-Wolf reluctantly opened her jaw and bounded back to Max.

"No!" Armand shouted. He began an incantation but the first wave of flyers struck, slicing into his shoulder, arm and cheek. He dropped the spell and tried to knock them away and then the crawlers reached him. A dozen of them leapt and crawled up his body and Zack was forced to look away as Armand fell to the ground with a muffled scream.

Bast pulled at Zack's arm. "C'mon, I need to get the gate closed."

Zack nodded and the two ran towards the grey oval.

Jackie's face grew puzzled as she maintained the dome over the swirling vortex of fire. "I thought the flames would have gone out by now."

"Why?" Kimmy asked.

"Because I'm not letting any fresh oxygen inside, and fire can't burn without it."

"Nah," Kimmy replied. "Put enough juice into it and magical fire can keep going."

"Oh," Jackie said. And then her eyes grew wider. "Oh!"

She waved her hands and the shield-dome dropped. Tabitha and Kimmy looked at her with alarm. The fire flowed outward, but without the speed it had before. Kimmy incanted and gestured towards the flames, which responded by calming and shrinking until the last flickers sunk into the puddles of melted snow. All that was left was the charred remains of the Fire mage.

"Oh no," Jackie said, her eyes locked on the body.

"What?" Kimmy asked with clear confusion. "I thought this was the plan. And it was brilliant."

"No," Jackie replied. "I thought the fire would use up all the oxygen inside the dome and then it'd go out and then maybe we could kind of choke hold him a little."

"Right." Kimmy nodded. "Nope. The fire used up all the oxygen alright. But then it kept burning and idiot here passed out before he snuffed the fire and then… well then, the fire snuffed him, I guess."

"Kimmy!" Tabitha wrapped an arm around Jackie. "You did the right thing, Jackie. You saved us."

"Hey, Kimmy!" Bast shouted from the gate. "I could use some cleansing fire over here!"

Zack and Bast had reached the gate, but there were too many of the creatures around for Bast to get it closed. Zack was doing his best with the bat, but he was struggling to lift it and they just kept coming.

Kimmy jogged over. "I swear you boys would be lost without—" Her eyes fell on the creatures pouring through the gate. "What in my unholy night terrors are these things?"

Zack wheezed as he spoke. "Art will probably name them later, but can you burn them away from the gate?"

Kimmy took a deep breath. "Yeah, I think I've got enough in me for that."

Her fingers flicked through the air and a two-metre column of fire roared into life next to the gate. At Kimmy's direction, it swept around the grey oval and wherever it struck the creatures, they ignited and crumbled to ashes.

Bast turned his attention back to the gate and began his own incantation. More creatures streamed through, but Kimmy's flames were waiting for them. The gate shrank and shrank until it disappeared.

"Right," Zack said with a sigh. "Now we just have to finish off the rest."

"Or not," Bast said, pointing.

The remaining flyers had crashed to the ground, crumbling into disconnected bones, while the crawlers had collapsed in place. It was over.

CHAPTER 33

THE TRAVELLER

The memory of Sara's voice echoed in Zack's mind. *Unlike your friends, your work does not end with returning to the Tower.* He looked with envy at where Kimmy and Bast had plonked down on the ground to catch their breaths, but he had a job to get on with. With whatever fumes he had left in the tank.

"Do you two have anything I should take care of?" Zack leant forward with his palms on his knees as he spoke.

Bast shook his head while Kimmy looked Zack up and down. "Plenty of scrapes and scratches, but nothing that can't wait."

Zack nodded in thanks and trundled over to where Tabitha and Jackie sat down with Art, Charlie and Max. The two canines were huddled in beside each other and Zack didn't bother asking before he directed streams of Life towards them both. Charlie first and then Max, he stopped the bleeding and closed up the worst of the wounds, including the torn muscle and ligaments on Max's leg. He could sense a cacophony of bacteria present, but his temples were already throbbing from the effort. He'd have to clean that up after he'd rested.

Charlie-Wolf nuzzled his calf as he stood back up.

"You're welcome," Zack replied. "Are you planning on changing back any time soon?"

Charlie shook her head, which looked odd on a wolf, but Zack was grateful. There was just no way he could help if it went wrong.

"Okay, you next, Art. Give me a look at that arm."

"Nah, mate," Art replied. "It's fine and you look like you're about to fall over."

"Shut up and stand still," Zack said. "We don't know we're safe yet."

Art nodded reluctantly and Zack stepped closer to him. He ignored the cuts and deep bruising and directed Life towards the bone itself, knitting together in seconds what would have taken the body weeks. His vision was spinning when he was done.

"Anybody else?"

"We're fine," Tabitha said, even though her burns and bruises were evident. "And we're a whole lot better than them."

Zack looked at the mutilated form of Armand, only slightly obscured by the crumbled bones scattered over his body. "Well, he's never getting up. But maybe some of the others can be helped."

He took a step towards one of the bodies lying nearby, but Art stood up and put his hand on Zack's shoulder.

"Mate, no. You can barely stand. You try to do any more and you'll risk doing serious damage to yourself. They made their choice."

Zack's shoulders dropped because he knew Art was right and he let his friend help him down to the ground. His body collapsed but his mind played over what Armand had said and done.

"Armand could use two different Schools of magic, right?"

"Not necessarily," Tabitha replied. "It was more likely a trick."

"Not a trick," Bast said. "I could feel it. Old mate there opened up a portal."

"Well, maybe he's some kind of freak," Tabitha said.

Zack held up his hands. "I'm not saying we work this out today.

I'm definitely too tired to think it through. But maybe we keep this bit secret from the Tower."

"Secret!" Kimmy's eyes widened and she spun around. "Mr Shanks! Where are you?"

Charlie-Wolf padded past her and stopped at a mound of muddy clay, pawing at it. Kimmy dropped to her knees and carved into it with her fingers. After half a minute of furious effort, she tore the filthy knife free and released it to float in front of her. It wiggled its hilt in enthusiasm.

"I'm so sorry you got trapped in there, but you were very brave," Kimmy said.

"I've never heard her speak that nicely to a living thing," Art whispered into Zack's ear.

"You know," Kimmy said. "If you let me set your blade aflame, this probably wouldn't have happened."

The dagger shook its blade back and forth.

"But the mud probably would have just burned off."

The shaking increased.

"Fine." Kimmy opened her jacket. "Have a rest, you deserve it and I'll give you a good clean when we get home."

The dagger floated back into its pocket.

"So, what do we do now?" Art asked.

"I think we rest up until Bast is ready to take us home," Tabitha said, "and then we see if we can get back into the Tower."

Bast cocked his head to the side. "Actually, I think the Tower's coming to us."

He pointed to the side and, a second later, a large gate burst open. Erik strode through, his axe ready, accompanied by five other Tower mages. The burly Water mage scanned the mountain top before his gaze settled on the teens.

He rolled his eyes dramatically.

"Why am I not surprised to see you lot in the thick of this?"

"Hey, Erik." Tabitha waved. "I assume you're the cavalry?"

"You might," he replied. "I assumed I was the vanguard. I'd ask how you got here, but I have a feeling I'm not supposed to know. Everything has been dealt with here?"

"We think so," Tabitha answered.

Erik looked to one of his companions and nodded in the direction of the gate. The woman ran back through the portal and returned moments later with Junie and another dozen Tower members. Zack recognised two from the School of Life.

Junie strode toward the teens, leaving the others behind. The teens rose to their feet as she approached.

"I'm glad to see you have survived," she said, "but I need details now."

Tabitha answered, "Bast had worked out some information from the photos we took, so we came to the Tower to share it with you, but we couldn't get in. We guessed it meant they must have started their plan, so we looked at the map and noticed there was an intersection point here. Figuring that most of you were trapped in the Tower, we hoped to come here and work out how to let you out. They were doing some kind of ritual that opened up weird gates. We stopped them."

Junie surveyed the mountain top as she listened.

"I am in awe of the seven of you. We will have a much longer, more detailed discussion soon, but by all indications you have done the world a great service today. Head back to the Tower and to the infirmary. I'll come find you there when I'm done here."

She didn't wait for a reply and returned to the others and directed them into action. The teens trudged their way toward the portal. Erik clapped Art on the shoulder as they passed him, but even Art seemed too tired to respond. Zack was looking forward to some time on an infirmary bed and maybe, if he was lucky, a shower.

The Lifers on duty in the Tower infirmary were able to heal their wounds and breaks, but it was the shower and a fresh set of clothes that had Zack feeling human again. Groups of mages hurried up and down the stairs, while Junie and the other liaisons compared intel and issued directions, but in between controlled chaos, Zack and his friends had learned more about what had happened.

As they had suspected, Junie had informed her superiors and then she and a few of the other liaisons had gathered dozens of response teams, waiting for any sign of activity. And then the Tower had been cut off. When the connection was returned, the wards had gone berserk, with multiple breaches scattered around the Middle East, north-east Africa, southern Eurasia and west Asia. And in the centre of it, the mountain top in Iran. The teams were mobilised to manage the breaches and Erik had been sent in to investigate Iran. The teams were getting it under control, but it was likely that the magical aftershocks would ripple out into more breaches for days to come.

Just as Zack and his friends were learning about what happened, the story of their own battle had filtered through the Tower and more than one group passed them with a look of deep appraisal.

It wasn't enough for Kimmy, who was keen to be part of the continued cleanup effort, but before that was even possible, they all needed a good night's sleep. They trundled out of the Tower and into the nearby parking station. Zack didn't need to use his mind to feel how exhausted his friends were, which was good, because he would have been hard pressed to do even that much magic.

"You did well on the mountain, young heroes."

The voice came from behind a concrete column and brought with it enough adrenaline to slap away Zack's fatigue.

A man stepped out with his hands open and raised. He was dressed in a long trench coat and, while his wild unkempt hair and beard made it hard to pinpoint his age, Zack guessed it to be around 50.

He moved no further.

"I saw the absurdity that Armand unleashed. I am relieved and impressed that you survived."

"Who are you?" Tabitha asked him in a sharp tone.

"Most importantly, I am somebody who means you no harm. I am known as the Traveller."

Zack remembered the overheard conversation when they were captives. "You knew them."

The man nodded. "Worse than that, I'm afraid. I brought them together. I even taught some of them. But they started listening to Armand when he became obsessed with this idea."

"Why are you here?" Kimmy asked. "What do you want?"

"What I wanted was to get there in time to stop them. But Armand has always been a slippery bastard and used the ritual to lock me away. I imagine that's why your overseers in the Tower weren't there at first either."

"What do you know about the Tower?" Tabitha asked.

"More than you, I'm afraid. I can't stay long. I don't like to get this close to one of their entrances as it is. But I'll say this before I go. They are lying to you. The Tower is not what you think it is. I'll come find you again soon and we'll talk more."

"Why should we trust you?" Art asked.

"You shouldn't." The man drew lines in the air beside him and a gate appeared. "But you shouldn't trust them either. Until next time."

He stepped through and the gate snapped shut behind him.

"I don't know what to even think about that," Bast said.

"Is he actually gone?" Tabitha asked.

"I think so," Art said, rubbing his temples with the palms of his hands. "But I'm not sure I can reliably pick up my own thoughts right now."

"I'm not picking up any danger," Jackie added.

"What now?" Charlie asked.

"Maybe we should go back and report it," Tabitha replied.

"I don't know." Zack scratched at the back of his head. "He's right about one thing. The Tower has lied to us. What Armand did shouldn't have been possible."

"It's probably more complicated than that," Tabitha said.

"Too complicated for us right now, that's for sure." Art pointed to Jackie and Zack. "I've got to get these two home before I pass out. This will keep."

"Yeah, okay." Tabitha pulled Art in for a hug. "You did good out there, psychomancer."

Art hugged her back, an awkward smile on his face. "You did too, captain."

Zack hugged Tabitha next, then Kimmy, Bast, Charlie and even Max, goodbye before plonking down in the back seat of Art's car. While Art concentrated on the road and Jackie dozed in the front seat, Zack's head was a whirlpool of thoughts.

After spending a few short seconds with the Traveller, questions and doubts flared in Zack's mind like spot-fires, threatening to ignite what he'd thought of as truth.

The sun had long since set, as Art drove through Sydney and the year had not long left either. The next year lay open in front of Zack with as many possibilities as the city streets rolling past his window. The railings that had defined this past year — high school, Charlie, his grandmother — had fallen away. And now the Tower, the foundation on which he had been planning to build his future upon, was being called into question.

He needed time. Time to rest. Time to mourn. Time to think. And time to plan.

Zack turned away from the window and looked toward Art and Jackie and thought about the others making their own ways home.

He wasn't going to do this alone.

www.ingramcontent.com/pod-product-compliance
Lightning Source LLC
Chambersburg PA
CBHW040215170726
48295CB00014B/686